MÉNAGE

La Belle sans la Bête Ménages

Serena Akeroyd

MENAGE AMOUR

Siren Publishing, Inc.
www.SirenPublishing.com

A SIREN PUBLISHING BOOK
IMPRINT: Ménage Amour

MÉNAGE MATERIAL

ISBN: 978-1-63258-955-2

First Printing: February 2015

Cover design by Harris Channing

Printed in the U.S.A.

PUBLISHER
Siren Publishing, Inc.
www.SirenPublishing.com

DEDICATION

Forgive the award-ceremony list of thanks, but this day has been a long time coming.

To Mum and Nanna. No words, not even a thank-you, is an adequate dedication. So, I'll say this: I might have looked like I wasn't listening, but I always was. I might have rolled my eyes, but I took your advice. (And it almost always was the right thing to do. In fact, delete the "almost.") I might have been a pain in the ass, but I was *your* pain in the ass. :D Cheers, my dears.

Granddad, I didn't know you. You were taken from me far too soon. That doesn't lessen the influence you've had on me. Mum made sure she passed along your teachings, you know, always having ten bags of sugar in the cupboard. Just in case. I love you, and I wish we'd had more time together.

To the people who have helped me along the way. Katrina, Caryn, Nicole…and to those of you I haven't mentioned—THANK YOU. I'm humbled by your help.

And finally, to Trever, for smelling, snoring, and insisting on stinking bits of dried tripe—no soap in the world gets rid of that stench from your pinkies. You may be just a dog, but there's no *just* where you're concerned.

MÉNAGE MATERIAL

La Belle sans la Bête Ménages

SERENA AKEROYD

Prologue

Your money.

Your wife.

Or your LOVER.

100,000 euros to keep quiet. To keep your sick secret hidden from the papers.

You have five weeks to figure out which means more to you.

Tick. Tock. Tick. Tock. Tick. Tock.

I'll be in touch. And I'll be watching.

-An interested third party.

Chapter One

Devvy Jacques was no idiot.

She held a PhD in cosmetic science, and while it could be said her line of study was more of a pseudo-science than a legitimate field, she was also a botanist, studying plants and their pharmaceutical uses. Still, her choice of careers never entered into arguments of her intelligence. After all, it wasn't as if she had to be a member of Mensa, which she was, to see that something was wrong in her marriage. She knew, point-blank *knew,* her husband was having an affair.

Okay, point-blank might have been a *slight* exaggeration, but a woman *knew*, didn't she? She could sense it, and every ounce of female intuition Devvy possessed was screeching a red alert.

"This is what happens when you aim high, Devina Jacques. You should have stayed in your own sphere. Stayed among the pond scum and not aimed for Darwinian perfection." Her voice was glum as she stood in her home laboratory, combining witch-hazel with tea tree oil to a solution that would eventually become a bar of facial cleansing soap aimed at teenagers with acne-prone skin.

It was all right telling herself it had been a dumb move to marry Sebastien Jacques, but actually coming to terms with it was another thing entirely. Unfortunately for Devvy, she loved the man, had loved him ever since she'd first set eyes on him at a cosmetics convention in the city that would become her marital home, Paris.

Sebastien was the owner of the only international brand of cosmetics free from animal testing, made with one-hundred percent natural products, and marketed around the world. What had started as a small business in a tiny suburb of Lyon had exploded into one of the fastest-growing cosmetic companies France had ever seen.

La Belle sans la Bête beauty line was a hit among the socialites and the struggling single mothers—it breached all of society's barriers and was popular with every income bracket. The snazzy name, Beauty without the Beast, said it all. The brand combined nature's bounty with reasonable price tags while producing products that actually worked, more so than the chemical-laden glop most women slapped on their faces, and all without animal testing.

Sebastien's success was legendary in the industry.

At forty-five, he was nearly twenty years her senior and even though two decades separated them, he was still a nine out of ten on the gorgeousness scale, whereas Devvy, with no amount of help from the *La Belle sans la Bête* product line, only just brushed a seven.

And that was on a good day.

When, at the Parisian cosmetics convention, Sebastien had headhunted her and offered her a dream role at his company, she'd dived right in. Not because she believed in his brand, even though she did and had admired his work for a long time, but because of him. Sebastien.

Nearly a foot taller than her own five six, onyx black hair with salt and pepper at his temples, olive skin that gleamed with vivacity and augmented the stunning amber-brown of his eyes, Sebastien was a hunk. Or, as the French said, a *bellâtre*. He was masculine beauty personified and to Devvy, who from birth had been a skinny, geeky non-entity, he'd been a total cliché.

Adonis, in the flesh.

Hell, scratch that. He'd been a walking advertisement. He might as well have had a sign on his head—*female orgasm distributor*. No BOB could ever match a guy like Bastien Jacques. Damn his gorgeous hide.

It had taken all of her reserve not to stutter in his presence. Not to flush or stammer or wring her hands with awkwardness whenever he was near. She'd been utterly beguiled by him. From the almost feminine curve of his mouth, to the lines that crinkled at his eyes whenever he beamed a grin her way. She'd fallen hook, line, and sinker for the man.

So, when he'd approached her with a contract that would take her from her sunny Californian hometown to Paris, the city for lovers, she'd been hard-pressed not to leap at him, to snatch the papers from his hands, and sign on the dotted line before he could retract the offer. She'd managed to hold back. Just. Her pride hadn't even twanged with self-importance at the fact he'd selected her for his company, when his choosiness at staff selection was as world renowned as his product line. She hadn't cared on a professional level. It had all been very, very personal.

Two months into her contract, he'd asked her out. Four months after their first date, he'd proposed. And Devvy, existing on cloud nine ever since he'd deigned to ask her out for a coffee, had nearly wept at the idea of actually being married to the man.

She should have realized there'd be a catch.

No man with looks like Sebastien could settle for someone like her, not unless he wanted something. In this instance, it had to be her brain, and the many cosmetics formulas she'd developed over the years.

He probably thought he could marry the non-entity and have a decent woman in his bed outside of his wife's knowledge. It was a very Gallic attitude. Almost par for the course.

Just not Devvy's course.

While he'd probably prefer it if she were unenlightened as to his extra-marital activities, she knew something was wrong. No amount of regrets, of wishing she hadn't been so damned foolhardy as to leap into this life with Sebastien—a life that had taken her away from everything and everyone she'd ever known, as crappy as it had been—would change a damned thing.

Oh, she could settle. Endure the shame of having a husband who needed a lover to see to his needs, because his ugly duckling of a wife couldn't satisfy him.

Or, she could fight…. Retaliate.

With her eyes focused on the solution in her glass beaker, for a moment, she allowed herself to think of fighting. And winning. Of having the courage to face her husband, of making him admit to her she wasn't enough to please him.

Then, her shoulders slumped.

Devvy was about as confrontational as a Koala bear. In fact, they had a bit more gumption than she did. She was a geek. She loved her science, her work. Before Sebastien, she'd lived for it. Now, it was only one aspect of her days. Sebastien had filled every other part. Such a pathetic admission shamed her but she couldn't help it.

He was a force to be reckoned with and under his protection, Devvy knew she'd flourished. In their two years of marriage, her experiments had consisted of success after success. In his environs, she bloomed. Until now, he had made her happy. How could any woman not be affected by that? Happiness was more addictive than sugar. Except now, it was starting to taste like saccharine, bitter.

The glass-stirring rod tinkled and sang as it scraped against the beaker in her hand. She made the stirring motion absentmindedly. Her eyes switched focus from the anti-acne solution to the herb garden upon which her lab faced. Fronds of lavender, pungent leaves of basil, and rampant sticks of mint as well as dozens of other plants perfumed the air, but behind the window, her nose had to rely upon sensory memory to remember the rich scents of her garden. There was a calm to be found from Mother Nature's treasures, but no amount of sniffing could make Devvy feel calm at the moment.

Two years, she'd been married to Sebastien. Two years in which he'd actively encouraged her to work from home, where she was happiest. Reproducing a small but highly advanced laboratory on their land, she'd taken the gift as a compliment. The amount of money he'd spent on ensuring her happiness…it could only have been a present for a woman who was loved.

But now, she wondered if it was to keep her out of the way. Tucked up at home, he could do what he wanted at the office. Maybe he was having an affair with his assistant, Adéle. With Devvy at home all day, he could fuck his personal assistant to his heart's content on company time, and without his wife being any the wiser. He could take solace in the curvy beauty that was his aide, try to imprint Adéle's looks on his retinas so he could pretend it was her when he deigned to take Devvy to bed.

The thought had her choking back tears and she slammed her hand down, shattering the beaker containing the plant extracts she was preparing. The astringents sloshed over the counter as the glass exploded into hundreds of tiny shards, some shrapnel digging itself deep into her palm. Even the pain of the cuts, combined with the sting as the witch-hazel and tea tree solution went to work on cleaning the wounds, didn't bring a halt to her train of thoughts.

"I'm not the Hunchback of Notre Dame," she told herself, pushing the discomfort of the cuts to the back of her mind. "I'm no Marilyn Monroe but I don't need to be hidden away like some kind of goddamn savage." Her lower lip trembled at the very idea. "I don't deserve this. I *don't.*

"He doesn't touch me, hardly talks to me. He's so goddamned uptight all the time…!" She sucked in a breath. "It could be work," she muttered to herself and to the labs' walls. They were used to her one-to-four conversation. "You don't get where he is without a lot of stress and tension invading his life. Just because we haven't slept together in…" She groaned as she did the math. "*Four weeks*? That isn't possible. The last time was after we went to Marie de Haviland's god-awful soirée…" With her hand still weeping blood and giving her floor a crimson, polka-dot makeover, she strode over to her wall calendar and looked back over the few occasions they'd had to go out. Sebastien hated high-society events more than she did. And that was saying something.

"Oh God, it's worse than I thought," she mumbled. "*Five*! Five weeks!"

Eyes flooding with tears, she fluttered her lashes in an attempt to hold them back. She managed. Barely. Sucking in some harsh breaths, she forced herself to be calm, and then, when her breathing was back on track, moved to the sink where she methodically cleansed the small cuts on her hand.

The only reason she'd started thinking about Sebastien being with another woman was because this morning, she'd been—as much as she hated the goddamn word, it described her to a T—horny. Being horny was not a state she was accustomed to. Sebastien liked sex.

A lot.

A lot, lot.

There were days they'd make love in the morning, before he had to leave for work. Sometimes, he'd take her in the shower after breakfast. He came home for lunch at least three times a week—something else he'd ceased to do over the last two months—but when he did come home, he'd usually take her then. Before dinner, *after* dinner, after he finished his work in the study…any spare time at all was used by them sharing mutual orgasms on whatever piece of furniture happened to be close to hand!

How could he go from being, well, *rampant* to *nada*? Zilch?

After a minimum of once a day—and just once was unusual—for the last two years, she'd never had to wait so long before, and her body was going nuts. Shit, she was more accustomed to being sore down there than needy! Going five weeks without made her feel like a nun.

Okay, teeny-weeny exaggeration there, but how could her sex-loving husband suddenly be okay to go without? Unless someone else was giving him what she wasn't…

And that, ladies and gentleman, was why she was upset. Another woman seemed to be the most likely, if heart-wrenching, story.

She hissed as a shard of glass stubbornly clung to torn flesh. It ripped her thoughts away from her husband and back to the pain in her hand.

The monotonous act freed her mind from the emotional tidal wave battering her, letting her focus on the physical discomfort. By the time she'd finished digging out the shards of glass from her hand and then bandaging it, her alarm clock beeped, making her jump. She almost slammed her hand on the counter, back onto the shards she'd just pulled out of her palm, but she remembered just in the nick of time.

Usually in her lab, she was totally focused on her work. The only way she would remember the strict dining hours their housekeeper insisted on, was to have an alarm clock warn her twenty minutes beforehand. The sound of the alarm was always accompanied by her jumping in shock. One time, she'd actually fallen off her stool. Her butt had had bruises for a week.

She left her work where it was on the counter. That morning, in an attempt to clear her mind and to figure out what was wrong with her husband, she'd started a new recipe for the anti-acne soap she'd been working on for the last four months. The last clinical trial of the previous version had worked in ninety-four percent of the people tested, but it had caused some dry skin in too large a number of the women using the product.

The conundrum had allowed her to focus and it was here, at her worktop, where she'd realized her husband had to be having an affair. Somebody else had to be giving him what he'd needed for so long, because he sure as shit wasn't getting it from her!

And now, she had to go and face him. Sit opposite him as they dined on food that could have come from an award-winning restaurant. She'd have to stop herself from choking on each bite that passed her lips…as well as maintain the low level of chitchat she knew Sebastien was used to hearing from her.

Dazed, wooden, and heartsore, she trudged out of her lab, locked the door and crossed the lusciously green lawn toward the home she shared with her husband.

Italian Renaissance and rococo architecture made love as they adorned the two-hundred-year-old mansion. The twelve-bedroom behemoth, tucked away in the heart of the sixth arrondissement, was a history lover's wet dream. In Paris, yet, in its own acreage of land in the space-poor city, Sebastien and Devvy lived in the metropolis yet out of it. It really was the best of both worlds.

As she crossed the lawns and ran up the three steps onto the terrace dotted with pruned teardrop-shaped bushes and lined with creamy stone balustrades as old as the house and survivors of the French Revolution, Devvy looked in each of the first floor's ten sets of double-fronted windows, for which the house was named *Les Fenêtres* or The Windows.

She searched in vain for sight or sound of her husband, but saw no one glancing through the sparkling glass onto the garden, which was unusual for this time of day. In the evenings, after the stresses of the working day, he stood in his office, a glass of red wine in his hand, leaning against the wall as he looked out onto the gardens at twilight. It was his favorite pastime.

She wondered if the woman doing the nasty with her husband knew *that!* Although it wasn't like Sebastien would need her to be aware of anything other than his sexual preferences. All a lover had to know was how to please her wealthy partner, not what made him happy after work.

Stomach churning at the thought, she entered the house through the portico, a small porch that sat bang in the middle of the property's back façade, and which let her into the main hallway. The light and airy space smelled of fresh air and recently picked flowers. There was nothing more than a round, gleaming walnut table in the center of the vestibule, loaded with a heavy vase filled with late-blooming hyacinths. Doors lined the circular room, apart from the east wall, which had a large arterial staircase. It split, after twenty steps or so, and led to the two different wings of the house.

Bastien and Devvy slept in the west wing. The guests, the few they'd ever had, went in the east.

She scurried up the stairs, passing doorways leading to elegantly appointed suites and priceless paintings and artifacts that adorned the corridor of their private wing. Hurrying into the bedroom they shared—for the moment, at least—Devvy pulled up short when she came across Bastien seated on the bed.

Their suite was a masculine haven. She hadn't liked to change anything, not wanting to spoil the look Bastien had obviously chosen for himself. He'd lived in the house for ten years before she'd moved in, and she'd altered very little in her time spent in the mansion. It was a masculine abode and she'd left it that way, only changing the rooms he gave her as an office and salon. But she spent little time there, preferring her lab or Bastien's study, which had a large open fire in winter and the best air conditioning in summer. As well as the man himself.

Devvy didn't care how many Manet's or Pissarro's they had lining the walls, her husband was the prettiest thing to look upon in the entire house. And she was a California girl. Being a geek didn't make her blind. She'd seen some hunks on her native soil, but not a one compared to Bastien.

Creams, beiges and blacks were the soothing shades of the bedroom, but they obviously weren't soothing Sebastien. His hand was at his nape and he was massaging his neck with a grimace twisting his handsome features.

"Would you like me to massage your shoulders?" Devvy's voice was hesitant, her new uncertainty about her importance in his life throbbing through every word.

Sebastien's taut smile was his first answer. He was usually very aware of her changes in mood, but in his pain, she could tell he hadn't sensed anything wrong with her.

She wasn't sure if that was a good or a bad thing.

"Please, *ma belle*," he whispered, the grimace twisted again, gentling with his appreciation as she stepped toward him.

"How long have you had it?" Devvy asked, knowing from experience he had one of the migraines he suffered from time to time. They were debilitating. Sometimes, he couldn't even leave the bedroom, and woe betide anyone who dared to open the curtains.

"Since last evening."

As she climbed onto the bed and knelt behind him, she tutted under her breath. "You should have told me," Devvy chided. "I could have rubbed your neck last night."

When she'd first learned of his migraines, she'd taken an online course in massage to ease his suffering during times like these. For her, it was a win-win situation. She got to help him and touch him at the same time. And she loved touching him. His skin was supple and like silk underneath her fingertips. A massage was a mutually pleasurable experience and where he was concerned, Devvy was a glutton.

Today, fear tinged her pleasure. Was another woman giving him something she herself couldn't? And if it wasn't another woman that was keeping him away from her, what was? Questions, questions everywhere, and not an answer in sight. She kind of knew how the Ancient Mariner felt. Only without the severe dehydration, and the albatross.

She was clueless, unless she built up the courage to actually come out and ask him what was going on…

Did she have the balls for it?

Technically, no. But was Devvy too lily-livered to approach her husband about a fundamental part of their marriage? For the last five weeks, the answer had been an unequivocal *yes!* With the idea that another woman was floating around in the background, giving her husband massages as well as other things…well, the situation had tilted a little too far. Even for Devvy's non-combative nature.

As her hands began to rub and smooth down the tension in his neck muscles, Bastien's groans echoed around the room. They were almost sexual, so deep and at such a bass, the pitch set her own sex to quivering with need. His hard frame drooped under her touch and her lips twitched as his fingers worked at the buttons of his shirt in a move filled with desperation, one that indicated he wanted her to work on his back with skin-to-skin contact.

She hummed with pleasure as his toned flesh was revealed to her. She took great enjoyment out of smoothing her hands over his skin, manipulating it and rubbing so as to ease his tension. For how long she worked, Devvy didn't know. She only stopped when her fingers started to ache and the cuts on her palm started to sting and even then, she trailed the digits gently over the back of his neck.

The sounds of his low, rhythmic breathing pleased her. She'd managed to work out the worst kinks, and from the lax curve of his spine, she'd done a good job.

"Dinner will be ready, Bastien."

He hummed his understanding under his breath and then, in a move that shocked her, for he was never overly tactile outside of sex, he tilted his head back and rested the heavy weight against her breasts.

Devvy closed her eyes as her nipples instantly peaked. She'd been inexperienced—not a virgin—on her wedding night and ever since that first time together, Bastien had awakened a passion in Devvy that she'd never imagined existed. Around him, she was a starved creature and he was her banquet.

She never asked him to make love to her. She waited for him to act. Uncertainty had always kept her at bay, had always stopped her from coming on to him. Aggression had never been her thing, but it might start to be if he didn't satisfy the knot of desire he had unearthed in her body.

She swallowed, wishing he'd turn his head to the side and tug at one of her nipples. It wouldn't hold the same punch as flesh-to-flesh contact, but it would be enough to send excitement buzzing down her nerve endings.

Trying to regulate her breathing so as not to disturb him was difficult. Especially when her mind was keyed on sex, and his was on the pain burrowing through his skull. As she looked down, his head bobbed a little with the swaying motion of her breasts, but he didn't seem to mind. His long, black-onyx lashes fluttered a little before they opened and their gazes clashed.

Few people ever held eye contact with Devvy because hers were strangely colored. Almost white, so light blue they had a silvery hue. She knew most found them unnerving. Akin to a husky's piercing orbs, especially in comparison to her coloring.

Her hair was a muddy shade, not like her husband's, whose blacker-than-black hair was softened by light golden-hued flesh. Devvy was more of a dirty blonde, where strands of chestnut and gold came together. And not always successfully.

Unlike Bastien, she was pale as linen. Some nights, after they'd made love, he'd trace the blue veins under her skin, for they were as visible as the few freckles that spotted her body.

She'd truly felt beautiful on occasions like those. Her husband worshipping her body, making her feel things she'd thought to be mythical.

It was amazing, or depressing, how, in five weeks of having not an inch of his attention, self-doubt could set in.

Devvy watched, almost in awe, as his pupils dilated at their prolonged eye contact. She knew he was about to reach up and kiss her, knew it and was on the brink of welcoming it, when those seeds of self-doubt demanded to be heard. It was bad enough feeling pathetic for needing her husband's touch as much as she did, but it was even worse when he didn't share her craving.

She couldn't help it. In her miserable anger, the words just blurted out. "Are you cheating on me?"

His slumberous eyes shifted, darkened somehow, and then he shot up and off the bed.

The behavior of a guilty man? Devvy wasn't sure. He *had* broken eye contact, and that was never a good sign, was it?

She watched as he began to stride back and forth at the foot of the bed. Each time he passed, he almost walked into the trunk that sat there, and she wished for his grace, because, clumsy oaf that she was, she'd have knocked her shins a dozen times by now.

His discomfort, the very unease he exuded, told her the truth, but she didn't feel sorrow, or misery. She felt nothing. Just a strange blankness. Hurt was there, waiting to come out, but it was dampened. At the moment.

The belief that he might be seeing someone else had only just popped into her head this morning. She'd been seeking an excuse for his peculiar behavior. The late nights, the drop in activity in the bedroom…his short temper, even, when she knew him to be a very patient man. Especially with her.

She'd had no real evidence that he was cheating. Nothing but a gut feeling. Despite herself, Devvy wished she could take the question back. Wished to bury her head in the sand, because once the truth was revealed, it could never be hidden again and she'd have to act. No one could hide from such a shameful truth and still retain a measure of self-worth.

And while Devvy knew she'd been silly to think a marriage between herself and a man like Bastien would ever work, she valued herself too much to stay with someone who wanted her for her abilities in the laboratory. Now the bedroom, she'd have accepted being shuffled into that role. Willingly! But apparently, she'd started to bore him in that department.

Mortification triggered a silent throb in her brain. She felt her cheeks start to heat, her body quiver with horror at the times she'd thought him to be enjoying himself in bed, when he must have been putting on an act.

His silence was unnerving, especially now she'd worked herself up to hearing his admission of guilt. She wanted him to get on with it but when he spoke, he didn't say the words she'd thought she'd hear.

"It isn't what you think."

With humiliation battering her, it would have been too easy to take comfort in those words. Because of that, and to be contrary, she decided to do the opposite. "It isn't?" she sneered. "Explain it to me, then. I'm all ears."

"I chose you for two reasons."

Chose? Fuck, what a verb. Almost like he'd been picking a broodmare. An old-fashioned concept but Sebastien was a wealthy industrialist with no children to inherit the fruits of his hard work. The thought hit her brain with the power of an ice pick.

Please, God, don't let him say because I've got childbearing hips!

"You're different from most women."

"Thanks, Sebastien. I really appreciate that! Different, how? Like a monster, different? An alien?" she snapped.

"No!" He held up his hands. "Listen to me. I'm not trying to offend you, simply trying to tell you the truth." He sighed. "You don't simper, or flirt. You have a brain. You listen and advise. You're wise. Your intelligence is attractive, especially as I know what you're capable of."

The least sexy part of her body, her brain, and that was the part that turned him on.

Great. Just fucking great.

"And the second reason, because Alexei felt the same way."

"Alexei," Devvy repeated, frowning as she failed to register the name. "Do I know him? Should his opinion be important to me?"

He shook his head. "No, but we've waited two years for you to finally meet him. And I hope, eventually, that his opinion *will* be important to you."

She swallowed at that news and whispered, "He's not like a son, is he?" Another shake of the head. "Or, locked up in one of the attics?"

Okay, so, she was reading *Jane Eyre* at the moment, but still, it was a valid question. Kind of. And maybe her imagination did tend to run away with her, but hell, she was just trying to make sense of what he was spouting out!

He frowned at that, and then chuckled. “And there you have why I find your mind so appealing. No, I do not lock him up in the attic, because he is mad, bad, and dangerous to know,” he mocked. “He is a man I very much care for.”

It didn’t take much for the truth to sink in after that remark.

“You’re gay?” Devvy barked, jumping off the mattress and nearly falling flat on her face in the process. He grabbed her just in time and righted her before she could hurt herself, but she shrugged him off, pulling away from him to stare at him with horror.

“No, of course not.” He was so calmly assured that confusion thrummed through her.

“You’re not?” She hovered in front of him, wondering what the hell was going on. She had an answer, of a sort, yet it resolved nothing. She was as clueless as five minutes before.

“Well, not technically.”

Devvy closed her eyes. “I can’t believe I’m hearing this. You married me as a ruse, didn’t you? As a patsy. To hide what you really are from the rest of the world.”

“I had no idea you were prone to melodrama. Exaggeration, yes. Hyperbole, no!” Sebastien snapped, cutting through her hysteria with the skill of a swordsman. “I did no such thing. I married you intentionally, yes. Do you know how difficult it is for two men to agree on the one woman? It’s borderline impossible.”

At his irritation, her eyes popped open and she gawked at him.

“Why would two men have to agree about one woman?”

He pulled a face, his lips twisting with self-directed anger. “This wasn’t the way we were going to broach this subject,” he complained. “You were supposed to meet him first, and then we’d explain. *Together*. I’m no good with words. Alexei is the charmer.”

“I don’t want charm. I want the truth. And what were you waiting for? Two years, we’ve been married. Two! When was I supposed to meet this Alexei?”

“Next month,” he retorted glumly as he resumed his pacing. “We needed to make sure you were happy with me. If you weren’t, if you couldn't settle in Paris, away from everyone you knew, then we would never have broached this topic."

Feeling like she'd entered some strange kind of parallel universe, Devvy shook her head. When the movement felt heavy, like she was wading through maple syrup and not air, she lifted a hand to cup her forehead. "So I've passed muster, because I've endured your moods and my solitude for two years?"

He surprised her with a wide grin. "I love your tongue, chérie. It's wicked. As sharp and as cutting as a knife."

Her cheeks flushed, and had she been able to control the involuntary reaction, she certainly would have. The last thing she wanted was to be complimented on her tongue. Good God, the man was French. Surely, he realized her humor and her brain were the last things a woman wanted to be admired! Trust Devvy to pick the most complicated and least charming Frenchman in the country.

Before she could do more than grumble at the thought, he was suddenly there. Right in front of her. No longer pacing back and forth at the foot of the bed, but five inches away. Touching distance. Her heart, the treacherous thing, started to pump like a piston at his proximity. There was something in his eyes, something that was the catalyst to her sudden arousal. She didn't understand it and from the mention of this Alexei, she wasn't sure she wanted to!

"Alex knew you would be at that convention and directed me your way."

And just like that, her arousal disappeared. Vanished, without a trace. If anything, she felt slightly nauseated. "Alex," she repeated blandly. From the depths of her desire for him came a torrent of fury. He might be taller than her but she didn't give a damn. Index finger erect and ready to point, she jabbed him in the chest and stepped forward, urging him to step back if the pair of them weren't to collide. "Just who the hell is Alex? Explain what's happening now, or I'm leaving!"

Even though he'd been preparing for this moment since he'd first proposed to Devvy, the timing of this ultimatum came as a shock to Sebastien.

He had thought to introduce this topic over a long, evening meal. One where romance was in the air and Devvy was soft and relaxed after an afternoon spent between the sheets.

He'd imagined countless ways of informing her of the truth behind their marriage, but he'd never thought she'd ask him if he was cheating on her. He'd never believed she'd be the one to bring the subject to a head.

Was he relieved the truth was about to be revealed?

He couldn't deny that he was. After all, he and Alex had planned this for so long, had been waiting for her for over a decade. What they wanted was unorthodox. The pair of them knew that, and knew only a special woman would accept them and their desires.

Bastien was certain they'd found her in Devvy.

Gentle, warm, welcoming Devvy. With her big heart and big eyes, eyes so blue that they pierced a man's soul and made him see himself for the true creature he was.

She would be good for both of them. God knew Alex needed an extra something in his life. Something to live for aside from his science. Someone who could understand the dedication required in his scientific calling but would push him, make him expand his boundaries.

Alex and Bastien had been together too long, had settled so comfortably into their roles that neither could change, for they were both stubborn men. They weren't in a rut. Their relationship wasn't stale, and they weren't seeking outside help to kink things up a little, to add some spice. No, they accepted each other. Flaws and all.

Just as Alex accepted that Bastien, in times of stress, would push himself to passing out on the treadmill, or bursting a blood vessel as he tried to lift weights as heavy as his own body, Bastien understood that his lover found the outside world to be one of chaos and disorder. In his apartment, the wide-open spaces, Alex was liberated, free.

Devvy would change all that. She had slowly started to change him, and she'd do the same for Alex.

When Bastien's work caused him stress, the gym wasn't his only port of call now. He'd find himself in Devvy's lab, pleading for her soft but strong hands to work their magic on his shoulders or spine—he'd been heading there this very afternoon, but she'd popped into the bedroom before he'd had a chance.

He could easily afford the best masseur in the land, could have him or her shipped in from whatever city they lived in just to tend to his needs when he required it. Instead, he preferred the hesitant and inexperienced but loving touch of his wife.

He knew Devvy would break the patterns the two of them lived in. Alex would slowly find order in the chaos of the world, because Devvy would make him. Christ, in summer, she practically lived outside so if Alex wanted to get within an inch of her, he'd have to leave the house and venture out.

Her garden was her source of peace, and Bastien had found himself out there more and more often. Because of her. In the evenings, he'd taken to looking out, finding his own brand of pleasure in the land, something that only happened because his wife had opened his eyes.

No, change was definitely coming. And he embraced it, wholeheartedly.

All that mattered was bringing Devvy, his orthodox and prim Devvy, around to their way of thinking. That meant he'd have to manipulate her, and the thought didn't sit well with him. It would be worth it in the end, and he could sweeten the bitter taste in his mouth by saying that the end justified the means, but he loved Devvy, and didn't want to have to manipulate her.

Oh, he knew she believed he didn't love her. She was a strange creature. So confident in herself as a scientist yet so unconfident in her position in his life. He hadn't failed to notice that the house was exactly the same as it had been three years ago, before she'd moved in. There was no feminine stamp on any of the rooms. Only her own quarters had been altered to suit her tastes.

She wavered in and out of his life, willing to step back so as not to crowd him for fear of annoying him, and he let her get away with it. It wasn't that he wanted her to be insecure. It was that he didn't know how to stop it.

He might be a master manipulator in the boardroom but where his wife was concerned, he was soft as putty. And that was a major problem, considering he'd have to call on all of his skills to make her see that the triad he and Alex wanted to forge between the three of them was a path that led to their mutual happiness.

Love weakened a man. This was a fact he'd learned upon meeting Alex, and falling for his wife had merely confirmed it.

But there was a bigger picture at play, and Bastien knew he would have to push aside his tendency to yield around his wife, if he were to attain every single one of his and Alex's hopes and dreams for the future.

He was used to duty and stress. He wore the mantle of power easily. But in this, he felt like Atlas. The globe on his shoulders, the weight of the world on his back.

He just prayed success was in his future. He wasn't sure Alex could stand the disappointment, and if he lost Devvy, if she asked for a divorce, Bastien could honestly admit, he wasn't sure how he'd cope without her. After two years, she'd inveigled her way into his heart, and the holes she'd leave behind if she left…they'd be there until he died.

Success or failure. The responsibility rested entirely with him.

For the first time in his life, fate held Sebastien in its hands, and he didn't like it.

Chapter Two

Devvy wasn't one for ultimatums. In fact, demanding that Bastien tell her the truth or she was out of there was the first one she'd ever made in her twenty-six years. The fact that it didn't actually work, she blamed on inexperience. The next time she made one, he'd damn well listen, she vowed.

That ultimatum, however, was the reason for their departure from the bedroom and their sojourn to the formal lounge. Sebastien had called down to the kitchen and postponed dinner. She didn't have to see the grimace on Bastien's face to know that the chef would have complained. Loudly.

It was France, after all. Good food, good wine…it was to be treasured and savored. It didn't matter that Bastien was the man's employer. Food should never be wasted. Especially not in favor of an errant wife's demands.

Not that the chef knew that she was to blame for the delay. He was just pissed that his creation, a meal he'd spent a day preparing, would be wasted.

It didn't matter to him that his employers' marriage was on the rocks. No, he just cared about his goddamn stew!

Devvy was sulking in an armchair, slouched in the padded leather of a moss green Chesterfield. She had propped her feet on a low, mahogany coffee table and refused to look at an irritatingly calm Sebastien, who was on the matching sofa to her left, one ankle settled on his knee. Instead, she focused on the elaborate fireplace, the hearth filled with flowers cut from the garden and the painting above the mantelpiece, a scene from a hunt.

She hated this room. Very rarely used it unless Sebastien invited guests over, and then, she had little choice but to sit here.

In reaction to her demand, Sebastien had picked up the phone and contacted this "Alex." After, they'd traipsed down here and were currently waiting for him to arrive so all could be brought out into the open.

Whatever was going on, by using this room and not going into her lounge or his office as they would ordinarily have after dinner, Bastien was being very careful to show her that Alex was a guest in their home. In a way, she appreciated that, but disliked the necessity of it. The sooner she knew what was going on, the happier she'd be.

Even though she knew it would be wiser to keep quiet until the mystery man himself arrived on the scene, she'd been unable to help herself when the words had spilled from her lips seconds after he'd cut the call with this "Alex."

"Are we going to split up?"

At his frown, she'd continued, "Will this conversation mean you'll want a divorce?"

He'd sighed and tucked his cellphone into his trouser pocket. The man had been half-undressed, his torso bare after her massage, yet he still managed to look cool and calm. "That choice will be yours, Devina."

His use of her full name had made her stiffen. Nobody, apart from her father, called her by her full name. And only then, because her dad had been the one to choose the horrible title, so he had to!

Part relieved, part unnerved by the odd reassurance, Devvy had merely nodded, then watched as Sebastien gathered his shirt from the floor where he'd flung it earlier and dressed himself again. Once decently covered, he'd held out a hand to her. She'd studied it and him. Her eyes had drifted up to his face to take in the blank expression covering his features. He'd given nothing away, not even one emotion. She'd frowned but accepted the courtesy, and tucked her fingers in his. And there they'd remained as they walked down the stairs and stepped into the salon.

For the last twenty minutes, they'd been seated here in silence, and it was the most peculiar twenty minutes of her life. She knew the world she'd created for herself here in Paris rested on the next few hours. Whoever this Alex was, whatever he was to Bastien, and whatever he would ultimately be to her, would make or break her life here.

That discomforting thought alone had made her relieved for the postponement of dinner.

When the doorbell rang, both of them shot up from their seats, spines rigid as they turned as one to face the salon door. Their ears pricked for the sound of Louise, the maid, answering the summons. They heard the door open, the slight mumble of a greeting and then, a faint boom as she shut out the outside world again.

Two sets of feet tapped against the polished parquet of the hall, and then Louise hovered in the open entryway, murmuring, "Monsieur Ivanov is here, Monsieur."

"Show him in," Sebastien told her.

The pair of them watched as Louise stepped out of the way and a man filled the doorjamb. As soon as her eyes caught a glimpse of the stranger, of the other man in her marriage, a man she'd seen in countless science journals, Devvy choked. "*Alex?*" she gasped out, her horrified eyes seeking her husband's. "You call Alexei Ivanov 'Alex'?" Leaping to her feet, she strode across the room and forcibly took Alexei's hand and shook it. "I know something weird is going on with you and my husband, but at this moment, I don't care." She blinked up at him, not seeing him but the scientist's version of the superstar he was.

The man had just created the first functioning prototype of a breathalyzer that could test for the presence of no less than six different types of cancers. He was a genius—well on the way to finding a cure for the more common cancers—and he was in her living room.

Her frickin' living room!

"It is a pleasure to finally meet you, Devina," he murmured, taking her hand and raising it to his lips. He brushed the back of her fingers with a soft kiss that had something burning to life deep inside her belly.

Her cheeks bloomed with heat as she shook her head in bemusement. Alexei Ivanov actually wanted to meet her! It was a pleasure, he'd said.

Heart on the verge of palpitating, and knowing she'd have to back down from her schoolgirl crush, she bit her lip then blurted out, "Call me Devvy. Only people who are mad at me call me Devina."

His smile was amazing. It lit up the somber lines of his face in a way that told her he didn't smile frequently. And that pained her. It shouldn't have, as he was only a stranger, and up to no good with her husband, but it was the truth. His somberness hurt something in Devvy, and she had to stop herself from rubbing her heart with the ache of it. Weird, or what?

Alexei Ivanov was not a hunk. Not in the traditional sense, at any rate. He was not handsome in the way that society measured attraction, but to her, it was like looking at an idol. Better, even.

He was younger than Sebastien, thirty-seven. Lines scored the sides of his eyes, his forehead and mouth. His head was covered in a thick pelt of silvery blond hair and his coloring was pure lab—i.e. he very rarely stepped outside, living his life in his laboratory. He was pale and should have looked washed out, but that thick mane of his made him look vibrant. Combine it with the deep, almost violet-colored eyes, and Devvy had a hard time controlling her attraction to the man.

No, he wasn't good-looking in the Hollywood way. But every single molecule in Devvy "Devina" Jacques's body sat up and listened now that he was in the room. And her molecules were already used to standing to attention. Her husband was gorgeous, after all.

At the protracted silence on her part, Sebastien commented around a chuckle that Alexei shared. "I think she has been struck by hero worship."

She refused to blush, instead ducked her head, and shot a glare Bastien's way.

"It is charming to be so appreciated," was all Alexei said.

"Take advantage of the peace. Devvy is not a quiet woman."

Huffing, she propped her hands on her hips and said, "Why not discuss all my flaws to a complete stranger, Sebastien? Where are your manners?"

Before he could reply, Alexei tugged at one of her hands and cupped it within his own. "But I do not wish to be a complete stranger for long."

Confused, Devvy snapped her gaze between the pair of them. She told herself it was wrong, that hero worship—something Bastien had correctly guessed was an affliction of hers where Alexei Ivanov was concerned—did not mean she could curl her fingers into this man's hand while in her husband's line of sight. The man she loved, even if he was keeping secrets from her.

No amount of reasoning stopped her though.

Her fingers acted of their own will and they speared through Alexei's, linking them in a fundamental way. A part of her wondered what she was doing. She'd never been so brazen with anyone in her life. Not even Bastien, and she'd made vows to him, for God's sake!

But this was Alexei Ivanov. The science world's version of Brad Pitt.

It was a wonder she hadn't flung her panties at him!

From the corner of her eye, she saw the pleased smile gracing his mouth and felt something deep inside her bask in the warmth.

"This has gone better than I expected. I wish I'd realized you had a crush on Alex, we needn't have wasted two years."

The wryness in Sebastien's voice had her frowning. "What do you mean?"

"Do you remember that cosmetics convention you attended, where you met Sebastien for the first time?" Alexei prompted and at her dazed nod, continued, "I'd seen an article about you. Your science, your methods. Your genius. There was a picture of you, looking serious and stern but those eyes of yours…" With his free hand, he traced the sharp jut of her cheekbone. The gentle touch had gooseflesh swimming the length of her spine. "And beneath the lab coat, you were every man's wet dream. It said you'd be at the convention, and I told Bastien to go there and to meet you."

"But why? If you…" She hesitated.

"If *I* was attracted to you?" he spoke the words for her and she nodded gratefully.

"If you were, then why didn't you come and meet me yourself?"

"Alexei makes a point to never attend a convention of that sort. He's been nominated for a Nobel Prize, and he probably won't be there either."

It was strange, because she could sense neither approval nor disapproval about this on Sebastien's part. He was carefully blank, and whatever her husband was, he was an instinctive creature. He'd made a fortune on his financial insights. That told her whatever he truly felt was carefully buried.

"I dislike crowds."

Sebastien snorted. "He's agoraphobic."

Alex's eyes flashed at the other man, and Devvy was startled to see anger and panic in his gaze. He quickly looked at her, and she could tell he was nervous about her reaction to Bastien's words.

"Is he telling the truth? Do you fear outside places?"

Alexei swallowed, and almost defiantly spat out, "Yes."

"Only the promise of telling you the truth made him leave his home tonight, Devvy. If I want to see him, I have to go to his apartment."

Devvy frowned and used her free hand, for the other was still being clutched by Alex, to scrub at her forehead. "I'm confused. You saw my picture in a magazine and because you won't leave your apartment, you had your friend date me instead?" Her words had her taking a step away from her idol and demanding her hand back.

"He's more than just my friend."

Her eyes darted toward her husband. "I thought you said you weren't gay."

"It's complicated, Devvy." Bastien rubbed a hand over his nape, and from the flash of pain that had him frowning, she knew his migraine was still there or coming back.

"So explain," she retorted, voice cool, ignoring his discomfort. He wasn't the only one with a tension headache waiting in the wings. "I want an answer."

"You won't like it," he muttered.

"Tough. I don't like *this*! You're frightening me." Maybe fright wasn't the correct way to describe how he was making her feel with his comments, but it summed up her nervousness.

A burst of French cascaded over the room as Alex and Bastien started to yell at one another. Devvy had a basic understanding of the language. She might be one of the top cosmetic scientists in the world, but the Romance language just escaped her at every turn. Something she bitterly resented as Alexei and Sebastien engaged in a war of words right in front of her, and she couldn't understand a fucking word.

"Enough!" she barked, digging deep and finding a previously unknown source of courage at her very heart. She was not known for her confrontational side. If anything, she was likely to flee from an argument, not dive right into battle. "Explain. I've already waited longer than I said I would, Sebastien. I think I deserve an explanation."

The two broke off, looking guiltily at each other, before Alex cleared his throat and said, "We enjoy the opposite sex."

"We enjoy the opposite sex," she mimicked, glowering at the pair of them. "I should damn well hope so considering you've just spent the last two years married to me, Sebastien." A thought popped into her head and she choked out, "Is that why you haven't touched me for over a month? You've stopped *enjoying* the opposite sex?"

Sebastien snapped, "I haven't touched you because *La Belle sans la Bête* was under threat of a hostile takeover! As much as I love losing myself in your body, *ma petite*, sometimes the spirit might be willing but the body is weak."

"Why didn't you tell me about the takeover?"

He rolled his eyes. "Women. You can't win either way!"

"If it stresses you out, then it stresses me out. Is that so hard to understand?" she directed the question at Alexei, who held up his hands in surrender.

"Don't get me involved. I've already had this argument with him. Many a time. He knows how I feel on the subject."

The pair of them directed their gaze at Sebastien. "Don't keep scowling like that. The wind will change and then you'll be stuck that way forever!" she told him, watching him try to fight a smile at the nonsensical advice. Something her grandmother had told her long ago.

"And do you care for my pretty face, *mignonne*?" he asked, the smile breaking free and tugging at his lips.

"Maybe," she retorted, unwilling to stroke his ego. "Look, I'm still waiting for an explanation. I think I've been more than patient."

"And your patience shall be rewarded, Devvy," Bastien muttered, sinking back into the sofa with a sigh. "We might as well relax while I tell the tale." He waited until Devvy and Alexei had taken a seat, his wife moving to the place beside him, leaving the armchair free for Alexei. It was a small act of possessiveness that both men recognized instantly.

"Firstly, you must realize, Devvy, that neither of us meant you any harm. If anything, it's the contrary."

She frowned. "What do you mean?"

"We both wanted to love you."

Stunned, Devvy sat forward, half-stood up, and then sat back down again. "Both of you?"

Alex nodded. "Yes. I have known Sebastien for nearly twenty years. Before he was the rich industrialist we see now."

"You've been friends? Or more than that?"

"More," Alex murmured, voice gentle.

"Oh."

"Don't look so broken-hearted, *mignonne*," Sebastien whispered, seeing his wife's beautiful features crumple with her pain made the tension at his temples beat to a tune of its own. "I am not a stranger now I have made this revelation. This is simply another facet to my nature."

"A rather large facet," she snapped. "You've had a male lover for twenty years and you didn't think your wife might appreciate knowing that?"

"I'm telling you now."

"It's a funny time to start being honest. What changed?"

"You asked if I was cheating on you."

"And I was bang on the money, wasn't I?" she spat, her anger making itself known in her hissed retort, before it whooshed out of her and she collapsed back into the sofa.

"Technically, he has been cheating on me with you," Alexei pointed out and shook his head as her eyes shot a warning his way. "I do not say this to hurt you, Devvy. It is simply the truth."

"One that *does* hurt!" she cried, unsure whether the tears pricking her eyes were from anger or sorrow.

Sebastien grabbed her shoulder and gently began to knead. It was a sharp contrast to the way she'd cosseted him only ninety or so minutes ago. She wanted to move away, shove his hand off, but Devvy didn't want to hurt him. Unlike the way he'd hurt her.

"I'm sorry, *chérie*." Bastien sighed. "But there is more to this than pigeonholing me as gay. What Alex and I have together is not strictly monogamous. Before you, we took other women to bed, but not men."

"So you're bi?"

"I hate labels, Devvy. We are what we are."

"God, this belongs on some bad soap opera. What do you want me to do? Condone the fact you have a male lover and just put up and shut up?"

"No," he murmured softly. "I wish you to take my male lover, as you label Alex, for your own."

This time, Devvy didn't hover. She leapt off her seat and strode over to the fireplace to gawk at them both from a distance.

Sebastien's jaw took on the characteristics of concrete. "We are not contagious."

"I take it back," she muttered, shaking her head and ignoring his pained anger. "This isn't a soap opera. It's a goddamn porn movie! Why the hell should I want to take a lover? Until now, I've been happy and damned busy keeping up with you!" She raised her hands and hugged herself. Self-comforting was the only way to go when she had two men wanting something from her that she had no idea how to give.

"I would like to see you with him." His anger had bled out, making his voice a soft rasp that sent shivers down her spine even though she told herself to man up and add some starch to her bones.

"Why?" she whined. "That can't be normal," she added, mumbling more to the room than the two men in front of her.

"What is normal, Devvy?" Alex slotted in.

"Well, what the pair of you want sure as hell isn't."

"I would like to see you with him," Bastien continued, almost as though the pair of them hadn't interrupted. "I would like to share you with him. I would like us both to love you and to pleasure you. And for you to love and pleasure us."

For some reason, only one thing popped in her head and she gasped out, "At the same time?"

Alex made a muffled sound and from his ducked head, she could tell he was fighting not to laugh.

"This isn't funny!"

"No, it isn't but you are such an innocent." Alex sighed and it was strangely redolent with pleasure. How she could sense that, she wasn't sure. She just knew she'd pleased him somehow. His next words confirmed it. "When I saw you in that article, I *knew* you'd be like this. Innocent, naïve, so intelligent you'd keep the pair of us on our toes. Creative, passionate, sexy." Another happy sigh. "I was not wrong in my judgment."

"You damn well were if you think I'm going to sleep with both of you at the same time!"

"There will be very little *sleeping*," he murmured silkily.

She stomped her foot. It made her feel like a toddler, but goddammit, he wasn't listening to her. "Look, I'm not interested in your perverted little games."

"Perverted?" Alex cocked a brow. "I think not. We do not wish to harm you, or do something that is morally abhorrent."

"Where I come from, wanting to share a woman *is* 'morally abhorrent,'" she hissed.

"Then America is not as enlightened as I thought." He sounded almost disappointed. "We French are far more open to such things."

"A ménage à trois might be a French term but I doubt there are many households of three in this country," she retorted, borderline snootily. Her nose popped up in the air as she made her cutting remark.

"Ah, so you do know of the phrase."

"Of course I do. I'm not totally out of touch."

"I fear you are."

Alex rose from his position and stepped toward her. She backed into the fireplace as he neared, ultimately leaving a sparse two inch gap between them. He was so close she could smell his aftershave. Could see a small graze on the firm, lean line of his jaw where he'd nicked himself shaving.

She could see the expensive cut of his clothing, a cut that was tailored to his body, and showed that while he might be on the cusp of agoraphobia, and while he might subsist in his lab, the man was built. His shirt rested against the flat plain of his stomach, and underneath, there were corrugated ridges.

In Cali, she'd seen many six packs, but had never thought any of her lovers would possess them. She'd imagined fellow lanky geeks would be the sort of men she'd take to her bed, and her first lover had been the epitome of a nerd. Like a beanpole, thick-rimmed glasses, bony, and with no clue of what to do between the sheets. She'd almost resigned herself to an unsatisfying sex life for the rest of her days as she herself was no babe. Then, she'd met Sebastien. Who not only had a six-pack, but biceps nearly three times the thickness of her own.

Sebastien dealt with stress in the gym.

And she thanked God every day for that fact.

Why she was thinking about lovers and Alexei in the same breath, she didn't know. It didn't matter that he had a six-pack. She wasn't some vacuous slut who could be swayed down a path she didn't want to take, because the man doing the asking had muscles on top of muscles.

At least, she didn't think she could.

This was Alexei Ivanov, for God's sake.

One of her idols. A scientist beyond repute. A man who had shocked the world with his discoveries, and who had only lived for less than four decades! The man was brilliant. So brilliant, his aura—not that she believed in auras—glowed with his genius.

When it got down to it, this entire conversation was taking place because he wanted her. A man with a reputation that would someday rival Einstein's, and he wanted plain-Jane Devvy Jacques.

"This is some kind of practical joke, isn't it?" she whispered.

Somehow, the idea that he could want her was borderline painful. It would make more sense if this were a mean prank.

She'd already hit a home run by marrying Sebastien, even if he had some weird perversions. The man was gorgeous and rich. He'd settled her in a mansion that had been the home to countless families in the two hundred years of its existence in the French capital. He'd installed a laboratory here, so she could work in peace amid the flowers and herbs in the garden she adored. Anything she wanted, she could have.

He was a modern day Prince Charming and he'd chosen the ugly duckling for his princess.

To think that Alexei Ivanov might want her as well…

Devvy could only believe that this was some kind of trick.

But no, Alex slowly shook his head. "Why would you think this is a game?"

He brushed against her, narrowing the two inches between them until they were no longer separate entities. At the contact, she jumped. And then, she jolted again when she felt his erection.

Devvy blinked and shook her head. "You want me?"

"I wanted you two and a half years ago, Devvy." He growled under his breath. "I showed Bastien the magazine, and told him to get you for me."

She frowned. "You make me sound like a bar of chocolate."

Alex chuckled, and she glared around him as she heard Bastien laugh too. "You are as decadent as the finest *chocolat*, Devvy. But no, you are not something to be bought, sold, or traded. I did not mean it as an insult. Sebastien has a way about him that few can resist."

"Strange, he said you were the charmer."

His snort had her jerking with surprise. It was such a down-to-earth sound, and it shocked her silly to think Alexei was capable of such a…*human* noise.

He was a God of science. Such a mortal sound had her ears, her goddamn ears, throbbing with pleasure. She hadn't even realized ears *could* be pleasured. It would seem anything was possible where this man was concerned.

"Another aspect the pair of us agree to disagree on," he eventually said.

"Am I the first woman you've asked to do *this* with?" she asked, as the thought popped into her head.

Alex hesitated but ultimately shook his head. "No. There have been two others. One who disagreed," he told her, before she could butt in and ask. "Another who joined us and was with us for around eight or so weeks. But that was a long time ago."

"Why haven't you asked anyone else?"

"Because it is rare that the two of us agree on a woman."

"And you both agreed upon me?" she asked, her disbelief evident in her scornful tone.

"*Oui*."

The pair of them spoke simultaneously. Not even a second's difference between their uttering the same word. More than anything, that made her realize, as mad as it was, they were not lying.

"But I'm so ordinary," she mumbled, hating herself for making the comment but needing to understand. She was not a vain woman, and knew the truth of her looks. She had long since come to terms with them. Christ, her mother had told her every day what her faults were, and how she had to counteract them with some piece of cosmetics—hell, that was what had flung her into the beauty industry in the first place!

Her hair was neither blond nor brown, but a dirty shade in between. Her heart-shaped face was attractive, but her eyes were too big and with the freaky light blue, they gave her an exoticness that was more strange than appealing. Her figure was decent. Curves in all the right places, a bit too much padding on her butt, but she ran three times a week to combat her body's leaning toward extra softness.

Every *flaw*, as her mother called them, Devvy had accepted and embraced. But a little self-doubt was only natural, she thought, when two guys as hot as these were trying to make out she was more than what she was.

"That is where your appeal lies, my sweet. The very fact you do not realize what a gem you are."

"You can't bullshit me, Alex. Or charm me into thinking I'm something I'm not. I'm very comfortable with who and what I am, but I know the pair of you are in a whole different league to me."

"What league is this?" Sebastien snarled, suddenly sounding very French.

She rolled her eyes. "You don't have to defend my honor from myself," she told him. "I just don't see how you could have seen my photo in a magazine, Alexei, and decided you wanted me."

"Want is a strange verb in the English language. There are too many different meanings. Did I desire you? Yes. And did I want to know you? Yes. But I knew that Sebastien would vet you. You could have been completely unsuitable and in that case, we wouldn't be standing here today.

"I didn't want you like a child wants a toy. I wanted to explore the possibility of the promise in your eyes."

"Okay, I can see why you say he's a charmer, Sebastien," she muttered, at a complete loss as to how to reply to that loaded statement.

"And that is all you have to say?" Alex snapped, finally losing his patience with her. It was only then she realized how calm he'd been. But then, she was the one who should be in hysterics, right?

Or in the twenty-first century, were women who learned their husbands were gay supposed to blithely accept it? Almost like they hadn't ruptured the cozy little matrimonial bubble in two?

That being said, she had handled all this very well. It was almost like she was waiting for the other shoe to drop, only Devvy didn't think this could get much worse.

"What do you want me to say?" she asked, her tone bleeding with her confusion. "You want something from me that I can't give. You can't charm me into it. It's too…*alien* to me. Things like this just don't happen. And not just to people like me, but to *anyone*. What you want…it's so out there! You're asking for too much from me."

"We shall see what is too much, Devvy. I ask only one thing of you."

"Just the one?" she mocked.

"Yes. Just the one."

"I'm not entirely sure that I owe you anything, but…" In a tone that said she'd rather leap off the Niagara Falls in a barrel, she asked, "What is it?"

"I would like the chance to become your friend."

The instant those words passed Alexei's lips, Sebastien knew they had her. There was no way on God's green Earth Devvy would pass up the chance to know a man she'd idolized from afar—damn, he wished he'd known about her crush. It would have spared them a lot of time. The way she'd reacted the instant she'd seen him…if he'd known, he'd have brought them together sooner.

The original plan had been to introduce them, let them get to know each other. Start a friendship and hope sexual attraction would work the rest of its magic for them.

Instead, with her coming out and asking him if he was cheating on her…

Sebastien was quite capable of lying. For the last two years, he'd hidden his relationship with Alex and felt little guilt. But when asked, point blank, if he was cheating…he hadn't been able to lie to her.

Time would tell if honesty truly was the best policy.

The only saving grace was the fact Alex wasn't just any crush. He was a man who lived at the very top of the scientific social stratosphere. Bastien should have realized she would never pass up such a chance to talk to the twenty-first century's version of Einstein. He'd been very shortsighted by failing to realize that, something which was unusual for him.

His belief that Devvy would comply with Alex's request was confirmed when she muttered, "Okay. But no funny business."

Alex chuckled, once again reminding Bastien of every single reason the man had held his heart for the past two decades.

Alexei, with his mane of blond hair, the amethyst eyes that haunted Bastien's dreams. The tall, borderline-lanky frame that he padded with muscle, because he knew Sebastien loved his lean, strong length. The man who spent far too much time indoors, who feared the outside world, had cast Bastien under a spell a long time ago, and he had no desire for that particular enchantment to be broken.

The man was a complex puzzle. Vague with the trivialities that were a part and parcel of daily life, yet razor sharp when it came to innovative scientific formulae. The two contrasts appealed to him greatly. Alex didn't prevaricate. He considered it a waste of time. He spoke the truth, usually of the painful variety, and he spoke it always.

In fact, when his lover had selected Devvy, neither of them had been aware of how similar she was to Alex. Devvy didn't understand bullshit.

There was only black and white, no gray, and to a man who lived in the business world, where everything was a shade of gray, her integrity was infinitely appealing. She lived with her head in the clouds, as did Alex. The pair of them would wander off, mentally, as they tried to solve the latest conundrum that challenged their massive intellects. Bastien was the one with his feet firmly on the ground. He was the kid who had one helium balloon in his hand, and who wanted to add another one to his coterie.

He didn't mind that he'd be the one to have to coordinate almost every aspect of their lives. And that, regardless of his business concerns, when the babies came, he'd be the one to have to organize the doctor's appointments or school registrations—and he firmly saw the future that way. Devvy, with her head of shaggy, dark blonde locks merging with Alex's white-gold gorgeousness in the shape of a little girl. And those dirty blonde traits of hers mingling with his own saturnine coloring to create a tiny little *brun* boy, swarthy olive-colored skin and chestnut hair.

The thought made him shudder with longing.

How long had they been waiting for this moment? How long had they been waiting to make a family together with the one perfect woman who could complement them both?

Too long.

The only thing that stood between Alex and Bastien's desires was Devvy's innocence—ironically, this was where she was polar opposite to Alexei. Her innocence was still going strong, even in the face of his own experience, and the amount of sexual acts Bastian had introduced into their bedroom.

He could still remember her shock when he'd first sunk his cock into her butt, spreading the tightly ringed muscle that clung hungrily to his shaft, no matter that he'd prepared her with his fingers and lube. As he'd readied her for him, he'd thought to the day when Alex would be a thin membrane of flesh away from him. Fucking her pussy as he claimed her ass.

She never disappointed. When he'd spanked her for some trumped-up misdemeanor, she'd squealed and rubbed her behind. Then, had trembled on the spot before she'd muttered how much that had "turned her on."

The truth was the only language Devvy knew. No matter how awkward her response was. And Bastien was fully aware that she meant it, when she said she wouldn't, *couldn't* accept what the two of them wanted from her.

For the moment, that is.

She might believe that Alex had only friendship on his mind, but there was a slither of deviousness running through his lover's nature. It only came out to play when there was something he or someone he loved wanted.

And they both wanted Devvy. Between them, above them, below them. Any which way they could have her. They were far too used to winning to concede defeat now.

She'd been shocked by his words, by his declaration, but she hadn't stormed out. Or demanded a divorce. Which, after all, she might have done. Christ, she was entitled to! Not many women could keep it together after discovering they weren't the only person in their husbands' lives.

He wondered if she realized how telling it was that she hadn't walked out, and how the pair of them would use it against her.

She would be theirs.

Eventually.

Close to fifteen years of waiting made a man patient. They could wait a little longer to have Devvy where they both wanted her.

Chapter Three

Devvy knew that for a woman in her position, she was saying all the right things but she wasn't necessarily *doing* them.

Oh, she told Alexei she wouldn't engage in a threesome with them, but had that stopped her from sharing a bed with Sebastien last night? Had she slept in one of the many spare bedrooms?

No.

Had she demanded a divorce on account of Sebastien's perverse demands?

No.

Had she dined with the two of them after she'd agreed to work on a friendship between herself and Alex?

Yes.

Talk about sending mixed messages. She was confused herself, and a good night's sleep—because yes, her marriage might be on the rocks, but Mr. Sandman had still visited her as though she didn't have a care in the world—hadn't lessened her confusion.

After dining on *coq au vin* that had tasted lovely to her but for which the housekeeper had apologized, as it had been left to overcook—Devvy still wasn't sure how that was possible with a stew—she'd promised to meet with Alex at his apartment the following day. Had he been a normal man, she'd have agreed to meet for coffee. Considering leaving his home and coming to theirs was like asking him to fly to the moon, she thought it wise for her to see him on his home ground.

Oh, she knew that she shouldn't be doing anything of the sort with the person who was the other man in her marriage. The very fact she'd said yes still perplexed her. Why hadn't she stormed out? Dropped more ultimatums like nuclear bombs?

Why had she sat down to dinner and dined with the other man and her husband?

That wasn't normal, was it?

Christ, it was anything but. So why hadn't she broken down in tears at Bastien's revelation? Why hadn't she felt scorned and abused and manipulated?

The only answer she could find was the fact that the man in question was Alexei Ivanov. Despite the vows she'd made to her husband, Alexei was probably the only creature who could make her break those promises.

Groaning with self-disgust, because she was acting like a science groupie, she slunk down in the back seat of the car taking her to Alexei's apartment. She couldn't drive and Bastien didn't particularly want her to. For some reason, he preferred her to have a chauffeur, and Devvy wasn't about to complain considering motorized vehicles and she had never been the best of pals.

On the brink of scrubbing a hand over her face, she froze, remembering the light dab of foundation, and the lip-gloss she'd applied before leaving the house this morning. That act alone spoke of Devvy's complete and utter discombobulation.

She never wore makeup.

Never.

After years of her mother forcing her to wear the horrible stuff, the minute she'd left for college at fourteen and had gone to live with her aunt in Boston, her rebellion had started. Being a genius had its advantages at times. It meant that she could leave home, live with an aunt that didn't mind if Devvy kept to herself, and she could start slouching around the house. Like her mother had never allowed.

Considering she'd hated wearing makeup herself, the cosmetics industry was a weird one for her to have chosen. But then, she was contrary at times. At least, that was what her dad had always said. Well, that, and difficult. Something to which her mother agreed. Although that was mostly because Devvy had been a breech birth, as well as the direct cause of Miranda Nelson's inability to drop down to a size four again.

Devvy didn't like to think her character was built upon something that had happened on her journey down the birth canal, but this decision did display a certain contrariness. Because to meet up with Alex Ivanov, for what was essentially a chat over coffee, she'd not only put on some of her own homemade mascara, kohl and lipstick but she'd dressed up too. Gone were her jeans, shirt, and sneakers. In their place was a skirt, an honest to God skirt, and a camisole. Both in black, because that seemed to strip away the dirty-blondeness of her hair and make it seem a bit more tawny. It also highlighted the delicacy of her pale skin, and slimmed down the too-large curve of her behind—or so her mother had always informed her.

She'd made an effort to go and drink coffee with Alexei. Her actions, in this instance, were speaking louder than her words.

She'd said no. She'd rejected their demands. Refused to sleep with Alexei. But she hadn't demanded he stop "seeing" her husband—if seeing was what they did behind her back. And she hadn't refused to set eyes on the man again. In fact, she hadn't acted like the hysterical wife, a role she deserved to play.

Christ, Devvy's reaction to learning her husband had a secret male lover had been far more relaxed than the treacherous SOBs deserved.

Why *was* that, though?

Because it was Alexei Ivanov—a man she'd idolized and drooled over for far too long—and that made it okay?

Devvy had a horrible feeling that was the exact reason her anger hadn't detonated.

As the car crossed the Seine, which would take them from the sixth arrondissement to the eighth, where Alex lived, she caught a glimpse of the Louvre. The pyramid glistened in the early spring sunlight. The Palais-Royal played peekaboo through the traffic, but she ignored it the instant they turned away and headed toward the Champs-Élysées. Alex lived in the Triangle d'Or, one of the most expensive residential areas in the whole world.

His wealth didn't impress her, nor did his address, but still, it was a huge achievement. Few scientists attained such a position, but then, this was Ivanov. It still astounded her that she'd been in his presence. Never mind the fact he'd handpicked her to be the stuffing in a Sebastian and Alexei sandwich.

The thought made her lips twitch and rather than feel repulsion, she felt something else. Something at the other end of the spectrum. Something that had her crossing her legs and clamping down on her inner thighs to stop the insidious feeling deep in her belly from spreading.

It was with a sigh of relief that the car pulled to a halt beside a *pharmacie*. She told the driver in her best pidgin French that she'd call when she was ready to leave, and then she stepped out into the dynamic, bustling street—that bustle was contagious. No matter the *quartier*, there was a vibrant energy she'd never experienced anywhere else, but that was distinctly Parisian.

On this street, it was a shade different. Here, there were none of the more laissez-faire, bohemian types. This was all money. All elegance. The shops reflected the zip code's wealth. Expensive jewelers, restaurants and boutiques lined the streets but she ignored them and looked up.

The building was old. Stylish and elegant. From another era. She recognized the Haussmann style simply because Bastien was an architecture buff and she was a Sebastien buff. Whatever interested him, she tried to share it. Pathetic or what?

Wrought iron railings, ornate with swirling curlicues. Tall windows with elegant cornices framing them. The beige stone had worn well over time. The carvings were as sharp as ever, the decorations still a strong part of the building's appeal.

Deciding she was procrastinating, she found the entrance to the building and pressed the bell to Alex's apartment. Barely a minute passed before he buzzed her in, and she set toward the elevator. Inside, there was a restrained air of wealth. As well as silence. Her heels tapped on gleaming checkerboard tiles and the elevator, when it came, was one of those kinds that was modern but had been made to look antique. More wrought iron.

It was a smooth and fast ride to the top floor. Too fast. She barely had time to reconcile herself with what could only be a disastrous meeting, before she was there. But she was in for a surprise. The elevator hovered, and opened up directly into the apartment. Her eyes darted over to Alexei's, and to the subtly, but expensively furnished foyer behind him.

He owned the entire floor?

Wow.

Now she was impressed, and she lived in a mansion.

The décor didn't really interest her, but the man himself did. Yesterday, he'd worn a shirt and dress pants. Today, he was in a T-shirt and jeans. He was also barefoot. And Devvy truly believed that she'd never seen sexier feet in all her life.

Quickly, she flickered her gaze from the elegant arches, because who found feet attractive aside from fetishists? The thought made her hope she wasn't one. Before Alexei's toes, she'd found most feet repulsive. Especially men's, which always seemed to be battered or wonky from the sport they played. Either that or sweaty with broken nails from poorly fitting shoes. Yuck.

The overall decision after taking in Alex's clothes was that she was overdressed for the occasion. But she'd rather that than look dreary.

"You're here," he murmured, voice soft. She could tell he was pleased, but at the same time, faintly surprised. He must have thought she'd renege on their bargain.

Huh, why hadn't she thought of that?

Fuck, she really had dived in headfirst, hadn't she? Somehow, visiting Alex had seemed like the only option open to her, and she didn't even know why. It hadn't even crossed her mind that she could cancel. That she didn't *have* to visit with him today.

"This is all very confusing," she replied, crossing her arms in front of her belly.

Her awkwardness made a smile tug at his lips.

At least it was amusing somebody!

"It is, but there's no need for you to feel uncomfortable. Come. I had my assistant fetch us some lunch."

"Oh, you didn't have to do that!"

In the act of walking down the vestibule, he stopped and turned to look at her. "There was every need."

His eyes were filled with heat, and a corresponding warmth kindled in her belly. She moved a hand, and pressed down against her lower abdomen. He recognized the gesture for what it was, an act of suppression, and took a step toward her, then hovered. The pair of them stood like that for at least a minute, staring at each other, letting their eyes drift over the other's form.

"This is wrong," she whispered, breaking the silence.

"No, it is what I knew would happen. If we both want it, then it can't be wrong."

"I'm a married woman. I shouldn't be feeling this way."

"Bastien will be kissing the ground you walk on for feeling the way you do." He shook his head, the gesture impatient. "What exactly is it you're feeling, Devvy?"

Her cheeks heated at the idea of telling him the truth, and she ducked her head, needing to say, "I want you," instead repeating her words of moments before. "Fuck, this is wrong. So wrong."

"Be honest with me, and with yourself. You can't be ashamed of the truth."

She sucked in some air and begged for calm. But there was no calm. This was no peaceful meeting between two people, a woman who idolized a man for his intelligence, and a guy who was interested in a chick's conversation. This was no friendly chat. This was a woman who looked at a man and thought about digging her feet into his ass as he pumped his cock into her. This was a man who looked at a woman and saw her legs spread, pussy lips parted as he sucked her clit.

Sex lay at the heart of the glances they shared. And they both knew it. Even if Devvy wanted to deny it, she couldn't. Just looking at him, from the rumpled white-blond hair to his bare feet, she needed to be close to him. It was difficult to reconcile that need with action, though.

Oh God, this wasn't her. This wasn't who she was. Who she'd been raised to be, dammit.

She loved her husband. She wanted him. How could she want this man, too? This…stranger, who she felt like she'd known all her life. Who she'd already argued and dined with. Talked to and lusted after from afar.

"I'd be cheating on him," she told him instead of giving him the words he wanted to hear. She couldn't allow him to sway her from the idea that what they both wanted, that what their clashing glances inferred, wasn't adultery. It was.

"It isn't cheating, when he wants it. When he wants you to want me."

"It feels like it, whatever you say. And that just makes it all the weirder. What kind of husband wants to share me?" she spat, feeling angry at Bastien for permitting this. For making her question herself.

"It isn't a sickness, Devvy," he retorted, evidently pissed off at her words. "There's nothing wrong with him. We all have our own kinks. This is ours."

"That doesn't justify it, Alex!"

"Maybe not, but we can't help it. We can't help wanting each other and wanting you."

She groaned. "Stop bullshitting me!"

"It isn't bullshit," he snapped. "It's the truth."

She ran a hand through her hair and froze when Alex reached up and played with a strand. God help her, the instant he touched her—just her hair, for God's sake—her pussy softened in reaction as her scalp tingled with pleasure at the simple touch. "I should go. I shouldn't be here, allowing you to think I'm okay with this."

"That's the problem, Devvy. You *are* okay with this, but a lifetime's teachings are telling you this is wrong. Screw what the people outside of these walls think. Do they matter? No, of course not. Sebastien matters. The man who married you, the man who loves you. He isn't judging you for wanting me."

She glared at him. "Who says I want you?"

He grinned. "The fact you nearly melted when I combed your hair behind your ear."

Devvy's mouth pursed in irritation. "This isn't right," she continued stubbornly.

"Who said it isn't? What goes on behind closed doors is our business. Now, I know you do, but you need to admit it. Do you want me, or not? If not, then leave. No recriminations, no angry words. Are you here because you want to be, or under some kind of force? Don't think about Bastien, don't think about anyone. Think about you, and what *you* want. Because, *bébé*, that is all that counts."

Her insides twisted, going into revolt at his tiny dip into French. Did it make her a slut to want him and to want her husband? Something wasn't right with her to need them both, surely?

She nibbled her bottom lip and whispered, "I don't understand it, but I do. Nobody forced me to be here. I'm here under no duress. That doesn't make it any easier to accept, Alex."

He sighed and narrowed the three steps between them so only a wisp of air separated them. His hand came up to cup her cheek. "At least you feel something for me. Even if it's just hero worship."

Devvy couldn't let him think that. "It is a little bit, but it's more than that. I don't understand it, and I can't believe I feel the way I do when I'm so head-over-heels in love with Bastien, I'm practically doing a headstand twenty-four-seven!"

At his chuckle, she whispered, "I'm not like this. I don't *do* things like this. I made Sebastien a promise and I never break my promises." She blew out a breath. "Damn the pair of you for doing this to me."

"I'm sorry, Devvy."

"No, you're not."

He grimaced. "No, I'm not sorry you feel this way. You're not wrong. But I am sorry it's hurting you."

"Think of this. You have these feelings for me, not because you know me, but because you know what I've done. What I've achieved and accomplished in my career. You're attracted to me because of that. You don't really know me, just like I didn't know you when I saw you in that magazine. But deep down, I *did* know you. Just like you can sense something about me—something that connects us. Binds us together."

"We're scientists," she groaned. "We can't be talking this way. About some ethereal connection between us. Soul mates don't exist."

"Why can't I talk like this? It's the truth. Soul mates don't exist for everyone…but maybe we're different. We've always been different, haven't we, Devvy? From the day we were born right until now." His eyes caught and held hers. They burned a hole in her soul. One so deep she knew he'd scar her for life.

"It's a weird kind of truth," she retorted, choosing to bypass his other comment both verbally and physically—she lowered her head to break the clash of their gazes. Their close proximity meant her forehead inadvertently brushed his chest. She froze at the contact, and on the cusp of jerking back, she sucked in a shaky breath and relaxed against him. His hand came up to cup the back of her neck, and the touch of his fingers to her nape made her pussy clench down. How could such a simple touch be the catalyst for such a complicated reaction?

"You're at ease with me, Devvy, and I think that's rare for you."

He was right. It had taken a good month or so after her wedding for Devvy to stop wringing her hands and sweating whenever Bastien was in the vicinity and wanted to talk to her. She'd been so certain he'd realize he'd made a mistake and demand a divorce on the grounds of *non compos mentis*!

After four weeks, she'd stopped second-guessing and ceased to worry about whether he thought he'd made a mistake. The weird thing was that he'd done nothing to make her feel that way. Christ, on their honeymoon, if they'd left the bedroom for more than an hour at a time, it had been a miracle! She'd seen close to nothing of any of the major cities they'd visited. And afterward, back home, he'd showered her with attention.

After two months of being married to him and of living in France—thousands of miles away from her mother—she'd begun to change. She wasn't sure if Bastien empowered her or if her mother had always been the one to drag her down, and finally being a continent away from her had made all the difference. Either way, she'd settled into her marriage happily.

That is, until her mother called and reminded her Bastien was far too good for her.

Something she did on a regular basis.

Inwardly, she snorted at last month's fortnightly call from her darling mom. The soirée both she and Sebastien had attended—the last time they'd had sex—a picture had made it into the press over in the US. Apparently, her ass was too big for the dress she'd picked, and her arms had looked like Popeye's post-spinach.

The fact that Sebastien had thoroughly fucked that ass after that particular party had made her grin as her mother condemned her poor fashion sense.

Then, after the lull in the bedroom, she'd started to wonder if her mother had been correct. If she was too fat for him…

And so recommenced the vicious cycle.

With Alexei, there was awkwardness, just no discomfort. And that made a huge difference.

She knew she'd batted a home run and scored way above her league the day Bastien had married her—she had eyes in her head and there was no point in lying to herself. Yesterday, she'd had doubts, because he'd been distant for a while, but at heart, she knew he found her attractive. Whatever her mother said. Now, this man thought she was hot, too.

That alone should have made her start stammering. Instead, she lifted her head and looked up at him. Two pairs of jewel-like eyes, one diamond-blue, the other amethyst, clashed. Tension arced between them, pulsating with power.

"I can't do this if Bastien isn't here," she croaked out, knowing she was agreeing to something that only last night she'd refused and classified as insane and perverse.

Today was a different day. Her feelings were different.

Devvy was different.

Why, she didn't know and couldn't say. But the emotion ping-ponging back and forth between them meant something. Whether it was the ethereal connection Alex insisted upon, or if it was base lust…Devvy wasn't sure. Whatever it was, it set her heart to pounding like she'd just run a marathon. To act on this strange emotion, she needed Bastien. Somehow, by having him there, it would justify her behavior. Otherwise, she'd just feel like a cheating slut.

He tucked her against him, pressing her length to his, and the instant their torsos connected, her nipples budded and poked through the camisole. He grunted as they pressed into his chest, the noise slight but all the more powerful for it. His hand reached down and suddenly, there was a cellphone tucked against his palm. He tapped the screen, Bastien's number popped up, and he connected the call.

His voice was strained when Sebastien answered, "I'm busy, Alex." She could hear him down the line.

"You're not too busy for this. Devvy's here."

"I know. I was there when you made the arrangements. How's it going? She's okay, right?"

Sebastien's sudden concern for the reason behind the phone call literally powered down the line, and it made tears burn at the back of her eyes.

He cared. She knew he did. He'd even told her he loved her and, until recently, he'd shown her. But hearing it spoken to someone else made it all the more powerful somehow. He really meant it. *She* meant something to him.

"She's ready. But only if you're here, too."

The pause on the other end of the line was long. She hadn't realized silence could say so much. "*Je comprends pas.*" I don't understand.

"What's to understand? She's here and she wants us."

There was a long pause, almost as though Bastien were registering Alexei's words, then came a low sigh followed by a quickly sucked in breath. “I’ll be there as soon as I can. I’m leaving now. If the traffic isn’t too bad, I’ll be there in twenty or so minutes.”

A second later, when Bastien had disconnected the call, she whispered, “I can’t believe I want to do this.”

“You feel the pull, I feel it, and so does Sebastien. It was inevitable.”

“I didn’t exactly put up much of a fight.”

“You’re far too rational for infighting,” he teased, and trailed his hand down her spine.

“We haven’t even had coffee. Or any of that lunch your assistant picked up.” Somehow, that shamed her more than anything. She pulled away, and lifted her hands to cover her hot cheeks. “How can I swing from thinking you were both perverts to wanting in on the action? This is your fault,” she groaned. “Why did you have to be Alexei Ivanov? Anyone else I could have handled. I’ve had a crush on you since I was in high school chemistry and I had to write a paper on you.”

“I’m very glad I’m Alexei Ivanov if it has broken the ice between us. Although, please don’t mention your being at school and studying me. It makes me feel very old.”

Despite herself, she snorted at that. A chuckle bubbled up and burst free. “If you feel old, then how must Bastien feel?”

“Like he’s robbing the cradle, I imagine.”

She shook her head. “There’s only nineteen years between us.”

“At nineteen, most people are considered adults. The age gap is rather large, but”—he shrugged and it oozed with his Gallic sensibilities—“the heart wants what the heart wants, and the body knows what the body needs. And you need each other just as I need you, and as we’ll come to need each other.”

“How can you be okay with this? I don’t even understand it. I’m working on instinct here, and tomorrow I might very well regret all this.”

He sighed. “I met Sebastien when I was eighteen and in college. He was twenty-seven. I lied to him about my age and he believed me, because I’d been at *l’université* for three years already. He didn’t know I’d been fast tracked.”

Devvy grimaced. “Fast tracking sucks.”

“Ah yes, I remember reading that we’d shared that particular nightmare. How many years for you?”

She blushed. "Four. I was studying my Masters when most kids would have just started their undergraduate studies."

"Then you understand. The need to fit in with people in your year but never being able to do so, because you're still a child in comparison to them."

Devvy nodded. "I understand completely. It's why I'm so damned shy." She sighed. "The feeling of being accepted is so important at that age, and when no one can, it does a real number on your confidence. College was one of the worst times of my life but one of the most exciting too."

"Yes, you know you are on the brink of breaking free into your own world. Where that acceptance you crave is no longer of any importance. We'll always be outcasts, Devvy. We're older than our years and because of it, younger. More naïve."

He was right. There were times when she felt very old, and at the other end of the spectrum, very, very young. Last night, when she'd confronted her husband, she'd felt the latter. And all throughout those tense hours with Alex, that feeling hadn't dissipated.

In the face of their experience, of their knowledge of each other, once more, she'd felt like an outsider. Being confronted with the fact Alex could understand how displaced she felt at times was remarkably freeing. Instead of being a round peg forcibly pushed into a square hole, here, in this luxurious penthouse, she finally slotted into place. Even if it was only temporarily.

"Did you meet Bastien *at* college?" she asked, rather than tell him any of that. He was already so certain of her, when she was anything but.

"No. I worked in a café at the train station, and he used to come in every morning after his train came in and every evening, before."

"Love at first sight over a coffee cup, eh?"

He chuckled. "No. Anything but a *coup de foudre*. The age difference between us was a huge problem for him when he learned I was nearly nine years younger than him." Alex grabbed her hand and started to tug her forward. "Come on, I don't fancy having this conversation in the hallway."

He half-dragged her through the first door in the hall, which led to a rather stunning lounge. From the top floor, the windows overlooked a short breadth of Paris. Not enough to see some of the great sights and monuments, just enough to see the lifeblood of the city in the distance.

But the sight of trees and other buildings, a glimpse of the Seine, wasn't the impressive part. The lounge was practically empty. There was a large L-shaped sofa in a bright, almost tomato-red linen. It sat squarely—or as squarely as an L-shaped piece of furniture can—on a cream woolen rug. Tucked into the naturally occurring corner was a coffee table.

That was it.

The huge, cream lounge only contained those three items, and they were bang in the middle of the room. That is, unless you failed to count the enormous, ivory grand piano in the corner, positioned in front of a window so that it looked out onto the world. It was a stunning piece. Something that made even more of a statement due to the sheer emptiness of the space.

"You don't have a TV," she murmured.

He laughed at her observation. "I have one in my bedroom."

He guided her to the sofa and when she sat down, almost primly—knees tucked together, one ankle angled behind the other like her grandmother had taught her—he bent a leg and fell back into the corner seat so he was sitting on his foot. In comparison to her, he looked completely at ease. "Feel free to play mum if you want something to drink. Or eat," he told her, pointing at the coffee set on the table in front of her.

The tray was laden down with a cafétiere and cups, a carafe of water and glasses, as well as a plate of triangle-cut sandwiches, some croissants with extra pats of butter and slices of Brie and ham. She ignored everything, but picked up a slice of ham and nibbled on that, then poured herself a glass of water. "Do you want anything?" she asked and sat back when he shook his head.

"Are you nervous, Devvy?"

"Yes. Do I look it?"

"It was the ham that gave you away," he teased. "Most women don't nibble on ham when they're talking to a soon-to-be lover."

"That's your mistake, Alex," she murmured, her words husky. "I'm not most women. Although, you're almost right. I'm very nervous. In fact, I feel sick. I thought it might settle my stomach."

"You don't need to be nervous, Devvy. We won't pressure you into anything."

"But Sebastien is coming here. He's left work for this." It was only as she said it she realized how much pressure she'd placed herself under by insisting he was here with them.

Alexei shrugged. "And? Sometimes, a wife has a need for her husband."

"I've never called him out of work before," she muttered, then bit her lip as guilt assailed her.

"Then he is very fortunate! I think I shall have to teach you not to be a mouse around him. You can roar. He won't break, and he won't throw you out." He spoke with wisdom and a shrewdness that had her narrowing her eyes at him.

"What do you mean by that?"

"Even if you did not agree to this today, he would not ask for a separation. You would have to make the request. He approached you because of me, but he did not ask you to be his wife for the same reason. You didn't have to be his wife for this relationship of ours to work. He asked you to marry him of his own accord."

"He wanted me, you mean."

"Yes." He shook his head at her scowl of disbelief. "Is that so difficult to understand?"

She hooted. "You ask me that when we had a similar experience at college, Alexei? Try losing your virginity at twenty-three, because you were jailbait to every single guy in your class—even when you started on your Masters! As inexperienced as I am with sex, I'm even worse with men. You might as well be Martians. In fact, I'd probably have more fun trying to understand you if you were!"

Alex's lips twitched. "I see what he means now."

Devvy scowled. "About what?"

"You have a tendency to run off on a tangent and then throw the strangest comment into the mix. Charming," he breathed and leaned toward her.

"Well, I'm glad being a social pariah is a turn on for both of you. It looks like my luck is finally in!"

"Oh, it was two years ago, Devvy. Today is the first day of the rest of your life, *mignonne*. Whichever path you choose to take is up to you, but know we will be here for you. Either way."

"I'm sure."

"Your cynicism wounds me."

"If an American guy said that to me, I'd probably ask him which Jane Austen novel he fell out of."

"Then it is a good thing that I am French, *non*?"

"Maybe."

The fact Bastien was French sometimes worked against her. Trying to argue with a man with an accent as sexy as her husband's was counterproductive. Not that they argued often. As Alexei had rightly assumed, she tended to stay quiet even if something annoyed her.

And the fact that he was right on the money pissed her off all the more.

Now, she was adding another man to the mix. She'd never get anything done! The thought almost made her groan at the very idea of what they would be doing instead of arguing…

She sighed, forced herself to stop thinking about French words being muttered in her ear as Alex rutted away on top of her, his mouth brushing her ear, her entire being surrounded by his scent, his power. Devvy cleared her throat and said, "Anyway, you were telling me about how you two met."

"I am wise enough to change the topic for the moment, *ma petite*. But be aware, you are not powerless in your marriage. In fact, you hold a lot of power. And now, you hold even more. If you allow me into your life, into your partnership, you will have two men who want you. Who need you. Just remember that, *hein*?"

At the very French "filler" word, *hein*, Devvy had to withhold a sigh. Those sounds were incredibly sexy, especially to a non-speaker of the language. There were times when just listening to Bastien on the phone made her want to climb onto his lap and ravish his mouth with her own.

Not that she'd ever done that.

Sighing at her lack of balls, she took another bite of ham. Maybe Alex was right. Meekness had gotten her nowhere in her life.

Why did she have courage as a scientist but not as a woman?

She let Bastien get away with blue murder. All out of gratefulness.

It was time for that to change.

"Neither of us have leanings toward men, Devvy," Alex dropped that little bomb and blasted her thoughts of her uselessness as a woman away.

She choked on the ham and grabbed her glass of water. Croakily, she muttered, “Then I completely misunderstood what the two of you mean to each other.”

He laughed. “No, Bastien and I are lovers. In every sense.”

“Then, what do you mean?”

“What I said yesterday. I do not like to be labeled and neither does Bastien, mostly because we’re neither gay nor straight nor bisexual. We like what we like and we want what we want. For twenty years, I’ve wanted Sebastien. And now, I want you.”

“Have you slept with any other men?”

He eyed her, pondering her question. “Why do you want to know?”

She shrugged. “I’m just curious.”

“There have been three men in my life. Bastien is one of them. But I’m fussy.”

“Bastien does that to a person,” she mumbled.

Alex’s grin nearly split his jaw in two. “Yes, he does. I am fortunate, am I not, that you find me attractive for my brain. Otherwise, I would be standing in the shadow of our great industrialist.”

“Not just for your brain,” she replied, speaking the truth. Even if it was embarrassing.

“That is nice to know, *chérie*.”

“I’m just being honest.”

“I know and I thank you for it.” He sank a little deeper into the cushions and studied her. “As you correctly assumed, none of my lovers even compared to Bastien. But, he has one failing.”

“He does?” She cocked her brow at him, her curiosity piqued.

“He does not have a *chatte*.” At her frown of confusion, he waved his hands. “A pussy, I think you call it?”

Laughter gurgled out of her, and she nearly spilled her glass of water down her front. “No, I think I’d have noticed if he did.” Grinning at him in return, she asked, “And you like pussy?”

“I do,” he told her softly. “Very much.”

His eyes flared at her, the lids widening slightly, exposing her to those violet orbs. They were truly beautiful. Enough to lose herself in them.

"You want mine?" The awkward question came out breathless, and had her stomach cramping with lust. It flashed through her, setting her skin to tingling with gooseflesh.

"Very much," he repeated. "Are you going to give it to me?"

Devvy scored her bottom lip with her teeth as she looked at this man, a creature who made her feel things not even Bastien had made her feel. Edgy, nervous, needy.

Bastien was rough. Not in a mean way, but he took. He conquered. When they had sex, afterward, it was like she'd been steamrollered. Every part of her ached, in the best possible way. Her pussy pulsed with the aftermath of the orgasms that throttled through her. Her breasts and nipples were sore from his teeth and tongue, the mouth that could suck those nubs of hers until she'd cum from that alone. He'd drag her over his lap and spank her. Roll her onto her knees and fuck her in the ass.

She was borderline passive with him. Letting him do whatever he desired, taking serious pleasure in letting him have his way with her. But she was with him at each step. Wanting more, needing everything he could give.

Devvy had a feeling Alex was a different kettle of fish. She could sense that he would tease and toy with her. He'd push her over the edge and then drag her back before she could fall, only to force her over once more.

Sebastien would let her fall. He'd glory in her tumble down to an orgasm.

Alex would make her beg for it. He'd make her work for every single sensation.

That hypothesis, based only on this conversation and his silky tone, was hardly concrete. But as with yesterday and her belief that Bastien had been cheating on her, Devvy's instincts were solid.

She sensed it and knew he was as different to Bastien as night was to day, and not just where their coloring was concerned.

She also knew that if she walked away from him, if she didn't experience his touch, just the once, she'd forever regret it.

At her prolonged silence, he merely stared at her, waiting for an answer. Until finally, when the doorbell rang, the sound jolting the pair of them, he gritted out, "Well, Devvy. Will you?"

She could do nothing less than nod her compliance.

Down the rabbit hole I go, she thought, almost fatalistically, but knew she'd be a willing player in the madness that was to come.

Chapter Four

He'd have been lying if he'd denied being thrilled by this unexpected outcome. But that was just what it was. *Unexpected.* And damned if Alexei Ivanov didn't want to kiss Devvy Jacques's feet for giving him one hell of a surprise.

Her coming at all today had been a shock. He'd expected an apology call, or an irate one saying that she couldn't go anywhere near him without her divorce lawyer present. Although if that had been the case, Bastien would have called him. Probably in tears.

Their marital dynamic was beyond peculiar. In fact, it was intriguing. Both granted the other one more power than either realized, and felt as though they were the weaker, or less powerful, one in their relationship.

Devvy had absolutely no idea of the hold she had over Bastien. Who yes, had instigated the relationship on Alex's say-so, but who hadn't proposed for the same reason. Their cosmetics magnate had managed to skip the bonds of matrimony for over two decades, but with Devvy, he'd decided to cement it with a ring. Apparently, Alex was the only one to see the meaning behind that.

As he stood and murmured to a shell-shocked-looking Devvy, "I'll just go and open the elevator for him," Alex pondered how interesting it would be to enter the unusual dynamic the two of them shared. He couldn't help but wonder how the power would shift and who would retain the most of it.

Bastien had been born a leader. It was in his blood. He wasn't cruel, and while he had a domineering streak, he wasn't dominant per se. He could be rough, and sex with him could cause a person to walk awkwardly the next day, but the man's arrogance was ingrained.

Devvy, on the other hand, was a loner. There was a power in that. She was self-reliant and accustomed to doing things for herself. That made her strong. Incorruptible. While he knew she valued herself, he also knew she didn't see her own attraction. Unusually, this wasn't because society had worked its magic on her. Her belief in her own lack of appeal stemmed from her adolescence. The time when her sexuality should have started to blossom, and instead, she'd been among a too-old crowd. To Devvy, she was still the young teenager amid the twenty-somethings, and therefore, unattractive and unappealing as well as awkward to the average guy. That in turn made her susceptible to Bastien, because she thought herself lucky to have him.

It was interesting that yesterday she'd refused their overtures even though it seemed like she gave in to Bastien a lot. Out of gratitude for him having taken her on—something that would rankle Sebastien if the other man were to learn that his wife was *grateful* to be married to him. Just the thought made him chuckle, for Sebastien's arrogance would weep at that.

Alex had appreciated Devvy's show of strength. That display of self-worth in the face of what she believed she could lose for saying no. And after their conversation this morning, it came as a relief to realize she was here for herself, and not to please Sebastien.

He could have doubted that if her body hadn't sent him the message. Loud and clear. One his own had reacted to, and responded to in kind. For the first time in his life, being Alexei Ivanov was a blessing, and not a curse. This woman, this amazing creature, lusted after him for his smarts. Oh, it wasn't the first time it had happened, it was just the first time it counted.

Alex moved out of the salon and into the hall, opening the downstairs door after a quick glimpse at the video footage, and at Bastien's tense if gloriously handsome face. He stood and waited for the other bell to ring, the one that told him someone wished to come to his floor, and then released the lock when the elevator pinged.

Bastien entered the apartment looking…the only way Alex could describe it was flustered.

It was amusing to see him that way, *and* touching. They'd both invested a lot of their hopes and dreams in this one woman, and to see them coming to fruition, even if it was only the first step down that path, was something worthy of celebration.

"You should have used your key," was all he said in the face of Bastien's meltdown, as he pressed a kiss to his lover's mouth.

"I didn't want Devvy to think I was sneaking in."

Considering that made no sense to him, he wondered what the hell his lover was thinking about, but shrugged rather than make a comment that would set Bastien off. "Well, she definitely knows you're here now."

"So she hasn't left?" Bastien sighed, literally sagging with relief as the elevator doors closed gently behind him. "Where is she?"

"In the salon."

"What the hell made her change her mind?"

Alex watched as Bastien raked a hand through his hair and from the dishevelment, it wasn't the first time he'd done so. If Devvy saw their mate now, she'd realize how tightly she had Bastien wrapped around her little finger. Alex foresaw a future where he was just as whipped, and rather than dread the prospect, he reveled in the idea, because she was his.

Like Devvy herself had said, they were scientists. Scientists didn't believe in the ethereal notion that soul mates existed. But Alex had, and *did*. The minute he'd opened *Science, NOW* and read the article-cum-bio of one Devina Nelson, he'd been hooked.

Her biography had interested him. Their shared past and experiences of being pushed through their school years so both graduated at an early age had come as a relief. They were both outsiders to their own peer group. Her article on the underestimated study of plants and flowers for medicinal purposes hadn't been as hokey as it might have been. Her arguments had been sound, intelligent, and her reasoning tight and loophole-free. She'd appealed to his intellect with every single justification. Then, he'd turned the page, and fallen hook, line, and sinker for a woman whose eyes were eerily beautiful. They'd leapt out at him, almost off the damn page. Those aquamarine orbs, so light in her pale face that she should have looked washed-out. Instead, she looked stunning. *Had* stunned him.

He wasn't an emotional man—for survival, he'd frozen the most tender parts of his nature—but Alex admitted his heart had stopped at that moment. Only a deep gasp had brought him back from his shock. He'd had to know her. To meet her had become imperative. Then, he'd seen the comment that she would be in his country, his home city. To him, that had been a sign from above. She would be here, in Paris. He'd made Bastien attend a convention, a place he wouldn't ordinarily be caught dead, just so they could start the ball rolling.

That act alone told him something he'd already known. Bastien's love for him was deep and true. As well as accepting. For a man as powerful as Sebastien was, Alex knew his agoraphobia could be viewed as a weakness. There was no doubting it was, but in his lover's eyes, it could have been unacceptable. Yet, not to Sebastien. Alex's flaws were simply viewed as one of his quirks, and were always handled with loving patience.

For a love so pure on both sides, they shouldn't have needed a third. But like he'd told Devvy, Sebastien's lack of a pussy was a major problem. His lips twitched at her amused reaction to his comment.

Just like Sebastien, Alex needed a woman's touch in his life. As complete as his lover made him feel, there was something missing.

And Devvy was that something.

"What are you smiling at?" Bastien snapped. "Answer me. What's made her change her mind? She's usually so stubborn! I thought we'd have a real fight on our hands to make her accept us."

"It's lucky for you that you want to share me with Alexei."

Devvy's hesitant and bad French stopped Alex from replying. The pair of them spun around to face the woman who would complete their circle.

Sebastien swallowed, his Adam's apple bobbing. "*T'es certain*? You are certain about this, Devvy?" he replied, reverting to English for her sake.

His croaky tone had the corner of her mouth lifting. "No. I'm not certain at all. In fact, I'm terrified."

She wrapped her arms about her belly in a display of vulnerability that made Alex ache. He couldn't help it. He strode over to her, and wrapped an arm about her shoulder. She nuzzled her face against his side in a way that made his heart swell and his cock stiffen.

"You don't have to be scared," Alex told her, pressing a kiss to the top of her head.

"I know but I still am. I have no reasonable explanation as to why I want to do this with you, *both* of you. Yesterday, I was certain my marriage was over. Last night, I had confirmation. Then this morning, I needed to see you, Alex. It didn't even cross my mind that I could cancel until you mentioned it. I had to visit. I needed to know you."

"Why do you think this whole thing started, Devvy?" Bastien murmured. "Alex saw you in a magazine, and there was an instant connection. I thought he was insane." He chuckled. "You will learn he has his quirks, and most of them are not to be trusted. But in this, he was so…" He sighed, looking for the right word. "*Ardent.* There is no other way of putting it. It was imperative that I meet you, and see how we gelled. The minute we met, the same happened for me. It was instant, and it was almost unbelievable.

"I'm too old to believe in love at first sight, Devvy. I mocked Alex for rambling on about you. I read the article you wrote, and while it was well written, I didn't particularly think anything of it…"

"You can see I married him for his compliments, can't you?" Devvy interrupted, throwing Alex an eye roll that once again had his heart swelling. She kept on treating him as though they'd known each other a long time. And the amazing thing was, it felt that way.

Bastien grinned, and it was the version of his that was worthy of a patent. Alex felt Devvy stiffen beside him, and hid a smile of his own—that grin affected her just as it did him.

There were few moments when Bastien was truly joyful. He was not only a busy man, but an important one, too. Upon his shoulders, he had the responsibility of a large conglomerate as well as two lovers. As powerful as he was, Alex was sure the two lovers caused him more aggravation than the conglomerate with its multiple offshoots.

"I told you Alex was the charmer."

Devvy grunted.

"But it's the truth. Until I saw you in the flesh, I didn't realize. Once I did, that was that. Tell me, Devvy, why do you want Alex?"

Her cheeks bloomed with heat.

"Don't be embarrassed, *ma petite*. It is important that we are honest with each other."

Devvy moved away from Alex's hold, and turned her back on the both of them. They watched as she stalked out of the hallway, and retreated to the salon. As they shared a look, Alex commented, "It is only natural she has trouble expressing herself."

"Why is it?"

"She is a creature of science, *cher*. And from what I can gather, this is the most emotional she's probably ever been. Come," he muttered. "We're wasting time."

The pair of them followed Devvy, their eyes tracking her movements as she stalked from one side of the room to the other.

"We might as well be comfortable," Bastien remarked, and took a seat on the sofa.

"Why don't you have any furniture in here?" Devvy demanded during her hike from the piano to the end wall and back. With her arms crossed and head down, she looked harried and Alex was sorry they'd made her feel that way.

He had no doubt it would be worth it in the end, but he disliked causing anyone discomfort. Especially someone as important to him as Devvy.

"Because when I play the piano, the music rings around the room," he told her easily, letting her change the subject as she tried to come to terms with her emotions.

He hadn't expected her to accept this arrangement easily. As Bastien had already admitted, they had expected many arguments and many attempts at seduction. As it was, Devvy had altered the timeline considerably, and now she looked as though she regretted it.

While his cock mourned the loss, Alex didn't. This was far more important than a shag. This was the future.

"Why do you need a woman, Bastien? Why isn't Alex enough?"

The last question had her looking at Alex with beseeching eyes. He immediately understood and sought to appease her discomfort. "You have not wounded me, *chérie*. Don't worry."

The visible drop of her shoulders conveyed her relief.

"Alex *is* enough," Bastien responded. "I love him very much. There have been times during our relationship where, had he not been a part of my life, I do not know how I would have coped. But I am not a man who will fit himself neatly into a pigeonhole to suit society. I know what I want.

"Just as I want Alex, I want you. Society says that's wrong. That just you or just Alex should be enough. I say fuck society.

"Maybe I'm greedy, selfish even, because I make no bones about wanting it all, but I don't care. I want what I want and I make no apologies for it."

Devvy glared at him. "That's no answer! What did you want before I came onto the scene? Would any woman have been enough for you two? Or is this about children? Am I going to agree to this…relationship, end up pregnant, and then find myself being divorced because my usefulness is over?"

Alex's temper was piqued at her remarks but Bastien just chuckled. He looked over and grinned. "Did I not tell you she was melodramatic?"

"Don't talk about me like I'm not here!"

Bastien held up his hands in surrender. "I'm sorry, love, but it's true. Where these ideas come from, I do not know. I swear, you should be a writer." He shook his head. "If Alex and I wanted a child, do you think we are not rich enough to beget one without involving an innocent woman? There are many less naïve women out there who would gladly sell us their baby if that were what we wanted. Surrogacy does exist in America, doesn't it?"

She flushed.

That gave Bastien all the answer he needed, and his pointed look said so. "Any children resulting from our union will be celebrated. But they are a natural by-product of what we all want. They are not the reason." He sighed. "Look, why does a gay man want another man?"

Devvy bit her lip. "He just does."

"Exactly. Asking me why I want Alex and a woman is exactly the same. I just do. I can't explain it. It's something entrenched in my DNA, just like my black hair. Maybe it's perverse in normal society, but like I said, I don't give a damn. I'm rich enough to live in a world of my own choosing, as is Alex. I'm going to assume you tackled him with these same questions?" When she nodded, he asked, "And what did he say?"

"That you don't have a vagina."

Bastien laughed. "I'm sure he used that exact word," he mocked, cocking a brow at Alex.

"Actually, I said pussy."

Sebastien just smiled. "But there you have it. He feels the same. We both need you, just as we need each other."

Devvy stopped her striding and hovered in front of the sofa. She looked vulnerable, and Alex wanted to tug her down onto his lap, and embrace that vulnerability away. On the brink of doing just that, she stopped him by muttering, "But why would I want two men?"

"Double the pleasure," Alex said, and received a cutting glance from Bastien for his pains.

"While he is correct, there is a simpler reason. What you feel for me, *chérie*, could you feel for Alex?" At her shaky nod, he continued, "And the way you respond to Alex, the attraction you feel for him, have you ever felt that before or with any other man?"

"Just you," she mumbled.

"There you have your reason, *mon ange*."

"Maybe it just means I'm a slut."

Alex snorted. "Finding two men appealing does not make you a slut."

"I shouldn't feel this way when I'm married."

"Why do affairs happen? Because people start to want someone else. Now, in this instance, had you met Alex, at a scientific gathering for example, and you had these feelings for him, you'd feel guilty but you'd act on them. It would be as inevitable as the moon waxing and waning. Sometimes, these things cannot be helped."

"Affairs are unforgivable."

"Yes, they are. They're a betrayal, because you're going behind someone's back. Someone you made vows to. But with us, you're not betraying me. I asked you to open your mind to the idea of sharing yourself with Alex. You refused. Yet this morning, you found yourself here. Why? Because he makes you feel something so rare, its value is precious.

"It is sheer good fortune on our parts the man you have fancied from afar is the man I asked you to consider. Then again, perhaps it is not fortune but fate."

"Oh, don't you start on about destiny!" she muttered crossly, to which he simply chuckled.

"You cannot hide from it, *mon amour*. You simply cannot. Feel lucky you can have us both, that you can love the two men who do something for you no other has. Do not reject it or call yourself horrible names for needing two men. *Embrace* it."

Could she? Was it possible to so easily accept Alex into her bed?

She already felt like a pushover. They hadn't even had to convince her into doing this. Her body had done the convincing. The minute she'd seen Alex this morning, she'd wanted him. Her entire being had come to life.

Bastien was right. How could she ignore that?

If Alex and she had happened upon each other at a conference, would she have been able to fight the attraction? Or had last night's suggestion made her body susceptible to the idea of being able to have both with no recriminations?

Devvy couldn't say for sure. And it was that that convinced her.

Life was short. *Too* short. So few were fortunate enough to feel this way for one person, never mind two, and Bastien was right again—not that she'd tell him. His head was large enough. Her feelings for him could easily extend to Alex. She couldn't explain it. There was no rhythm to it, no rhyme. It just was.

Standing in front of the two most handsome men she'd ever seen, she whispered, "Okay."

Elation flashed over Sebastien's face, and as her eyes flickered over to Alex, she saw a gut-wrenching relief. A relief so deep that she was humbled.

What had she done to deserve this? Devvy didn't know but she hoped she lived up to their expectations.

"Where do we go from here?" She bit her lip as awkwardness tugged at her confidence.

Bastien patted the sofa beside him. His smile was gentle when she complied. "We go at your pace, *mon amour*."

Devvy nodded, and then found she couldn't stop nodding. Until, that is, Bastien grabbed her chin, held it with his fingers, and slanted his mouth over hers. The instant their lips connected, the nervous energy seemed to slither out of her veins. He always did this to her. Made her forget herself, made her drown in emotions and sensations that, up until now, only he'd created.

He was gentle at first—highly unusual for Sebastien—his lips tugging and pulling at hers, drawing her tongue out to play. He dragged his against hers, little flickering laps that had her holding her breath as hunger ravaged her. She moaned against his mouth, lifted her hands to hook around his neck, and the instant she did that, another set of hands were there, cupping her breasts. For a second, she stopped breathing, and then she groaned as Alex began to knead her flesh as he lapped at the side of her throat, and at her nerve-laden nape. He bit down, suckled and continued to do so as he manipulated the warm giving flesh of her neck with his lips, tongue and teeth. She tingled as pleasure rained over her nerve endings, and then whimpered as he pinched the nipples budding through her shirt.

Needing more, but not knowing how to express it, she suddenly felt Sebastien's slender fingers tugging the neckline of her camisole down. They blindly worked at the catch on her bra until her breasts spilled out into the loose cups. Alex's hands supported them for a few seconds, before he moved the cups out of the way, and then bare flesh touched bare flesh, and every inch of her sat up in reaction and hovered with tense expectation, waiting for his next move.

Alex's fingers continued their kneading, only now, with slight calluses scoring the tender skin, the sensations were doubled. As they razed over her nipples, teasing them into tighter buds, she sucked down on Bastien's tongue then grunted as, in response, he began to thrust in and out, fucking her mouth like he'd fuck her pussy. He took control, dominated her, demanded everything she had, until she could do nothing less but give him her all.

Alex clamped down, nibbling at her throat, and from the heavy sucking, she knew she'd have a hickey in the morning. The thought didn't bother her, but his constant pulling motions did. She squirmed in her seat, unbearably excited at having two sets of hands touching her, two mouths tormenting her. And that one of those pairs belonged to Alexei Ivanov made her cream in her panties that little bit more.

Her adolescent crush was touching her, tasting her, supping from her flesh. Devvy didn't think anything, not even Bastien, could get her hotter than that.

She broke free of Sebastien's mouth as Alex suddenly pinched her nipples. Her head fell back, feeling too heavy for her neck but it found a support of its own on Alex's shoulder. He was directly behind her, a scorching hot presence along the length of her spine.

For a second, she reveled in the dual heat, in being pressed so totally between them, until Sebastien ducked down, and his lips pressed open-mouthed kisses to her breasts. She looked at him, watched his mouth playing and tormenting her greedy flesh, feeling dazed at the thought of the pair of them attending to her. When she saw Alex's hands offering her breasts to Sebastien's mouth, she jerked upward, and sent her hands to the hem of her skirt. She wriggled and dragged it up, up, until she could spread her thighs. The instant she could, she sent them around Bastien's hips, widening them even more.

With that one desperate act, she knew what she was inviting and she froze. The hands, lips, tongue and teeth continued their insidious magic.

They made her breathless with want and need but she wasn't ready. She wasn't. No matter how much her body wanted them, both of them, this wasn't Devvy. They'd taken her out of herself, transformed her into a sex-fueled creature.

For the first time in her life, Devvy wasn't the prodigious scientist. She was a sex-starved beast, wanting only cock. These two men's cocks.

The scientist had reared its head, however, and croakily, she whispered, "Bastien?"

He hummed around her nipple, making her cunt cream a little harder, and her body need that much more. She could so easily throw herself into this. So easily let him fuck her as she rested against Alex, using him as a back support. But if she did, she'd regret it tomorrow.

"Bastien, stop," she grated out as Alex pinched her nipple so Sebastien could tug at the tip with his teeth.

At her words, he obeyed, releasing her nipple with a panting breath.

"I need…," she managed to say, and then sucked in another breath. "I need to see you two kiss. I"—just saying the word had her toes curling—"I really need to see you both together."

She didn't want this to end, but she just couldn't let it end the way her body needed. If she succumbed to the pair of them today, not even twenty-four hours after their shocking suggestion of a ménage à trois, she'd never forgive herself for rolling over so easily. She didn't want to be coerced or seduced down the path they'd spent years constructing. She just needed time to adjust, and to be frank, Devvy didn't think that was a lot to ask!

In the meantime, her body was pissed off. The only consolation that would ease the deep ache in her pussy was the sight of them together. She'd never thought she'd like to see two men kissing, but this was Bastien and Alex. Devvy didn't think there could be anything more glorious.

Alex chuckled against her throat, and the vibration made her blood run a little hotter. It also distracted her, so when Bastien dragged her legs around his waist, and when he lifted her so she was pressed tightly against him, she could only squeal with shock. As soon as he moved, Alex did too, and what she thought would happen, didn't.

Sandwiched between the pair of them, she was in sensory heaven. Alex's lean length cushioned her back, and Bastien's bulky muscles were a heavy weight above her. To put the cherry on the cake, over her shoulder, the two of them kissed. She turned her head, and awkwardly gawked at the pair of them as they kissed over her. Only when Sebastien rocked his hips slightly did she realize what he'd done. Perfectly aligned his cock along the parted lips of her pussy.

His erect cock.

Beneath her clit, where she needed it most.

The sounds in her ear, the sight beside her…she didn't care if she ended up with a permanent crick in her neck. She couldn't stop watching.

It was tenderer than she'd imagined. Slower. Sebastien didn't really do slow. At least, not with her. He tended to fuck her silly, saving the gentle kisses for afterward. But here, he was different.

They gently rocked their mouths, rubbing their lips against the other. Then, she saw a quick peek of Bastien's tongue, and the man she knew suddenly came to the fore. His tongue worked at Alex's. He raked his down the other man's, nibbled and tangled the two together. He pulled away only to bite down on Alex's bottom lip. When Alex groaned, Bastien's hips rocked upward, and that started the rhythm. That groan was the catalyst, because Bastien didn't stop rocking. His cock continued to work at her panty-covered cunt, dragging back and forth, back and forth, until once more her head was rolling against Alex's shoulder. It turned out that was the perfect position for watching the pair of them devour each other.

Up until that moment, Alex had taken Bastien's aggression, accepted it with enjoyment. That was until Devvy had started to whimper and mewl at the contact of Sebastien's shaft where she needed it most, a touch that was just right but not enough to get her off.

The sounds incited Alex, which in turn thrilled her. To see his reaction to her arousal made her blood start to sing and she watched, in awe, as he started to fuck Sebastien's mouth with his tongue.

As impatient as ever, Bastien allowed it for thirty seconds at the most, and then he was forcing the pair of them backward. The press of his chest to her bare breasts had her groaning and she barely noticed as Alex controlled the movement, slowing down the pace until he was flat on his back on the sofa with her above him. Bastien had more freedom now and he removed her legs from about his waist and knelt on the sofa between her thighs. Then, he was there. The pressure at her core had her back arching as he began to fuck her, only without penetration.

He seemed to realize she wouldn't be able to cope with that until she'd grown more used to the idea, but he also knew she needed this. Only this would break down her barriers. Sure, she'd be embarrassed afterward, but it would be the start of her tumbling down the slippery slope, and even in her current state of need, she was well aware that was all Sebastien wanted from her. Once it started, it would snowball until she craved them and would agree to all their demands.

At that moment in time, she didn't give a shit. And she gave even less of a shit when a hand shoved in between Bastien's hips and hers, and fingers fought their way into contact with her sex. Suddenly her panties were dragged out of the way, and the digits burrowed down.

It was Alex. She could tell by the calluses.

Every part of her sat up and danced at the knowledge his hands were inches away from the entrance to her body. For all intents and purposes, his fingers were on her pussy, and didn't it just welcome him? She literally felt the moisture slip down her channel and coat her pussy lips.

The abrasive quality of Sebastien's expensive pants against her clit had her shrieking, her head lolling from side to side. It was only then she noticed they were still kissing at the same time as they were driving her crazy.

"More, more, more," she mumbled, dazed with a need she didn't know how to soothe.

But Alex did.

His fingers slipped down and he began to play with her pussy lips. He ignored her clit, because Bastien had that part of her covered, and she felt him start to coat the digits with her cream. The touch was enough to have her feet burrowing into Bastien's backside. She thought, hoped, prayed he'd fill her cunt with them. But he didn't. They slipped down to her asshole, where he rimmed the tight pucker once, twice, and then shoved a finger in deep to the second knuckle.

Her vision turned fuzzy, like the gray snow on a dying TV set. As he pressed deep, the gray began to bleed out, drain away, leaving dark patches at the edge of her vision. Almost like her nerves were short-circuiting. When he slipped his thumb into her cunt, and between thumb and forefinger pinched down, taunting the thin membrane where one day Alex and Bastien's cocks would rub, her sight finally caved in and turned black.

A shrill scream escaped her and this time, her back arched up with such a force it jerked Bastien backward. Her head, resting against Alex's on the sofa, held all of her weight as Bastien's hips and Alex's fingers pinned her butt down.

She was surrounded. On all sides. By their bodies as well as their arousal. Their panting echoed around the room, but they seemed to swaddle her. Deepen their possession of her. The only hole that wasn't filled was the one that didn't really count, her mouth. At that moment, she was theirs. Taken and claimed by Alex and Bastien in the most simple yet effective of ways. She would never forget this moment. She would always crave the duality of their touch against her.

This was a memory in the making, one that would haunt her for life.

Time would tell if that was for good or ill.

* * * *

It was worth returning to the office with a hard-on as well as a fresh suit, thanks to Devvy's cum ruining the expensive fabric of his previous set of pants. A thought that had his dick twitching with the memory of what had just happened on Alex's sofa. Only those two could have him so hungry, so fast. It was a phenomenon the two of them shared. It made them unique to him. Special.

In truth, Sebastien had never been so happy to have an aching cock. It was well worth the discomfort. And besides that, he was on top of the world. She'd actually taken part in their first "scene" together, and afterward, even though she'd been shy, another kiss from Alex had made her cheeks stop their blushing, and she'd simply sagged into his hold, going completely limp.

Seeing the two of them together—Bastien wasn't ashamed to admit—had lodged a lump in his throat.

All the years of waiting, planning, and hoping, and they'd found *her*. She wasn't a faceless woman, a stranger. She was Devvy. The only person he could ever love as he did Alex and did, in fact, even though in comparison to his other mate, Bastien had only known her for two short years.

When a person entered your life, took over, and you didn't mind, that was serious stuff. From the very first, Devvy had been that person. She'd sat at the front of his mind, vying for position with Alex. Sometimes winning, because he'd been so certain she was the one to finally complete the pair of them, and his judgment hadn't been wrong.

Today was the first step down the path to all of his and Alex's dreams being fulfilled.

God, he was a lucky bastard.

He didn't even care that someone was trying to blackmail him. He was walking on air, because the journey had begun.

That being said, he'd have to deal with the blackmailer sooner or later. There had been vague threats over the years. Exposés he'd quashed by revealing all to the press, and cutting the blackmailer off without a cent. He was as honest as a businessman could be, and where his company was concerned, he had nothing to be ashamed of. He made certain of that.

Being an ethical producer of cosmetics was hard for many businesses, but not for him. He'd started in the industry thanks to family. In his case, his great-great-grandmother. She'd had a book loaded with ancient and old-fashioned remedies.

When he'd gone through a punk phase, he'd nearly destroyed his hair by over-bleaching it. Not one of his proudest teenage memories. Especially as his grandmother had made him douse his hair in her grandmother's special shampoo. Regardless of his adolescent horror of smelling like a *bouquet garni*, it had worked. The rosemary, basil, and mint shampoo had done what expensive hair repair masks hadn't. She'd sorted out a pimple cream for him too, and when he'd started his job at a frozen foods factory, her honey and lemon balm had stopped his skin from becoming chapped.

When she'd died at the grand old age of ninety-nine and left him her book of magic potions, he'd decided to get out of the frozen food industry—packing up revolting excuses for chicken goujons had not been his career of choice—and had started a little market stall selling her recipes to the public. His products had been popular, because they'd all worked. Organic, locally sourced, and doing what they said on the label, he'd soon been earning enough to start classes at night school. Business classes.

Soon after, he'd hired a helper, one who had sold his produce at the local markets while he kept up with the demand on the products. Then he'd hired another assistant, this one to help him in the kitchen as he produced the remedies. Over the next few years, there had been the rental of a shop and then another, and another. He'd had to outsource to a local laboratory that could make his preparations *en masse*. A laboratory he'd eventually purchased.

It had been a long and hard road to success, but five or so years in, when ethical beauty had hit the masses as the ultimate in importance, his little Lyonnais brand had suddenly gone national thanks to Julia Angel, one of France's highest paying actresses, who had mentioned *La Belle sans la Bête* on a chat show one Friday night, declaring it a miracle brand, and the major reason for her clear skin and natural beauty.

Combine that with the internet, and sales had boomed. So much so, his brand had gone international. He was no longer a company, but a conglomerate with many fingers in many pies. But through it all, he stayed true to his grandmother and the family recipes.

In this instance, the blackmailer wasn't interested in exposing the source of his basil for the hair-repair shampoo, but in the fact he was a married man with a male lover.

Having to reveal all to Devvy couldn't have come at a better time. If the blackmailer were to get impatient or renege on his so-called promises, she wouldn't have to learn about Alex thanks to some gossip column or two-bit rag.

Not that he wanted the truth about Alex to come to light. Not yet, at any rate.

He hadn't lied when he'd told Devvy he didn't give a damn about society, and their views on the kind of relationship he wanted with her and Alex. He'd made it to the top and with a hell of a lot of millions to cushion him from life's blows. If the news were revealed about their ménage, well, he'd ride it with ease. Alex would hardly be disturbed, because he never left his bloody apartment! But it was Devvy who would be most affected, and at the moment, she was too uncertain, too insecure in his love for her to cope with a revelation of that nature. She needed Alex's reciprocal love to further cement her place in their world.

She didn't know what she meant to him and there was nothing Bastien could do to rectify that but hold out, remain strong, and know that eventually, she'd know who and what she was to him. What she meant to him.

Which was nothing less than the world.

Chapter Five

"Don't go there! Don't do it! You stupid bitch, get out of the way!" Devvy's shrieks had Alex laughing.

"She can't hear you."

"Even if she could, she wouldn't listen. Why would you do that?" she asked him, deadly serious. "Why, when you know there's a serial killer outside your door, *why* would you open it and try to run for safety? For God's sake, that's like rule number one in the 'how to deal with mass murderers' handbook! How can anyone watch this crap?"

"We're watching it, *ma petite*."

She sniffed and with great aplomb, grabbed the remote and pressed the OFF button. "We're not anymore," she said, her words oozing with satisfaction. "What a load of shit."

"You won't hear me disagreeing," he retorted, eying her from his position on the bed.

Sitting up against the bedhead, legs flat out and crossed at the ankle, hands together and resting on his belly, he looked cool, relaxed, and sexy as hell. An inch away from his hands, his cock butted against the fly. He had an erection. In fact, every time they were together, he seemed to have a hard-on.

For the most part, she ignored it. Well, she *looked* at it but never commented or acted on the silent promise of his arousal.

After two weeks of dating Alex, she had to ask herself why she was holding back, and also, if she was insane. The man was perfect for her. So perfect she knew she'd be hard-pressed to choose between Bastien and Alex. *If* she ever had to.

A month ago, the very idea of wanting another man more than Bastien would have made her snort with amusement at the impossibility of that ever happening.

Two weeks ago, she'd have doubted it or felt guilty at the very notion.

But today, she knew it was a step in the right direction.

The very basis of this relationship was the fact that she didn't have to choose. She could have them both, and that her feelings for Alex could, with time, level with those she had for Bastien meant a great deal. It was a promise of the things to come.

And she loved it.

She was flourishing under their care.

For the first time in her life, she was secure in herself as a sexual creature. She no longer felt immature, incapable of handling Sebastien, never mind Alex, too. She was ready for this. She was ready for the next level.

Bastien had had to fly to Napa this evening. There had been a crisis on one of the vineyards he owned, and even though he could have delegated, the situation had merited his attention because this year's harvest rested on his decision. Rather than have the details shuffled over the internet or via phone, he'd decided to go out there himself and deal with it personally.

His mind had been focused on the bug currently eating through a quarter of his crop, when she'd packed up some clothes for him. He'd absently told her the details as he prepared his briefcase. In fact, the only time he'd given her his full attention had been with the goodbye kiss.

Hours later, and she was still horny because of that tongue-on-tongue action.

The driver had honked the horn before he could say anything more than, "Be good." And he'd left her to it.

She could have stayed at their house. A month ago, there would have been no question about it. But tonight, she hadn't wanted to. She'd waited for the driver to return from dropping Sebastien off at the private airfield where his jet was housed, and she'd asked him to take her to Alex's.

He'd been shocked to see her, but pleased. They'd only parted a few hours earlier, when they'd dined on bo luc lac, a Vietnamese beef dish, and bitched about an article they'd both read in *Science, NOW* on a group of scientists who refused to believe in global warming.

The pair of them had enjoyed yelling at each other and arguing as they ate, and she'd returned home to go back to work on her anti-acne soap. A project that had definitely gone on the backburner of late.

The prospect of a night alone when she could be with Alex had seemed churlish, so off she'd gone, driving through the effervescent sparkle of Paris on a Friday night. Promise burning through her veins of what the night could hold alongside the thrill of being with him again. Only as she stood in front of the console, ready to press his buzzer, had the doubts come. Maybe he wouldn't want to see her without Bastien, maybe she should have called first, maybe, maybe…. She'd eventually screwed up the nerve, thanks to her nose feeling like it could drop off in the sharp, chilly wind, and, thank God, Alex had greeted her with open arms.

This was the first time she'd been in his apartment at night, and there was a definite difference in the atmosphere.

Tonight, things would change.

She'd instinctively known the minute she'd made the decision to come here that their relationship would step up a notch. How high a notch—as the last two weeks had shown—depended entirely on her.

She was in control here, and it was pretty damned awesome.

From her position at the foot of the bed, she rolled over onto her back, as she'd been watching the TV on her belly, and sat upright. When Alex had informed her that his TV was in his bedroom, she hadn't realized he had a seventy-inch monster on his wall.

Alex was certainly a fan of minimalism and statement pieces. His bedroom consisted of a bed which, to her untrained eyes, looked like three single beds strapped together. It was huge. But comfortable. The mahogany headrest was cushioned and covered in a dark forest green fabric. The sleigh style bed sat comfortably in the large space. Covered in a huge down quilt with bedcovers the same shade as the headrest and tons of squashy pillows, it looked directly onto the behemoth TV set.

On either side of the bed were two tables. Round, about the size of a dinner plate, with inlaid mother-of-pearl and ebony. Two round orbs were the only lights. They were like translucent versions of crystal balls.

Aside from that, there was a door that led onto a narrow but wide Juliet balcony. She'd looked over onto the still-busy streets, when he'd guided her in here two or so hours ago to watch a movie together.

There was something about his extreme method of interior decoration that pricked her curiosity. She was no psychologist, had no leanings toward the dissection of human emotions or the actions they instigated, but this extreme minimalism said something. It spoke to her. Devvy just couldn't understand the gobbledygook, even though she knew it was important.

"Do you want to watch something else?" he asked easily, breaking into her thoughts and forcing her to stop thinking about the *real* Alex.

In reply to his question, she sighed and shook her head.

"What's wrong?"

"I'm antsy."

"Antsy?" he asked, cocking his brow.

"Yeah. It means I'm on edge, I guess."

"Nervous?" he stated, asking for clarification. The guys spoke English fluently, but sometimes, she'd throw in words that had the pair of them looking at each other in confusion.

To be honest, she'd started saying slang words just to confuse them. They did look adorable with their matching frowns.

She nodded.

"Why? There's no need to be."

"I know there's no need to be, but it doesn't stop me from feeling that way."

"Do you want to go home?"

"No." She made a bridge with her fingers and stretched her arms over her head. "I don't."

"Are you worried I'll jump on you?"

She snorted. "Of course not!"

"Then what?" he muttered, rolling his eyes.

"My mind is saying one thing, and my body is asking for another."

That had his frustrated scowl turning into a smile. "Ah."

Just that one sound and he managed to load it with way too much meaning. It was her turn to scowl.

"Yes. Ah," she grumbled.

He shrugged. "I am here. At your disposal, *mon ange*."

"That doesn't make the decision easier, Alex," she mumbled, only just managing not to groan.

He grinned. "I know."

"Pussy tease." She couldn't fault him. He was always honest.

"Yes," he admitted with a wink. "I'd like to say that you think too much, but you would not be the woman I know you to be if that weren't the case. And if I'm a pussy tease, then you're a cock tease, *ma petite.* You're not the one who has had more cold showers than coffee this past two weeks."

"Been horny, have you?"

He grunted and corrected her, "I have needed you."

"Good answer," she retorted.

"It wasn't a line."

"I know. That's why it was so good." She tapped her fingers against her knee, drumming them as she hovered between the right and the wrong path.

She'd been lucky with these two. They never pressured her. Always made her feel at ease. And they'd been more than generous. Every time the three of them were together, they made her climax. While they always walked off. With a boner.

She'd have liked to have asked them to make each other cum, but her confidence wasn't ready for that move. Instead, she'd watched them kiss and once, Bastien had grabbed Alex's cock through his jeans and jerked him off a little. To her disappointment, Alexei had stopped him and shoved his hand away, instead pushing it down her panties and urging him to get her off.

It was amazing how one could be sexually replete yet still need. She could only imagine how Alex was feeling, and it was the thought of how he must indeed be feeling that had her moving upright and onto her knees. She crawled to his side before lifting a leg and settling herself astride him. Low down at mid-thigh level.

Their eyes clashed. Her new position and his slouched one meant that she looked down on him. Subjectively, she knew it meant nothing. But that didn't stop her feeling as though she was in control.

Swallowing at the thought, she forced herself to calm down. A few deep breaths and she was ready as she'd ever be. Her hands moved forward, almost of their own accord, and she reached for his belt buckle. His own snapped down to catch hers and he murmured, "You don't have to do anything you don't want to, Devvy."

The very lack of pressure worked against her. Maybe she was being difficult, but she wanted him to roll her over and take control. Make the decision for her. And it was for that reason, she knew he wouldn't. That would be for next time. Just this once, he would let her take each step for herself with no coercion.

Even though she wished differently, it asserted once again that if there was another man for her out there, besides Bastien, it was definitely Alex.

"I want this." She wet her lips. "You've no idea how much. I wanted you that first day. Badly. But it was a lot to come to terms with. Going from rejecting the entire thing to wanting it in the space of twelve hours…I had to be sure, and now I am."

"As long as you're ready, *chérie,*" he rasped, his voice guttural as she went to work on his belt buckle, shoving his hands out of the way.

"I am."

The certainty in her voice had relief washing over his features. That tension was replaced with need. Need for her.

The thought made her feel like a kid in a candy store, and as quickly as her hands would work, she pulled off his belt and threw it on the floor. The buckle jangled as it connected with the carpet. She ignored it, kept her focus on his fly. The stubborn ass thing wouldn't budge an inch, and as her exasperation grew with each failed, fumbling attempt, she had to force herself to stop, take a few cleansing breaths to calm herself down, and keeping her eyes away from Alex—just in case, and she highly doubted it, he was smiling—she managed to work the zipper down.

His cock was reassuringly hard regardless of her miserable fumbling, and as it popped out to say hello, she felt her mouth water at the sight of it. It was the first time she'd seen it. The pair of them had remained fully clothed for the last two weeks, while she'd been in various states of undress. Sebastien hadn't even fucked her at home. She'd orgasmed more times than she could count yet she was ravenous for this. She needed Alex inside her. Deep.

His cock was different to Bastien's, who had an extremely thick and medium-length shaft. Sometimes, as he worked his way into her, filling her with his width, it was borderline uncomfortable. He seemed to spread apart her tissues and make them sit up and wave. The very thickness always had her pussy lips spreading and baring her clit, making it pop out of the hood.

Alex's was thinner but longer. She knew, just knew, he'd fit perfectly in her ass. She could almost feel it. Sebastien in her pussy, Alex in her butt.

Both of them touching places the other couldn't, and each of them driving her insane with want and need.

Her hand shot out to grab his cock and as she clenched down, both of them groaned. Deep inside, everything turned to hot mush, whereas Alex's corrugated belly clenched down. She could see it through his shirt.

She dragged her hand up and down his shaft, glorying in the silky sensation and the faint beads of pre-cum that had started to ooze out of the tip. Her mouth watered at the sight and she bent down, hovered and let her breath wash over the head. She waited one, two, three seconds and grinned when his hand gripped the back of her head, tugging at her hair. He was more patient than Bastien though, not that that came as much of a surprise. A beggar at a feast had more patience than her husband! Alex simply urged her head lower, and she accepted the slight pressure, slipping the tip between her lips and sucking down hard. His low groan and slight jerk of his hips encouraged her to continue in the same vein.

She pulled at the glans with the pressure of her mouth, sucking the very essence out of him and only giving him some relief when she flicked the flat of her tongue over the crown. He hissed out a breath as his fingers gripped and tugged at her hair. The sting caused a delicious zing of pleasure to whip through her.

Releasing her hands from his cock, she burrowed down between her own legs and tugged at the fly of her jeans. She seriously hadn't planned this night right by coming to Alex's in pants. What the hell had she been thinking? Why hadn't she changed into a skirt?

Her grunts of exertion vibrated along his shaft and the tingles at her scalp as he pulled her hair had frustration replacing the pleasure as she couldn't get the fly down. Fuck, ask her to make a goddamn anti-wrinkle potion and she was your gal. Pulling down a zipper apparently required an extra degree from college!

Her teeth scraped over the sensitive head of his cock as she whipped her head away. She practically leapt off the bed in her haste to rid herself of her jeans, and once standing, she managed to release the catch and in seconds was shucking free of the tight denim and her panties. Naked from the hips down, she climbed back onto the bed and moved astride him. She didn't mess around, didn't try to prevaricate and tease. She needed to feel his cock deep inside her too much to waste time.

She grabbed his dick and slid it along the length of her cunt, wetting the shaft with all the cream soaking her sex. Only as he nearly penetrated her did she remember a condom and froze. "Tell me you have a condom. Please God," she gritted out and watched as he froze for a second too, before jerking his head in a yes.

His hand shot out and he fumbled for a second, blindly grasping something under the bed. He dragged out a box and the condom wrappers crinkled and sang as he grabbed one and handed it to her.

She sank back onto his thighs as she ripped open the packet with her teeth and spread the condom down his shaft, jerking her hand once, twice, before retreating to her earlier position.

As she slid down, filling herself with him, she stilled. For a second, the sensation of a cock so different to the one that had been fucking her for the last two years was so deliriously hot she wasn't sure if she could come from that alone.

Alex's shaft hit completely different places in her pussy. From the current position, her pelvis resting against his groin so that every inch of him was deep inside, Devvy realized she was content to just sit like that, impaled on his cock. Of their own volition, her inner muscles started to flutter, manipulating his shaft with a deep massage. They sucked down, rippled and played about the intruder invading her. Her head fell back and she used her hands, pushing them down against his belly, to keep her upright. It was only then she realized Alex was still dressed and she still wore her shirt. She'd have liked his hands on her tits, pinching her bare nipples, but she didn't need it enough to move and make that happen. Devvy was quite content to just sit there, almost skewered by his long shaft in the best possible way.

It was only as she took stock of her body that she realized her eyelids were actually twitching with the overwhelming flush of exhilaration. Pleasure was too weak a word to describe the singing nerve ends that sizzled with the scorch of his penetration.

She lifted those twitching eyelids and stared at him, saw the strain on his jaw, the white tension that spoke of his own excitement. He was one of the sexiest men she'd ever seen. And that it was Alex Ivanov's cock deep inside her, had her cunt clenching down on him with the force of a clamp. The resulting groan had her hissing with satisfaction.

She thought of the years she'd spent gawking at his pictures. Her pathetic teen crush on him had had her crawling the net for news on his experiments and the man himself. And here she was. He was fucking her.

In fact, *she*, Devvy Jacques, was fucking him.

The thought of her surname was a reminder of Bastien but it didn't diminish her pleasure any. Instead, her mind leaped ahead, picturing a time when all three of them would be together and that image prompted her to roll her hips for the very first time.

"Yesss," the pair of them hissed out in unison, backs arching as sensation shot down their spines.

Devvy whimpered as she lifted herself free from his shaft, hovering with only an inch of him in her cunt, before slamming herself down again. She repeated the move, enjoying the sensation of emptiness and then, fullness. She worked herself up and down, ignoring the ache in her thighs, using Alex's taut belly as support and he just let her. He let her do whatever she wanted. He let her tease herself, let her use his cock for her own pleasure like she would have used a dildo.

And then, he snapped. As she rolled her hips, descending down his shaft in circular moves that had him touching all sorts of interesting places deep inside, his hands shot out to grab her waist. He pushed her down, sheer force slamming their sexes together. Before she could do more than whimper, he'd rolled upward, over, and then pushed her down so she was flat on her back.

He grabbed her legs and spread them, wide, holding them at the ankle and with sheer brute force, lifting her butt off the bed. When he fucked into her, his cock slid deep, deeper than before and she squealed. Her head lifting off the mattress and slamming into her chest with such speed, she knew she'd have a bruise above her breasts in the morning. He fucked her, fast, hard, taking every inch and claiming it as his and just like that, with no direct stimulation to her clit, no pinching of her nipples, she came.

Everything inside her clamped down. Her stomach muscles reversed into the mattress, her butt fought to retreat to the bed and her pussy, swollen with orgasm, turned into a vice. As he struggled to penetrate her, that struggle only jacked up her pleasure, so the blackness in her vision seemed to glitter and glow at the edges. Fire stole over her nerve endings, making the ones at the back of her eyes burn brightly, blindingly.

Suspended for countless moments, she was flung back into the moment as Alex yelled, his voice breaking as his body froze, his climax hitting him with the same one-two punch as had happened to her.

She watched, drugged from her own orgasm, as he was battered in the same pleasure storm as she had been.

Slowly, he sank down. First, his hips against hers, then his arms released her legs, and finally, his torso kissed her own. He slumped on top of her, and she reveled in his weight. In the heaviness of his frame. The deadweight of his lax body counteracted the battle of his softening cock. Their proximity ensured a few inches of him stayed lodged within her, and with that slight feeling of fullness, with his heaviness pushing her into the bed, with her blood singing with remembered pleasure, she finally dozed.

* * * *

Alex knew he was too heavy to rest on Devvy the way he was doing, but selfishly, he ignored the knowledge and reveled in her clinging arms and legs. She obviously wanted him as close to her as possible, and he used that to soothe the pangs of guilt.

She was like hot silk, every part of her that touched him. She branded him with her own innocence and he knew he'd never be the same after tonight. In that one act, the simple connection of cock to pussy, he reevaluated his sex life.

He enjoyed kink. Whether it was tying Bastien to the bedstead or being tied down himself. Be it a quick fuck in the elevator, wondering if someone was going to press a button and intrude or on the rare occasions they went out, giving Bastien a hand job under the table in a restaurant…. The sexy acts seemed sordid in the face of that innocent union. Of that tender connection that joined a man and a woman together with the sheer power of their mutual pleasure.

Oh, he knew he'd corrupt her eventually, and he looked forward to it. In fact, taking Devvy outside onto the terrace and fucking her as they stared down at the busy, bustling street, clamping a hand over her mouth to keep her quiet as she came, made his drained dick twitch a little inside—something that had her mouth pouting into a happy smile. For sex, he always overcame his agoraphobia—it was worth it! And he didn't doubt

Devvy would make it more than worth his while. It was those moments of naughtiness that were part and parcel of learning every lover's hot spots.

But this…it transcended what he'd imagined.

A part of him had always sought a third for Bastien's sake. Alex was not the right partner for a man like their lover. He was selfish where his science was concerned, stubborn where his refusal to leave his apartment came into play. He loved Bastien with a depth that disturbed even him, but because of that love, he accepted that the other man would need something else in his world. Someone normal. Some hint of softness that Alex couldn't seem to bestow upon his lover. Oh, they embraced and hugged and, in the aftermath of sex, their arms would tangle and their bodies would cling. But in daily life, Alex and Bastien might as well have been friends.

A part of him hoped that having Devvy with them, he'd be able to open up to a more affectionate kind of relationship with Sebastien. He both longed for that time and dreaded it. He'd never been an overly tactile person. His home life had prevented that.

His mother, divorced and shamed by it, loved him too much. As a boy, and a man. Only when he was little, there'd been no escape. She'd cling and grasp at him, trying to hold him back for fear of being alone, of being left once more by a man she loved. Frightened of his intelligence, jealous of it and the distance it placed between them. His early childhood had been a virtual tug of war. He'd been relieved when she'd taken a boyfriend, thinking she'd transfer the suffocating love onto her new partner. But that relief had soon turned to horror.

Alex tried not to think about it, tried not to think about the abuse, about what that bastard had done to him, but it was too late. He'd let the poison in, and now it was taking over. Invading his thoughts, memories, turning everything toxic. He tried to slam on the brakes, but to no avail. As usually happened, a question popped into his head, and it was that question that stewed his brain and triggered a meltdown.

Was his mother aware of what had been done to her once-precious boy? A son easily replaced by a man who had been the perfect partner, all of it for show, so his access to a small child would never be cut off.

The thoughts polluted the once-contented atmosphere of his post-orgasm buzz. The desire to be as close as possible to Devvy dissipated, and he pulled free, tugged away from her with a force that jolted her awake. He dragged himself off, sat on the edge of the bed and then, needing to hide from both her sleepy eyes and from the shame of his past, he sank down to the floor. Curling his legs up, he pressed them to his chest and bowed his head.

No amount of therapy could convince the little boy deep inside he'd done nothing to deserve such treatment. Rationally, he could blame the sick bastard his mother loved to this day. But feelings, emotions, memories…none of them were rational.

He wanted to scream. Wanted to rail with fury at those perfect moments of union being forever tainted by his past. Why had he thought of something that could never be changed? Why had he had to spoil such beauty with the stain of his childhood?

This was the major reason he'd been seeking a third for Bastien. Alex poisoned perfect moments. He couldn't cope with them. When everything was going well, one thought could trigger the past, and inwardly everything would shut down. His brain detonated, and the only escape was his lab.

So many times he'd been with Bastien, happy and relaxed, then something would happen…he'd see a man who looked a little Pierre Defreine, his abuser, or Sebastien would slide a finger along his spine just like that bastard had once done. In that moment, he'd freeze, then usually say something to trigger an argument.

He couldn't do that now. Not with Devvy, not when she was his and Bastien's salvation.

That knowledge didn't stop the pleasure of before turning to ice in his body. It only melted in the form of tears that spread along his eyes and slowly poured down his cheeks.

He nearly jumped out of his skin when a soft hand touched his shoulder. He froze, trying to remember that it was only Devvy, not Pierre Defreine.

"Alex?" she asked, and he hated himself for having created that quiver in her voice.

Over the last two weeks, she'd come to relax around him. She'd softened, become content in his presence. In one fell swoop, his behavior would change all that if he wasn't careful.

But even knowing that, the part of him that would forever be caged in ice wouldn't let him relax. Couldn't prod him to let his guard down.

"What's wrong?" she asked, her hand massaging his shoulder a little, kneading the tension gathered there.

"Nothing."

His brusqueness should have pushed her away. She should have retreated in a snooty fit. After all, what grown lover took to the floor, curled up like a rebellious teenager against the bed?

"You're lying," uttered as a statement and not a question.

The words "leave me alone" trembled on his lips, but he thought of Bastien and what Devvy's relationship to Alex meant to him. Alex had to give his lover Devvy. Her softness, her pure innocence would counteract the darkness in Alex's soul. Darkness no amount of love from Bastien could counteract.

His therapist had told him to share the truth of his childhood with Bastien. In a relationship as long as their own, secrets of this nature should not be withheld. But Alex couldn't do it. He couldn't share this with his partner. He couldn't taint himself in the other man's eyes.

At his continued silence, Devvy ceased her gentle massage. She moved and he hoped she was going away, to the bathroom, anywhere so long as he could have a little room to comport himself, to get himself back on track. But she didn't move far away. Instead, she crawled over the side of the bed and sat beside him, copying his defensive position.

"You're not upset about what happened, are you?" she asked, her tone conversational, as though they were still bitching about the crap movie she'd wanted to watch.

"No."

"Okay, that narrows it down. Are you frightened about Sebastien's reaction?"

"No."

"Do you think he'll be mad we didn't wait for him?"

"No." He forced his lips to move, knowing how important it was to answer this question correctly. "He'll be relieved. Happy. He wants this as much as we do."

"Did I do something wrong?" she questioned, only this time uncertainty had crept into her voice.

He hated himself for making her nervous and made himself answer, "No. It was wonderful."

She snorted. “Yeah, it really looks like it.”

Alex could sense her hurt, her confusion. The strength of her feelings battered him, and made him curl up a little tighter.

She rolled upward and sank back onto her knees. Tugging his fisted hands with both of her own, she swept her thumbs over the back of his hands, and just sat there with him. Slowly, gradually, she moved closer. Inch by inch, she crept forward. After around twenty minutes, she was pressed into his side, her arms awkwardly around him, tucked against him as though she were protecting him from the demons she didn’t know he possessed.

The crazy thing was…it worked.

Oh, the memories didn’t go. Nor did the oily sludge they left in their wake. But her warmth seemed to melt the chill deep inside and as slowly as she’d soothed and gentled him, he started to respond to her presence.

He swallowed, bitterly regretting the path his thoughts had taken him down. He hated himself for spoiling their first time. He imbued his regret and remorse into the kiss he pressed against her temple.

“Would you like to get under the covers?” she asked quietly, her voice as soft as the brush of a butterfly’s wings.

The inner ice surrounding his heart had sent a chill to all of his limbs. The room was more than comfortable, but to him, it felt as though the temperature were below zero. “Please.”

She nodded and started to move away. He surprised himself by reaching for her, and then forced his hands to stay by his sides as she climbed to her feet. She leaned over the bed and pulled the covers down and then bent over him, grabbed his arm and tugged him upright with surprising strength. She dealt with the wet condom half-falling off his cock. Pushing and prodding him onto the mattress, she—there was no other word for it—nursed him. Arranged him so he was comfortable and with swift hands, swaddled him in the duvet once he was positioned how she wanted him.

She retreated to the bathroom but was only there for twenty seconds or more, just long enough to dispose of the condom. He almost called for her to come back, another shock to his system, not actually wanting to be parted from her, but she’d returned by the time he’d dealt with his surprise at wanting her by his side.

Devvy switched off the lights, climbed into bed, and curled herself around him. She was softness, warm caring. Her very presence soothed the lost little boy that was still a part of the adult Alexei, the little boy who had been wronged. Why she calmed him down, he didn't know. She was still a stranger to him. A woman who he was slowly getting to know after selecting her out of a magazine for her intelligence and pretty face, the eyes that had spoken to his very soul.

Why did that part of him, the raw and ragged ache in his soul—the part Bastien wasn't even aware of because he'd hidden it—respond to her gentle nurturing?

She didn't say anything. Didn't ask anything of him. She just lay there, close to hand.

And after an hour in the dark, neither saying anything, both aware the other was awake, when he reached out for her hand, she slipped her fingers between his.

He slept, finally, with their fingers knotted, a bridge between two separate beings desperately seeking a lasting union.

Chapter Six

As the lights from the terrace glared behind his eyes, Alex groaned, wishing he'd had the wherewithal to close the curtains the night before. The thought brought with it a memory of what had happened, and he realized *why* he hadn't shut them.

He groaned with regret. Scrubbing a hand over his face, he tried to wish the night back but there was no use. The damage was done.

That thought was compounded when he turned to his side and found an empty space. A cold, empty space. She'd been gone a while.

His stomach twisted at the way he'd reacted last night. It was rare for the past to take hold of him, to grip him between clawed fingers, and throttle him until he was nothing more than the frightened nine-year-old being raped by a man his mother insisted he call uncle.

The years had a habit of falling away when the memories besieged him. Especially if he was feeling vulnerable, and Devvy certainly made him feel that way. She was special, this one. And he'd just fucked it up. Big time.

He climbed out of bed, feeling ancient as his bones creaked and complained. Padding to the bathroom, he pissed, and after washing his hands, splashed water on his face. The cool liquid soothed the tender throb behind eyes that had wept the night before. He decided to brush his teeth after he inhaled a full cafétiere of coffee. The caffeine was probably the only thing that would make him feel human.

Aside from Devvy or Bastien, of course.

He'd alienated one, and the other was on another continent. It seemed coffee was the only way to go.

Naked and feeling glum, he padded out of the bathroom and into the hallway. His penthouse was large. The bedroom at one side of the building, the lab in the middle, and at the opposite end, his living quarters. When he passed the lab, he heard the gentle tinkling of the piano keys, and at the sound, his heart literally fluttered in his chest.

To no other creature would he admit to a *flutter*, but the knowledge she hadn't left made him feel as though a ten-ton weight had been lifted from his shoulders.

He hadn't frightened her away. He'd probably freaked her out, but not enough to make her run.

Dieu merci!

Closing his eyes in thanks, he strode on ahead, uncaring of his nudity or morning breath. He just needed to see her. That would be enough.

He headed into the salon and saw her, shoulders and back bowed over the piano as she tinkled with the keys with a solitary digit from each hand.

Alex managed to enter the room and stand an inch away from her without her even realizing it. She jumped, her two fingers slamming down, when he cupped her shoulder.

"*Bonjour*, Devvy," he murmured, leaning down to press a kiss to the top of her head.

"Morning, Alex," she replied, literally radiating tension through every stiff limb.

Feeling guilty for spoiling her moment of peace, he sighed and sat beside her on the duet piano stool—Bastien played rarely, but did if Alex asked it of him. As he took a seat, she chuckled at the sight of his nudity, when she finally peeked his way.

"Didn't you think to put on a pair of pants?"

He shrugged. "No one to see anything. Apart from you and you've already seen it. Why? Does my cock offend you?"

She snorted. "We became quite good friends last night."

"It is hoping we shall become more than just good friends."

"I'm sure that's in the cards."

Her surety eased some of his own strain. When he didn't reply, she returned to her single digit playing of *Chopsticks*.

"You are a master of the piano, I see," he teased, and felt more of his tension disappear as she grinned up at him.

"I'm not a bad player actually. My mother forced lessons on me. She couldn't seem to understand that I wanted to be a scientist. That I wanted to take a role in what she considers to be a man's world. I think she's read too many Georgette Heyer novels…" She paused, frowned. "Or maybe not enough. Mom's certain the way to every man's heart is to play the piano, ride, sing, paint…everything a Regency heroine can do." Her words culminated with a rather impressive arpeggio that had him clapping.

"That's an odd take on life."

She shrugged. "That's my mom for you. She's very traditional, and because my father humors her, and because they're quite wealthy, she gets away with it."

"You would have to keep the relationship between us a secret, then." He made the statement knowing it would be true, but wishing it weren't. "If she's very traditional, I mean."

She paused, hesitated over a chord, then peeked up at him again. "It depends."

"It does?"

"On how deep we go."

"What do you mean?"

"If…" She bit her lip and switched her gaze to the piano keys.

"It's okay, you can talk to me."

"If this works out, *really* works out, then I'd tell my mom and dad. I don't think he'd really mind. So long as Bastien was cool with it. Dad's quite important at his bank. He appreciates wealth. If Sebastien didn't want a divorce, if he was happy with it, Dad wouldn't give a damn. Especially as we're in France and nobody would know in his circle.

"Mom would freak. Probably call me all kinds of names. But if I come to love you, I won't deny you."

"You say that now…"

There was a bitterness to his tone, one that he hadn't intended to be there. But her shake of the head was sharp. As was her answer. "No." She slashed her hand in front of them. "If I love you, if you love me, I won't hide you. I'm not like that."

Touched, also feeling guilty at her lack of guile in the face of all his lies and secrets, he placed a hand on her knee and squeezed. She smiled at him and he sighed. "I'm sorry about last night."

Her gentle humor disappeared and concern replaced it. "You don't have to apologize. I should be the one to say sorry. I must have done something…I don't know what…to make you feel like that…" At her hesitation, he squeezed her knee again.

"You did nothing wrong. You were perfect, Devvy. As perfect as I'd always imagined."

She flushed. "It was wonderful, wasn't it?" she confessed, eagerly peeking up at him for confirmation.

"*Oui*. It was. And I spoiled it."

"Well, I wouldn't say *spoiled*."

He grunted. "What would you call it?"

"I don't know." She jerked her shoulder. "I'd have said it was some kind of breakdown but, I'm not sure why it happened."

"You and me both."

His muttered words had her frowning. "You don't want to talk about it, do you?" she asked, astute in her reading of him.

"No. Not really."

"Will you tell me what happened?" When he didn't reply, she added, "One day?"

He didn't want to lie to her so he pondered the thought and wondered if he could share something with her, when he'd never told another living soul save for his therapist. And the therapist only knew, because once upon a time, Alex had tried to commit suicide. After having his stomach pumped, the hospital insisted upon therapy. He'd been with the same psychiatrist for over two decades.

Alex could have pandered to her, all the while knowing he never would reveal the truth, but Devvy didn't deserve that.

He fully intended on making her fall in love with him, and if that was the case, she'd share the truth of their relationship with her parents. Regardless of their negative reaction to such a revelation. In the face of that, how could he lie? How could he withhold the truth from her?

Alex knew that at some point in his life, he would have to share his past with his lovers. A part of him knew he could never tell Bastien. Maybe Devvy could do the telling for him?

Playing the messenger wouldn't be pleasant, but Bastien wouldn't shoot her. He might want to shoot the man who had abused Alex, but considering the man was six feet under, little damage could be done to the stained bones of a pedophile long since dead.

Having Bastien know the truth might add a level of peace to their relationship. They'd never settled together or lived in the same place. After twenty years, that was beyond bizarre. And he knew it was his fault.

He needed his space. Needed room to be himself. Here, in his penthouse, he was central. In the middle of it all. Close to the hubbub of the metropolis but able to lock himself away from the outside world. His assistant and her assistants intruded his bubble, attending to his needs, ensuring he never had to leave his home unless it was urgent or as Devvy would call it, for a booty call. He liked his life that way. The sense of freedom soothed the ragged, soul-deep ache. He might once have been weak, exposed…but now, he was untouchable.

Devvy was the harbinger of change.

His neat world had always been a hair's breadth away from implosion. With Devvy and her ways, he knew the implosion had already begun. It just hadn't reached its full momentum yet.

And in truth, he embraced the change. He wanted it. For Bastien.

Seb deserved at least one normal partner.

Alex knew that could never be him.

He'd long since grieved the sad truth, and part and parcel of that grief had been to find a solution. That solution being a third. It just so happened he'd found her. And she was perfect for the role and for him. He'd always imagined their woman would soothe the ache in Bastien's soul that Alex couldn't reach. He'd never thought she would work her magic on him as well.

The Alex who replied was well aware of what he was doing, of what a promise he was making, when he said, "Yes. I'll tell you what happened. Some day."

* * * *

"Does he ever call you when he's away?"

Alex eyed her, caution definitely buried in his gaze. "Why?"

Waving the spoon loaded with macadamia nut brittle and vanilla ice cream, aka orgasm in a bowl, she wafted his concern away. "I just want to know."

"You're not going to turn into a jealous harpy, are you?" he asked, swooping down, stealing the spoon *and* the ice cream.

"You're lucky I came twice last night. Otherwise, I'd have to kill you for that." In fact, after four days in Alex's bed, she was thoroughly sated. Not a tense muscle in her body. That didn't mean she couldn't threaten the man for stealing her favorite ice cream.

The deadly seriousness of her tone had him chuckling. "Ah, so you'll kill me for stealing ice cream but not for swiping your husband?"

"I think you'll find I swiped him from you," she teased, turning around to pinch the spoon from him and then moving to rest her arms on the back of the sofa so she could watch him wield a whiteboard pen with the precision of a scalpel.

The first time she'd entered this room, she hadn't noticed the whiteboard. Considering the room was white and the whiteboard took up the entire back wall, she guessed it was easy to miss. Only when the light shone on it a certain way did you even notice it.

"So, we're getting down to the nitty-gritty," he mocked, using a phrase she'd taught him a few days ago.

"Yes, it's all in the details," she told him primly, savoring another spoonful of ice cream.

"To answer your original question, before we were bombarded with minutiae…"

She butted in, "How is it you know what minutiae are but not nitty-gritty?"

He shrugged. "Selective learning. I read medical journals, *ma petite*." He scribbled something on the whiteboard and she watched him ponder the calculation before muttering, "Sometimes, he calls me. But only if he needs a sounding board."

"I refuse to believe sounding board is in a medical journal."

Alex just smiled. "You shall have to see to my English education, Devvy."

"Does it involve me being a teacher and you a naughty pupil?"

"Depends if there's spanking involved."

The deadpan statement had Devvy's heart flatlining. She sputtered around her ice cream. "Are you being serious?"

He cocked a brow. "I'll try anything once."

"Oh fuck, you didn't just say that," she said in a breath, excited beyond belief at his blasé comment.

"Research is my life. No matter the subject."

She shook her head. "You're insane. Do you know that?"

"Well, not certifiable."

"So reassuring."

"Does he call you when he's away?"

"No. Never."

Alex frowned at her as he bent down, retrieved the spoon and scooped up more ice cream. "Are you mad that he calls me?"

"No. I probably should be. But then, I should be a lot of things and I'm not."

"You mean this entire situation should disturb you?"

"Yup. I should be totally freaked out."

"But it doesn't?"

She snorted. "I'd really be here if it did, wouldn't I?"

"True. I've never purported to understand the inner workings of the female brain."

"Oh, ho, *purport*? The average American would think you're talking about some kind of marine life." At his scowl, she clarified, "Porpoise."

"I'm sure you're underestimating the English-speaking world."

"I promise I'm not. I foresee plenty of cult films in your future, Alex."

"Not more *merde* like we watched the other day."

"Yep," she told him cheerfully. "But look how it turned out. You got your end away, didn't you?"

"True." He pondered the thought. "Okay. I shall watch the movies you deem fit. But I need to work on this for the moment."

"And I'm distracting you?"

He grinned. "If I admit to that, I'd never get my 'end,' as you so charmingly phrased it, away. Ever again."

She winked. "What did I tell you? I'm not your average woman. I'll just shut up and have my foodgasm in peace."

Alex grunted but returned to the formula he was working on, yet another piece of the puzzle that was cancer. She let him work, left him to his thoughts as she lay sprawled back on the sofa, spoon and ice cream tub in hand, eyes staring at the ceiling.

She'd spent these last weeks pondering if there was something wrong or something very right with her. She'd yet to decide which was the case.

She had no doubt there was something skewed in her sexuality. Devvy just had the feeling it was only skewed where Alex was concerned. Had Bastien introduced anyone else to the mix, she'd have told him where to go and at what speed to travel. It was Alex, her Achilles' heel, that had enabled her to adapt to the idea of a threesome. As it was, she was looking forward to seeing the two of them together.

Devvy had never watched porn, so she'd certainly never seen man-on-man action. Aside from the kisses and heavy petting she'd witnessed with her lovers, she had no other images or memories to fall back on. Her imagination was strong, and now, having finally seen Alex's cock, she could piece together a picture of her own.

It was hotter than hell.

Enough to make her stomach twist and clench.

The new, daring Devvy wanted to do something completely insane. In her mind's eye, she saw her hand slip down between her legs, saw her fingers start to play with her clit.

She wondered if she had the balls to jack off whilst Alex was staring at the whiteboard. The idea in and of itself was crazy. It told her how far she had come in the few weeks she'd known Alex.

The thought made her question how deep the corruption would go, and while corruption had negative connotations, she looked forward to it, to being deep under Alex's influence, because if he were anything like Sebastien, she'd enjoy every single minute of it.

"I can hear your brain ticking away." Alex's voice disturbed her thoughts and she chuckled.

"Is it too loud for you? I didn't realize thoughts made a sound."

"They don't. But it depends."

"Depends on what?"

"On what you're thinking about, of course."

"What do you mean?"

His pen squeaked across the board. Slashing blue symbols and periodic elements that at a glance, she understood, but the entire amalgamation of chemical formulae just blew her head off. With a bit of research and a bit of study, they wouldn't be beyond her comprehension, but this was most definitely advanced cancer research, something outside of her specialty.

Just knowing that the man was on the brink of something revolutionary had that melting thing going on down below. If her pussy had felt red-hot moments before, now, it felt as though the conflagration had already started.

The man's brilliance was hotter than any six-pack abdomen or solid-concrete pecs.

Saying that, Alex had both.

Fuck, she was a lucky woman.

His squeaking came to a halt, and the sudden cessation of sound dragged her from her thoughts of Alex's double-whammy hit to the female population—gorgeous *and* smarter than Einstein, was there anything sexier?—as he recapped the pen and turned around to face her. "You're wriggling around on the sofa."

"And? Am I not allowed to fidget?"

"Fidget," he murmured the word, puzzled it out for a second and then nodded. "Of course, but you are not fidgeting. You're wriggling."

"What's the difference?"

He grinned. "Fidgeting implies discomfort, a subconscious act to burn off unnecessary or excess energy. But you, *you're* not uncomfortable, you're thinking about sex." That grin of his had widened and had her smiling back at him.

She shook her head and said, "How big a fool would you feel if that weren't the truth?"

He shrugged and the gesture was so French she almost swooned. Americans shrugged both shoulders. Quick and meaningless. The French, on the other hand, slowly jerked a shoulder. Giving so much meaning, so much poignancy to a simple gesture that it was almost alien in comparison to the American version. Poems should be written about that Gallic shrug, she thought whimsically.

"I would not feel foolish, because if you said you weren't thinking about sex, I wouldn't believe you."

"Charming!" she snapped, sitting up and glaring at him with outrage.

"What? Do not take offence, *ma chérie*. There is nothing to be offended about. I, too, am thinking about sex."

"Men always think about sex," she butted in.

“Maybe some or most men do. But not me, nor Sebastien. We are too busy in our minds”—he tapped his forehead with his finger—“to waste time constantly thinking about sex.”

“So, you’re telling me that even though you’re working on pretty important research and ordinarily your mind would be focused on that research, you’re thinking about sex as well.”

“*Mais oui*. How could I not be thinking about that? What are you wearing, *ma petite*?”

She looked down at her shorts and T-shirt. Hardly the clothes required to win a beauty contest, but from the way he was looking at her, it was like she was wearing lingerie. Frilly, lacy fripperies that showed more than they hid.

Devvy laughed. “You can’t find this sexy?”

“Why not? I can see all your legs. If I look, just so…” He tilted his head. “…I can see your panties.”

She squealed, crossed her legs and pressed her hands down against the apex of her thighs. “Alex, what are you doing looking there?!” she chided, although her reprimand was spoiled by the faint giggle in her tone.

“It is mine to look at, is it not?” he stated as though black were red and white were blue.

“Does that mean I can look at your cock when I want?”

“*Naturellement.*”

She shook her head, not understanding his logic. “These are some weird-ass rules. I’ll have to learn them. You need to write them down for me.”

“*Non*, you do not need rules. We both know how we feel for each other.”

“We do?” she asked, her amusement disappearing in the face of that statement. It was so concrete, so certain, and she was feeling anything but, where Alex was concerned. Not that he did anything to add to her uncertainties. It just seemed wrong to feel so much for him in such a short space of time.

“Yes.” He rolled out the one syllable word.

“What is it we feel for each other, Alex?”

He frowned. "We are falling in love with each other, of course. *Un coup de foudre*. Or," he paused, "it *was* a *coup de foudre*. These are the aftereffects."

"It's too soon for that, isn't it?"

"It's never too soon. That's the whole point of the lightning blast. A connection is all that is required. We have that. It just takes time to develop.

"We've only known each other for close to four weeks and for a lot of that time, you have been confused about the state of our relationship, of your part in this triad, the way that this ménage will work. This is not a porn film, Devvy. This is not about sex." At her cocked brow of disbelief, he sliced his hand through the air. "Sex is an important part, but it isn't the whole. It's a piece, as there are many pieces to the whole."

"Do you think we can make it work, Alex?"

"I see no reason why not."

"That's such a blanket statement. There are many reasons why all of this could fall apart. We're all volatile, even myself and I think I'm pretty relaxed in comparison to the pair of you. We all work crazy hours. How do we make time for each other? How do we make it work? Not only that, but you're here. Whereas Sebastien and I are at *Les Fenêtres*."

"The house isn't far away," he returned.

"It's far away enough. My lab is at home. I can't be here all the time. In relationships like this…" She sighed. "Maybe I'm being stereotypical but I imagine it's the woman who has to do a lot of giving and taking. The one who has to be malleable, because she's the glue, and in our case, that's the truth.

"If you were happy to be a couple as you've been for so many years, you wouldn't want me. So, I'm the one who has to adapt, I'm the one who has to change. How can I when I'm at *Les Fenêtres* and you're here? On top of that, do you intend to be here all the time? Will you come and live with us?"

Alex held up a hand. "These questions are important, but they're not vital. The problems you mention have a habit of working out for themselves, but we must not force them. These things must go at their own pace."

He uncapped his pen and returned to his whiteboard. From that alone, she knew she'd touched a sore spot in his armor, because his return to work spoke louder than words. He wanted to change the subject.

Devvy just wished she knew for sure which sore point she'd touched. She could only assume it was to do with her asking where he'd live, eventually. She'd have to make it a point to ask Bastien on his return about why the pair of them had never lived together. Devvy knew for a fact Alex had lived in this penthouse for the last eight years, ever since his first scientific breakthrough had paid for the multimillion-euro property.

From this discussion alone, she had the feeling that where Alex lived was not a subject up for discussion and for some reason, maybe because she could be as stubborn as her lover, Devvy knew this would be a point over which they all battled.

If they wanted her to live in a permanent ménage à trois, then that was just what they'd do. Live. Together. All three of them and damn the consequences.

Perhaps they would gain a certain notoriety, but as Bastien himself had said, he didn't care what society thought. He was rich enough to live above it, to dance to his own tune. In this, she would not be the only one forced to adapt to this new situation—if they wanted this to be for life, then it would be just that.

One for all, all for one.

She could understand why the Musketeers had adopted that particular phrase.

Perhaps it was too soon to be thinking about this, to be wondering about the living arrangements, but none of this was normal. Nothing was going at a normal pace. Her feelings for Alex were turbocharged, and the security and peace of mind she felt in his company were entirely unusual.

If Alex's instincts spoke to him and told him they were falling in love, then Devvy's were telling her this was for keeps.

As crazy as it seemed, that was the way it was. She wasn't blind, as Alex seemed to be. These relationships…it would take a lot of work. Hard slog. A normal partnership was rife with complications, and adding another person to the mix only made it so much more difficult. All of them would have to adapt. Otherwise, what felt so right and so promising would just sink into the quagmire that was life.

Sebastien, for all his dominant ways, was not domineering. If anything, he was flexible with her. He worked long hours and she didn't want that to change, because he enjoyed his work. It made him happy, just as her own research and Alex's gave them both much pleasure.

However, Sebastien wasn't the pivotal point in this relationship. He was a kind of cement. The central role, though, would be the newer pairing. Her and Alex's connection would always be the weak part, where strife could arise, simply because it was the newest joining and therefore unpredictable.

While her research wasn't as vital as Alex's, and while creating an anti-acne soap might not be groundbreaking, to her it was important, and to teens around the world suffering with zit-pocked skin, it was imperative.

She would not be the one to always travel to him. Regardless of his agoraphobia.

She felt like a bitch, but if Alex wanted this to work, he would have to meet her on her own ground.

It was time to make him see sense. And once he did, he wouldn't regret it, because the first thing she intended to do when he moved into *Les Fenêtres* was fuck him raw in the middle of her herb garden.

She closed her eyes at the thought of a hot, sun-filled day. The pungent smells of basil and thyme filling their nostrils, the birds tweeting in the distance, the grass staining their knees as they fucked each other…

No, she'd make him overcome his phobias just to enact that particular fantasy.

Devvy grinned wickedly at the thought, and wriggled a little deeper on the sofa.

* * * *

The next day, and decidedly against her Machiavellian plot to make Alex face the future, Devvy awoke to an empty bed. For the first four days of Bastien's visit to Napa, she'd slept at Alex's. Or not slept, as was the case.

She'd chosen to stay with him, because she'd wanted to see how the pair of them would gel. How the two of them would get on without Sebastien's presence. Until yesterday, things had been going swimmingly. She'd dared to ponder the future, and Alex, while he wanted this and while he wanted *her*, didn't welcome changes to his own living environment.

As such, his selfish desire for the status quo to remain just as it was had led to a few…she couldn't call them arguments. "Heated words" was probably the best way to describe the altercations that had occurred between the two of them. Especially in comparison to the relative calm of their first discussion of the day which had taken place as she ate ice cream for breakfast and he worked on his research.

She thought back to yesterday, when she'd awoken to his mouth tugging at her pussy lips, his tongue slurping up her juices, torturing her with lashes against her clit. The thoughts had her instantly getting wet and wishing he were there with her. But he wasn't. He was in his apartment, because he refused to come to her house. He refused to leave his flat.

Devvy hadn't pushed him and she wouldn't. She'd take it nice and slow, because she realized the pressure he was under. Pressure that stemmed from his phobia as well as his research. However, she'd made the suggestion he come and stay the night at *Les Fenêtres*, so she could work in her lab and have him close to hand.

Devvy had told him she had her own whiteboard, which he was free to use. He could have worked there as easily as he did at his own place. But he'd refused. In fact, he'd done more than that. He'd snapped at her.

It was amazing the man could be patience itself, cool and collected as he stared at the firing line, yet on this point, he'd been so adamant and stubborn, so quick to flare.

His arrogant obstinacy had pissed her off. She wouldn't lie. But she hadn't stormed out, as she would have done had it been Sebastien. Even when she was content to be the doormat of a wife, her temper had often gotten the better of her and if he'd said anything to exasperate her, she'd let Bastien know by storming off, refusing to look at him.

With Alex, she'd very calmly held out both hands, palm up in surrender, and said, "Calm down. I won't talk to you when you're like this. I made this suggestion because I want to be with you, and it seems silly to be apart when we can be together. But if that's what you want, then that's what you want. I'm going home now."

She'd backed out of the room, keeping eye contact with him until she'd hit the doorjamb—not literally, thank God. How humiliating an exit would that have been?—and then she'd walked to the elevator and waited for it to appear. As she'd taken a step inside, pressed the button to take her downstairs, he'd called out from the lounge, "I'll phone you tomorrow."

He'd just been visible through the doorway and she'd merely nodded as the elevator closed in front of her, staring him out all the while. Without even meaning to, she realized she'd scared him. She thought back to her words, wondering if she'd said something that indicated she was saying this was the end. It was a testament to how precarious their relationship was that he'd jumped to such a conclusion.

Rolling flat onto her back, she snuggled down into the covers and let the birds outside bring her to wakefulness. The down feathers weren't as comforting as being cuddled into Alex's arms, but she would settle for it today.

There was one advantage to being the boss's wife. She never had to get up at the crack of dawn to go to work. It was bliss! She was definitely not a morning person. If anything, she liked to get up around noon. These last eighteen months, when her lab had been at home, Devvy had been able to indulge that particular preference.

As she thought of what she intended to do today, of what path she'd take with the soap she was working on, her phone vibrated beside her. She was tempted to ignore it, but considering Alex's parting words, she reached blindly behind her and grabbed it from the bedside table. Around a yawn, she answered the call—without checking the Caller ID, something she immediately regretted. "Hello?"

"Devvy, darling! I'm so glad I caught you."

Grimacing and wishing she'd ignored the call, she muttered, "Mom? Is everything okay? It must be pretty late over there."

"Not really, sweetheart. It's only eight or so."

For her parents, namely her mother, that was very late. Her mom kept the hours of a five-year-old. Miranda Nelson tended to be in bed by eight on the nights she wasn't entertaining her husband's business associates. Devvy didn't think she actually slept, but for as long as she could remember, her mother had always left to go to bed at seven thirty, almost every night.

Devvy shared her love of books with her mother and she had the notion that Miranda escaped to her bedroom so she could read. In peace.

Had she been a regular child, one that made a lot of noise, one that lived with their toys or played noisy games, Devvy would have understood her mother's craving for silence. But considering she'd been a quiet child, always living inside her head, she'd always just felt out of it where her mom was concerned. Borderline unwanted. A nuisance.

That feeling had never gone away. Distance would always separate her from her parents. And not just in the physical sense. She could be in California, living next door, and a chasm as wide as the Atlantic would still separate her from her mother and father. She'd never been close to her family, just as she'd never been close to anyone at school. She'd always felt like the cuckoo in the nest.

In truth, Devvy had grown quite used to feeling as though she belonged nowhere. Even with Sebastien, she'd believed him to be too good for her and she'd always believed he'd come to his senses eventually. For the majority of her married life, she'd been waiting for the other shoe to drop. A belief her mother shared and perpetuated.

As it was, that shoe had dropped and created an avalanche of admissions. Said avalanche was the source of what Devvy believed would be the only place she'd ever belong.

Between Alex and Sebastien.

Her gut, even after only a short time "together," told her there lie her future and it was why she was calmly accepting of this unusual relationship. Deep down, she knew this was her place. They were her men.

It was ironic that she came to that decision while on the phone with her mother.

A more bigoted creature, in all her travels, she'd yet to meet.

"Is there something I can help you with, Mother?" Devvy asked, when Miranda seemed quite content for silence to shadow the line.

"Not really, dear," came the quick reply. "Can a mother not just want to talk to her daughter? Her only little girl?"

As soon as she said that, Devvy knew Miranda wanted something from her. And usually, whatever Miranda wanted, she got. That was her father's fault. Because of it, Devvy had paid the price far too many a time.

"Well, it's lovely to hear from you. Thank you for thinking of me," she murmured, playing the game as was expected of her.

"It's been so long since I heard your voice. I just wanted to make sure everything was fine over there. On the other side of the pond."

Ha, it had been ten days since Devvy had endured yet another lecture. Hardly long enough in her opinion.

"Well, you got it right. Everything's great."

"And Sebastien? How's he?"

Devvy knew right away that she wouldn't be telling her mother Sebastien was in Napa. If she did, Bastien would be extended an invitation to visit her parents' home, and if he didn't accept it, which he wouldn't—he'd never said anything, but she could sense he didn't like her family. She could hardly blame him when it was a sentiment she shared—she'd never hear the end of it.

"He's fine. Working hard as usual," was all she said.

"Well, I hope you're looking after him."

"As much as he'll let me," she retorted, amused at the idea of Bastien needing someone to take care of him. He was one of the most self-reliant men on the planet. One of the reasons why she'd always felt unneeded by him, surplus to requirements, as it were.

"Good, good." There was a long pause. "I was wondering…if you'd heard of an Alexei Ivanov." Miranda butchered the name, making Alexei sound more like laxative and Ivanov like enough.

Devvy frowned at the ceiling, her limbs tensing at the weird note in her mother's voice as she mentioned Alex's name. "Yes, of course, Mother. He's a specialist in the treatment of cancer. He's world renowned. I'd say most people have heard of him." Aside from her Regency-romance-loving mother. Not that there was anything wrong with a good romance. But it was time to change genres when you started forgetting this was the twenty-first century, not the nineteenth.

"Do you know him personally?"

How to answer that? With the truth? Ha! Way to cause her mother's mental breakdown!

"I know of him, and I've met him. The man might live in Paris but that doesn't mean to say I know him well. Paris is larger than you think."

"Of course, I don't expect you to know every scientist, Devvy! I just wondered. That's all."

"Well, we're not close friends." That wasn't exactly a lie. They weren't close friends. Yet. As Alex had said yesterday, it took time for these friendships to develop. Especially as at the moment, they were lovers, rather than anything else. “Why do you ask?”

“Oh, no real reason. Irene Van Der Bossche just happened to mention him and Sebastien in the same breath. That’s all.”

“Maybe Bastien’s company has funded some of Ivanov’s research?” Disliking the direction of this conversation, Devvy steered it on the right track. “Sebastien has his fingers in many pies. It wouldn’t surprise me if he’d donated to the cause. Anyway, since when were you and Irene Van Der Bossche friends? You always called her the most frightful gossip.”

Devvy was pleased when her mother rose to the bait. “Of course I’m not friends with Irene! But she came round to dinner last week and I just didn’t like what she was inferring.”

“And what was that? I’m sure she was just being nosy.”

“It was almost like she was saying there was something going on between the two of them.”

“Undoubtedly,” Devvy stated, making her voice as bland as possible. “Business.”

How was it that people in California were discussing her husband and Alex as though there were some deep connection between the pair of them?

Maybe it was because Devina Nelson, boring and bland as the soap she made, had managed to snag a man like Bastien. There had to be something wrong with him in the first place if he’d marry a little wren like Devvy. In that same vein, there must be something else marring his so-called perfection.

To the elite society of Portola Valley, circles in which her parents traveled, Bastien’s being declared gay would be all that Devvy deserved for daring to marry outside her tedious little world.

A part of her was certain that was the root of Irene Van Der Bossche’s malicious comments to her mother. The other part just wished such gossip didn’t hang on Alex’s shoulders.

In this case, where there was smoke, there was most definitely a fire.

“Well, that’s what I told her!” Miranda declared. “I don’t know what her filthy little mind was suggesting but I’ll set her straight the next time I see her.”

“Good! If it makes you feel better, I’ll ask Bastien if he knows Ivanov well. That way you can put an end to whatever bull she’s trying to spread.”

"That would be marvelous, sweetheart. Before I go, I wanted to ask if you started that diet I told you about."

"Not again, Mom!" she snapped, glaring at the armoire as though it were her mortal nemesis. "My weight is fine. I'm perfectly healthy!"

"Healthy doesn't mean attractive," came the confidence-bashing retort.

"Maybe not, but in my case, I don't need to lose weight. Seb likes me just the way I am."

Miranda huffed down the line. "Every man says that to his wife. He'd be an idiot not to! Don't believe him. They're all liars when it comes to the way they like their women to look."

It was too early in the morning to be dealing with her mother's bullshit. On top of that, for once in her life, she refused to let Miranda demolish her newfound pleasure in herself, her body and her sexuality. Rather than let her ride roughshod over her, she gritted her teeth. "Well, I'm sorry Dad's like that, but I'm lucky, Mom. Sebastien *isn't*. Now, if you've finished insulting my husband, as well as myself and the way I look, I think that's all we need to say to each other for a little while! Good night!"

And with that, for the first time in her life, she disconnected the call and hung up on her mother.

For a second, horror trickled through her veins. It was an unspoken family rule that everyone pandered to Miranda. Devvy had no idea why, but everyone from her own father to her great-aunt Netty always treated her gently. With care. Like she was made of the most fragile of crystal.

Before the horror could stick, resolve replaced it. Her mother had no right to talk to her that way, no right to belittle her appearance or the way her husband viewed her. Every phone call with Miranda usually ended with her traipsing to the bathroom and stepping on the dreaded scales. Well, not today! She refused to let the insidious words toy with her mind, as her mother's so-called sagacity usually did.

Enough was enough.

Whatever the repercussions of her harsh words to her mother, be it a pissed-off call from her father, or to go through a phase of Miranda sulking with her, it was worth it. She'd had enough of her mother's bullshit. Twenty-six years of being pulled down was quite enough, thank you! Especially when she was starting to feel like she was finally settling in her own skin.

Mouth firming with purpose, she forced herself to get out of bed and to kick-start her day. She refused to think about the repercussions of her rudeness, and instead focused on the reason behind her mother's call. The gossip about Alexei and Bastien.

Refusing to worry, she resolved to wait until Bastien returned home. He might have some idea as to why this particular piece of gossip had made it over the pond and to her parents' circle. Until then, she'd just have to wait and there was no point in going around in circles asking herself questions she didn't have the answer to, was there?

Chapter Seven

Devvy stretched her back, glorying in the delicious tug of muscles as she tried to loosen the tension in her shoulders. She'd been working hard on the anti-acne soap ever since Wednesday morning, when she'd returned home from Alex's. They'd spoken on the phone since then, but she could hear the pout in his voice.

He was most definitely sulking.

The distance worked in her favor, though.

For one, she knew he missed her. The truth of it was that she missed him. It was weird how she'd grown so used to him being there, when she'd only stayed at his penthouse a few nights.

Another reason a bit of space between them was working *for* her, was the fact that it gave her time to think. She'd brushed off Alex's anxiety attack when he'd promised her he'd share the reason for it when he was ready. Losing herself in her work was a natural way for her to problem-solve, and her thoughts had naturally drifted to the reason behind Alex's behavior that first night they'd spent together.

With her mind going around in circles, she couldn't deny she was getting very impatient. Devvy didn't want to wait. She wanted to know what was wrong *now*. Not some nameless day in the future, as he'd promised.

It was only in the calm environment of her lab, with the lulling peace from her herb garden, that she realized how different she was to the Devvy who had worked at this same project a month before.

Under the care of her two men, she was starting to change. Nothing drastic. Just little things. A few weeks ago, she'd never have had the balls to tend to Alex the way she had the night of that weird anxiety attack. She'd have hovered. Uncertain as to how to act. Not wanting to disturb him for fear of him battering her with his anger.

As it was, she'd taken charge in a subtle way. Gradually getting closer to him and then cosseting him with her care. She'd enjoyed it, too. Not his anxiety, but being able to care for him. To show him how she felt. Somehow, it had been easier to show than it was to tell. Telling meant understanding and even now, days later, she was no closer to making an admission of her real feelings for Alex.

She didn't know why she was shocked she cared so much, so quickly. Hadn't she fallen for Bastien with a speed that had astonished her?

Six months after their first meeting and they'd been dashing into a *mairie*, a town hall, and making vows to one another. The cautious Devvy of old had disappeared in the face of Sebastien's unheard-of eagerness to wed. She'd been caught up in the magic of it and even though she'd had her doubts, she'd never, not once, regretted agreeing to be his wife.

Up until now, she'd gone through her life with blinders on. Not seeing much, hiding from the rest. Then her husband had appeared and that had all changed. With his bringing Alex into their relationship, he'd simply tilted their world on its axis.

Devvy smiled at the thought that the world toppling over hadn't been cataclysmic. If anything, it had been *orgasmic*.

"That smile's devious. Should I be scared?"

"Bastien!" At his words, she spun a complete circle on her favorite ballet pumps to face the door. Spotting him there, leaning against the doorjamb in a travel-worn suit, collar unbuttoned and the knot of his tie loosened, legs crossed at the ankle and arms folded across his chest, he looked delicious.

She loved him like that, all rumpled and approachable—not the man who spent ninety percent of his life perfectly turned out. And the fact that he'd come to see her first before getting changed had her heart beating faster.

She rushed over to him and into the arms he uncrossed and held wide open for her. Tilting her head, she accepted his kiss and gave as good as she got. Within seconds, her lips had parted and his tongue was thrusting against hers, simulating the same thrust of his cock into her pussy. That ignited something in her bloodstream, like a bomb being detonated, and made her want to climb him and have him fuck her against the wall.

Devvy shuddered at the thought but knew she couldn't be selfish. As much as he shared her desire—the urgent nudge of his cock at her belly told its own tale—the man had just come back from the airport. He'd crossed time zones and was probably swaying on his feet. Still, that didn't stop her from shuddering as she pulled back and dotted a kiss to his cheek.

"That's my favorite kind of welcome home," he commented, voice husky.

"I aim to please."

He chuckled then sighed, the sound replete as though he was really content to be there with her. "You've no idea how good you look."

"Neither do you."

He cocked a brow. "A travel-crumpled suit is the way to your heart?"

She winked, then standing on tiptoe, pressed her lips to his ear and whispered, "Makes me want to fuck you raw."

"I shall try to always come back looking a mess if that's what my lady wants."

Amused, she shook her head. "Our ideas of a mess are completely different."

"That they are. I'll never understand women," he remarked with a wry grin, then brushed his lips against her temple. "Come on, I'll let you fuck me raw. But I want a bed. My bed. No matter how much you spend, a hotel mattress just doesn't compete." As a yawn cracked his jaw, he looked around the lab, a sleepy cast to his gaze. "Do you need to finish up before we go?"

"No, I can leave everything. I just need to lock up."

As they left the lab, she did just that and he hooked his arm around her shoulder. Together, in a comfortable silence, they walked up the lawns, through the neat pungent squares of her herb and flower patches, and toward the terrace that gave the house its name of *Les Fenêtres*. Only seeing all of the double-fronted panes of glass could anybody understand why the house had been given such a title. She was just relieved she wasn't the one responsible for washing them all!

A few more steps, another staircase, and they were in the corridor leading to their bedroom.

The minute they crossed the threshold, Devvy sat down on the bed, shucked off her shoes, and lay down on top of the covers. She intended to watch the show of Sebastien stripping off. She knew from experience he *might* want her but his body wouldn't let him. He'd fall asleep as soon as his head hit the pillow.

Every time he traveled to the US—in the two years of their marriage, he'd only done so a few times—he did the exact same thing. Only, on the very first occasion, she'd been mortified. Had thought him bored with her, or disinterested enough for him to fall asleep practically on top of her. After the second time, she'd realized it was just something he did, and she'd let him get on with it. Humoring him by always coming up to bed and taking a nap herself. He'd usually wake her up with his cock sliding home.

Just the thought had her smiling once again and as he removed his jacket, Sebastien commented, "You seem happy."

"And *you* sound shocked!"

His lips twitched as he pulled off his tie and shrugged out of his jacket. "I suppose I am. I wasn't sure what to expect when I got back. I was away a lot longer than I'd intended."

He studied her for a moment and she knew he was wondering what had happened between her and Alex. Seeing no point in prevaricating, she murmured, "I had company this time. When you go away, you've no idea how boring it is around here."

"Well, I'm glad I'm useful for something, even if it is only keeping you entertained. Has Alex been the one keeping you company?"

"Yeah. I've been at his apartment every day."

"That's good. You're enjoying being with him?"

Amused at his desire to know what had gone down between the pair of them, yet his inability to come out with the question, she told him, "I am. That first night you flew out, I went to his apartment." She sucked in a breath, hoping Alex had been correct and that Sebastien wouldn't be mad at his not being there that first time. "We slept together."

Bastien paused in the act of pulling off his belt. "Ah."

"That's all you have to say?" she asked with a pout. She'd expected more than that for a reaction!

"It depends. Do you have any regrets?"

"None."

His answer was a grin. A relieved and happy one. "I'd hoped that you'd take the opportunity to get to know each other when I was away. I just wasn't sure if you'd get to that stage. I'm glad you did. How…? Did…? *Zut alors.*" He grunted, and rolled his eyes at his own stuttering. "Did everything go okay?"

Charmed at his fumbled question, she nodded. Unsure as to whether or not to mention Alex's "episode," she kept quiet about that and simply said, "It went perfectly."

The dopey grin had returned. He swiped his hand over his jaw. The sound of his skin rubbing against stubble was audible in the quietness. "You know, I never imagined you'd accept all of this so easily. Don't get me wrong. I'm not complaining. I'm just…relieved."

"I don't understand it either, but I feel like I've known him a very long time. It's made it easier to get to know him, and I didn't lie when I said it's because of who he is. I've had a crush on him for so long. Since I was a teenager. Other kids drooled over singers or actors. I drooled over Alex. And then, you offered him to me on a platter…. It has all worked in your favor."

"It has, hasn't it?" He chuckled.

Curious, she asked, "I know you're tired, Bastien, too tired to talk about anything serious, but this thought has been bugging me. Who first mentioned the idea of a third?"

In the act of shrugging out of his pants and boxers, an act that had her attention switching to his semi-hard cock, he paused, a frown on his face as he contemplated her question. "It's hard to say. We've talked about it for so long. Wanted it for nearly fifteen years or so."

"Who pushed for it though?"

His eyes were distant, remembering. "Alex, at first. When we got together, he was still pretty young." Bastien grimaced. "Both of you are far too young for me."

"Most men wouldn't make that sound like a complaint!"

"I'm not complaining," he denied. "Just…I'm too old for both of you."

Devvy snorted. "You know our backgrounds. We're used to being around mature people."

"Mature. Read ancient." He rolled his eyes. "You're wonderful for my ego."

"Being twenty years younger than you is as big a sop to your ego as anything."

His chagrin was swallowed up in his laugh. "I'll stop feeling sorry for myself. I see I'll get no pity for my antiquity from your quarter." He climbed into bed, going under the covers, grunting with relief as his spine hit the mattress, and the duvet cosseted him in its soft, giving warmth. She maneuvered herself so she could climb underneath the sheets too, and the minute she did, he curled onto his side and grabbed her to him. He settled his face into the crook of her neck, hooked his arm over her waist, and pinned her back to his chest. They'd fall asleep like this, but as time progressed, they'd pull apart and stick to their own respective sides.

Devvy was, or so Bastien accused, a bed hog.

"Alex was about twenty-four when he mentioned it the first time."

"How did you react?"

Devvy wasn't entirely sure why this mattered, but she was sure it did. Two men, happily in love, whether they were bi or not, didn't just decide to look for a third partner to complete the circle. Something had to happen to instigate the process, right? She could have been wrong, and if that was the case, there was no harm done in asking a few questions. There was something here, she could feel it. Her instincts were on red alert. Instincts that had been triggered by Alex's behavior.

She couldn't say for definite if the reason behind the threesome idea was in any way connected to the other night's anxiety attack. She just felt as though it could be a possibility.

On the other hand, there was something Devvy was certain of. Alex's style of interior decoration might be minimalistic, but he was not a minimalist creature. He amassed clutter. Alex had shown her his lab the other day. Proudly shown off his spores and other material he was researching. He'd introduced his PA, a rather harried-looking woman by the name of Kate. She'd had no time to do anything but smile a greeting before she went around clearing up after Alex.

There was a reason behind the almost manic emptiness of Alex's apartment.

A man didn't buy a penthouse, in Paris no less, that was the size of an entire building's story and keep it empty for no reason.

The piano room, maybe. But the rest of the apartment was obsessively bare as well.

There was a puzzle to be solved, whether Alex wanted it solving or not.

Had he not broken down in front of her, she might never have suspected anything was amiss. As it was, she knew something was happening behind the façade he presented to the world at large and to the pair of them. He was a charmer. It was a part of his nature. But there was something else. Something he was hiding.

She was dead certain Sebastien was unaware of it.

Which meant Alex had been keeping secrets. For a very long time.

If Sebastien had expected Alex to break down after they consummated their relationship, he'd either have warned her beforehand, or he'd have asked after Alex when she revealed the truth.

Were she to share the news that Alex had leapt off the bed, terrified, then huddled up on the floor like a little boy seeking shelter from the bogeyman, she just knew Sebastien would be astounded by the revelation.

A part of her wondered how Alex could hide something so major from his lover for so long. The fact they lived apart probably helped. After so long together, she had imagined there were very little surprises to be had.

What the pair of them had shared together that night…Devvy wasn't being a romantic, when she thought of it as momentous. A meeting, a *clashing* of two bodies that had quakes quivering their very souls. She had the feeling she'd made him vulnerable, and that weakness had allowed one of his secrets to come to the fore and wreck the perfect harmony of those moments.

Without doing some more research of her own, she didn't intend to tell Bastien anything. Yet.

Her thoughts had carried away with her and so had Sebastien's. At first, she thought he'd fallen asleep, because he'd taken so long to reply to her question, but his words were pensive, ponderous, as he muttered, "I'll be honest and say I was shocked when he first mentioned it. We'd been together for nearly six years. I'd been thinking about asking him to move in with me, and almost on the same day, he brought it up. I didn't ask him to live with me in the end. I thought, because of the difference in our ages, he must have wanted to explore still. I didn't mind. Much. The idea turned me on."

"Have you never lived together?"

"No. Alex lived in a sardine-tin studio at first, and even though I'd just bought an apartment, he refused to come and live with me. It was a dump, as well. But he was almost proud of it. I don't think he was very happy at home."

"Think?"

"Alex never talks about it. I know his mother's alive. He goes and visits every four months or so. A duty visit, he calls it, and I know he hates going." He sighed, squeezing her a little in his embrace. "After the studio came an apartment of his own, and then he made that first breakthrough with the cancer drugs."

"The antimetabolites medicine."

He snorted. "I forgot I've got my own little Ivanov groupie in bed with me."

She pinched his hand. "I'm a scientist. When someone widens a once-narrow channel in cancer research, everyone sits up."

"Yeah, yeah. I'll believe you, when thousands wouldn't." The pair of them laughed, but Sebastien's laughter eventually turned into a sigh. "If I'd thought he'd wanted to, we'd have moved in together a long time ago. He never seemed ready for it, and I stopped thinking about it to be honest. Just moved past it. Being a couple but apart never did us any harm. And when he wanted to look for a third, it excited me and I guess he convinced me by using my own sex drive against me."

"You really love him, don't you?" she asked, voice soft, as neutral as could be. Devvy didn't want him to think she was jealous. In truth, she wasn't. A month ago, she probably would have been if she'd known Sebastien had a lover whom he loved. Now, that lover had a name. He was Alex. And how could she begrudge Sebastien when she herself could easily feel the same way?

"Yes. He's different, Devvy. To both of us. Although, you're more like him than I realized. His agoraphobia is getting worse. I know how hard it is for him to even get out of the house, but he convinces himself he's in control, because the few times he goes out, he can manage it.

"Like I said, he's probably due a visit to his mother's soon. He'll have to prepare himself for it, but he'll do it. The fact that he can will convince him he's okay. When I called him a month ago about you, I wasn't even sure if he'd come. I think he knew he had to, not only because of the reason behind my call, but because he knew I'd mention he was getting worse if he couldn't make it."

"What would you do?"

"I want him to see a therapist. I accept his other quirks, always have and always will. But this? This is getting serious now."

She pondered that a moment. "You accept my quirks, too."

He pressed a kiss to her head. "As weird as you are, Devvy, you're normal in comparison to our Alex."

Our Alex. She liked that. More than she cared to admit. "As complimentary as ever, I see."

"I left my charm phrase book on the plane."

Ignoring that, she inquired after his trip. "Did you manage to sort the problem with the vineyards out?"

He grunted. "No. They've been completely decimated by phylloxera. We're going to have to pull the vines, replant with a different variety, a hybrid that's resistant to the bastards."

"I'm sorry, darling."

"It's life."

"Still."

"That was my favorite vineyard, as well. I was proud of it. It was the flagship organic vineyard of my brand. All that damned work down the drain."

"You'll make it bigger and better. You know no other way."

He sniffed. "You're just saying that to make me feel good."

"Is it working?"

"Yes."

"Well then, my wifely duties are done."

He growled and nibbled her throat. "You'll be done after we wake up."

"I'll look forward to it."

Chapter Eight

Lips tugging at her clit, a tongue prodding and piercing her pussy, teeth nibbling at the sensitive wet flesh of her cunt, were her alarm call.

She luxuriated in the sensations rolling through the lower half of her body for a few moments before surging into wakefulness. The languor coursing through her was almost drugging, but it felt so damned good. Bastien was taking his own sweet time about pleasuring her. Gentle tugs, little sips, tiny bites. Each one intended to drive her higher and higher but not take her to the brink of orgasm.

The lack of haste was, in itself, pleasurable. The lazy sleepiness of the moment had her hips wriggling against the mattress and she sighed as he clamped his hands against her thighs and held her down.

"*Bonsoir, chérie.*" The words were mumbled against her clit and the vibration had her squealing, thighs lifting her hips into the air only for them to fall back down, her toes digging into the bed. Wishing he'd removed her skirt so she could spread her legs wider, Devvy reached down and grabbed his head, smashing his face into her cunt. His chuckle only made the ache worse, and what had once been lazy and drugging suddenly became intense.

She groaned when he moved away, pulling her hands off his head. Glaring at him, her voice was hoarse as she bit out, "Where are you going?"

His grin was wide as he grabbed her hips and tossed her over onto her belly. Before she even had a chance to squeal, he'd arranged her. Her stomach touched the mattress, her arms were overhead, and her legs were flat out. His weight was suddenly upon her. Her back to his chest, her butt to his hips. His legs surrounded hers, and when she felt his cock drag down the crack of ass, instead of flinging herself over and onto her back as she'd intended, she froze and waited for his next move. He bypassed her butt and slipped his cock into her pussy, just the tip and as always, she had to bear down before he could sink in deep. It was like the sex-organ version of choking. After a few weeks without his cock deep inside, it was hard to take him in, and she butted her forehead against the mattress, refusing to panic when her pussy had accepted him so many times.

This position seemed to make each inch feel that little bit bigger, and by the time he'd thrust all of his seven inches in deep, she was sweating and biting down on the comforter. The sick thing was, around him, she was gushing. Her juices flowing. But he was so goddamned thick, his dick acted like a plug!

His arms came around to bracket her sides and his weight settled atop her in a way that was comforting. He was heavy but she liked him there. His cheek nuzzled against the side of her face, and he brushed his lips against her temple, before whispering in her ear, "Cross your legs."

Curious, she did as bade, then grunted as his cock seemed even larger, her pussy transformed into a vice by this new position.

Slowly, he thrust his hips. This extra tightness making his every inch drag against her quivering channel. As he slid back home, she shuddered, feeling incredibly full and with him surrounding her, every part of him touching her, inside out, it was an almost claustrophobic feeling.

Each thrust added to her pleasurable torment. Each breath was harder to make. Her body was taut, throbbing, on the edge, and he seemed content to just slip in and out. His slow but steady thrusts were calculated to drive her insane. When she could take no more without slipping over the edge of madness, she began to thrust her hips back as he pulled out.

She probably looked like a fish out of water, flopping about on the bed, but every hip jerk of her own caused a burn at the very heart of her sex. That burn slowly began to spread, sending flames shooting down her limbs, until the flames exploded making her scream out, her cunt fastening tight on his shaft, making him work hard for every thrust. Harder than mere moments before.

When he climaxed, his low yell reverberated around the room and his hips seemed to hammer her a little harder as he milked himself of cum. The banked fires deep inside were more than mere embers. It took little to have the flames burning hotly again, especially with his rough thrusts. She screamed as he rode her, burying her face into the covers, hands scratching at the fabric, needing him to pull out and to leave her alone, yet wanting him to keep covering her. Surrounding her with him.

He answered both silent calls. Pulling out, but staying a heavy weight atop her.

The pressure soothed her as she came down from the high of her second climax but she still felt like tearing his hair out. Aggravating, hot, intense…. She needed to go back to sleep after that.

She said as much, mumbling the words into the comforter and grunting at his chuckle. "You're heavy," she complained.

"Tough," he retorted, knowing she was bitching at him, not particularly wanting him to move.

"What is it with you two? Acting like human blankets around me?" At her inadvertent mention of Alex and her in a sexual position, a very interesting thing happened. His cock hardened at the crack of her ass. She gasped, and then laughed. "Someone likes the idea of Alex and me together."

"Fuck," he gritted out. "I'm too old for this shit."

Devvy giggled. "A part of you doesn't agree."

He kept his hips tight to hers by grabbing her and pulling her up onto her knees. She complied, thanking God to be out of the other position. The instant she added starch to her arms to keep her upright, her elbows gave way and her face smooched the blanket again. He began to fuck her. Cock slamming in hard, hips butting into hers. One hand slipped underneath her, between her legs and hovered above her clit. Sensing his fingers there, her eyes opened and she gawked at the patterned fabric of the duvet. Waiting. Willing him to touch her there. He shocked her by spitting, the sound echoing around the room and she felt the spit gather between her butt cheeks. When his thumb pressed deep and then angled down inside her ass to rub his cock, a high cry escaped her. The fingers of his other hand went on the attack and he pinched her clit.

With those two moves, she was out for the count. A hurricane couldn't have woken her as mind, body and soul worked against her. Ecstasy throttled her, choking her, strangling her with its power. Her entire being shut down. It was either that or have each and every molecule in her body go for a quick journey around the room.

* * * *

"How did it go in the US?"

Sebastien balanced his cellphone between his ear and shoulder as he shrugged into a robe then stepped out into the hall, not wanting to disturb his wife from her slumber. Ever since he'd left the bed, she hadn't moved an inch. He'd fucked her to sleep.

Feeling rather proud—pathetic, but still a man counted his blessings when his wife was nineteen years younger than him—he closed the bedroom door and made his way to the study, as he answered Alex, "It couldn't have been worse." His French was sharper than a stiletto, staccato and filled with his anger at the waste of time, resources, and what had looked set to be a fine vintage. "The damned insect had managed to infect the roots. Half the crop was riddled with fungal infections and the rest…" He grunted. "We had to raze the entire field to ash."

Alex clicked his tongue. "I'm sorry, love. I know that was your favorite vineyard."

He sighed. "It was a bloody shame. I can't deny I'm gutted. Although, Devvy greeted me with good news. You two finally did the deed, correct?"

Alex laughed. "We did. More than once."

"And? Spill the details."

"I wish you could have been there that first time, I won't lie. You'd have loved it. I don't think Devvy becomes the aggressor very often…"

Thinking of her slumped form upstairs, the complete annihilation of her energy reserves after his session as the aggressor, he merely murmured, "No. You wouldn't be wrong."

"Well, I let her start. I thought it might give her confidence in herself."

"Like she needs more," Bastien grunted. "The woman has me wrapped around her finger. You too by the sounds of it."

There was silence and then, Alex huffed. "You really mean that, don't you? Do you know your wife at all?"

"Of course, I do! It's the truth."

"Bullshit. Before you introduced her to me, she spent half her time thinking you were going to leave her!"

In the middle of pouring himself a large Scotch, Bastien swore as he spilled most of it on the tray. "I nearly killed myself trying to keep up with her and she thought that?" He shook his head, refusing to believe it. "You can't be serious."

"Deadly."

"I always knew she was on edge, but she thought I was going to leave her? She told you that?"

"Not in so many words, but she's insecure as hell. Letting her be the aggressor was a kindness."

"Saint Alexei," Bastien mocked.

"Now, now. No need to be jealous of my halo."

"With my horns, it wouldn't fit anyway!"

"True," Alex conceded with a chuckle. "Anyway. I thought my cock was going to explode before she managed to get my zipper down. God, it was worth the wait. Her mouth…" He groaned. "Fuck, just thinking about it…"

"I know." Sebastien smiled to himself. "She doesn't have much experience, but I think a vacuum has less suction than her mouth. We ought to patent her."

"She'd kill us if she knew we were talking about her like this."

Sebastien shrugged. Not that Alex could see it. "We're talking about her skills. I doubt she'd complain about that."

"You really can be an arrogant dick sometimes, Bastien."

"It's why you love me." His claim was so secure, with not one ounce of doubt in his words, Alexei had to laugh.

"You're fortunate I have the patience of a saint! Maybe you're right. Saint Alexei has a nice ring to it."

"True," Bastien admitted easily. "As much of a pain in the ass as my flying off to California was, it seems to have fast-forwarded the timetable. I'm relieved. I didn't want her to back down out of nerves."

"You should have had more faith in her."

"I know. I've learned my lesson."

"Until the next time."

Bastien sniggered. "You know me too well."

"I think we should carry on at this pace. Letting her discover for herself the beauty of this kind of relationship."

"I agree. We've achieved so much by letting her go at her own speed. I'm still shocked at her about-face. Pleased and relieved, but still surprised."

"The power of Ivanov, you see. She couldn't resist my biography."

"Your ego's never going to deflate, is it?"

Alex hooted. "As if yours would! Devvy is one of the sexiest women we've ever known, and she's had a crush on me for God knows how long."

"Lucky bastard."

"Being a genius has its advantages."

"Yeah, two thousand square feet of red-hot Parisian property is small fry for a genius."

"Ah, but what is a penthouse in comparison to the beauty of a woman like ours?"

"Incomparable," Bastien said with no hesitation. "I can't deny I like that…a woman like *ours*."

"We're nearly there, love."

"I know. I still feel as though I should pinch myself."

"Wait, and I'll do it for you."

"Smart ass." Bastien growled.

"Listen, I was thinking. Next week, I have to visit my mother. I was thinking about taking Devvy with me."

Despite himself, Bastien stiffened. Unusually for him, he had little to say but his silence spoke louder than anything he could have said.

"If it would hurt you too much, then I won't," Alexei commented after a long pause.

"Why do you think it would hurt me?"

"Don't play the big man, Bastien. I'm sorry my mother is a homophobic bitch. I'm sorry she'll accept Devvy but not you. I'm sorry you've never met her. I thought it would do Devvy some good. She might feel more settled if she thought I would like her to meet my mother." Alex groaned as Bastien remained silent. "If you don't want me to, then I won't. It was just an idea.

"When we were talking the other day, she said she'd tell her parents about us. All three of us. I thought it fair if I reciprocated. Even if it was only a little."

"I've only met her parents a handful of times." He grimaced at the memory of those odd dinner parties. "Her father's all right. A bit arrogant, pompous, and self-important, but her mother, Miranda, is…peculiar. Always watching Devvy, almost like she's waiting for her to make a fool of herself. Odd woman."

"She sounds like a bitch."

"You wouldn't be wrong. I think I'm the only one with a decent family."

Alex snorted. "Maybe, but when was the last time you visited them?"

Offended, Bastien retorted, "I'm busy!"

"Never too busy for me or for Devvy, though, *hein*?" Alex said slyly.

Bastien rolled his eyes and ignored that provocative little statement, preferring to return to the topic of Devvy's mother. "I overheard them talking once. I was supposed to be in the dining room with Derek, Devvy's father, but I followed them into the kitchen."

"Miranda was being unkind?" Alex asked, perceptive as ever.

"Unkind isn't the word."

To this day, Sebastien still felt on edge when he recalled that night. When he'd heard a systematic play-by-play of everything Devvy had done wrong in her mother's eyes that evening. Everything from eating too greedily and having two rolls of bread to her lack of interesting conversation.

He hadn't wanted to embarrass his new wife at the time by commenting on what he'd seen, even though he'd felt like a cad for brushing it under the carpet. He knew how mortified Devvy would have been if he'd mentioned it, so he'd kept quiet and reacted in another way. He'd made sure their visit to Portola Valley had been "accidentally" cut short, and that subsequent visits were also short and very, *very* infrequent. The last time they'd traveled over to see her parents, he'd reserved them a hotel suite. Preferring that than to lodge with them.

He sighed, disturbed as always by the memory, and eventually said, "Let's just say, I'm not sure how they'd react to a relationship like ours."

"Devvy said if she comes to love me, she won't deny me. Her words."

Bastien raised his glass to her in the empty room. While Alex always came across as confident, his lover had some major issues. A fear of rejection was one of them, and Devvy had managed to counteract that with her promise. "She's a brave little thing."

"She really is. We're lucky." He paused. "I think when things are more settled between the three of us, we should have a more spiritual ceremony for you two. Rather than just one at the *mairie*. I'd like to attend this time!"

Bastien grunted. "You're a wily bastard. Making me feel guilty for that when you were the one who suggested you stay out of the ceremony in the first place. I told you I'd have you as my best man."

"Yes, well, we all have our crosses to bear."

"Meaning I need to deal with Devvy meeting your mother."

"That's right. Do you think I want to introduce them? Devvy is as sneaky as she's courageous. She'll figure out, somehow, that I'm going to visit my mother, and if I don't invite her…well, it might offend her! That's the last thing we need."

"Do it. Maybe she can soften the old she-witch."

"Only my father could do that, and considering the bastard left her thirty years ago, I don't think I'm going to get much help from that quarter."

Bastien sighed. "I'll be over tomorrow."

"Miss me, did you?"

"Of course. Do you think Devvy would like to watch?"

Alex chuckled. "Do bears shit in the woods?"

"Maybe it's too soon for her." Bastien pondered that a moment. "We don't want to rush her."

"She'll be curious, *mon amour*. Even if she isn't ready, she'll want to watch, just to know what happens between the two of us. That is, if she hasn't already done some research online."

Even though his cock was thoroughly limp, Bastien felt tingles at the base of his spine at the idea of his innocent little wife watching porn. He groaned and Alex hooted at the sound.

"We'll have to make sure we don't disappoint."

Bastien, ever confident, grunted, "Porn stars have nothing on us."

* * * *

"Two days in a row! I am blessed."

Devvy's comment had Bastien's brows lifting. "I often visit you here!"

"Since when?" she demanded, planting her hands on her hips.

He pursed his lips and she could see his brain ticking, calculating how many times he'd visited her at her lab. She saw the exact moment he realized he couldn't turn the argument around so he'd win. "Often."

She clucked her tongue. "Bullshit."

"I'm a bullshitter." He held up his hands. "I make no bones about it."

Shaking her head at him, she asked, "What do you want?"

"I'm going over to Alex's. I wondered if you'd like to come."

She stilled in the act of adding a few clear drops to the solution she had bubbling over a Bunsen burner. Her hands shook as she placed the dropper onto the counter. Her voice quivered as she asked, "Are you going to fuck him?"

"Does that upset you?" he asked, surprised by her reaction. He'd expected rosy red cheeks, visible signs of rapid breathing. Instead, he saw what looked like disgust.

Her eyes were glassy as she shook her head. Switching off the gas to the burner, she muttered, "Let me clear up. I'll be ten minutes."

"Come over to my study, when you're ready. Alex's clear all afternoon."

A small mewling sound escaped her throat and those glassy eyes of hers suddenly grew wide. Her cheeks started to flush and her tits trembled as she started to breathe heavier. Pleased that she was excited by the idea, he left her with a small smile.

Had her husband understood the thoughts roiling through her mind, he would probably not be smiling. If anything, Devvy was frightened, uncertain by what was about to happen. She was approaching this situation with the Band-Aid philosophy—pulling it off in one yank rather than torturing herself with several tugs.

She needed this to be over and done with. Even though she felt certain she'd enjoy what she was about to see, she was scared about the effect it would have on her.

Having never watched any kind of porn, Devvy, ever the researcher, had decided to rectify that situation. After all, how could she approach a sexual encounter with Alex and Sebastien completely blind? Entirely unaware as to what was about to happen?

Which is how it would have been if she hadn't gone online and forever sullied her search history. The things she'd seen and heard had been a definite eye-opener.

And while the pneumatic porn stars—with their huge breasts and impossibly tight stomachs, the perfect pussies, the instant orgasms, and the built men with their XL cocks and delineated, steroid-esque muscles—had provided a lesson, they hadn't acted as stimuli. As soon as Devvy had replaced the stars with herself, Bastien, and Alex, a miniature volcano had erupted inside her veins.

Her heart had winked out of existence and the organ had no longer been pumping blood, but lava that melted her veins and sent her temperature through the roof.

Perhaps she was a little strange, but the porn sites she'd found had left her cold. Outside of research matter, she'd felt no desire to touch herself from what she'd seen. They'd been reference material. As embarrassing as it was, she'd just wanted to know what went where, how it happened and what it looked like, because while in her head she understood the mechanics, seeing it really was believing it.

A few days before Sebastien's arrival home, she'd asked herself how deeply the pair of them would corrupt her. It was only as she'd watched a woman's pussy being stuffed with two cocks, as she'd witnessed a man being sucked off by another guy and a gal, she'd realized there was no going back.

What did she mean by that?

Well, it was one of those moments, where it just felt like it would be a defining instance of her life. Something she could never take back. It would forever change her. It might only be sex, but the staid Devvy, the woman of old, the traditionalist, who hadn't really partaken in an active sex life prior to her marriage even though there'd been offers from fellow nerds…that creature was borderline disturbed by what she'd seen online.

The two sides of her nature were at war. The side that had popped out fully formed, like Athena from Zeus's head, a creature that had appeared upon her marriage to Sebastien…well, she reveled in the idea of being possessed by two men. Of Bastien being fucked by Alex as he pumped his cock into her. She welcomed the idea of both men going down on her. Or of Alex sucking her clit, while Bastien licked the other man's balls. Devvy had come to title this creature the slut.

A harsh label and an unfair one. She doubted Alex and Bastien had felt as though they were man-whores for sharing a woman. It was a very prudish tag to give herself. The double standard that society gave woman who slept around by denigrating them yet celebrating men who sowed their wild oats had done a number on Devvy.

Oh, she wouldn't let it stop her. The instant Sebastien even mentioned it, she felt like a kid being taken to a theme park for the very first time. The cautionary side of her was telling her not to go on the Big Dipper, the biggest and best rollercoaster in the park, but it was either go big or go home, and Devvy certainly did not intend to return to *Les Fenêtres* by herself!

She was, therefore, subdued on the ride over. Her thoughts amassing in her brain, collecting and building, until she felt as though her head were a pressure cooker on the brink of explosion. It was a relief to just stare out of the window as the chauffeur maneuvered them through the early evening traffic. Workers, making their way home, added to the number of cars causing chaos in the capital.

If she opened a window, the stench of diesel and gasoline would fill her nose. As it was, cool air from the air conditioning unit circulated around the back, and in truth, she needed the chill. It was a mild day but she felt flushed and the hand that was joined to Bastien's was slightly sweaty. Enough so that she tried a few times to disentangle her fingers from his, but he wouldn't have it. Perhaps he could sense her nervousness, her doubts, her fears, for he never let that connection drop. It grounded her in a way that she would never really be able to explain. Because were it not for this man, she would never be slaloming into a world she'd never even realized existed.

Sebastien was opening the doors to a whole new way of life. It was only now that she really felt overwhelmed. A part of her wished she'd never looked at the pictures, never watched the videos, never seen or heard the sweating, pumping, debauched scenes, because all they'd done was freak her out.

Devvy wasn't as liberated as she'd thought herself to be.

Being with Alex, by himself, had felt deliciously naughty.

The very first day, when she'd visited him in his apartment, and at the sexual vibes, the need humming between the pair of them, had asked him to call Sebastien so he'd come round, she'd done so, because she'd believed having her husband there would make her feel as though she weren't cheating on him. Now, that feeling hadn't dissipated, but the idea of being with them both was like a bomb to the brain.

She tried to focus on passersby. On the chic vibrancy of the arrondissements they were passing through, intermingling with the shabbier areas that still held Parisian flair, making even the drab glitter and shine. Small and large streets, wide avenues, huge courtyards. Paris had it all. Even though she'd been here two years, she'd never really explored. A part of her wanted to play chicken, to ask Sebastien to cancel, to ask him to take her around the city, to show her its magic.

Several times throughout their marriage, he'd made the offer but work had always gotten in the way. Only the knowledge that he'd yet to see Alex made her hold her tongue.

The road to their lover's home, a road she'd traveled on quite frequently this last month, popped into her line of sight. As they maneuvered down it, nervousness overwhelmed her and made her feel slightly sick.

It was with relief when five minutes later they'd been dropped off outside the apartment block and had made their way to the penthouse. She just needed to get on with it. She'd built it up in her head, so much so that the hype was petrifying her.

The instant the doors of the elevator slid open, she rushed from it, and into Alex's waiting arms. Minutes later, feeling selfish because her lovers hadn't had the chance to greet each other, she started to move away from him but he tutted and continued the gentle stroking of his hand down her spine.

In her ear, he whispered, "If you are not ready, *ma petite*, you must only say."

"I don't know what's wrong with me," she whispered, not seeing Sebastien's concerned and surprised glance at his wife's quivering self.

"You are nervous. It is quite natural. You've never done anything like this before. It is, how you say, a momentous occasion."

Even though she still felt nervous, Devvy chuckled against his chest. Pressing her nose into the crisp linen of his shirt, she scented the pure essence of the man. He wore a pair of freshly laundered slacks, the shirt, and nothing, as usual, on his feet.

He looked, felt, and smelled richly casual. A wealthy man in complete control.

The same went with Bastien, who wore a thin silk jumper in a shade of cream that augmented the amber of his eyes. Underneath, a white, V-neck T-shirt peeked out at the throat. His jeans weren't the thirty-dollar bargains that she herself sported, but five-hundred-dollar, designer gear.

In comparison to her work clothes of a ratty T-shirt and discount jeans, she was sadly underdressed.

A feeling of inadequacy assailed her, but she knew it was her nerves talking. Working against her. Undermining her defenses. It was a voice that sounded just like Miranda Nelson's. A voice that picked and prodded. A voice that demanded perfection at all times, and Devvy was anything but.

She shivered a little when Alex's hand slipped further down her spine to roll over the curve of her behind. She pressed her face into his throat and nuzzled slightly. They'd spoken on the phone, but she'd refused to visit him these last few days. On principle.

It was good to simply breathe him in and realize how much she'd missed him. How deeply he'd entrenched himself in her days, and in the shortest space of time! She recognized at that moment she'd reached the "no going back" part of a relationship. This man was hers now, just like the one behind her was.

Once she got today out of the way, once her nerves were settled, she knew this was the beginning. And the idea thrilled her. Just being with him made her earlier fears dissipate. The rest would go as soon as she saw the two of them together, because now that she was here, she was very confident of that.

He smelled of aftershave and man, as well as soap with a faint hint of O-zone from his lab. A peculiar combination but one that made her tingle nonetheless.

The soft skin of his throat beckoned her lips to press against the sinews and she rubbed them back and forth, feeling daring when they parted and her tongue slipped out to gently swipe across the delicious expanse of recently shaved flesh.

A faint groan escaped him and that sound acted as a trigger. Sebastien was suddenly behind her. Close. So close, she could feel his cock nudging her butt.

He pressed his torso to her back, completely sandwiching her in between the pair of them and just like that, her uncertainties fell away. Her nervousness disappeared.

At front and back, there were two cocks pressing against her with urgency. Active reminders that as inadequate as she might be in her mother's eyes, a vision she'd brainwashed Devvy into sharing, these two men wanted her. They wanted the unpolished creature who slobbed about in cheap jeans with stained patches on the knees from her work in the garden. The ratty T-shirts that were a few sizes too big, and that were misshapen from over-washing.

She remembered Alex's reaction to her in a pair of shorts a few days ago.

How the pair of them were reacting now, when she was hardly at her most elegant.

The simple truth of it was that they *got* her.

They clicked with the real woman.

And just the thought had heat flushing through her, with, as Alex himself had said, the acknowledgment of this momentous occasion.

"I want to watch," she whispered, carefully tilting her head back to rest against Bastien's shoulder. Her gaze ricocheted between the pair of them. "I need to watch you both together."

Just saying the words made her heart pump a little harder. When she saw Alex's devious grin, the wickedly amused slash of his lips at her perverse need to play voyeur, she flicked her finger against his shoulder and said, "Don't tease!"

The grin disappeared to be replaced by a look of innocence. "I wasn't!"

She rolled her eyes. "You were so! I know it's strange to need to see you both, but I'm interested. Intrigued is a better word, I guess."

Behind her, Sebastien chuckled. "I think we are experiments to be viewed and studied, Alex. Specimens. Does that bother you?"

Alex shook his head, a wide grin on his chops. "Not at all. I'll willingly dedicate my body to science."

When Bastien laughed again, Alex stepped back, and the instant he did, Devvy realized how much she'd relied upon him to support her. Her legs jolted, the muscles trembling at his abrupt departure. She had to stiffen her knees and spine to keep herself from falling forward. Not that she needed to worry. Bastien would have caught her if the starch in her joints had completely disintegrated.

Sebastien moved away too, lingering to make sure her legs hadn't turned into limp spaghetti, but reaching for her hand within seconds. The pair of them followed Alex as he moved away from the elevator, and they all walked down the barren hall, passing the lounge, the lab, and the gym, all to approach the bedroom. All places Devvy had explored frequently during Bastien's absence. Not that there was a lot to see.

The minute they crossed the threshold, Sebastien squeezed her hand, then released her fingers. He strode forward, the steps rapid, urgent, filled with need as he neared Alex. From being separate entities, suddenly their arms clung at one another and their torsos smashed together in an effort to be as close as physically possible. Mouths fought, clashed. Lips nipped and caressed. Tongues played and teased.

She'd seen them kiss before, but never like this, because this would have a satisfactory ending for both of them. Before this, they'd kept it relatively innocent. For her benefit. But that was gone now, in the past, and there was an urgency and a need to love one another. That need ratcheted up by the length of time they'd been apart.

Their chests arched back as they began to tear at each other's shirts. Buttons popped, threads groaned as they were stretched. Alex gripped the hem of Bastien's sweater, tugging it up, baring the corrugated expanse of muscle. His fingers plied and massaged his abdomen. Sebastien's own fingers went to work on Alex's lower back. Those digits had kneaded her flesh, teased and caressed her. And while she was both astounded by the aggressive tenderness—an oxymoron, she knew—Devvy was also energized by the display.

The desire, the lust inherent in this…they'd invited her to see it. They wanted her to be a part of this beautiful madness.

Panting breaths tore them apart and Bastien took the moment to tear at his sweater and T-shirt and practically rip it overhead. She grimaced as the misshapen garment, no longer as pristine as it once was, thanks to Alex's fumbling fingers, landed on the floor. Bare skin kissed bare skin. Hard, male nipples brushed against hard, male nipples. Cocks, hidden behind slacks, rubbed against each other as their hips jerked back and forth, inciting more need.

The groans they made, the deep, bass sounds echoed through her, down to her very soul. She rested against the doorway, using it as a support, but when their hands went to their belt buckles and fingers tore at zippers, and cocks appeared, weeping heads screaming of their torment as they popped out behind their flies, she slowly sank to the ground. Her body humming with need.

Alex's hand shot out and he grabbed both their dicks. He made a tight circle with his fist, and the pair of them rocked their hips, forcing their shafts through that tight surround. She just knew the pair of them were imagining fucking her, only the thin membrane between her ass and pussy separating them. The thought had her biting her bottom lip, gnawing on it as desire flushed through her veins.

As lips and teeth clashed, pained grunts escaped them as their lust for one another reached fever pitch. Desire throttled them, she could sense it, and when Sebastien muttered something in French, something to which Alex chuckled, she knew it was the beginning of the end.

Alex pulled away and knelt in front of Sebastien. Devvy's entire world caved in as he took Bastien's cock between his lips. She watched in awe as he slurped and swallowed, sank down the shaft, swallowing him whole. She saw the protrusion at his throat as Alex took every inch of him. More pained sounds escaped from Bastien—it was hard to believe that they were pleasure-filled.

His hands wafted inelegantly in the air, clenching and de-clenching. At one point, they reached up to grip his hair, and they tugged as though insanity were a mere breath away. Then one dropped down and fingers pulled and played with Alex's soft silky locks.

"*Pas plus! Pas plus*! No more!" he shouted when Alex ignored him. He jerked back, forcing Alex into releasing his cock. It glistened, almost purple as it throbbed and quivered an inch away from Alex's plump, wet lips.

For a second, he hovered there and Devvy knew her husband was trying to regain control. Then he strode over to the bed and pulled out the tray Alex kept under the mattress. It nearly shot out across the floor in his haste, and he swore a litany of curses as it slid over to Devvy's side of the room.

His steps were measured, slow. He was fighting for control and winning. He bent down, and amid the paraphernalia Alex kept on the tray, he grabbed the lube. As he drizzled it over his shaft, ensuring every part of him was wet with the solution, his eyes caught hers. Fire fought fire. Her eyelids fluttered down to half-mast at the hunger in his face.

At that moment, she could have stepped in. Asked to play a part in this. She chose not to. Intent on seeing the pair of them together without her interference. It almost killed her to stay back, every part of her singing with the desire to be at the center of both men's attention. The prudish creature of before disappearing in the face of such glory. She forced herself to remain silent and realized, when Sebastien nodded at her, he'd been checking in. Even at that intense moment, he'd wanted to make sure she was okay, that she was with them, not freaking out.

Somehow that made it harder to stay quiet. Alex had once told her that she had power over Bastien, and it was only now she realized he was right. She mattered to her husband. She was important.

With his cock sopping wet from lube, he returned to Alex's side, grabbed him by the arms and with a force that shocked her, pushed him onto the bed. Alex laughed, the sound light, carefree. A sound she knew was rare. Something that only escaped him when he was in Bastien's company. And now hers.

Bastien forcibly turned Alex over onto his belly and dragged his jeans down to his ankles. He stood to the side so she could watch as he poured lube down the crack of Alex's ass. She watched as the pucker tensed and released, Alex's hiss telling her how cold it was, and how very much it aroused him.

Sebastien's fingers prodded and thrust deep, fucking him with the elegant digits. Alex had spread his legs slightly for balance, but Bastien kicked them closed. There was little play, because she could tell both men were on the edge. Soon, Bastien's body was in the way, but she heard Alex's small cry as he was penetrated, the low groan as Bastien's cock forged deep, and she herself knew how that felt. Knew how intense a feeling that was. Something that almost made every part of her scream with need of her own.

Bastien's hips shuttled back and forth, his butt clenching as he began to fuck the man that both he and his wife had taken for a lover.

Alex's grunts and moans were a song of their very own. A song that made Devvy stand on trembling knees, every step difficult to take as she neared them. Her muscles were weak, quivering as she forced herself to move around the bed. She climbed up onto the mattress to watch them from the front.

Her husband's face, beautiful as always, was filled with the pleasurable pain that only sex could bring. Alex's eyes were clenched shut, his mouth working as ecstasy ripped him in two. He kept on shaking his head as though physically rejecting how good his lover was making him feel. As though it weren't possible to feel so much.

She continued crawling forward until her breath brushed his lips, and only then did his eyes pop open. There was a dazedness to those luscious amethyst orbs. When he realized she was there, inches between them, a hair's breadth between their mouths, flames suddenly shot into the striations of his eyes. As beautiful as they always were, at that moment, they seemed iridescent with color.

She caught his gasp with her mouth and tongue. Forging a path of her own in his mouth. She refused to close her eyes, as she wanted to see everything, didn't want to miss a second. And as she looked up and saw Bastien watching her, a look of pride and intense relief on his face at her acceptance of what was happening, the feeling she'd known would come when she was with these two appeared.

Belonging.

Devvy Nelson had found the place she belonged.

Her doubts of an hour ago seemed foolish now. Her fear that they were taking her down a path to what her mother would class slatternly behavior held merit, but she didn't give a damn.

This was her place.

Seeing them together and realizing how magical they were as a pair made her feel all the more cherished. She couldn't understand why, when they were so perfect a match, they needed her. Yet, they'd brought her into this. They'd asked her to become a part of this magic. And a part she would become.

Bastien forced his eyes to stay open. Even as pleasure battered him, he continued to stare at her. Alex's lips were slack, quivering as she fucked his tongue with her own, and Devvy only had a few seconds to enjoy the two at their most vulnerable before both men, seconds apart, screamed their pleasure.

Chapter Nine

After a few days of emotional highs and lows, the stress of watching porn—who knew it could have such adverse effects?—the aftermath of watching her two lovers together was rather anti-climactic.

They didn't spin her over onto the mattress and make her see stars of her own.

They didn't clutch her in their embrace.

Or, if they did, Devvy wasn't awake to notice any of it.

Like switching off the light, Devvy had fallen asleep.

She awoke in Sebastien's arms under the covers. Minutes or hours later.

At first, she thought they were in their own bedroom. A part of her wondered if she'd dreamed the entire thing. Then, she smelled the starch in the sheets and recognized the scent as coming from Alex's bed linens.

He was the only man she knew who preferred to have crisp cotton beneath him as he slept.

And this wasn't just a little starch. The sheets were like cardboard. On the verge of being uncomfortable. Especially in comparison to the bed linen Devvy herself preferred.

When she'd married Sebastien, she'd had no choice but to switch to luxury thread counts. Sheets that cost a small fortune. As a singleton, she'd had old bedclothes, because in her opinion they were the best. The ones with the nubby balls from overuse and over-washing. She'd found they were the softest and the best for snuggling. As such, waking up with her face pressed against sheets like paper, she instantly recognized where she was.

Her eyes popped open to the semi-darkness of the room. Half of it was in shadow, half was illuminated by the caramel-colored glow from the streetlamps. She wasn't sure what time it was, but either way, sounds of life could be heard from the streets below.

It was amazing how sound traveled. While Alex was relatively far away, distance wise, from the road, there were still some pedestrian and traffic noises that slipped through the soundproofing. As it was, she could hear a gaggle of French women. Just like the geese she'd likened them to, they spat, hissed, and shouted at one another.

It was only as she'd visited France, then gone on to Spain and Italy for her honeymoon, that she'd realized how the Romance languages all sounded so beautifully aggressive. It was amazing how two people could be having a regular conversation, and yet they all sounded like they wanted to kill one another.

Sebastien spoke French, Italian, Spanish, English, German, and some Mandarin. She'd used his skills as a translator to eavesdrop as she people-watched on their honeymoon. She could easily remember a couple who had looked on the brink of throttling one another discussing who had turned the dishwasher on that evening.

As the gaggle of women disappeared, a jet sounded overhead, soaring from Charles de Gaulle to some far-flung place, and as a planeload of people left the capital, a car tooted its horn. Brakes squealed in reply, there was another burst of angry French, and then there was silence. From that alone, she reckoned it to be early morning. Paris was rarely silent. It was too alive. Silence was death in a city like this, where noise and activity were the lifeblood coursing through the city's veins.

It seemed incredible she'd slept for so long, but the last few days had been pretty tense. It was a tension of her own making but that hadn't made her feel any better. She'd caused that argument with Alex, forcing him to think about their future in more than just a transitory way. Then had come the telephone conversation with her mother, as well as the click onto the porn site where she'd petrified herself. As it was, even though the situation needed resolving with Alex, and the gossip on the other side of the Atlantic needed addressing with Sebastien, Devvy felt a hell of a lot better.

It was also lovely to awaken in Bastien's arms. He'd never really been a cuddler. In fact, he'd never been all that affectionate. She hadn't minded, simply because she wasn't used to affection anyway. Growing up in an emotionally distant household did that to a girl, so entering another one upon her marriage hadn't disturbed her overly, even if she had wished things were different.

But now, to have awoken in Bastien's embrace, one of his hands proprietarily resting on her belly, the other on her boob, was a great feeling.

That belief from before, that she'd found the place she belonged, Bastien at one side, in Alex's bed, even if the man himself wasn't here, returned.

She wriggled out of Bastien's grip. Still jet lagged, he merely grumbled, mumbled something in low French, and then flung himself onto his back before sinking back into sleep.

She rolled out of the bed, inelegantly as always, and managed to stop herself from falling over the side. Standing up, carefully trying not to rock the mattress, she realized they'd taken off her sneakers and jeans, and left her in her too-large shirt.

She padded barefoot out of the bedroom, using the lights from the street to guide her. In the hallway, she saw the glare coming from Alex's lab and walked toward the glowing doorway. She opened it, blinked at the bright light in comparison to the pitch black of the corridor and, rubbing her eyes, started trying to focus on the large room. In truth, it was more than large. It was huge.

Her own lab at *Les Fenêtres* wasn't exactly tiny, but this was an average person's bedroom times three. So big was it, that on first glance, she couldn't actually see him and she had to step deeper into the room in an effort to find her wayward lover.

The equipment and machinery she passed made her whistle at the cost. All of it brand-new and gleaming, she'd seen it before, but it still reiterated Alex's importance. The sheer quality of his instruments told her without words the miracle he was reaping here.

A smell of O-Zone pervaded her nostrils, making them twitch, and a dryness in the air appeared, the closer to the center of the lab she walked. Devvy found him working with some distilling equipment. She didn't even bother to question why he'd decided to work on a night such as this one. She just tapped her knuckles against the counter to warn him she was there.

His head shot up, his fierce frown of concentration slipped away, and was replaced by a warm, gentle smile that worked wonders on her heart.

"Devvy," he murmured and her name had never sounded so beautiful. Each letter was imbued with his own language in a rumbling purr that set her nerves alight.

Not with lust or need. But with a gentle heat.

It would be so easy to love this man, and for the first time, she wondered if she was already there, like he insisted they both were. Regardless of the length of time they'd known each other.

He looked tired, his eyes drawn, and her own dropped down to his lab-coat-covered shoulders that he wore over a naked torso and a pair of boxers.

"I guess a regular lab wouldn't accept that for a uniform," she teased.

"We both know there are many advantages to working from home."

Devvy smiled and nodded. "The grounds at *Les Fenêtres* are large enough for a lab of your own. You needn't share with me, if that's what's bothering you."

His frown soon returned, and she was saddened to see it. She hadn't meant to cause him upset. The thought had popped into her head and she'd seen no harm in saying it when it was the truth. There was plenty of land to spare and if it made Alex happy to have his own working environment then she and Bastien would do whatever necessary to make sure that happened.

Subconsciously, Devvy realized she was being pugnacious, stubborn, and maybe a little premature, considering how long they'd actually known each other. But something inside her knew this subject needed addressing. She hadn't mentioned it in the three or four calls that had passed between the two of them ever since she'd left his apartment. And now really wasn't appropriate but these things couldn't always be planned.

"I am happy where I am, Devvy," he told her gently.

"Would you prefer us all to move in here?" she asked, taking a step closer to the counter he was working on and perching her panty-clad butt on a stool.

His eyes widened in horror and she chuckled.

"This penthouse is large enough for a family of twenty, Alex. It's huge! People rarely have so much room. You're fortunate."

"I like my space, Devvy."

"I know you do. I may not have known you long…"

Before she could continue, he butted in, "You may not have known me long, ma petite, but you know *me!*" He imbued the last word with a lot of meaning.

As silly as it seemed, he spoke the truth. She did know him. Just like he knew her.

Maybe it was the scientist in them, the genius. The fast-tracked kids who had always been too smart for their peers. They connected in so many ways and those ways still had a habit of shocking her.

She thought he'd continue to shock her for the rest of their lives together and if anything, rather than frightening her, the thought pleased her.

She knew there was no such thing as a guarantee in this world. Things could happen. Things could change. Love could die and hope could be lost, but she saw no reason to be a pessimist in such a matter.

At heart, she was a realist. With her feet planted firmly on the ground. It was why she'd always been so filled with doom and gloom where Sebastien was concerned, because she knew the score of things. But now, the status quo had changed. Tilting everything on its head. Making her see the world through different eyes.

What the three of them had, while in its infancy, was unique.

And special.

She could feel it, deep down. She tried not to think too far ahead in the future, but it was so easy to see herself settling down. A blonde little girl on one hip and a dark-haired little boy clutching at her fingers as they wandered through the gardens at *Les Fenêtres*. She imagined Sebastien watching them from his office, a contented smile on his face, a smile that came from his love in his family. She saw Alex, lines of strain at his eyes, as he escaped the lab, only to follow her and their children through the gardens. She imagined her son squealing as one of his fathers chased him around the garden, and then the soothing sounds Alex clucked from under his tongue after that little boy had tripped and grazed his knee.

She was not the sentimental sort, had always been far too analytical for that. Where these two were concerned, she felt every single one of her X chromosomes come to life.

She didn't care that she'd probably be an outcast in her family.

She didn't care that having two children with two different sets of coloring would declare to the world the type of relationship she had with the two men she shared a house with…

She intended to grab every second of happiness she was lucky enough to be given, and if that meant prodding Alex up his ass, she'd do it. And being prodded up the ass was something he obviously enjoyed if Sebastien's earlier demonstration was anything to go by. She smirked at the thought and he glared at her.

"What are you laughing at?"

"I'm laughing at you." She sighed. "I'm not going to give up, you know. You like this apartment, fine. But you are going to live with Sebastien and me. I don't care if we have to leave *Les Fenêtres* and find somewhere else in the city. Somewhere that suits you."

"Why are we even talking about this? We've only known each other a month."

She snorted, unoffended. "It's amazing how we've only known each other a month when it comes to talking about this kind of commitment. But when you want me to remember the connection between us, time is irrelevant." His lips pursed. "Look, you can be just as weird there as you are here!"

At her earnestness, even though the topic obviously irritated him, he laughed. "Oh Devvy, only you could use that to try to persuade me."

She shook her head, refusing to be disarmed. "No, it's the truth. Sebastien is really flexible, you know. He is with me, when I get up in the middle of the night to go and work on something. He won't make any demands on you. You can live exactly as you choose, how you please. You don't have to share a bedroom with us. If you need your own space, there's plenty of it at *Les Fenêtres*."

"Why is this so important to you?"

"I don't know." She shrugged. "I'm not asking you to do this now. Not even in six months' time. I want this to be the future. I want us all to be together. It's the one normal thing we can do. Share a roof. Otherwise…" She sighed. "You can't be happy feeling like the other person in a marriage. An extra cog in the works, when you're an integral part. Why feel disjointed when you don't have to be?

"The way you pull away from Bastien…even tonight, I know how it is when inspiration strikes, but tonight was important, and what do I find when I wake up? Bastien's asleep, and you're in here, working. This was the first step toward everything you and Sebastien want. And when I asked him, he said it was you who pushed for a threesome, at first. It was you who raised the subject.

"So, why are you pulling back?"

"I'm not doing anything of the sort," he retorted.

"Yes, you are. You're distancing yourself from us. I just don't understand why." She pulled a face. "Look, I don't want to get into this. I just want you to realize I won't let this go. It's too important. Six months, a year, eighteen months, whatever…down the line, all three of us will live on the same property. Get used to the idea."

With that, she strode out of the lab. Ignored the beeping, humming machines that held answers to one of the deadliest diseases to mankind. She bypassed them all and returned to the bedroom, climbing carefully onto the mattress and placing her hand in Bastien's, so as not to disturb him but still wanting a simple union with him.

She stared at the ceiling, watching as the streetlamps glittered and flickered, and how beams of light would trace across the cornices in the ceiling, creating a miniature light display.

She couldn't say for certain how long it was before Alex returned to bed. She couldn't put a number on the minutes, but it was just that. Minutes. At a guess, she'd say ten. Just enough for her words to penetrate the thick skull of her genius lover, and for him to climb into the bed beside her. The instant he lay down, he pulled her against him, and into his arms.

She fell asleep like that, but a part of her consciousness knew Alex remained awake. His brain cogitating her earlier words.

Once again, she'd discovered another sore spot. A point that acted as a trigger for Alex. One by one, she'd challenge them. One by one, she'd challenge *him*. Because for that sense of belonging, that unique knowledge, it was worthy of a bloody battle.

Chapter Ten

The next day, when Bastien awoke to the tangle of arms and limbs on the mattress, he grinned and leaped out of bed with a spring to his step.

He was hard-pressed not to start whistling. The only thing that stopped him was the idea of waking the two sleeping beauties on the bed.

God, life felt good at the moment.

Really good.

In fact, good was an understatement.

As time passed, with Devvy and Alex's relationship flourishing, he was only just starting to realize how hard it had been before Devvy knew.

It was his own fault. He'd entered their relationship knowing he'd be telling lies to his wife for however long it took to enlighten her to the truth.

He was well aware that made him a bastard.

A bastard with good intentions, but nevertheless, he was fortunate Devvy had been so tolerant and so deeply infatuated with Alexei as a scientist and the man himself.

Otherwise, he knew there would have been a completely different ending to this particular tale. He would be in Alex's bed now, waking up to the realization that he'd pushed one of the best things that had ever happened to him out of his life.

He'd be grieving now. Probably would have had a meeting with his attorneys scheduled, because she'd have set the divorce train rolling and he'd have no choice but to accede to her wishes, because he was to blame. For everything.

Instead, he felt great.

For the first time in a long while, he felt whole.

Being with just one of them had felt as though he were splitting himself down the middle.

He'd long since recognized that Alex was his soul mate. Alex, being Alex, was difficult and even though it hurt, Bastien knew the feeling wasn't reciprocal.

He wasn't enough for Alex.

He'd long since come to accept the pain of that, and was accustomed to the sting of rejection. He was loved by Alex, and that was enough. Truly.

Throughout the years of their searching for a third, for him, he wouldn't lie. The search *had* been tinged by bitterness. By the knowledge that he wasn't enough for Alex and that his soul mate needed someone else.

When Alex had found Devvy, seeming to have some kind of strange epiphany over a goddamn magazine article, Bastien had reluctantly agreed to meet up with her. For Alex's sake.

The instant he did, he realized a man could have two soul mates. Seemingly impossible, seemingly the truth.

That first day, it was like being hit in the chest with the lightning bolt. Bang. Instant connection. Just like he'd experienced with Alex.

From that very first moment, sharing himself between the two of them had been painful. Only now, when they were together, could he feel at ease.

Before Alex, Bastien had thought love and soul mates to be bullshit. What guy in his twenties didn't? Just like his peers, he'd thought with his cock. A cock that gravitated toward women. Until Alex.

That first, life-defining moment had pushed away the clouds of bullshit, and made him see the truth of it. That love was real, that it hurt, and that it was wonderful.

It could make you feel alive, and by the next breath, make you feel like death.

It could fill you up, fill all the holes in your heart, and then leave you feeling empty.

He'd never experienced as much as he had with Alex. Until Devvy.

That feeling of fulfillment, of feeling lucky for Devvy's forgiving nature and her crush, went with him through the morning.

He left the two of them to sleep off the night before, knowing he'd be meeting Devvy for lunch later anyway, and went to work. A huge conglomerate was interested in *La Belle sans la Bête* and said interest had been causing a huge stink at the office.

He'd been putting in extra hours to cope with the fallout of a hostile takeover, instigating safeguards to protect the company from other corporations.

Then had come the goddamn decimation of one of his favorite vintages.

Work, of late, hadn't been the pleasure it had always been.

He wasn't so blind that he failed to realize the slippery slope had started when he met Devvy.

Fulfilling dreams had a habit of changing your priorities. Work was getting in the way.

That being said, he headed a meeting with *La Belle sans la Bête's* lawyers and the financial directors. Plugging in the holes in the companies defense was taking far longer than it should have taken, but *c'est la vie*. He accepted the increased workload, and felt only relief to get out of the meeting with a small headache.

Another dampener on his life at the moment.

The headaches.

As he strode down the corridor toward his office, ignoring the view and the palpitations that came with being thirty stories up and being acrophobic, scared of heights, he tried not to be too obvious as he rubbed his temples.

The fact he was acclimating to the pain was perverse.

Sighing, he entered his office, and immediately walked over to the windows to pull the blinds shut. The room's darkness helped, but the ear-splitting screech of his cellphone ringing didn't.

It was his personal line so he didn't grumble. In fact, hearing from either Devvy or Alex would undoubtedly cheer him up.

Christ, he was turning into a real sap.

He snorted at the thought. He already *was* a sap.

Checking the ID, he grunted with disappointment that it was neither of them, then immediately felt guilty because it was his mother.

Picking up the cell, he murmured, "*Bonjour, maman.*"

"Sebastien, *mon petit*, it is that time of the week."

His lips twitched. "Your weekly checkup call, *hein*?"

"Yes," she admitted cheerfully. "How's the head?"

"Fine," he lied.

"Still hard as ever, I see." She sounded unconvinced. "It's a wonder you suffer with migraines at all, considering it's as tough as concrete."

"I'm fine," he repeated.

Her snort told him she didn't agree. "Your voice changes when you lie, *mon fils*." When he kept silent, but narrowed his eyes, she chuckled. "It does. You growl. Subconsciously, you're trying to make the lie sound true, but I know you too well."

Ever since Suzette Jacques had retired, she'd started studying online courses. Anything from learning Mandarin to psychology classes.

Sebastien and Henri, his father, had been suffering ever since.

"I'm sure you're right, *maman*, but I'm fine. Even if I do have a headache at the moment, so please don't make a fuss. I really don't need it."

She sighed. "The doctors have found nothing?"

"They're still looking," he muttered. He didn't suffer from a fear of small, closed-in spaces like Alex did, but that MRI scan had been tough work.

He hoped to God he never had to go through one again.

"Are you taking the medication?"

"Sometimes." At her tut, he grunted. "They don't always work. Especially if I take them for every little twinge. I try to save them for the ones that make me feel ill."

From the back of her throat, there came a helpless catch. He knew if he wasn't careful, she'd start crying.

Suzette was the type of mother who blamed herself for what she viewed as his faults. It was her fault he had to wear contacts. It didn't matter she had perfect vision and his father was the one with the specs. She blamed herself.

When, at eight, some of his baby teeth had dropped out and crooked replacements had appeared in their place, she'd blamed herself and spent a small fortune on visiting an orthodontist.

His *grand-mère,* the one that had led him down the path which would eventually lead to *La Belle sans la Bête*, said that Suzette blamed herself for the rain falling and felt guilty when it was windy.

She'd been right.

It was all out of love. He'd been a late child, appearing when his mother had been on the brink of turning thirty-five. In her day, that had been uncommon and she persisted on believing his faults came because she'd been an older mother.

Her paranoia, for the most part, was sweet. Just not when he had a headache.

"*Maman*, please do not worry. It's work. That's all."

"Of course, I worry! I'm your mother. It's my job."

He'd never convince her of the alternative. He'd stopped trying. "If you say so," was all he said, knowing she would be hurt if he tried to argue the difference.

"How is Devina?" came the next question.

Now, a smile creased his lips. "Marvelous, as usual."

She chuckled. "You might have scared your father and me by waiting so long to get married, but you chose wisely, *cher*."

"I know I did," he replied, tone confident.

"And what of Alex?" Suzette asked. She was treading cautiously, but there was no need.

They might not speak every day, a weekly five-minute checkup call the most they connected, followed by a monthly in-depth one, but he tended to discuss these matters with her.

A lifetime of motherly curiosity had made it a habit.

Even as an adolescent turning adult, that difficult phase when kids hated the world and their parents, he'd still shared what he'd perceived as his woes with her.

It had been an ingrained habit, one that had never died out.

"He's fine, too," he said, as nonchalant as possible. Teasing Suzette was par for the course.

She mumbled, "What did I do to deserve a difficult son?"

He laughed. "It must have happened in a past life. You're far too angelic to have done anything so bad."

"Stop teasing," she retorted. "Tell me. Any closer to the goal?"

She hadn't approved of his marrying Devvy while remaining with Alex, but she'd understood Alexei's frailties.

That psychology course had come in handy, then.

Being on the cusp of eighty-two, his mother should have been ultra-traditional. To a certain extent, she was. But, she'd spent most of her life trying to be youthful, trying to keep up with her young son. Forever feeling like the mature mother the hospital had labeled her, she'd done as much as possible to remain in the know.

"She knows about him, *maman*," he told her, his excitement finally bleeding into his words. It was the first chance he'd had to tell her, thanks to the chaos of the hostile takeover and the impromptu visit to the States, and sharing the news made more elation bubble through his veins.

There was silence on the other end of the line. Cautiously, she asked, "Does she accept what you two want? It is rather unorthodox, *mon fils*. You must be patient with her."

His mind switched to his view upon awakening this morning. "I am, *maman*, never fear. But she is gradually coming to terms with it."

On the other end of the line, Suzette blew out a breath. "We'll keep this between ourselves, Bastien. Your *papa* tries, but I don't think he'd understand Alex's need to have a *ménage à trois*..."

He interrupted. "It isn't just Alex's need."

Not anymore.

Another sigh. He knew she wanted to understand but couldn't. It didn't make her judge him. She loved him too much for that. "No, but still. It was hard enough when you brought Alex home that first time."

His father, now nearing eighty-five, had been a perplexed sixty-seven-year-old when Bastien had turned up at the house with a boyfriend.

Bastien, once again, had been fortunate. His parents' love for him was absolute. Henri had never ceased to be confused, but he accepted Alex, simply because Bastien loved him.

Not that Suzette would have let it be any other way.

Unlike his lovers, he was lucky. His parents loved him, regardless of his flaws, and they went out of their way to understand him.

He was a bastard for being so distant. It wasn't intentional. The last two years, he'd spread himself so thinly between work, Devvy, and Alex, he'd had little time to spare.

He resolved to rectify that.

It was hard to remember his parents' ages, at times. They had both gone out of their way for so long to be young. To never come across as fuddy-duddies that it always came as a shock to realize they were elderly now.

"How was I so lucky to have you for parents?" he muttered, more to himself than Suzette.

She laughed, the sound belonging to a woman half her age. "The stork decided to be kind," she teased.

He smiled. "It was more than a kindness. I'm sorry I've been neglecting the two of you recently."

"You're a busy boy," she said, immediately defending him. "We understand that."

Her defense of him just made him feel guiltier. "Devvy and I will come for a visit. *Soon*. I promise."

"We shall look forward to it," she murmured, sounding content. "And I'm glad Devvy understands, Bastien. I'd have hated for you to lose her. She is a good girl."

He eyed his computer, ignoring the hundreds of unread e-mails in his inbox, and settled back into his desk chair.

"She is, *maman*. Don't judge her for accepting us. She almost didn't."

"Well, I'm not surprised she found it hard to acclimate to this new situation. But I'm relieved she didn't walk out. I was around in the sixties, Bastien," she retorted, sounding amused. "Far worse things went on back then, you know. I don't judge her and I won't. Not even your father would. He just wouldn't understand. That's all. And I don't want him upset."

"But you can handle it," he teased, not even making it a question.

"Of course! In time, you will realize Devvy is your backbone," she mocked. "Just as all strong women are."

"She'd probably disagree. You know how self-effacing she is."

Suzette tutted. "With two men at her side, she'll soon grow out of that."

"*Maman!* What are you implying?" His grin was so wide, his jaw ached.

She sniffed. "You don't all sit around watching television, do you, Bastien? I might be over eighty but I'm not an idiot!

"No woman with that amount of physical attention, could ever stay shy! And that is all I'm going to say on the subject."

"Silence never was your virtue, *maman*. When do you go to Greece?" he asked.

"Next week."

He grunted. "I'll try to make it over before you go. If not, as soon as you get back I will. You'll call me when you get there."

"Yes, *cher,*" she murmured, amused. "There's no need to check up on us."

"There's every need," he countered. "What's a phone call?"

"Don't worry, I won't miss our calls! Now, I have to go. Be a good boy, *non?*"

"Never," he retorted with a smile, easily using their code words for "I love you." "Stay safe."

When she promised she would, he disconnected the call and immediately eyed the clock. He looked between the time and his inbox, hesitating over how long it would take to sort through them.

Deciding it wasn't worth it, he switched off the computer and asked his PA, Adéle, to call for his car.

She handled his request with only a faint tinge of surprise in her voice. It was becoming a frequent occurrence for him to leave the office before he should. A perk of being the boss, he told himself. But he knew his love of the game had disappeared, and that was the reason behind his leaving earlier than he ought.

As he made it out of the private elevator and into the lobby, he spotted one of his top chemists flirting with the receptionist.

Lucian Davidson was a serial flirt. He'd worked his way through a few dozen skirts in his lab and down through the secretarial staff. For the most part, Bastien left him alone, even though Lucian's man-whore ways, as Devvy would call it, had actually been brought to his attention by a few departmental managers.

Perhaps he should intercede, but Lucian ruled the labs with an iron fist. His service record had never suffered, which was why he tended to leave him alone. And even though he wanted to get out of the building, he veered over to the reception desk and stood behind Lucian. Deciding that a nudge now was better than a rebuke later, especially as this was the first time he'd seen the other man in action.

The receptionist, a girl who according to her name tag was Sophie, saw him and blanched, her smile disappearing. Lucian spotted this and turned around with a frown that turned into an easy smile when he spotted the boss looming over him.

"Good morning, Sebastien."

Bastien nodded, his features set in a serious cast. Only the execs were allowed to call him by his name. Technically, Lucian wasn't one of them, but he'd never made a move to rectify the other man's tactlessness.

"Don't we have a deadline on the new anti-wrinkle cream?" he asked, tilting his head to the side in a mock show of concern.

"It's all under control."

Lucian's confidence had Bastien's eyes narrowing. "And how would you know that if you're downstairs chasing skirt?"

His gaze flickered to Sophie, in rapid French, far too fast for Lucian, he ordered, "This company does not pay you to be picked up, or to be asked out on dates. Get on with your work."

He felt like a bastard, when Sophie looked on the brink of mortified tears, but those tears were fewer than the ones that would fall when Lucian got her into his bed and then dumped her.

He was saving her from herself. She just thought he was being a bastard to work for. Sometimes being the Good Samaritan was a real pain in the ass.

Bastien turned his attention to Lucian. At the same as Devvy had come to work for *La Belle sans la Bête,* he'd been recruited from a pharmaceutical company in Britain. Apparently his accented French worked a real number on the ladies.

"Well, Lucian?" Bastien asked, polite as can be.

The other man's eyes narrowed, his head jerking in an irritated nod. "I'll just go and make sure everything is how I left it five minutes ago."

"You do that," he retorted pleasantly and waited for Lucian to head to the elevators, and physically leave the lobby.

Sophie's head was bowed over the papers she was collating. Bastien rested an arm on the desk and said, in a much softer voice, "Sophie, he might look and sound pretty, and a huge chunk of the female work staff probably agreed with you at one time." Her eyes widened, her naiveté astonishing him for a second before he continued, "You don't want to be another notch on his belt, do you?"

She shook her head.

"Stay away from him, then." He smiled to lessen the inappropriate advice he shouldn't be handing out, and then strode away deep into the hall. Aware at all times that it was his wife's influence that had made him help the girl. Devvy had never liked Lucian, didn't like working with him or his arrogant ways.

While she'd never said anything, Bastien believed Lucian had come on to her at some point. Getting her away from the male slut had been a major factor in his decision to build her a lab on the grounds of their home—as was her comfort, the fact that she hated getting up on a morning, and the fact that he didn't want her to be bothered by the commute.

He came from a traditional enough background to not want his wife to work. That she loved her research was the only reason he hadn't gently suggested she become a "lady of leisure." Devvy and botany went hand in hand. The idea of her not working on some soap or unguent was impossible to imagine. So, he'd settled for a solution that would please both of them. Devvy could work in her own environment, close to nature, and away from colleagues—she wasn't the most sociable of sorts. He, on the other hand, could rest easy, knowing she was safe and happy in her lab.

Striding down the lobby's long corridor, Bastien acknowledged that this was his favorite part of the building, and mostly because his wife had helped him to appreciate the luscious indoor garden that ran down either side of the path leading to the reception desk. It had cost a fortune to install, never mind maintain. Enough so that most of his directors had thought him insane.

Thanks to Devvy, he even recognized some of the plants. In all his years of making his grandmother's recipes, he'd always bought in the ingredients, never grown them from scratch, unlike Devvy who always used the flowers from her garden in her recipes. He didn't possess a green thumb but he was slowly growing to appreciate those who did, and the beauty they created for people like him.

Considering the company was founded on nature's bounty, Sebastien had only thought it wise to ensure they didn't lose touch with what they were actually doing. The first impression of the company was of this indoor garden, and *La Belle sans la Bête's* desire to use nature instead of man-made chemicals wherever possible, to use nature to enhance and rejuvenate, was reinforced.

The greenery soothed him as he walked past fragrant flowers, and heard the spit-spat of the automatic watering system. He nodded at one of the gardeners as he pruned a bush. The lobby reminded him of Devvy's pride and joy, her herb garden. There were less pungent scents here, but the flora did improve his mood.

The journey to Devvy's favorite restaurant had that mood plummeting a little. Traffic, road wars, jams…the beeps and honks of horns, the stress, and the flustered air of the city at midday, made him wish they'd arranged to eat at home.

Usually, he did. But once a month, they dined out.

Devvy was just as bad as Alex in some ways. She tended to stay at home a lot. Before Alex, she'd rarely gone out at all. Now, she wasn't as house-bound as before, but he saw no reason to break the habit. Meeting with his wife once a month for a private lunch was certainly no hardship. And thanks to the emergency over in his vineyards, this month's date was later than it should be.

The car slipped stealthily through the traffic. The smooth ride was painless for him, but Bastien could only imagine how stressful it was for George, his driver. Had he wanted to, Bastien could have afforded a fleet of cars, and he could have driven through the city himself.

But, for the same reason he preferred Devvy to use a chauffeur, the stress of driving through the city took any pleasure away from owning a luxury vehicle. And he didn't give a damn if he was the only person on Earth to think that way.

His two Bentleys and George were quite adequate for their needs. Something that was hammered home when a car shot out of nowhere and nearly blindsided them. George swerved out of the way just in time, and it was with relief that minutes later he pulled up outside of *Esprit*, Devvy's favorite bistro.

As soon as he stepped out onto the street, the noise bombarded him once again. He refrained from wincing, just, but slipped on his shades as the light pierced his eyeballs with the precision of a red-hot poker.

Grimacing, he escaped into the bistro. The maître d' spotted him, and immediately guided him over to the private room they always hired when they came here. The corridor they took bypassed the main hall of the restaurant.

The instant he saw Devvy, her back to the door, looking through the two-way mirror that overlooked the dining room, his heart sighed at the sight of her.

That sense of something loose inside finding its other half, once again reconnecting, had a smile twisting his lips as the door shut behind him.

The best thing about *Esprit* was the private room and the extras that came with it. For him and Devvy, they always took advantage of the intercom, where they made their orders without having to see anyone. There was also a dumb waiter, which meant they could serve themselves.

This extra privacy made it so Devvy had, more than once, acted as starter and main course in this particular restaurant.

It helped that his security staff had swept the room beforehand.

He was already plagued by threats and blackmail attempts. He didn't need footage of him fucking his wife in *Esprit's* private dining room to be floating around the black market!

Thrusting the current blackmail threat to the back of his mind, the deadline of which was looming, he murmured, "*Mignonne*, it is not like you to be early."

She turned around, a cheeky grin on her lips. "Are you saying I'm always late?"

"I would never be so rude," he retorted, taking in the dress she was wearing with a sigh.

He'd seen women in sexier outfits, tighter and shorter, showing more flesh, but nothing got him as hot as *his* woman in a dress.

It wasn't even skintight. It was summery and floaty, a light fabric that swirled about her legs as she moved. The fabric gently swept over her breasts, not cupping and not enhancing, but the deep V neckline was enough to draw his eyes down the length to her décolleté.

"To what do we owe the honor of a dress?" he asked, brows raised. More accustomed to seeing her in little short shorts that she considered lounge wear, but he considered prick teasers, the dress was definitely an unusual wardrobe choice for his wife.

Her grin twisted a little, a bloom of color rose on her cheeks, and her eyes sparkled with secrets, but she just jerked a shoulder and said, "I fancied a change."

Humming disbelievingly under his breath, he stepped closer to her, bent down, and scooped her up into his arms. He held her by the butt, she gripped his hips with her thighs, and, in that same position, he walked her over to the next best part about the private dining compartment.

In the dead center of the room sat the table. Dressed for fine dining with pristine white, linen tablecloths, and glass that sparkled like diamonds, the setting fit with the rest of the room. Creamy gold walls, abstract paintings that made no sense, and light fittings that were little glass balls of illumination.

Yet, in the corner, all was dark. Another table sat amid blackened crimson walls. Here, the lights were dim, creating shadows even at the time of day when the sun was at its highest.

Candles sat on this table, with its corner cubicle loaded with cushions, and made for comfort.

Considering he was friends with *Esprit's* owner, Jean Gauvin, he knew what the man's intention had been behind this tucked away corner.

Sex.

In public, but hidden.

Discreet, but still in the middle of a busy, celebrated restaurant.

Bastien grinned, headache forgotten as he took a seat on one of the high loungers. When her knees pinned him to the seat, and he slid his hands along the sleek curves, he murmured, "I think I like you in dresses."

She pouted. "You think?"

He shook his head. "Okay, I know." He leaned up and bussed her mouth with his own, a gentle kiss that ended with him nibbling her bottom lip. "But I like you to be comfortable too. So, tell me, why the dress? Because I know you hate them."

Her cheeks flushed again and she leaned closer to him, her breath brushed his ear as she whispered, "No panties, a skirt…you can be inside me so much quicker."

A few weeks ago, Devvy would have stuttered through such a statement.

Her shyness had been endearing and proof of her innocence. This creature, who was growing ever more confident, bold, and proud, just blew him away. It was as his mother had said. She was growing stronger just by being at the center of his and Alex's world.

Unable to help himself, his hands slid higher up the outer curve of her thigh. Farther and farther until he reached her hip, her strap-free hip.

He groaned. "You're not teasing."

She tutted. "And why would I tease? Why wouldn't I tell the truth?"

His grunt made her laugh. She rolled her hips, rocking them over his shaft and murmured, "I think someone's happy I'm not wearing panties."

Devvy reached between them, her fingers not fumbling an inch as she slid the zipper down and delved between the folds of fabric. When her hand encountered his cock, he groaned again, sweat already beading above his top lip. His head tilted backward to rest against the cubicle and he watched her face, the studious cast to her features, as she jerked him off.

That level of concentration always did him in. She put her all into everything, into pleasing him, and nothing got him hot as quickly as his wife's intent to please him.

Her fingers were strong and sure as they gripped his cock, sliding along the length, clenching down as they reached the base. One hand dropped and cupped his balls, while the other returned to the head of his cock. Nimble fingers tickled the tip, rubbing and caressing the glans, making his hips jerk every time she gently pinched the rim.

His breathing was fast, far too fast. She did this to him every time, yet she still doubted her power over him.

The thought, the only one in his brain now, rammed home. His hand slipped under her skirt and he reached for her wrist, gently halting her movements.

"*Mignonne*," he panted, feeling on the edge of coming but refusing to do so outside of his wife's pussy.

"Yes, *cher*?" she asked, her voice sultry, deep. So unlike the Devvy of old that his heart throbbed and his cock twitched in her hold.

"No matter what," he whispered, throat working as her other hand continued to play with his balls. "No matter what happens, I love you. You know that, *oui?*"

She smiled, the simple twitch of her lips so devastatingly sexy, he wanted to explode. "I do."

The two words, filled with cocksurety, had him grinning. "You do, do you?"

Devvy winked, leaned down, and pressed her lips to his. She rubbed her mouth back and forth, and then retreated to his ear again where she nibbled the lobe. "I love you, too."

Not by one inch did he show his relief. Instead, his other hand, the one holding her thigh, squeezed slightly. "I think you should show me how much."

Laughter barked from her. "I should?" she asked, the tilt to her head coy and all the more sexy for it.

She didn't wait for an answer, instead, arched up, her hips rolling back as his cock collided with the outer lips of her sex. He moaned, fingers and toes clenching down as she teased him. Sliding her pussy along the length of his shaft, nudging her clit with his cock head. She liked to do that, masturbate with his dick instead of her fingers. And he loved her to do it. Every single time, it got hotter. Dragged him to the brink of explosion.

As she worked herself on him, his cock grew wetter with her juices. Her hips started to jerk frantically and he knew she was close. He also knew this was another pair of pants ruined.

All in a good cause, though, *hein*?

He grabbed her hips and brought her to a halt. A sulky pout was his reward, but his hand slipped between their legs and he angled himself toward her cunt. Gently, slowly, so slow that it killed something inside him, he started to push home.

She mewled as he started to penetrate her, as always, taking his time to make sure she was ready for him. Her breathing whistled past his ear as she collapsed on him, tucking her head against his neck so damp skin could collide with damp skin.

The sounds she made were like a siren call. They egged him on while calling him back, forcing him to be in control, because he refused to hurt her.

It took a good minute for him to start the slide deep, and her cries had him clenching his eyes shut. Finally, when he was tucked inside her, the both of them sat there, already exhausted. Her muscles clamped down, milking him but he wanted her pleasure, too. Otherwise, it was bittersweet.

Devvy had different ideas.

She lifted her hips a scant few inches, and then dropped down. Her inner muscles pulled taut as she did. His hands clamped down on her waist, trying to stop her, but she shook her head against his throat, refusing to stop, telling him silently she was in control here.

He let her manipulate him, enjoying her confidence as she rocked back and forth, clenching down harder each time. She literally milked his shaft with her pussy, dragging out the cum, urging and encouraging it from his cock.

His cry of pleasure ricocheted around the room, as did his panting. Behind his eyes, where the ache of earlier had been, fire burned and branded him.

His wife's fire. His wife's brand.

He sighed as the pleasure drained away, all tension and stress with it.

Her gasps of need whispered past his Adam's apple and he tutted, "Why did you do that, *hein*?"

Her legs twitched as she continued to rock back and forth. "You had a headache."

He grinned. "You're my personal prescription of ibuprofen, are you?"

Her head shot back and she glared at him. "You're my husband. I'm supposed to take care of you."

"And you're my wife," he retorted. "I'm supposed to take care of you!"

Before she could answer, he grabbed her by the hips, dragged her off his limp shaft, and placed her on the edge of the table. Spreading her legs, within five seconds, he had his mouth buried at her cunt. He slurped at the juices, tasting himself, but mostly, tasting her pleasure. Her cries, now, were high-pitched, edgy, filled with need.

He sucked down against her clit, nibbling the little nub, biting it and teasing. He rimmed the small hole that had, moments ago, given him such pleasure. Slipping his tongue deep, he heard her moan of pleasure and flickered his tongue upward again. Sliding two fingers into her cunt, he drew those wet digits down to rub against her butt. Rimming the pucker, his mouth returned to its earlier task.

As he sucked down, the two fingertips edging deeper into her ass, she screamed. The sound made his ears ring, and his lusty chuckle vibrated against her most tender flesh, a move that had her nearly falling back onto the table and destroying a small fortune in glassware.

He grabbed her waist and kept her upright, enjoying the little spasms as she worked through the climax he'd just given her.

When her hoarse gasps had calmed, he returned her to her earlier position on his lap.

"I think we should eat like this, *non*?" At her tired nod, he just smiled. "Did you order us anything, or shall I order now?"

"Tapas," she mumbled, yawning around the word.

He grinned and nuzzled his nose against her cheek. "I'm going to check the dumbwaiter. I know a bell usually rings, but with all the noise you were making, we probably missed it."

Her head flew back at that and she glared at him. "You were making just as much noise, buddy."

He held up both hands in surrender. "I'm sure I did."

She nodded stoutly and on shaky legs, stood. He watched her weave a little as she walked over to the little elevator that brought their food from the kitchen. Inside, there was a tray and she shot him another glare at his having been correct. Both of them had missed the rather large bell that rang when food arrived.

He just shrugged. "At least we did it right."

Tray in hand, she chuckled. "Yeah, I guess if I'd been bored I'd have heard the bell."

He growled. "I'll take that as a compliment, *chérie*."

"Good," she retorted pertly. "It was meant as one."

Sniggering a little, he peered down at the tray of food she'd ordered. Before he could pick up the deconstructed chorizo, she perched herself on his knee, and wiggled around to get comfortable.

He just laughed as she reached for the chorizo, took a bite then fed him the other bit.

"How did you know I wanted that one?"

She grinned at him. "You'd be surprised how much I know about you."

"Oh?" he asked, brow cocked.

"Yep," she retorted cheerfully. "I spent two years hanging on every word and absorbing every detail. I know a lot about you, honey."

He scowled. "You thought I was going to leave you. Alex told me."

At his statement, she reached around and patted him on the cheek. "Maybe a smidgen."

He tapped the nose she'd crinkled. "I hope you now realize how foolish that was."

Devvy blushed. "Sort of. I asked Alex to move in with us last night."

He said nothing at the change of subject. Her boost in confidence only went so far, it would take far longer for her to feel secure in her marriage to him, and their relationship with Alex. At her other comment, his brows rose.

"I take it that went badly." He reached for an asparagus spear surrounded with Serrano ham and took a bite, before offering the rest of it to her.

His voice was strain-free, but it was a lie. It both pissed him off and saddened him the way Alex continually rejected him, and what he could offer.

After twenty years, he should have been used to it.

He wasn't.

"Kind of," she answered. "He was a little annoyed, but I was too. He got up, in the middle of the night, and started working! I mean, I know I'm bad sometimes. But I'm not *that* bad. I told him if he wanted to be an outsider in our relationship, then the way to go about it was to stay at the penthouse and not come and live with us."

"True," Bastien murmured softly. "I think a part of him wants to be an outsider."

She frowned at that and picked up a slither of peach topped with melted Manchego cheese. "I think you're right, but I won't allow it."

At her arrogant claim, he grinned. "Since when did you get all bossy?"

She rolled her eyes. "Since you introduced me into this wacko way of life. If we're going to do it, we're going to do it properly, Bastien. No messing around. He wants me to fall in love with him, he wants me to need him. Well, there are consequences if I do."

"Do you think you could love him?" he asked, voice quiet, his eyes caught in the ice blue of her eyes.

She nodded. "I'm halfway there." The admission was husky and rueful.

"I'm glad. He needs you. *I* need you."

She sighed and turned to him, resting a finger moist from the peach's juices on his lips. She trailed the digit around his lips and whispered, "For two years, I needed to hear you say that." Another sigh. "It really was as good as I thought it would be."

Pressing her forehead against his, she whispered, "I need you to take care of yourself, Bastien. Nothing can happen now that I've found you. Do you promise me?"

Wrapping his arms about his wife, thanking his lucky stars for having found a woman that could fill all of his blank spaces as well as Alex's, he kissed her gently and murmured, "I promise."

Chapter Eleven

Eight days later

Alex's jitters were starting to make Devvy uneasy and that was really saying something, especially after having to defend her PhD dissertation the way she had. She'd been fine all morning, not at all nervous at what today held, that is until Alex had left his apartment.

Not even the fact they were going to visit his mother discomforted her. But Alex's terror at leaving his own little bubble to walk out into the chaos of reality definitely put her on edge.

When Sebastien had talked about the times Alex left his home, there had been strain written into every single one of his features. He'd physically felt Alex's emotional tension, and Devvy could now understand and appreciate Bastien's concern.

She wasn't proud to say that twice she'd had to bite her tongue. Patience was a forte of hers but the stress he was under was being transmitted to her and it was contagious. Her temples were pounding, already, and they hadn't even left his apartment building!

"Alex, sweetheart, how did you manage to get to our house? Why can't you do it now?" she asked softly, only now just realizing how huge a deal this was for him.

It was one thing being told by Bastien how bad Alex's agoraphobia was, but seeing it in the flesh was another thing entirely.

His panic was an ethereal but existing form. So tangible, she could almost touch it.

She'd tried to coax him, tried tough love, but nothing was budging him from the elevator. They'd been up and down the damned thing so many times she was thinking about grabbing a chair from the penthouse and making herself comfortable!

If a person could *look* nauseated, then Alex was doing a pretty good impression of it. His face alternated between puce—a color she hadn't realized existed in the natural spectrum of shades the body was capable of emulating—bright red, then deathly pale. So white, he looked on the brink of fainting.

Usually, the white pallor came when they landed on the first floor and he could see out onto the street. His hands would clutch the elevator's hand rail, his head would bow, and the sounds of his breathing…she could only liken it to an asthma attack without the wheeze.

His panic was making her panic. She knew if they didn't get out of here soon, he'd either throw up or collapse. He was making himself sick. She'd never seen the like before and she hoped to never see it again.

"It was for you," he gritted out, eyes closing as one of the tenants sent for the elevator. As they shuttled upward, he whispered, "It was important. Had to see you. Had to make you understand what Sebastien and I wanted. I knew he'd cock it up if I wasn't there."

Despite herself, her lips twitched at that. Alex rarely said anything derogatory about Bastien. Not because in his eyes, their mutual lover was perfect, but Alex seemed to accept Sebastien's faults easily. She imagined it was because that acceptance was mutual.

Very few people would be able to handle the many hang-ups Alex had.

And Bastien wasn't even aware of some of them!

"Isn't going to see your mother just as important?" As soon as she said the words, she chuckled and shook her head. "Yeah, I take that back. Nearly fifteen or so years looking for a third for your relationship takes precedence. But still, you wanted to see your mother. We're already late."

"I'm always late to see her. She knows to expect it."

"How long have you suffered with agoraphobia, Alex?"

"Too long," he spat as the doors opened and a fellow tenant climbed in. All three of them shared brusque nods of greeting. The newcomer kept on peeking out of the corner of his eye at Alex's decidedly ill coloring but Devvy glared at him and the man soon stopped, preferring to stare down at the floor.

They shuttled downstairs, the doors opened, and the man departed. As he left through the main entrance, his gaze wandered back and he frowned at their lack of movement from the elevator before shrugging it off and going on his way.

The sight of the outside world had that horrid paleness reappearing, and she squeezed the hand she held in her own.

"Okay, different question. Since when has it grown so bad?"

He scowled but it was a welcome change from the weak terror clinging to his features. "How do you know that?"

"Well, you just answered it for yourself. I could tell anyway. Sebastien said you were bad, but he said you believed yourself to be in control of the situation. Now, either you feel you can let go with me—which I'm pleased about, don't get me wrong—or he doesn't know how bad you're getting."

The elevator doors closed, and the machine hummed as though going into sleep mode, awaiting the next user. At last count, this was the twenty-second time they'd hovered on the first floor.

It was a good job she wasn't claustrophobic.

They'd have both been ready for the loony bin by now!

He grimaced at her summation of his condition. "You are too astute, Devvy."

She shrugged. "I'm supposed to be analytical. It's a part of my job description."

"It's always bad when I have to visit my mother."

"Why go, then?"

"I have to."

His brisk answer had her rolling her eyes. "So, for future reference, this is as panicked as I'm likely to see you?"

She hadn't thought it possible for him to blanch even further. She'd been wrong.

"If I'm keeping you from something else, something urgent, then don't let me stop you!" he snapped.

"I think I'd have left on the fifth ride from the top to the bottom floor if that was the case, Alex," she retorted dryly, refusing to let his temper ignite her own. "I'm just wondering what I have to do to get you out of here."

Her words had him frowning. He tilted his head to stare at her, a question in his eyes.

She smiled slowly. "Yep, you heard right." Devvy pulled her hand from his and stepped closer, pushing herself into the personal space he'd set earlier when they'd first climbed onto this goddamn elevator. She'd tried to stand close to him, but he'd stiffened and moved away. Now, she pressed her chest to his and nuzzled his jaw with her cheek. Her hot breath had his throat working as she whispered, "What do I have to do to get you out of here, Alex?"

He swallowed again. "I don't know."

"I'm sure that's a lie," she remarked, insinuating her hand between the two of them to rub her fingers down over the lean line of his hip, following the muscular ridge of his obliques to smooth along the length of his shaft. Under her fingers, it began to twitch, as though coming back to life. "I think we need to do a deal, you and I."

Alex frowned. "What sort of deal?"

"Every time you have to go out, I'll do something for you. Whatever you want." A month ago, Devvy would have been mortified at the very idea of making such a proposition. Now, she felt her pussy start to quicken, heat setting deep in her belly with the promise of what was to come.

It was a sign of how she was changing, of how confident she was growing in herself and in her allure that she could make such a proposition with her body and not just with words.

"*Whatever* I want?"

She nodded.

"*Wherever* I want?"

Another nod.

"What if I said I wanted to fuck you on the balcony in my apartment?"

"I'd say yes, but that you were cheating, and that you could only fuck me after we'd gone out."

"Small print, *hein*?" He tutted. "You just can't escape from it."

She was heartened by his teasing. It was definitely a step up from outright terror!

He bent down and bussed her lips with his own. "I accept your challenge."

Devvy grinned. "Why didn't I think of this sooner?"

"I expect more of my overachiever. In the future, come up with inappropriate propositions earlier." He checked his watch. "We might have missed the rush hour."

His chiding had her rolling her eyes. "*In the future*, you're going to have to talk to somebody about this. Especially if it's getting worse, and you've already admitted that it has. Sebastien's concerned, and after today, I am too."

He grunted. "Don't spoil the moment, *ma petite.*"

"I'm not. I'm being realistic. Offering you carte blanche with my body can only work for so long!" Now that wasn't a sentence she'd say often.

"Surely not."

She frowned at him. "Be serious, Alex. You need to see someone. I'll get Sebastien to look into it. He'll find one that comes to the apartment."

She made to step out of the elevator, but he grabbed her arm and shook his head.

"No, don't mention it to Sebastien. Please. I don't want to worry him."

"Too late. He already is. He loves you, Alex. Of course he's concerned."

He winced at her words. "I never sought his love for this very reason."

"That makes it all the more precious that he gave his heart to you regardless of your hang-ups."

"I know. Even at twenty, a few years after I met him, I knew he loved me, and I knew I was nothing but bad news for him." He tapped his temple. "Something's never been right up here."

"We all have our own problems, Alex. They're normal."

"Mine aren't," he retorted gloomily. "They never have been. Do you think this is normal? I thought at one point you were going to sit on the floor to wait me out."

Her lips twitched. "I almost did, but the thought of what your neighbors would think stopped me."

A phantom grin fluttered over his mouth. "You won't let me take myself too seriously, will you, Devvy?" He sighed and slipped his hand up her arm to cup the back of her neck. He dragged her close until their torsos touched and whispered, "I need that. I think I've always needed you. Even when I didn't know you existed."

The muscles in her abdomen clenched down at his words. To be needed by this man was an honor. Resting against her, telling her his woes, sharing his problems, was one of the world's greatest scientists. The man who had found cancer's trigger, and determined how to stop it in its tracks.

When a normal cell mutated into cancer, it deactivated the body's ability to suppress tumor growth. For over ten different cancers, Alex had determined a way to counteract this deactivation. This stopped cancer in its tracks. By targeting the malignancy so early on in the disease's development.

And those ten weren't enough for the man who had effectively found a cure for one of the world's most worrisome diseases. He was working on more. Always working, always researching until his work became a cancer in and of itself.

She had to change that. He was right. He did need her. He needed her to bring him out of himself.

Because he was a man, and a busy one at that, Sebastien believed Alex's need to work was simply something he had a right to. Sebastien probably would have seen no wrong in Alex getting up that night after they'd taken their first steps toward a fully-fledged ménage relationship. He'd probably thought something had popped into Alex's head, and it needed to be hashed out.

He hadn't realized that was Alex's way of putting a barrier between them all.

He wouldn't have known, but she had, and Alex needed her to force him to change. It was folly to enter a relationship where the woman believed she could change her man. Devvy knew that. In this instance, it was imperative she make him see the light at the end of the tunnel.

Because Alex was dying. From the inside out.

She didn't know how she realized that. His mind was taking over as it had a way of doing with men of his caliber. His hang-ups were a part and parcel of his genius. He had every right to them. But those hang-ups had no right to torment and torture her lover, to twist him and to drag him down a path that could only end in tragedy.

These little oddities were what made him great, and as with any great man, he needed a great woman behind him.

She was no slouch in the intelligence department, but capable of nothing so miraculous as Alex. It was a pleasurable duty to realize she had to keep him under her wing. She had to keep him safe and to protect him from the bogeyman.

In a way, to be needed so intensely filled Devvy with warmth.

Bastien was so independent. So self-reliant. As she'd told her mother, her husband looked after himself. He didn't need her. Devvy hadn't known she needed to be needed, but the fact that Alex did, had something deep inside flowering. Blossoming.

It was early days. She knew that. But Devvy had the feeling she'd just found her purpose.

Her very reason for being.

To keep Alexei Ivanov on the right track. To stop him from drowning in his psychoses, and to stop him from trying to find a way out.

"If you need me, Alex, I'm here."

His breath fluttered against her lips and his arms slipped around her waist. "Will you leave me, Devvy, when I get too annoying? When I won't leave the apartment, and when I get churlish and refuse to move out?"

She pressed her face against his chest, breathing in the scent of starch and cleaning detergent, laboratory, and pure Alex. Her olfactory senses were in heaven. Absentmindedly, she remarked, "You can be as churlish as you want, and I won't leave you, because I'll make you move out. I'll tell you when you're pissing me off. I won't let you get away with murder just because you're Alexei Ivanov."

He surprised her by laughing. "Will you get out the whip and make me toe the line?"

"Only if you want me to."

His chuckle deepened. "I have many kinks but that is not one of them. Although it might be interesting to see you dressed from head to toe in leather."

"Well, if that's a fantasy of yours, you'll have to save it for when I want you to go out with me. It will have to be one of those occasions where I'll do whatever you want as incentive."

"You little manipulator," he teased.

Devvy shrugged. "I have to be to keep up with you. You'll keep me on my toes."

"And me on mine."

"When I get home, I'll tell Bastien to look out for a psychiatrist that does home visits."

"Back to that, are we?" he asked, gruffly. "Can't we just leave it for the minute? Your proposition might be the solution I've been looking for all my life."

"Sex isn't the answer, Alex," she retorted with a sniff. "You need to get to the root of the problem, and Bastien will be so relieved if he has to look for a psychiatrist. At least it's an active step toward a solution, and you know how proactive he is. It will make him feel better."

"It won't cure me, Devvy." He sighed. "I already have one."

She stiffened and tilted her head to look up at him. "You see a shrink?"

He nodded.

"Are you lying to get out of this?"

He rolled his eyes. "I do not lie, Devvy. I may manipulate the truth a tad, but I don't outright fib. I've been seeing the same psychiatrist for the last twenty or so years."

Devvy stared up at him, studying him a second. Slowly, she murmured, "I think I'll still tell Sebastien to look for one. You need a change. If you're getting worse in this man's care, then it's time for a fresh pair of eyes to look at your case."

"I'm happy with my current one."

"Tough. I'm not. You've said it yourself, Alex, things aren't getting any better. And they're not going to, are they?"

"They might. Our relationship is only new. The longer we're all together, the stronger that will make me."

"You need to know that you can rely upon yourself as well. Lean upon me as much as you must, darling. I'm strong enough, but you have to know, deep inside, that you're strong, too." She placed her hand over his heart. "Do this. For me."

He looked down into her eyes for countless seconds, enough for the elevator to be called once more, and dropped his head to buss her lips with his own. "If I must."

She nodded. "It will make me feel better. Now, this is the last time I'm staying in this damned box. So, what are you going to do to me to make me pay for dragging you out?"

His lips twitched and he was on the brink of answering when the doors opened. She ignored the newcomers, but saw Alex's head jerk in a nod of greeting. She heard two people conversing in French but continued to ignore them, staring instead with intent at her lover.

"After we visit my mother, we're going to go to *Les Fenêtres*."

Her eyes widened. "We are?"

He nodded. "Yes, that's where we're going. I'm going to fuck you in Bastien's bed. His sheets are going to smell of us, and when he gets home, all stressed and tense and probably with a migraine, we're going to rub him down and take all his tension away."

"Are you going to sleep there?"

The low throb permeating the elevator came to a halt and the doors jerked open.

"Do you know I've never stayed the night at *Les Fenêtres*?"

"No, I didn't know but I could guess. So, will you?"

He looked deep into her eyes and whispered, "Yes."

Chapter Twelve

Madame Ivanov was a strange woman.

In fact, she was more than strange. She was downright weird. And considering the majority of people in Devvy's acquaintance were a tad unusual, labeling Antoinette as odd was an understatement.

Dressed all in black, as though she were in mourning and not because the color suited her, she wore a dowdy skirt and a too-large, button-down shirt. Horrible they might be, but they were expensive. The quality and cut were there. They just did nothing to suit Antoinette Ivanov's sparse frame.

It was that very reason that made her look as though she were in old-fashioned mourning. Many women wore all black, but in this case, it was different. Devvy sensed it.

Her apartment in the sixteenth arrondissement was nothing more than Devvy expected from the part of the capital that was considered one of the best Paris had to offer. The elite lived here. The sixteenth was high society's most favorite place, and with views of the Palais de Chaillot, and the huge mass of green that was the Bois de Boulogne, Devvy knew Alex had bought his mother a piece of prime real estate.

It was strange how he provided for her, when he didn't particularly like her. Devvy had spotted that from the very start. He was distant, abrupt. Whenever she touched him, the muscles in his arms tensed as though he wanted to thrust her away from him. She spoke more than he did, and he listened with disinterest, his eyes wandering to the magnificent view of Paris.

If Alex was bored, Antoinette was anything but.

In truth, she was giddy with pleasure at seeing Alex. The instant they'd walked through the door, her eyes had been glued to her son as though she lived and breathed for these pockets of time he deigned to bestow upon her.

The dour face had been almost illuminated by her joy. She'd been so happy, it had taken a few moments for the older woman to even notice Devvy was there. Even then, she paid little attention to her.

When Alex had made the suggestion she come along to visit his mother, they'd agreed to introduce her as his partner but with her maiden name and as Devvy, not Devina. Even though Sebastien's name was big news and his marriage even bigger, he'd set security on her before and immediately after their wedding to ensure that the paparazzi wouldn't take snaps of her. To him, her privacy had been of the utmost importance. There was a fifty-fifty chance something had slipped through the tight net he'd sprung, but it was highly unlikely.

She had to wonder if he'd been so precautious because he'd envisioned the day when she'd have to meet Alex's mother.

His privacy drive ensured that no one, outside of people invited to the wedding and Bastien's acquaintances, knew what she looked like. Even the wedding guests had been politely asked to refrain from using the cameras on their cellphones.

At the time, she'd thought it peculiar. Now, it kind of made sense.

Especially if Antoinette was as dour by nature as she was by looks.

Christ, Devvy could only imagine the woman's reaction to the fact Alex shared a bed with a man, never mind a man and his wife! In fact, the thought was so amusing she covered her mouth with her hand until she composed herself.

As it was, she'd been given a cup of coffee in light china cups and sent to the corner of the terrace where all of them were sitting. She had then been promptly ignored.

"*Je sais que...*"

"English, for Devvy's sake, *Mère*. It would be rude, otherwise."

Antoinette nodded tightly and shot a glance loaded with dislike Devvy's way.

It wasn't the first time Antoinette had tried to talk in French, but the three other times she'd tried, Alex had barked at her in their shared tongue and his mother would shoot a glare at her before reverting to English for Devvy's benefit.

Devvy was growing quite accustomed to glares. It seemed to be the only look Antoinette was capable of bestowing upon her.

For the most part, she talked of charity functions, her friends and their foibles. Chitchat Alex definitely found boring.

It wasn't the most uncomfortable occasion of her life, but it was definitely up there with one of the highest. And she was the daughter of Miranda Nelson, for Christ's sake. There had been some real doozies in the past.

She was entirely and utterly unwelcome here. Antoinette literally exuded rejection. In fact, it was so strong she could have bottled it and labeled it, "Do not return."

The best part of this whole uncomfortable mess was the view. Heavy, sweeping clouds weighed down the skies, but a rich blue, shot through with shards of sunlight, played peekaboo. It bathed Paris in the most glorious light, and Antoinette's apartment was in a tall building on the corner lot, so she had a two-faceted view that made the horrible visit worth it.

"So, you are obviously seriously involved if you have brought her to meet me." Antoinette's voice broke Devvy's thoughts. So much so, she jumped in her seat.

Alex replied, "*Her* has a name. And yes. Devvy and I are serious."

His brusqueness had Devvy frowning at him. Alex was always slightly recalcitrant. Always a little difficult, an angular person rather than a smooth curve. His attitude toward his mother spoke of something else.

There were layers here.

On the surface, Antoinette appeared a loving if overly possessive mother. She seemed to live for the moments her son would visit. In between, she fiddled with charities and other social events to fill her time.

Alex looked and was acting like a brat. Especially in the face of his mother's genuine joy to see him.

Yet, why did Alex dislike her? If he did dislike her as much as he made perfectly clear through his behavior, why act the dutiful son and pay for his mother's way? Not that Alex had shared that pertinent fact with her. Bastien had.

It was all very confusing and she had the horrible feeling it was tied into Alex's behavior the first night they slept together. When Alex had leapt from her arms and to the side of the bed like a little child.

For good measure, why not add in this morning's farce in the elevator?

The pathological desire for space, be it physical or emotional. The need to be in control of his environment…

The path seemed to lead here.

She could be firing blanks but her instincts were pretty spot on where Alex was concerned. Something had happened to Alex as a boy. Something either his mother had caused or something she'd done to make him dislike her so deeply, that as an adult, he couldn't help but revert to the helpless child he'd once been.

The fact he paid for his mother's living expenses also spoke loudly. Alex didn't trust his mother, but whatever he believed her to have done, he wasn't certain of her part in it.

His feet were firmly on both sides of the fence.

She'd like to ask him for more details, but she had the feeling he'd clam up the instant they left his mother's building.

"What do you do, Devvy?" Antoinette spat, her eyes mean.

If eyes could be mean, that is. All narrowed and filled with malevolence.

Devvy knew it was a strange way to describe someone, but Antoinette did have a mean cast to her features. Combined with the all-over black, she had a very saturnine look about her. An almost…unholiness.

Now Devvy knew she was being over the top, a little extreme maybe, but Antoinette was once again exuding rejection like an anti-pheromone. Alex's mother had judged her, found her wanting on the basis of a handful of comments, and that was that. Devvy was not, in Antoinette's eyes, good enough for her son, and her attitude portrayed that.

"I'm a cosmetic scientist."

Antoinette sniffed. "Another scientist. Do not think to advance yourself by using my son's name, *hein*? He does not have the, how do you say, "free ride" tattooed on his forehead!"

The attack hadn't been entirely unexpected, yet it still came as a shock. Devvy replaced her cup of coffee onto the table.

"I can assure you, *madame*, I am quite successful in my own right. I've no need to use Alex to advance my own position in the scientific community."

"No one is as successful as my Alexei," Antoinette boasted, a zealous gleam in her eyes.

Alex snorted. "Don't be ridiculous, *Maman*. This isn't a competition." He reached for Devvy's hand and squeezed. His fingers clung to hers, and she didn't let go. "Devvy is a very successful woman in her own field."

"How long have you known her? How do you know you can trust her?" came more questions. A lock of hair fell from Antoinette's messily bundled hair and stuck to her brow. It was only then that Devvy noticed the other woman was perspiring.

Having her here, the ramifications of Devvy's presence and what she obviously meant to Alex was scaring Antoinette.

Literally. Physically.

Devvy shook her head at the notion and was about to reply but Alex stopped her by declaring, "Stop insulting Devvy. I brought her here out of respect to you, but I can see I was wrong to do so." He made to stand and Antoinette shook her head, quickly holding out her hands to pacify him.

"I apologize. I did not mean to imply anything."

"*Ça, c'est de merde*, you weren't implying, you were stating!"

Devvy reached forward and placed what she hoped was a calming hand on Alex's shoulder. Seated around a small, circular mosaic-patterned table, he was close enough to touch. "Calm down, Alex. I'm not offended." She wasn't. Her mother was quite capable of making similarly cutting statements. At least Antoinette seemed to have her son's wishes, and not her own, at heart. To Antoinette, she said, "I mean him no harm."

"Again, I apologize. I should not have made such a statement, but he is my son, and I want only the best for him."

Alex lifted their clasped hands to his mouth and brushed Devvy's knuckles with a kiss. "Devvy is what's best for me. I wouldn't have brought her to this inquisition, if our relationship wasn't serious."

Antoinette bowed her head. "I care for your welfare, *mon fils*. That is all."

She stood and retreated to the salon, which was separated from the terrace by a wall of French doors. Devvy watched as she disappeared and immediately prodded Alex with a finger.

"Why are we here if you don't want to be?" she asked, more curious than pissed at what Antoinette had said. She'd taken a lot more abuse over the years. College at fourteen had been a real joy.

"It is my duty."

"Bullshit. This isn't 1814. We're in the new millennium, don't you know? If you don't want to see her, you don't have to." Even though she made the statement, it said a lot about Alex that he was here, even if it was against his wishes.

"I don't have to do anything, but I choose to visit a few times a year. If I didn't see her, she would bombard me with her presence. This is a small sacrifice."

"What do you mean, bombard you?"

He grunted and tugged his hand free from their clasp. Standing, he strode over to the balcony rail and muttered, "Haven't you noticed? She has to hover. Over everything."

Yeah, he wasn't exaggerating.

She did smother. Hovering was too polite a word for Antoinette's behavior.

If she wasn't trying to fill his already full to the brim coffee cup, she was asking if he was hungry. If he wasn't hungry, she'd ask why he wasn't. Her overreaction to Devvy's presence was another example of her extreme ways.

It could have been seen as doting, but it was a little too avid to just be an act of love.

Feverish summed it up.

At one point, when he hadn't sipped at his coffee cup—because it was boiling hot and fresh from the pot—she'd asked him why he wasn't drinking it and before he could reply, had shouted for her maid. The ensuing barrage of words had almost had the poor woman in tears!

Alex had said something that shut his mother up and quickly drunk his coffee as though demonstrating it was perfectly all right. Only that had satisfied Antoinette.

To be quite frank, if Alex had psychological issues, Devvy was starting to see his mother was a direct cause!

"Has she always been like that?" Devvy asked.

"Always," he stated grimly, and then sighed. "That's not true. Before my father left us, she used to smother him instead of me."

"How old were you when he went?"

"Seven."

His tone had been grim ever since his mother had departed to, Devvy could only assume, compose herself. But now, there was a heaviness to it. A darkness.

It concerned her enough that she stood, walked over to him, and then wrapped her arm about his waist. "Hey, it's okay. You're all "*growed*" up now."

He jerked a shoulder. "The only reason she stays away is because she knows I won't let her into the penthouse. At first, when I moved in, she used to try. It sounds awful but I used to tell her to go away.

"I try. I always come here with good intentions, meaning to start afresh. It just never works out. She's…suffocating. It's like she sucks all of the oxygen out of the room."

It might have sounded a little dramatic, but after a lifetime of this, Devvy could easily understand.

While Antoinette's behavior could be deemed as slightly peculiar, it was the hectic energy with which she acted that made it worse. She was the most restless person Devvy had ever known. Jumping up and down in her seat, rearranging something or other, turning the tray just so, as though trying to make the scene perfect for Alex.

She'd lean over and touch his cheek, but it wouldn't just be a fleeting touch. She'd hold the pose for an uncomfortable amount of time.

She was the sort of woman people studied surreptitiously and silently asked themselves if their eyes were deceiving them.

"Before the agoraphobia became so bad, when I used to go out at least once or twice a week, she used to follow me."

Devvy choked out, "You can't be serious."

He grimaced. "I wish I was. She tried to keep a discreet distance, but after the first time I caught her spying on me, I saw her a lot. The café opposite my building was her hiding place. She used to wait for me there. "

"Is that why you don't go out anymore?"

He shrugged. "Maybe. But I've always appreciated my home comforts so the fault isn't hers entirely. You can see why I feel like I'm choking whenever she's around though, right?"

Devvy shook her head. "You're a better person than me, Alex. I'd have cut her out of my life a long time ago. Either that or made her see a doctor."

He snorted. “She won’t. You don’t think I’ve tried? She’s just obsessed with me. Always has been.”

Devvy frowned. “She isn’t *just* anything. She’s nuts! Christ, it’s not exactly normal to stalk your own child!”

The sudden sound of high heels had the pair of them stiffening with the knowledge she was coming back.

“Here we go again,” Alex muttered.

It felt like that. Like watching a car crash.

Devvy turned and smiled politely at the other woman. Even though it was the last thing she wanted to do after that disturbing conversation. Apparently, Antoinette had composed herself, but with Alex’s back turned, she saw no reason to be at all friendly. On the receiving end of a glare for her trouble, Devvy sighed inwardly and hoped for this coffee afternoon to be over. Soon.

Antoinette strode over to Alex’s other side and pressed a hand to his back. He immediately stiffened but she ignored that and stroked it along the length of his spine. It wasn’t motherly, it was creepy, and even though Alex grew so tense Devvy was certain he’d break out in a cramp, she kept on doing it. She finally stopped, only her hand continued upward and she played with the ends of his hair as she crooned to him in French.

Devvy started to move away but Alex’s hand shot out of nowhere and clamped her to his side. She relaxed into him, and his tension once again made itself known.

It was hard to pinpoint why Antoinette’s actions were so odd, but she finally figured it out. Her gestures were inappropriate, so much so, they were almost a caress.

Her mind immediately flinched at the thought. Putting two and two together, she came up with what she hoped was five instead of four. Reasoning it out that if she’d molested Alex as a child, or behaved in anyway inappropriately with him, the adult Alexei would not provide for her.

At least, she didn’t think he would.

The very idea made her feel sick and uncertain. She longed to blurt out the question simply to erase it from her mind. Until she asked, it would continue to roil and churn.

"*Suffit*," Alex burst out after a few moments of having his hair played with and having French nothings murmured into his ear. "Enough. We have to be going now."

"So soon!" Antoinette immediately protested. "You only just arrived."

"Nonsense. We've been here a good hour."

"You normally stay longer!" she accused and then leaned around Alex to glare at Devvy. "Why did you bring her here if it would make you leave earlier? I see you so little!" And so the diatribe continued, once again reverting to the mother tongue.

Alex's face grew whiter and whiter, that grimness turning his face to hard stone.

"I don't want to hear anymore. I am well, you are well. That is all we wish to know. I shall call you when I am due to visit next time."

"Don't bring her!" Antoinette spat.

"Don't worry, I won't! You've embarrassed me today, *Mére*. I can only hope Devvy can come to forgive me for this huge mistake. I thought you would want to see the woman who is playing a large role in my life."

Antoinette snorted, the sound unladylike. Her hand shot out and she grabbed Devvy's. "She's married, you fool." She raised Devvy's left hand. "The ring might be gone, but that mark says it all. As well as the fact she never has a manicure," Antoinette scorned.

Neither Devvy nor Alex replied. Alex merely shook his head and murmured, "Forgive me, but my next visit will not be for quite a while."

She looked on the brink of stomping her foot but all of a sudden, the cast to her face changed. Turning from sulky to pouting. More weirdness ensued.

"Please, don't go, *mon fils*. I did not mean to criticize. We are French. The world is not black and white as we all know." She dropped Devvy's hand and made to cup Alex's cheek. He jerked back before she could touch him.

"You belittle Devvy and you belittle me," he stated.

"I apologize," she murmured, tilting her head in a way that was almost flirtatious. The thought dominating Devvy's brain once against popped up to the fore.

"Apologies aren't always the solution." He looked down at his watch. "It is, in fact, time to go. The car will be waiting for us."

"I understand, *cher*. But please, do not punish me. You know how excited I am when you're due to visit."

He stiffened and then released the tension from his body with a sigh. He looked almost defeated as he murmured, "I shall see you in two or so months."

Antoinette's delight was evident. She clapped her hands with jubilation and reached up to press a kiss to Alex's cheek.

Devvy felt him flinch and when his mother stepped back, she nodded politely at her and murmured, "It has been an interesting morning, Madame Ivanov. I wish you well."

She wouldn't lie and say it had been a pleasure, when it had been anything but.

This place and the woman living in it were toxic.

Devvy couldn't wait to get out of there and that feeling was shared by her lover.

The pair of them left with indecent haste and Devvy noticed Alex's agoraphobia did not extend to leaving his mother's building! The sooner he could leave, the better.

She could hardly criticize when she felt the same way, and she could easily understand why it had been so hard for him to leave his apartment in the first place. With the prospect of a morning like that, no wonder it had taken close to two hours to get out of the elevator! The morning would have been more successful if they were still in the damned thing.

As they sank down in the supple leather seats of Bastien's limousine, they both sighed with relief to be out of there. The mutual release had both of them bursting out with laughter.

"Was it as bad for you as it was for me?" Alex asked, chuckling. "I don't even know why I'm laughing! That could not have gone much worse!"

"Let's just say if I don't have to meet her again, I won't be upset. Thank you for introducing us, darling. I appreciate the gesture." Her smile was genuine as she reached over for a kiss. "I know what you were trying to tell me."

"That I intend for you to be a permanent fixture in my life even if I bitch about moving out of my penthouse?"

She nodded. "For you to even dare to introduce me to her…well, it says a lot, considering how volatile she is."

"Volatile isn't the word," he retorted.

His irritation had her asking a question she should have left until later, especially after the lightening of the mood by the humor they'd found in the weird interview between mother, son, and lover. But she had to know. It was imperative.

"Alex…," Devvy started, and then broke off. At his cocked brow urging her to continue, she whispered, "She didn't hurt you? As a child, I mean."

"Hurt?" he asked with a frown that slowly cleared as he understood her meaning, as well as her complete discomfort at asking the question. "Did she abuse me?"

Devvy licked her lips, feeling her nerves flutter through her with a speed that made her feel sick. "Yes."

His face had smoothed out. All tension releasing. All humor and the earlier traces of anger disappearing. He turned his head away to stare at the traffic. "No. She did not."

Somehow, that answer didn't reassure her. He said the right thing, but he wasn't *saying* it right. If that made sense.

Devvy didn't push it, though. Aside from the clearing of his features, he hadn't moved, but a brick wall was suddenly between them. Invisible, but there, nonetheless.

"Okay," she murmured and squeezed the hand they'd clasped moments before, leaving the subject for a future time. Knowing that she wouldn't be the one to raise the topic…because there was something here. Something that had that awful stillness appearing about him. And that said a lot.

Too much.

* * * *

The migraines were getting worse.

It was a sign, and Sebastien wasn't too foolish to take it as anything less than a warning.

With Alex's urging, he'd already been to the doctors. He'd been through CAT and MRI scans, blood tests and screens…if the preventative measure existed, he'd had it done to him.

The result was that he had the all-clear.

There was nothing there. No reason for fear or concern as to why the migraines were occurring or why they were causing him more and more pain. He didn't have a brain tumor, malignant or otherwise. He was healthy, just with debilitating migraines.

He still felt guilty about having undertaken hospital treatment without Devvy's knowledge. It was hardly a respectful way to treat his wife, by hiding the truth of his wellbeing from her. If she had done the same, he'd be furious, and when she found out, because he had no doubt the truth would eventually make an appearance, he deserved to be railed at. He'd accept her fury with grace. But he'd done so for one reason and one reason only.

Pride.

At forty-five he was closer to middle-age than his youth. He wasn't a sensitive man. His years didn't disturb him. All of his experiences had turned him into the creature that stood here now, a success.

But where his wife and his partner were concerned, the age gap was an issue.

One that only existed on his side.

Nearly twenty years older than Devvy, he hadn't wanted to unduly concern her over his health. She was young. He didn't want to barrage her with hospital visits before her time. If the result hadn't been positive news, then he'd have had to share it with her. Considering the results he'd received a day ago, he was glad he'd refrained from telling her about the tests.

Being married to a woman nearly half his age was good for the ego, but not for the soul. He didn't understand why anyone would put themselves through the agony of it if they didn't love their younger partner. Only love made it all tolerable, bearable.

As it was, he felt very old most of the time. Unless he was actually with her. Then the torment made sense.

He'd made a decision around four weeks before Devvy had questioned his fidelity. Hickle Corp, the muscle behind five of the biggest cosmetic brands on the planet, was looking for an in on the organic, free-from-animal-testing market. They'd approached the situation in a manner that Sebastien had recognized as the beginnings of a hostile takeover.

At forty-five, in the business world, he was still at the top of his game. He was considered young, in his prime at the head of a cosmetics brand that globally turned over ten billion a year. That put *La Belle sans la Bête* up with some of the biggest boys in the market.

No corporation in their right mind would believe the head of *La Belle sans la Bête* was ready to retire.

That is, until he'd contacted Hickle Corp and set them straight.

He'd played his cards close to his chest, not wanting them to realize he wanted out, merely that he was open to persuasion.

Their lawyers had arrived at the end of last week and they'd already started the negotiations.

In the middle of talks with the company, Bastien was attempting to tie them up in so many legal loopholes that they'd never be able to stray from the core beliefs he'd set down in stone at the very beginning of this venture…all those years ago.

He had demands and he'd only hand over his baby if they were legally obliged—with no sign of a way out—to continue with his methods.

As he'd grown ever more successful, it would have been easy to stray and settle on a business path that would have undoubtedly doubled the company's profits. Choosing chemicals over organic plants and herbs. Or settling for substandard ingredients in the lines. By maintaining strict regimes of quality control, the brand had grown steadily.

He would not have it sink upon his departure from the fray.

All he and Alex had wanted for the last thirteen years had been to find that elusive third. The women who would complete them. When he phrased it like that, Sebastien knew it sounded almost corny. Devvy, however, filled in all his and Alex's gaps. And there were many, for they were both complicated men.

Finding that one woman had taken a hellishly long time. Longer than either of them had imagined. Devvy was definitely worth the wait.

Would he cope without the hustle and bustle, the frenetic pace of his current life?

He'd have to. He was leaving to enjoy this new world before his health quit on him.

The migraines were a sign from whatever benevolent being gave a damn about him. They were telling him to get the hell out before his health really caved in. Bastien had too much ahead of him to waste his time on business.

He couldn't get any richer. Didn't expect or want any more success. He'd done it all, and now, he had other goals.

He wanted children.

He'd wanted a family for a long time, and while the three of them had some fun times ahead of them, a few years down the line, he wanted to be settled.

Bastien wanted Alex to integrate into a family environment. He accepted his lover's quirks and foibles, but it was time to change. If Bastien's health was emitting a warning sign, Alex's was as well and the cure was Madame Devina Jacques.

She was the glue.

She just didn't realize it yet.

She was in the dark where her importance in his life was concerned, something he was slowly rectifying. Maybe that was his fault. After all, hiding his trips to the hospital undermined that to a certain extent, even if he hadn't intended for that to be the case. Things would change when he was no longer the head of *La Belle sans la Bête. He* would change to be whatever Devvy needed. It was nothing more than she deserved for being the miracle that would take him and Alex out of themselves, and set them on the path to a rich and fulfilling life.

He sighed at the very thought of the future ahead of him, and a pleased smile settled on his lips as he rocked back in his chair. Ignoring the clean lines of his boardroom, he swung around to stare out of the windows onto the world class view of the city.

Few people realized it but he hated heights. It was an irrational and pathetic fear, one whose power over him caused him nothing but irritation. Its strength was such that when the company had transferred into its own high-rise, he'd manipulated the layout. Rather than have the Presidential offices at the top of the building, with the VIPs and other executives underneath, he'd put the labs on the top floor, and he himself had taken a story essentially in the middle but above the other executives. He shared the floor only with a PA, her assistants, and the boardroom.

Regardless, the views of the Seine were unsurpassable. Mostly because had he stood on the fiftieth floor, looking down at the river, he'd probably have been unable to appreciate the beauty of his adopted city.

As it was, here, he could see the *Tour Eiffel*, catch glimpses of the to and fro of this vibrant place. It was enough. Usually, it calmed him, and today was no different. His mind was wandering, and it shouldn't have been.

Hickle Corps's execs were here trying to hash out a deal. Bastien's lawyers were doing most of the talking and his presence wasn't exactly necessary, so he needn't have felt guilty about his failure to listen and digest the business chatter going on around him. He disliked wasting time, however, so he pushed his thoughts of the future to the background, ceased to ponder the view of Paris from his boardroom, and started to concentrate on the droning voices of his American visitors.

"...you can't seriously believe we'll allow you to monitor the business," Derek Wickham snapped.

Bastien's head attorney and longtime friend, Louis Rozen, merely settled deeper into his chair. His expression gave nothing away. Not by one twitch of the brow or pucker of his lips did he display any emotion at the other man's irritation.

It was why Rozen was one of the highest paid members of staff on the *La Belle sans la Bête* payroll. He was a bitch to play poker with, too.

"If you want the business, then you'll have to do more than consider the possibility. Gentlemen, your company has a reputation for using substandard ingredients."

"I resent that. Our products are all tested and meet international standards."

"That they might do, but they wouldn't reach *our* standards," Bastien inserted, voice silky. He usually refrained from speaking during these occasions, preferring to listen and leave Rozen in charge, but temptation to muddy the waters had overtaken him.

It was best to approach these situations with confidence. If he betrayed his eagerness to part with the company, it was almost guaranteed that Hickle's interest would dry up.

These relationships were very similar to those between man and woman.

A little play of hard to get worked wonders on recalcitrant partners.

Because he was who he was, Wickham bit his tongue rather than snap at him. His anger was quite evident. In fact, Bastien was shocked that this was Hickle's negotiator—he'd seen few men in such a role betray themselves so exuberantly.

"Why should we invest in a company where the previous owners still want to keep their feet dipped into the waters?"

"It's hardly an unusual request."

"It's very unusual. Ordinarily, honorary roles can be created to portray the idea the old management is still keeping in touch with the new, but there's little real interaction between the two sides. I'm afraid if you can't negotiate on this point, we might have to call a day on the talks."

At Wickham's statement, Rozen's eyes flickered over to Bastien's. A silence thrummed overhead as he processed the words the American made, and watched the smugness overtake the executive's face as the belief he'd cowed Bastien made itself known.

He smiled. "That is fine by me. Good day, Mr. Wickham. Ms. Roberts."

Bastien made to stand, when the other negotiator, Emma Roberts, spoke, "I'm afraid Derek has given you an ultimatum that goes against our company's better interests."

"Emma!" Wickham snarled under his breath but she slashed her hand in front of her, making the other man sit back in his chair like a chastened school boy.

Considering it was the first time the woman had spoken, she exuded a position of authority Wickham did not. It was interesting, therefore, that he had been acting as lead spokesman, when it was, in fact, Emma Roberts in charge.

"Indeed?" Bastien asked, settling himself back in his chair with an air of boredom about his person.

It wasn't feigned.

He *was* bored.

He wanted to go home, be with his partners. Not waste time here.

It was amazing how he was gradually changing. His decision, now cast in concrete, didn't have him meandering back and forth with regrets. He'd made his choice and now, more than anything, he wanted to act on it.

The very fact that he had to remain patient was a chore, but one he'd succeed at. While the company was coming to mean less and less to him, that didn't mean he would hand over years of his hard work to an undeserving corporation who would rape it of all its assets and leave behind an empty shell.

"We would still like to continue our talks with yourself, Monsieur Jacques."

"Please, formalities aren't required. I'm Sebastien." He smiled winningly, knowing Wickham was pissed that he hadn't extended such an invitation to him. "I understand that my terms might be considered unusual, but it's vital to me that I retain some control here. I do not wish to make changes. I wish to monitor the alterations you make to the company's running.

"If you could guarantee that you wouldn't mess around with our providers as well as the way we go about manufacturing the products, then that would be perfect.

"As it is, I don't think you'll agree to that. I need to have the authority to make the board change their ways if I see your company taking this one down a path that goes against everything the brand stands for."

It was the longest he'd spoken to either representative since the talks had commenced, and Emma pondered the lengthy speech before saying, "I can understand your misgivings. But you have to understand, the very reason we wish to purchase the company is for its moral standing. That is half the product you're selling. Were we to make any substantial alterations to the workings of the company, the product would change, and so would the market. Surely you can see that?"

"All I can see is that you would tell me blue was black to try to urge me into signing your contract. While yes, it is true, there would be a butterfly effect were you to mess around with the providers and the manufacturing process, that doesn't mean my methods are protected."

"If you're so insistent on retaining control, then why are you interested in stepping down?"

Bastien's eyes flared at the remark. He had to quash that particular train of thought in its early stages before it flowered and undermined his bargaining position. "I'm not interested in stepping down. When I noticed Hickle Corp was gearing up for a hostile takeover, I extended an invitation to talk. Nothing more. These negotiations have come into play, because your company requested it. Not us."

Emma Roberts merely pursed her lips and nodded. "I shall have to discuss this with my superiors." She looked down at the proposal Rozen had given her at the start of the meeting. "I don't have the power to say yea or nay to the requests you've made. My team will need time to work through your requirements. Can we break now and I'll contact your team in a few days to reschedule after I've spoken to the board?"

Bastien nodded. "Of course. You do what you see fit. I am willing to bend so far, Ms. Roberts. But this company will not be swept from under me. If your side thinks to return to the MO of hostile takeover, I've since taken steps to protect myself and my place of business from such an attack.

"Be warned, the only way to get a foot in the door is through the proposal in your hands."

With that, he stood, nodded at the Hickle Corp's representatives, and departed the boardroom.

He had things to do, and being stuck in his offices wasn't one of them.

Regardless, he returned to his suite of rooms, checked his e-mail and the messages his PA had left for him, before sending for the car.

As he checked his e-mail, a reminder from his calendar popped up. The deadline had hit. Today, he either had to pack a bag with a hundred thousand Euros in small bills and leave it at the Saint-Laurent church over in the tenth arrondissement or something about his relationship with Alexei would appear in tomorrow's papers.

Goddamn blackmailers. Dismissing them as scum of the earth was a complete and utter understatement. And in this case, the timing of it all couldn't have been much worse.

Were anything untoward to appear in the papers regarding his personal situation, a situation that was most definitely unorthodox even for the most liberal of the French population, he knew it would undermine his leverage with Hickle Corp.

At the same time, kowtowing to some anonymous schmuck's demands didn't sit well with him.

Being threatened was hardly a new experience for him. The only difference this time being he'd been handling this particular threat himself, and had not handed it over to the company's security department as he'd done in the past.

That alone told him he was treating this differently to the other threats he'd received over the years. But, he knew he'd be dealing with it in the same way.

No pay off would be made today. At least, not from his point of view.

The idea of having to tell both his lovers of the situation made him grimace. The knowledge that personal secrets could be in tomorrow's press was abhorrent to him, and so was the idea of having to pay for those secrets to be kept.

He could afford any number of payouts. It was the principle of the thing. He had to wonder if Devvy was strong enough, if she was secure enough in this new dynamic of theirs, to ride the waves.

What concerned him more than anything was the idea of what would happen on the other side of the pond. Miranda Nelson, Devvy's mother, already had her claws flexed into his wife's hide. As soon as any news about him having a male lover hit, she would make Devvy's life miserable. Or as miserable as she could when the Atlantic Ocean separated them.

He had the whole day and the evening to make payment. The church closed its doors at ten, and he had the money in his home safe if, upon revealing the truth to the pair of them, they decided they wanted to make the payout.

Well, that calendar reminder fucked up his original plans royally! From toying with the desire to play hooky to being forced to discuss some bastard's extortion attempts…this day was *not* going to end the way he'd imagined in the boardroom.

He spent a further twenty minutes in his office, half-expecting Rozen to come in and demand to hash over the talks with Hickle, but Bastien was in luck. He made it out of the glass revolving doors without coming into contact with anyone requiring his attention.

He had some bad news to share with his lover and wife.

He now knew what it felt like to be the Grinch.

Chapter Thirteen

To Alex, the world outside the doors of his apartment heralded chaos.

Noise. People. A manic, frenetic energy that sucked him in and spat him out, leaving behind a tangled, befuddled mess in both mind, body, and spirit.

The immensity of Paris should have been a repellent. As soon as he'd finished his studies at the Sorbonne, as well as the other myriad universities he'd attended, he should have escaped to a lab in the countryside. Tucked away in the middle of nowhere, nobody to bother him, no reason to enter the craziness of city life.

Those plans had changed the day he'd served Sebastien a cup of coffee to the sounds of trains screeching and braking.

That moment, the very first time his fingers had brushed Bastien's as he passed over the throwaway cup, his life had been set on a completely different path.

He hadn't been a virgin. His "uncle" had seen to that. But he'd never been taken with the gentleness of a lover, and Sebastien, in that sense, had been his first. The first to touch and kiss, to caress and cherish.

After his uncle's attentions, men should have repelled him. For the most part, neither sex had caused a spark in his adolescent sex drive. He didn't think of himself as asexual, merely relieved to be away from sex. For the first time in too long, he'd been free from sexual abuse and adding another relationship of the same, if less disturbing, nature had been the last thing on his mind back then.

At seventeen, he'd been six months or so into his Masters of cytopathology—the pathology of cellular diseases. Even at such a young age, he'd known what he wanted to do. His entire college career had had him studying up until his thirty-second year, a career that left him with a list of letters after his name and the ability to work anywhere in the world in a multitude of different positions in the scientific community.

When he'd first met Sebastien, his future had been all that concerned him. Gaining his degrees, attaining the requisite knowledge to dissect the disease that affected so many…. They had been his goals, and he'd striven for them. Worked night and day, took on extra jobs to fund his degrees. Ran himself ragged.

Then, Bastien Jacques had appeared and tilted his flustered, if structured, world on its head.

At that age, his hatred of entering the outside world had been a daily chore. He'd known it would have to be kept in check until his studying was complete, and until he had made enough discoveries to warrant a personal laboratory on the premises of his choosing. It had been hard, a struggle to get out of bed every day, knowing he had to penetrate a world that wasn't to his liking. Bastien had added to the pros, and eventually he'd transformed Alex's life to the point where leaving to live in the countryside had been an impossibility, as Bastien's work had been and always would be firmly entrenched in the city.

He had no regrets about living in Paris. After so many years, it was his home. He just preferred to see it from the safety of his own apartment. He couldn't deny, however, that the instant he walked into *Les Fenêtres* and the door closed behind him, that same sensation of peace overcame him as it did when he walked into his penthouse.

That boded well.

Especially considering Devvy was on the warpath.

Eventually, he would concede to her wishes. He *would* move into *Les Fenêtres* if that was what she and Bastien wanted. Not that he'd make it easy. Giving up his penthouse was to give up more than just his solitude. It was to give up a place that had been his haven for so many years.

But he understood her argument.

How could he expect this complicated relationship of theirs to function if he wasn't there? And considering how he'd toiled to convince her that this *ménage* wasn't about the sex, how could he now shift that around to his own advantage?

He couldn't.

Not without nullifying his every word.

It wasn't about sex. It was about the connection. It was also about providing Bastien with a peace, a harmony that he himself couldn't provide.

Alex was broken. Deep inside. Irreparable. He knew that, and knew Bastien's love for him would make him try to patch Alex up. He'd never stop. In all their years together, he'd always been a stalwart support, but Alex wasn't what Bastien needed. By introducing Devvy to the fray, he'd changed that.

Their little threesome would eventually be symbiotic. Each member of the trio drawing strength from each other. Alex looked forward to the day he could be an active partner, rather than a lead weight around Bastien's neck.

Devvy was the harbinger of change. She would be the one to forge a new Alex out of the wreckage of before.

She'd do as she'd done today.

Drag him out of himself, convince him to enter the chaos of the city by propositioning him with sex. She'd tease and entice, mock and amuse…be what he needed and when.

It was when she'd made that proposition that he realized he loved her.

The feeling had been there for a while. A slow burn in the pit of his soul. He'd known of its existence, but he'd pushed it away, believing it to be too soon even though he'd told her otherwise. She'd given herself to him. Prodded and chided, showered him with her concern, then shocked him with her suggestion.

How could he not love such a woman and be proud of that love?

The words had burned a hole on his tongue. The need to tell her, to gift her with his heart, imperative. Only the knowledge that he had the charade of a meeting with his mother enticed him to keep quiet.

And that particular rendezvous had been as terrible as he'd imagined.

His mother, in all the years, hadn't changed. Still insanely possessive, still a little unhinged. She was out of touch, still wearing widow's weeds even though her husband had only divorced her, not died and been buried away to disintegrate into the earth. Instead, he'd remarried and created a new family with a woman from Marseille. Alex knew because he'd had his father investigated the instant he'd earned enough money to pay for a private investigator.

His mother's traditional views extended to homosexuality. A sexual congregation practiced by perverts, was her belief. The irony being she'd invited a sick bastard into her home and life, enabling him to abuse her son…but Alex was the pervert for being attracted to a man. That is, she'd label him as such if she knew.

He could have told her. It would have divorced her from his life, but something…he didn't know what—maybe a sense of filial duty?—had kept him from doing so. He'd protected her from the truth, and would continue to do so. Just as he'd never told her about Pierre Defreine's attacks, he'd hide this from her as well.

Had he taken Sebastien to meet her and introduced him as his lover. Alex could easily imagine the beginnings of some kind of psychological meltdown. That would have been a barrel of laughs.

As it was, her reaction to Devvy had been atrocious, but a damned sight better than the alternative.

He'd heard Bastien's hurt the other week, though.

Bastien's parents were alive, well, cared about their son, but for the most part, led their own lives. He'd been introduced to Henri and Suzette eighteen months after their relationship had begun. Sebastien had never said anything about wanting a reciprocal meeting with Alex's own mother, but then, the little Alex had had to say about Antoinette, had easily described the fragility of her mental state.

That didn't make it right.

He hated having to deny the man who had kept him glued together for so many years. He wasn't just denying Sebastien. He was renouncing his very self. Just as he'd keep on doing until his mother died.

The day she did…

He felt like a bastard for even thinking it, but Alex would feel nothing on the day the call came. If anything, he'd probably experience a great welter of relief.

While his mother lived, Alex's past remained an open, festering sore.

He could never close ties to the past, because he wasn't certain if his mother had played a part in his ruination as a child. And if he wasn't certain of that, how could he trust any part of his relationship with her? She might have betrayed him in the most evil possible way. On the other hand, she might have been entirely unaware.

His gut told him it was the former that was the case, for how could a live-in partner leave a shared bedroom three or four times a week, in the depths of the night, without the other partner being aware of it? No matter how often he was on the verge of breaking all ties, with no real, concrete evidence, Alex remained in contact with her.

The thoughts were a trigger. He fought hard to stop himself from releasing the "bullet" and completely annihilating his plans for the day in a meltdown of his own. Alex managed to curb his emotions by focusing on Devvy's promise.

Such a simple offering, gifted freely and openly. It was clean. So lily white that the black in Alex's soul shriveled a little. Turned gray.

He turned his head to watch her as she shrugged out of her lightweight cardigan and handed it to one of the maids, Louise, if memory served. He himself gave her his leather jacket and she scurried away to tuck them in some closet or other, leaving them alone after completing her task and waiting to be summoned for further instruction.

The archaic running of Bastien's house was thanks to a housekeeper, Madame Joffet, who was nearing seventy and had a familial background of service to the rich and famous. Her grandparents had once acted as housekeeper and butler for some of Paris's most elite. As such, she took her teachings from them and had the staff scurrying around as though they would be whipped if Bastien or Devvy so much as saw them for more than a few seconds at a time.

Devvy didn't seem to notice, but he did. The idea of living with such a high number of intrusions made him shudder with the horror of it.

At the moment, living alone suited him. His PA, Catherine, came in and molded herself to his schedule, her PAs worked to ease her life and to further enhance the smooth running of his own. He only interacted with Catherine, and her staff worked on a telecom basis.

He preferred it that way. Catherine knew how he liked things done and she did them to suit his routine, often carrying out the heavy tasks when he was asleep or in the middle of an experiment. He ran her ragged, he knew that, but she never complained. Mostly, because he gave her freedom to come and go. As long as he was never troubled, she could work as little or as much as she chose, and whenever she wanted. He never checked up on her. Her wage was more than twice the average PA's, and she could adapt her job to suit the school run. As a single mother, such flexibility was vital.

As far as Alex was aware, Bastien had at least eight people working in his house. From maids to gardeners to drivers to maintenance people to the chef. As well as their assistants! In a way, having so many people under one roof was like inviting the chaos of the outside world indoors.

Would he be able to cope living this way?

As he pondered the question, he realized he was looking at it from the wrong angle.

Could he cope in a world without both Bastien and Devvy in it?

No.

That was the short answer.

The long of it was, Bastien loved Devvy and that love was returned. As Devvy had once told him, he was the outsider, because he pushed himself to the fringes of their relationship by living away from them.

He'd never thought of it that way. Even when he'd been Bastien's dirty little secret. He had just believed they were both waiting for the perfect moment and had been content to be hidden away.

Now…he wasn't content with the idea of his many foibles turning his lovers away from him. Especially after he'd realized his love for Devvy was as concrete as his love for Bastien.

A life without them was worse than a life of inhabiting a house such as this one, with a small pack of staff that kept it ticking like a clock.

Priorities.

Everyone had them and it was time Alex reassessed his.

As he pondered such a reassessment, his eyes wandered over to the catalyst for such change.

In the light and airy vestibule, with the central circular table loaded down with freshly-cut flowers that perfumed the room with a clean tinge of the season and the lights beaming into the room from the windows surrounding the door, Devvy's dirty-blonde beauty was highlighted to perfection.

The light golden tones in her hair shone and glistened in the bright, hot sun. The darker shades, the light chestnut and almost bronzy hues, were given extra contrast in the shadows of the hall. Her skin, the shade of magnolia tinged with the rosiness of a downy peach, gleamed in the muted, dusky glow from the windows.

She was unique and she was his. As he was hers.

In a way, it was a miracle. *She* was his miracle.

Intelligence was a burden as well as a gift. The higher a person's capabilities for brilliance, the higher the chances that same person could crack. Alex had more cracks than he could count, and he was on the brink of a Humpty Dumpty moment.

Only in his case, he could be put back together again.

If Devvy chose to do the repair work.

He was laying all of this on Devvy's shoulders and not Bastien's, because Bastien's love gave him a different kind of support.

With him, Alex was at peace. When they were together, the outside world didn't exist. But the instant they were apart, the demons returned. They attacked.

With Devvy, perhaps because she was just as brilliant as he, perhaps because they were both scientists, albeit in different fields, she kept the demons at bay. When he was with her, memories of the past, his nightmares would return, but she would dampen their effect with her unique outlook. And when she left him, while he felt lost, his lips would often twitch as his mind recapped a conversation they'd had as he worked on something or other in the lab.

They were two halves of a whole that would keep him sane.

"What are you staring at?" she asked, turning to him with a scowl. Her eyes glanced down as though she were looking for a stain on her shirt, and a smile graced his mouth at her lack of artfulness.

"The flowers," he teased, deadpan.

Her scowl deepened as her gaze flickered over to the pink-purple azaleas. "I didn't realize you were a flower lover."

"Whatever made you think I wasn't?"

She rolled her eyes. "The complete lack of anything green in your penthouse." She mock shivered. "I don't know how you can stand all the recycled air without some plants in there to rebalance and cleanse the space."

Alex shrugged. "I like them but they don't like me. We can't all have a green thumb, Devvy darling." Stood beside the table loaded down with the huge display of blossoms, she was in the center of the door-lined space. He strode over to her and calmly, presumptuously, wrapped his arms about her and pulled her close. "Don't change, *ma petite*."

"Why should I? I'd say I'm too set in my ways to go through a complete personality shift."

He grinned. "You say that and yet you're deep in the midst of a relationship that most would consider taboo." The dimness of the room had dilated her pupils, but the icy-blue orbs darkened further as his tone dropped into a husky growl, "You know what's going to happen tonight, don't you? When Sebastien gets home and finds us both here?"

Swallowing, she turned her head from side to side. Her eyes never left his, not for a second and he reveled in being at the center of this woman's glorious attention.

"He's going to fuck you. And as he takes your ass, I'll sink into your pussy. When we've flooded you with cum, I'll fuck him and you can suck his cock…" He paused, waited and watched as she sucked in a breath and held it with expectation. "Just think of all the different positions, Devvy."

"If you think I haven't already contemplated what you two will do to me, you're very much mistaken, Alex."

He grinned. "I'm glad to hear that you've been looking forward to it as much as I have."

"Damn right." She snorted, and then looked sheepish. "Well, I did freak myself out. Just a little."

He cocked a brow, urging her silently to explain, but she shook her head, untangled herself from his embrace, and then grabbed him by the hand. He let her lead him into one particular room and from the slight touches of femininity, he knew this was her lounge. He'd often heard Bastien complain about her refusal to change any of the other rooms.

"While you can't leave a statement like that unexplained, my curiosity has me changing the subject."

"Oh?" was all she said.

He hummed and looked around the white walls with the cream cornices and *café au lait* decorative touches. A light, moss green linen sofa sat squatly in front of the original carved stone fireplace. To the side, a matching armchair overfilled with stuffing had the best seat in the room to stare out through the double-paned French doors and out onto the gardens. Cream cushions with a silky texture had been plumped and arranged artfully on the chairs. Small, occasional tables dotted the room with pieces he could only assume were her favorites. Everything from an ornate, mahogany armoire the size of his hands, carved in an Asian style with jade-inset doors, to an elaborate plant pot filled with a plant he'd never seen before but had the most delightfully silky petals.

It was a woman's haven, restful, calming, and peaceful.

It shocked him but he knew he could sit in here and feel at ease. It wasn't overfull with stuff. The room wasn't at all cramped. In fact, for the amount of space she had, the room was rather over furnished. In comparison to his own haven, it was full, but still…. On an afternoon, while Bastien was out at the office, when he didn't want to be cooped up in his lab, he could imagine himself in here.

That was enough to have his stomach twisting with nerves.

"Why haven't you changed any of the other rooms? I know Sebastien asked you to." Her blush charmed him into crossing the room to caress the silky leaves of the unknown flower. "What is this?" he asked, before she could answer his other question.

She frowned at him, then down at the plant and absentmindedly said, "It's a camellia. Seb has them on standing order for me with a florist. They won't grow in our garden. I think our soil has too low a soil acidity for them. They're my favorites."

When he nodded his understanding and continued to caress the petals, the sound of a heavy sigh crossed the room. He turned, looked at her, and immediately interpreted this new flush as arousal. Hiding a smile, he trailed one finger down over the frothy bloom. She shivered at the touch, so he did it again. And again, until she stepped backward and sank onto the armchair.

"I actually think I could come from watching you do that," she whispered hoarsely, her honesty surprising but pleasing him.

"Perhaps I should stop."

"I don't think you should."

His lips twitched. "Why touch a flower when I can touch the real thing?"

At that, she grinned. "My grandmother used to call "the real thing" her "lady garden." Maybe my grandfather was a lot more adventurous than we realized."

Stepping away from the flower, he crossed the room, ignoring her sigh to sink down to his knees in front of her. Tucked into the armchair, she looked comfortable, even if he'd inadvertently put her on edge by touching the flower the way he had.

His hands slipped over her skirt-covered thighs and he sighed with pleasure as they fell apart slightly. He pushed them wider so he could kneel between them. "I do like this new habit of yours."

"What new habit?"

"In the last week, I've seen you three times in a skirt."

She blushed again.

"It isn't that I dislike you in jeans, because, *ma petite*, I can't deny your ass is perfect in trousers, but it means…"

"…easy access," she butted in before he could finish his sentence.

"Exactly," he murmured with pleasure. "Now, tell me why you won't change any of the rooms."

"It isn't my place to."

He snorted. "Bullshit. When I move in here, there will be a lot to change. That god-awful salon is the first to go."

She stilled at his words. "*When*?"

"Yes. I don't know when it will be, but I shall move into *Les Fenêtres*, Devvy."

It unnerved him to see tears moisten her eyes. "Thank you, Alexei." She reached forward and cupped his chin. He relaxed into her hold and rubbed his cheek against her palm.

"I should be thanking you. I can be stubborn, at times. I can't guarantee it will be soon, but I can guarantee it will happen."

"That's all I want." She sucked in a breath, obviously overwhelmed by his agreement and said, "I guess, the house does need a makeover. It still looks like a bachelor pad."

"Which is miraculous, considering Bastien has never been a bachelor."

Her mouth rounded at that, into a lusciously round O that had his cock pricking up to attention.

A chuckle escaped her. "Deliciously true." She grinned.

"You know you could have changed any part of the house and Bastien wouldn't have given a damn, don't you?"

She bit her lip. "I don't think that's the truth."

He shook his head. "You could have painted all the rooms bright pink and he'd have looked at it, grimaced, but wouldn't have said a word. He wants you to be happy here, *ma chérie*. That's all that ever mattered to him." When she still looked unconvinced, he shrugged and changed the subject. "I've been patient. Tell me how, in your words, you 'freaked yourself out a little.'"

She groaned, lifted a hand to her eyes, and then peeked between the small spaces in her fingers.

Alex grinned. "That bad, *hein*?"

A nod was his only answer. For a second, anyway. "I did some research."

Lips twitching, he murmured, "As any good scientist would."

"Exactly! I needed to see what went where. I mean, I knew what went where but I needed to see it. I didn't want to…"

"You wanted to see if it was attractive or repulsive to you," he commented, no inflection to his tone.

She nibbled her bottom lip. "Well, it might have been. When I watch you kiss, it turns my stomach out. I can't explain it. You're…" She sighed. "You're so beautiful together, but I didn't know if that side of it would be."

"Perfectly natural."

She looked relieved at his easy acceptance of what was, in truth, perfectly natural. The idea of two men together was a turn-on to some women and a definite switch-off for others.

"Well, it wasn't repulsive. Not at all," she assured him quickly. "But, when I watched the ménages, I knew when it was my turn to be in that situation, it would be a life-changing moment."

He frowned. "Hardly, *chérie.* These things happen all the time."

Devvy snorted. "To other people. On the internet. These things might be okay to some people, but you're forgetting, I grew up in a house with a mother as prim as Jane Austen, for God's sake! You're lucky I didn't pass out when you first showed up at the house!

"When I saw what it would be like, I knew it would define me. Or, it would change the way I viewed myself. I knew I might think of myself as some kind of slut." When he made to interrupt, she held up a hand. "No, wait. Look, I know that's a bit extreme. It was how I felt, but notice I didn't let it stop me. I was nervous, yes, I'll admit that. The other day, the idea of what was going to happen had me running hot then cold. When I watched you together, though, I didn't give a damn. I needed you both and I loved seeing you like that. It was so beautiful. Even hotter than just watching you kiss."

"I'm glad, *mignonne*," he told her, voice husky at the depth of emotion in her words. She really meant it.

Her smile was gentle as she continued, "Some people can easily accept situations like this, but I think the majority don't. I guess, considering who you and Bastien are, once we live together, the truth will come out. Like I told you before, I won't deny you, Alex. I couldn't do that. I—I love you, you see," she whispered, and damn near broke his heart. "Very much. If you love someone, you don't betray them by refusing to acknowledge them.

"My being freaked out wasn't just about the sexual side of things. But the way we'd be viewed in society. The way *I'd* be viewed in society. I mean, my mother probably will never speak to me ever again, which to be honest, might not be a bad thing!

"It was just a very overwhelming moment. Seeing the mechanics of it all, well, opened my eyes to more than just what we'd do together."

"It is true we French are more liberal in these matters, but I think to a certain extent, we will be outcasts among a certain crowd. This is something one keeps secret. Behind closed doors. Perhaps our wealth will smooth the way. On the other hand, it might not. And to be honest, my sweet, darling Devvy, I don't give a damn either. I love you, and for a love like ours, who needs the approval of anyone else?"

She cupped his cheek and traced her fingers over his jaw. "You two, sometimes, you make me want to pinch myself."

"Is that a good thing?" he asked, brow cocked.

"Oh yes. I can't believe how lucky I am. That's all."

"You're more than worthy, Devvy darling."

She grinned. "I'll get a big head, you know."

"I'm counting on it. It's about bloody time you started to value yourself. You're more than a match for Bastien and me."

"Did you talk about me?" she asked hesitantly. "The pair of you…before, I mean."

"Of course. We had a lot resting on your delicate shoulders, Devvy. He didn't betray your trust, *ma petite*. Bastien's not like that. He shared his concerns with me.

"We'd expected a lot from you by asking you to move away from everything you'd ever known. That was a great concern, wondering if you'd settle or not. Then, after you'd taken the job, making the first move was a huge topic of discussion.

"He seems so suave, but Bastien is, how you say, a clod. Especially with women. I should have been the one to make the introductions. I'm blunt, but I have common sense."

"He is pretty, though," she retorted, a wicked gleam in her eye.

"Oh, he certainly has his uses."

Devvy laughed. "Did he ask you for advice on how to handle me?"

He pulled a face. "That's dangerous talk. Remember, I'm the one with the common sense. Sebastien might be able to handle a company with over ten thousand employees, but with women, he's like a teenager still trying to get rid of his virginity."

"I'll be sure to tell him that."

"*Agent provocateur*!" he claimed, then spoiled his show of outrage by winking. "You think I have not told him this already? He knows I think he's useless with women. When I showed him the magazine with your interview and told him to go and meet you, we had a huge row. Both of us realized I should be the one to go, but if stepping outside my door is hard enough, entering a convention is like climbing Everest." He shuddered. "I just couldn't do it. Not even for that silent promise in your eyes."

"I'm sure I was just looking into the camera, you know. I don't think I was silently promising anything. Actually, I know I wasn't." She tapped her chin. "I remember that interview. The photographer was a pain in the ass. I had to change outfits three times before he was happy. I think, more than anything, I was pissed off."

A clap echoed around the room and both of them jumped as Sebastien's bark of laughter ricocheted alongside it. "All these years, he's gone on and on about that bloody photo and she was angry! *Mon cher,* now who is the fool with women, *hein*?"

Alex just grinned. "Eavesdroppers never hear good of themselves," was all he said. Piously, too. And pious was an achievement considering he was on his knees, tucked between Devvy's thighs, hands smoothing up and down the sleek curves of their woman's legs.

"So it would seem," Bastien retorted and stepped into the room, shutting the door behind him.

The instant they were closed in, a strange atmosphere overtook the room. Alex decided to break it by saying, "You weren't supposed to arrive home so early."

"Disappointed, *cher*?" Bastien cocked his brow and began to remove his tie.

As he tugged at the knot, Devvy sucked in a breath and Alex's eyes flickered over to hers. He grinned. "More than pretty, *hein*?"

Bastien rolled his eyes and shrugged out of his jacket. "God, it's good to be out of that." He flexed his shoulders, inducing another sigh from Devvy.

"I love it when he's all rumpled."

"Rumpled is a good word, *chérie,*" Alex admitted.

"You're both trying to distract me from the fact Alex is actually here, at *Les Fenêtres*."

Devvy's smile was loaded with triumph. "I made him a deal."

"Deals are more my forte," Bastien chided with a mocking grin. "I'm not sure if I like you overtaking my territory, *mignonne.*"

Alex snorted. "She has a way with words that you, *cher*, do not share!"

"Curiouser and curiouser!"

"Whatever he wants to do to me, he can, so long as he leaves his apartment."

Bastien smiled. "I can now understand why he's here. Well done, Devvy. Very imaginative." He winked at her.

She looked very pleased with herself, and Alex couldn't help but lean forward to bestow a soft kiss to her lips. "Come, I see no reason to wait now the main guest has arrived. It's time for you to work off your dues."

Devvy chuckled. "My dues? Christ, I want a hotter word than that!" She turned to Bastien with a cheeky smile. "Alex wanted to stain our sheets, but you got home too early. You spoiled the surprise."

Sebastien shook his head. "It's a good job I got here in time. He'll cost me a fortune in laundry bills." He stepped over to her, bent down, and pressed a kiss to her lips. "Run, little girl. Run."

She blinked up at him. "Run?"

He grinned, the smile wicked. "Alex likes a good chase."

Her eyes widened as they snapped between him and their lover. Alex moved out of the way as Bastien stepped forward, grabbed her hand, tugged her onto her feet, and slapped her bottom.

"Run," he whispered.

She studied him a moment, a frown in her eyes, but as her gaze flickered over to Alex, that frown turned into a hot burn that scorched the two of them. After a slow nod, she turned on her heels and did as bade.

Ran.

Devvy knew it was only a game, but she dashed up the stairs and ran from the pair of them as though the hounds of hell were snapping at her ankles. Within seconds, she heard sounds of laughter and pounding footsteps as they chased after her.

Alex rarely laughed. So when he did, the sound just buzzed along her nerve endings, as though she'd smoked a spliff. Giving her a strange kind of toxin-free high.

Bastien was just as bad for taking life so seriously. The sounds of his chuckles were music to Devvy's ears and knowing that she added this dimension to their lives just filled her with a sense of empowerment.

They'd waited for her.

All these long years.

And unknowingly, she'd been waiting for them.

Shuddering at the thought, she made it into the bedroom and, sedately now, walked to the bed and perched on the edge. After crossing her legs, she sat there, waiting for the ten seconds it took for them to catch up to her.

They burst through the door, took a look at her neat pose, and charged forward.

In a tangle of arms and legs and chuckles, they collapsed on the bed. Devvy, squished between the two of them, was immediately wrapped up in their love for her. She was cocooned by strong male arms, pinned down by thick thighs and nudged by hard cocks.

Laughter soon died out as mouths had more important tasks to do. Kisses and pecks, licks and sups. Amid the chaotic tangle of limbs, Devvy had never felt more at peace.

Alex suddenly disappeared. He pulled away for no more than fifteen seconds, and it took him that long to shuck out of his clothes and return to her, naked.

It was Bastien's turn to disappear and he too returned as bare as the day he was born. They kept their distance as soon as they were nude, staring down at her, wonder in their eyes as she wriggled between them. Needing them, craving them. Ready in every way possible for this next step.

She held out her arms, silently pleading for that mad tangle, but Alex shook his head, a wicked smile on his mouth.

"I think we should take advantage of that skirt, Bastien."

Devvy's husband's grin was wide as he nodded and knelt beside the bed, between her legs. He slid his hands up the silken length of her calves, back and forth, nudging the skirt's hem a little higher with every sweeping move.

By the time he was touching her inner thighs, just above the knee, Devvy had melted a little inside. She quivered, waiting for a more intimate touch, but Bastien denied her it. He kept on sliding his hands along the length of her legs, making gooseflesh rise up and stand to attention.

She shuddered when, after being content to watch Bastien at play, Alex decided to join in. His fingers immediately went to the panty-covered pussy Bastien had been ignoring. A moan escaped her, her back arched up as he touched her through the fabric. Letting his finger edge down between her pussy lips, penetrating her slightly before returning upward to nudge her clit.

A tremor worked through her as he rimmed the tiny nub. Other hands appeared at her pussy, only these were tugging at the clinging damp fabric. Bastien pulled them down, over her legs and over her feet. The instant she was free from them, he spread her legs further apart and dragged her down, so her pussy was right on the edge of the bed.

A perfect alignment for his mouth.

She cried out as his lips dropped down to press a kiss to her wet cunt, as his tongue played and his teeth nibbled. Her arms flew overhead, throwing her backward with the momentum, and she pinned them down to the mattress using them to keep her grounded, but it wasn't enough. Especially when Alex's mouth joined in.

She had to look. Had to.

She arched upward and stared down as two heads, one dark and one tow, made a feast of her cunt. She watched, in awe, as their lips met and clashed over her sex. Their kiss, at the most intimate juncture of her body, almost had her coming there and then.

She watched them. Bastien's mouth covered in her juices, Alex's just starting to get damp, as they devoured each other. A whimper worked free of her throat, followed by a mewl that caught their attention. She pushed their heads together before they could stop what they were doing.

Panting gasps rattled her chest, and she couldn't breathe. The sight of them…she'd seen them before. Countless times. A kiss, a snog…she'd grown accustomed to it. But not like this. Never like this.

They were celebrating their union. Celebrating it as they celebrated the new addition to their triad, and it set her bones on fire.

When they turned back to their original task, her stomach muscles were screaming from the enforced position. But it had been worth it. Oh, God, had it been worth it.

She sank back into the bed only to rear up seconds later as one of them nibbled her clit and the other thrust as deep as he could with his tongue.

Sounds of wetness, of moisture, filled the room. She was so wet, filled with juices, so ready for them, readier than she'd ever been.

Her legs had been lying limply against the side of the mattress, but now, she lifted them onto the bed and spread them as wide as she could. Her reward was a tongue prodding at her asshole.

Another shudder throttled through her at the sensation of that most sinful part of her body being tickled by a tongue. As one caressed there, the other prodded her clit. Slipping it between his lips and sucking down. Hard.

Her shriek let the entire house know what was going on, and Devvy just didn't care.

For this moment in time, she belonged to these men. The world didn't exist. Only the three of them did.

A finger slid between her pussy lips, rubbing back and forth in a way that let her know he was collecting her juices. She awaited the prod of the digit at her ass with bated breath, and the instant a fingertip made its presence known, she shuddered in delight. Bearing down, she let him in and quivered as he began to fuck her with his hand.

Tight, taut muscles clung to the digit and Alex's voice was a groan as he grunted. "Can't wait to get my cock in there."

Bastien chuckled. "It's worth the wait, *cher.*"

She didn't even have it in her to be embarrassed by such talk. She just needed. Craved.

When Bastien returned to supping at her clit, he licked the underside of the nub, flickering the tensile muscle along the tiny curve. The act was like detonating a bomb behind Devvy's eyes.

She was an inch away from climax, and she didn't want to come.

She wanted to come when her men did.

She didn't want a tiny explosion. She wanted an atomic bomb blast to hit her behind the eyes.

Nothing else would do for this first time together.

She began to struggle, her legs flailing and moving, and her arms, limp as spaghetti, attempted to move her away from their seductive caresses.

Their hands clamped down, but she glared at them. "Now!" she stated firmly, then less firm and more desperate, she whispered, "Now."

Bastien looked amused and touched. The emotions so tinged with his love for her that she melted a little more.

Christ, what these two did to her should be illegal.

"*Petite*, you're not ready."

"Oh, I'm ready, Bastien." She sucked in a breath, because, boy was she ready! "Do it. God, please. No more teasing."

Their eyes flickered toward one another, and she could sense more amusement on their behalf. She didn't take offense, because Sebastien enjoyed torturing her with foreplay. He could spend an hour on that alone, driving her wild, driving her insane with the need for him to just thrust inside her. To fill her.

In contrast, a few minutes of teasing were nothing in comparison to that. But ever since Devvy had watched porn and freaked herself out, ever since she'd seen the two of them together, deep inside, she'd been readying herself.

Life had been one whole heap of foreplay.

She didn't need to be caressed.

She needed to be fucked by these two men.

And the sooner it happened, the better.

"Fuck me, baby, please," she pleaded, her eyes huge in her delicate rose-tinged face as she held out her hands for Alex.

His chuckle was hoarse as he said, "I can deny you nothing, Devvy. Bastien, see to our *mignonne.*"

Bastien did as bade. He climbed onto the bed, settling atop the covers at the head and sinking down onto the cushions. He curled a finger, beckoning her to come to him and Alex helped her roll over and get onto her knees. How she managed that short crawl, Devvy didn't know. She was a mass of molten mush. So on edge, so ready, she kind of wished she'd let them bring her off just to get a little stuffing back in her joints.

She shuddered as she settled on her husband's lap. Just the sheer act of lifting a leg over so as to straddle him had her quivering. Her pussy lips parted with the gesture and that tiny movement had her clit throbbing.

She moaned when a hard cock immediately waited for entrance to her body. It nudged her clit, slid up and down, around and around the wet slit. When Bastien nudged in the tip, she grunted. No matter how wet she was, he was always so fucking wide.

Sucking in a breath, she bore down, pushing her stomach muscles into submission as her entire body went to work on accepting her husband inside. He wasn't *huge*, but she was small. Even after two years of his thick girth.

He lodged the tip in, something that always filled her with relief and had sweat popping out of pores from both of them. It took a few seconds more to simply slide down and lodge him deep.

She shuddered when he was seated inside. Her muscles clamping down, twitching and releasing in an intimate greeting. Now he was there, bound to her, and she collapsed against him, a willing victim to whatever the hell they were about to do to her.

His chuckle sounded loud against her ear, as he murmured something in French to Alex, who immediately laughed. She knew it wasn't *at* her, so she didn't mind. And even if she'd had the energy to chide them for switching to French, she wouldn't have. Bastien always reverted to his mother tongue during sex.

It was his weapon of mass orgasmic destruction.

The instant his grunts and groans, his whispered curses, turned French, she was a goner.

Every single time.

The sounds of their husky mutterings worked their magic on her, as they always did. Everything inside sat up in expectation.

The bed jolted slightly as Alex made his move onto the mattress, and she shuddered as his hand cupped her ass, sliding his callused palm over the silky flesh. His fingers ran down the crevice parting the two cheeks, and she whimpered as his fingers nudged at the pucker resting there.

The sound of liquid flowing was her only warning as cold lube splashed against her ass. Her grumbles were ignored and they were short anyway, as Alex began preparing her for him.

His fingers played with the pucker, spreading it, teasing it before retreating. He'd thrust finger-deep, and then pull all the way out, before thrusting in deep again. A mewl burst free as on one thrust, he pressed down. The move had Bastien hissing too and the pair of them shuddered against each other as Alex went to work.

Tucked against her husband's chest, her legs cupping his waist, she'd never felt safer and more ready to fly off the deep end.

With him here to ground her, and Alex at her back to help her soar, Devvy experienced a deeper sense of belonging than she'd ever known with these two.

Her mind wasn't up to deep, philosophical thinking. But her body knew the difference.

Today, these two men would be hers.

That's all she knew, and her very DNA clamored with it.

Wet with lube, Alex's fingers suddenly slid over the curve of her ass and she felt the bed shift as he pressed forward at a new angle. She knew now was the time and every part of her sang with the knowledge.

His cock head brushed the pucker he'd lovingly prepared. One hand kneaded her ass, while his cock began to nudge muscles aside to demand entry to her most forbidden part.

A thought fluttered through her mind as she waited, on the edge for Alex to take her…Why was it forbidden? And then, there were no more thoughts.

Slowly, but surely, Alex impaled her on his shaft.

It took a while. Every inch was hard-won, because Bastien's girth already filled her to bursting.

There were moments that were uncomfortable. Moments that had tears pricking her eyes and rolling down to dampen Sebastien's shoulders. But they were slow. They took their time and fingers belonging to Sebastien, she imagined, skated between them to caress her clit, as though reminding her of the pleasure to come.

When his shaft was deep in her ass, Alex's low keening cry echoed around the room. The strange pitch trembled along her nerve endings, putting her on edge in a way she couldn't understand.

A flurry of French rebounded between the pair of them. Sounds of grunts and groans, husky laughs and need-filled chuckles told her, without words, the depth of pleasure she was giving her men.

She didn't need the English. She just needed their mother tongue to work its insidious magic on her body.

With Alex finally in deep, rubbing against Bastien in the most intimate of ways, as he slowly pulled out, dragging against tender tissues and adding an incredible amount of pressure deep inside, her mind gave way.

She blew.

There was no fancy light show behind her eyes. No fireworks or fire. No supernova blast.

There was a one-two punch to her nerve endings. A punch so fierce they snapped, and in her very core an implosion had everything sparking.

The only color behind her eyes was blackness. A ceaseless obsidian that sparkled silver at the edges.

The instant Devvy outwardly went lax, inwardly, everything tightened down. Bastien's eyes widened as her pussy clamped around his dick, tighter than before and Alex grunted as her ass did the same.

He moved, thrusting twice, maybe three times, their shafts rubbing against each other through that deliciously thin membrane separating them.

They'd known this kind of pleasure before, but the difference, because it was Devvy, was unsurpassable.

Her laxness was almost worrying until out of nowhere, she reared upward, the momentum almost throwing Alex off, and a low sound, almost a deep roar, escaped her. Her hips started to rock as she fucked herself on the pair of them. Both men watched, in awe, as she did the work, taking herself to the upper limit. Dragging their shafts back and forth in the delicious vice of her cunt and ass, before throwing all of them over a precipice not a one of them had ever visited before.

Chapter Fourteen

The first time Bastien woke up, the clock read eleven thirty. Seeing he was too late to fulfill the blackmailer's requests, he sank back onto the pillow, guilt spearing him like a sword through the gut.

The only thing that made it all bearable was the sight of Alexei and Devvy's entangled limbs.

His lovers were in his bed, in his bedroom, and in his house.

Sebastien wasn't sure if a more satisfying sight even existed. All he knew was that he'd do anything to protect the pair slumbering away like the innocents he knew they weren't.

The second time he awoke, the moonlight pierced the windows of the bedroom and spotlighted the three of them in the bed.

With Devvy's face pressed against his chest, her soft breaths made his nipples hard. At her back, Alexei lay flat but as closely pressed to Devvy as physically possible.

In the large King-size bed, the three of them took up a slither of the available space thanks to their close proximity.

He returned to sleep, content with the knowledge that for the moment, peace reigned.

And after a full twelve hours' rest on their part, just before the alarm went off at six, Sebastien awoke for the third and final time.

The sun had just started to rise, shooting rosy glares through the glass and washing them all in a warm, pink bath of color.

A part of him dreaded actually getting up. The other part called him a fool for not having told the two of them what was going on and what could, potentially, be on today's headlines.

The instant he made it down to the breakfast table, the papers would be waiting for him. And Bastien had a bad feeling in his gut.

Things had been going so well, so smoothly. Devvy had easily accepted Alexei into her heart. All of their dreams had seemed so close to fruition. Bastien knew something had to spoil it.

It was a negative train of thought. Not a track of the mind he was used to taking. In this instance, his relationship was too important for the shit to hit the fan.

He wished, last night, he'd told them. Given them the choice and hastily fulfilled all the blackmailer's demands.

Instead, he'd thought with his cock.

The idea of finally taking Devvy to bed with Alexei there had been too much temptation. How could he have ruined the mood, when they were finally ready to take their relationship to another level?

He couldn't have.

But now, he was paying the price.

And what a price.

His head was aching by the time he made it out of the shower. So bad was the dull thud, he staggered over to the toilet seat and sat down heavily. He tried to rub the back of his neck, tried to ease the tension gathering like storm clouds, but it didn't work. Five minutes later, Devvy found him there. Sat on the toilet, shoulders hunched over, his face twisted with agony.

Instantly recognizing what he was going through, she rushed over and said, "Why didn't you wake me?"

Before he could answer, her hands were there. Rubbing his temples, gently smoothing over the taut flesh and running down over the lumps and bumps of his skull. Her thumbs dug deep either side of his neck, round and round they worked, massaging away the hammer-blows that were still attacking him.

She moved in front of him, standing between his legs for better access and he took advantage. Leaning forward, he rested his head on her belly and whispered, "*J'espere que tu me pardonnes, Devvy.*"

"Hey!" she grumbled. "No French. Not this early, not when I'm fresh out of bed. You're likely to convince me to get back into it, especially at this godforsaken hour. Anyway, what do you need me to forgive you for?"

He grunted. "Your French is improving."

"Not really. You spoke really slowly. But that doesn't bode well, does it? You muttering stuff when you think I won't understand." Her tone was chiding, but tinged with amusement. Her fingers continued their work as she asked, "What's going on? If it's caused this, it really isn't worth it!"

"I'm being blackmailed, Devvy."

She froze. Against his head, her stomach muscles clamped down, removing the warm, giving pillow of her belly. "Why? What have you done?"

"When the first threat came through, it was a threat to tell you about Alexei."

"Oh, well. There's no need to worry about that anymore." Her tone had cheered up a notch. "Considering he was fucking me in the ass last night, I don't think I could *know* him much more!"

"It isn't as simple as that, Devvy. It's highly likely the blackmailer went to the papers."

"*Went?* You mean, it's *fait accompli*? We can't pay the ransom demand?"

He groaned. "I meant to tell you last night. Discuss it with you and then Alexei. I never expected to see the pair of you together, in your salon. The thought of the blackmailer's demands just flew from my mind. You've no idea how hard it is trying to get Alexei to go out! Just seeing him here, with you, together…. My mind just drained itself of other thoughts."

"You mean you could have paid the payoff last night?"

His nod had his head butting against her belly.

She sighed, but her fingers didn't cease to rub tenderly at his head. "Well, we'll just have to deal with the aftermath, won't we?"

"You say that now. But what will you say when the news hits the US? It's bound to! What will your parents say? The papers will likely touch upon my relationship with Alexei!"

"Then, you'll just be confirming the gossip that's already floating about."

He tilted his head back to frown at her. "What do you mean?"

She jerked a shoulder. "I meant to tell you before, but in the scheme of things, it was so unimportant. Mother called me a few weeks ago. She said someone had commented on you and Alexei. She didn't actually say what the gossip was inferring, but reading between the lines, it had to be that the two of you were an item. I just told her you two had a business relationship. She accepted it. I guess this will only confirm it."

Bastien's arms reared up and he embraced her tightly, pulling her legs against his chest and wrapping her tightly in his embrace.

"I'm so sorry, Devvy."

"Don't be," she told him, sounding surprisingly cheerful considering the direness of the situation.

"If your parents suspect I'm gay, they'll expect you to divorce me."

She snorted. "Like that's going to happen. Don't be worrying about that. And if it causes a fallout between my family and me, then there's no love lost there anyway. Christ, it's the excuse I need to break things off.

"Do you realize how often my mother calls me?" she asked, cheerfulness now replaced by a sour note that made him frown.

"Once a month?" he guessed.

"At least once a week. And usually to gripe at me. To bitch. To ask how much I weigh or if I've lost weight. If she sees my picture, she tells me I need to go on a diet or asks why I wore the dress I did. She tells me I need to be careful with you, that I need to watch everything I eat, because I'm not good enough for you, so I have to make sure I'm skinny." She sighed. "Does that sound like something to be missed?"

"You never told me any of that," he snapped.

"It's embarrassing! Of course, I didn't! Do you take me for an idiot? But what could I do? She's my mom. A thirty-minute call, once a week, is endurable. If this breaks the ties, then it breaks the ties. I certainly won't miss her. If anything, it will be a relief. I won't be the one to do it. She'll have to be the one to cut me off. When she does, the fault lies with her."

Bastien shook his head. "I can't believe you're being so blasé about this."

She shrugged. "I don't really have a choice, do I?"

Her wryness made him close his eyes as guilt throbbed through him once more. "This is my fault for thinking with my cock."

"No, it isn't. Blackmailers never stop. Isn't that what they say? You could have paid this bastard last night and he could have still released whatever he's got on us to the press. Alternatively, he could have come back for more.

"That's no way to live our lives. Always looking over our shoulders, waiting for the next ransom demand. The only thing is…how do we tell Alexei?"

Before he could answer, a croaky voice retorted for him, "Consider him told."

A yawn echoed around the bathroom as Alexei stepped in and headed toward the washbasin. Devvy and Bastien watched as, completely unconcerned, Alexei ran the water and gulped up a few mouthfuls. Turning toward them, he jerked a shoulder. "What? I'm okay with it. Hell, it won't affect me either way. You're the one with the corporation, Bastien."

"What about your mother? You saw how she reacted to *me* yesterday. Never mind how she'll react to Bastien!"

Alexei grunted. "Do you think I'll miss those pity visits? We share the same sentiments where our family is concerned, Devvy darling.

"I won't cut the ties, but she can. I'll gladly be free from her." He shuddered. "It's about time anyway. The woman disturbs me."

"That woman is your mother," Bastien told him wryly.

Devvy shook her head. "Yesterday, I'd have agreed with you, Bastien. But she's really weird. I mean, psycho weird. *Hitchcock* weird, you know?"

Alexei chuckled. "It's nice to see I have someone on my side now. Bastien," he retorted, "we're not all lucky to have loving parents who leave us the hell alone and are happy to come together during the holidays."

Devvy grinned. "You're not wrong, Alexei. You *are* fortunate, Bastien. Suzette and Henri are so nice in comparison to my mother and father. Hell, we should invite them here more often." She grimaced. "Well, that is if they're still talking to us after the press opens the door to our lives." She sucked in a breath. "We'll deal with it. We have to. No other choice, is there?"

Her strength astounded him. Bastien let his head drop down to her stomach again and mumbled, "I deserve neither of you. I don't even deserve my parents!"

When Alexei's hand ran through his hair, he trembled a little. "Don't think about what you deserve, Bastien. You're a good man. You love us and you love your parents, even if you're absentminded where they're concerned. You're an easy man to love."

Soft lips pressed against his hair. "He's right, darling. You really are."

Bastien swallowed, ashamed by his sudden urge to cry. He cleared his throat and whispered, "Thank you. Both of you."

"Alexei, why don't you go to the breakfast room and get the papers. They should be on the table by now. Let's see what damage control needs to be done, because it *could* affect *La Belle sans la Bête*, Bastien."

He shrugged. "It doesn't matter. I'm looking to sell anyway."

Devvy sucked in a breath. "And you didn't think to mention that?"

He grimaced. "I need to learn to share more."

Alexei rolled his eyes but laughed. "You've got that right."

Devvy glared at him, and said, "Bring the papers up, Alex. I'll sort out our secretive SOB's migraine."

"Now, now, Devvy. You can't compliment Suzette on the one hand, and then call her a bitch on the other."

Devvy just grunted. "Get the papers, Alexei."

He strode off, cheekily patting Devvy's bare butt as he walked off. He grabbed Bastien's robe and covered himself in its folds before leaving the bathroom. The sounds of his whistling could be heard as he entered the bedroom and started to move down the hall.

"I'll never understand that man," Bastien complained.

"I don't have a hope in hell of understanding him if you don't after all those years together!" She shook her head. "Anyway, you! Don't change the subject. Go and lie on the bed. All your shoulders are knotted. I need you to lie flat to work them out."

Bastien nodded his acquiescence and stood up the instant she moved out of his path. He heard her open some bathroom cabinets as he made his way over to the bed and crawled onto the soft, warm sheets.

He'd have liked to belly flop, but the ensuing wobble of the mattress would have been the final straw to his still-throbbing head.

Sometimes, confessing one's sins didn't help a man atone. Or in this case, a man's body.

Feeling forty years older than he actually was, he spread himself out on the sheets and waited for Devvy to work her magic.

She returned in seconds, carefully climbed onto the bed and settled herself atop his ass.

The sensation of her warm pussy lips rubbing his butt had his cock reacting predictably even in his current state of pain. Grunting at his body's foolhardiness, he tried to ignore his erection as she poured oil down his back.

The torture continued, however. Every time she moved her arms, massaging away his ache, she created another of a different ilk. He wasn't too far gone to feel those soft, silken lips had started to grow moist. Every time her hips rocked, the gentle sway enabling her to rub his shoulders or neck, she'd grow a little wetter.

By the time Alexei returned, his feet padding down the hall, her breathing was soft and flustered.

Little hiccups of sound burst free every time her hips twitched and his cock, already suffering, started to dig a hole in the expensive mattress.

It was either that, or break.

Alexei's soft chuckle sounded from the doorway.

"Well, well, well. Bastien always told me how your massages worked miracles, Devvy. Now, I realize why!"

A soft whooshing sound told Bastien Alexei had removed the robe and that it now lay on the floor. He groaned at the thought of his lover being naked, of the hard-on he'd probably be stroking as he watched the two of them cavort on the bed and all under the guise of a massage.

"Let him roll over, Devvy. I think Bastien needs a different cure for his migraine."

A breathy sigh was her response as she stood on shaky legs on the mattress. When Bastien rolled over, his ruddy-purple dick told a tale of its own, a tale that had Alexei laughing.

"Bastien has another ache, Devvy. Maybe you should massage that away, too."

Bastien grunted as she settled astride him once more, only this time, a little further down.

He'd expected her soft, greased hands to jack him off. But when her mouth supped at the leaking tip of his shaft, he wasn't going to complain.

She licked at the pre-cum gathered there, then popped the glans into her mouth and sucked down. Hard.

His hips reared up off the bed at the sudden pressure. The move had his cock sliding deeper into her mouth, ensuring all of his length was encompassed in that hot, pressurized cavern.

Now, tears really did gather at the corner of his eyes. The need to come was inches away. His climax of the previous night seemed to have occurred a lifetime ago. His balls throbbed, pulling tight into his body with the need for release. When a callused pair of hands fondled them, before grabbing them and twisting roughly, an embarrassing whimper escaped from him.

"Now, now," Alexei cautioned. "Not so fast, Bastien." To Devvy, he said, "Don't let him come too soon, *mignonne.*"

She pulled away from his shaft with a breathy moan.

"If he needs to cum as badly as I do, then you're being cruel, Alex," she told him, her voice high.

"Soothe the ache, *petite.* You're more than welcome to some pleasure. Bastien needs a little punishment, *non*? After all his secrets, he can wait a while longer. It might teach him to be more honest with his lovers!"

Devvy chuckled breathily at Alexei's pithy remark. She climbed higher up Bastien's lap and settled herself so her pussy was an inch away from his cock.

He grunted at the sensation of heat gathered just a few centimeters away and groaned as her hand captured him.

He prayed for the silken cunt that had pleasured him so often during his marriage. Instead, she tortured him. Sliding his cock through the clinging lips of her sex, using his cockhead instead of her fingers to rub her clit. Her panting breaths increased his torture as she used his dick to get herself off.

The sounds reverberated around the room. They were pleasure-filled and so beautiful because of it.

It amazed him that such a dire start to the day had led to this, but he wasn't one to look a gift horse in the mouth.

He let Devvy "punish" him for his secrecy. Hell, it was the least he deserved. Not that his cock agreed.

Her pussy was slippery with her juices as well as his own. Every time she tapped the glans against her clit, or almost breached the gate to her cunt, his heart came close to stopping.

How long she teased him and herself, he didn't know. Only when his breaths had turned into heavy gulps did he contemplate saying something. Then, Alexei moved. Their lover had been quite content to kneel on the bed, hand on his cock, desultorily stroking himself as he watched Devvy tease Bastien.

Almost as though he sensed Bastien's surrender, Alexei moved. Within seconds, Bastien had a cock in his mouth. The shaft's length hit the back of his throat before he could even say, "Please!" And Bastien greedily gobbled the throbbing cock. Sucking and licking, pleasuring and torturing with little nips, hard sucks and flicks of his tongue.

For a minute, he was distracted. Then, Devvy moved.

He felt his cock head at her cunt, felt the glorious pressure as she struggled to accept his girth. The amount of times he'd almost come from that alone, her body's acceptance of him, was a joke. That tight pressure had him closing his eyes and grunting as she worked herself on him, slowly impaling herself on his cock.

Her frustrated cries and high mewls told their own tale. She had little patience, did Devvy. It was usually why he was in control of penetration. The few times she'd ridden him, she'd managed to burst into tears before she'd managed to get his cock inside her. This time wasn't much different.

With implosion imminent, it was with relief that her cunt finally accepted him. She slid down, taking all of him in, and crying aloud at the sensation.

His groan vibrated along Alexei's shaft, causing him to cry out too.

The sounds were a delicious accompaniment to the sexual tableau occurring on the bed.

His eyes were closed, the bright light of the morning making them ache. But blindness just enhanced all of his other senses.

His ears rang with the sounds of their pleasure. His nose was filled with the earthy scent of Alexei's cock, and in the background, the sweet, floral essence of Devvy's juices teased his sense of smell.

He could taste Alexei's musk. That unique scent that triggered thousands of memories. Some sexual, some sweet. All loving. The pleasure of those sensory memories made his hands fist. When he released, and pressed his fingers between Devvy's legs, intent on touching her clit and driving her to madness of a different nature, one that had nothing to do with anger or irritation, he felt the slippery slide of her skin against his. That silk was softer than the robe she wore after her shower. It was sleeker than the softest velvets and more satiny than the most tender of flower petals.

A sudden groan from Alexei dragged him from his thoughts. Combine it with Devvy's fingers nudging his, their slickness telling him half a tale, he opened his eyes, curious to see why Alexei's groans had grown deeper, harder.

He saw that Alexei had moved. No longer astride his shoulders, simply fucking his face. Now, he'd toppled over onto his hands and knees, giving him a perfect view of Alexei's dangling balls and a slender hand moist with her own juices, making mischief with their lover's butt.

From nowhere, Alexei began to fuck his mouth. His hips bucked, sliding his shaft into Bastien's throat.

As cum spewed from the tip, Alexei's groans turned into degenerative grunts, while Devvy milked him for all he was worth.

The panting sounds of Alexei's endless orgasm combined with the tangy taste of his lover's cum, had Bastien's own hips rocking. He fucked Devvy, not waiting for her to once again take control. He slammed his butt into the bed and thrust. She sobbed as he pulled out, then fucked her deeply, going in to the hilt.

Three more thrusts like that and she shrieked, a fourth one combined with her clamped-down muscles, and release poured through him, too.

As ecstasy ricocheted behind his eyes, erasing any and all traces of pain from his head, he grunted with relief. When Alexei finally moved away, taking his cock with him and emptying Bastien's mouth, he whispered, "I think we've discovered another way to get rid of my migraines."

The comment had Devvy and Alexei sniggering. Bastien was too damned tired to do more than grin.

As his orgasm freed him from the earlier tension, burning away the shadowy memories with fiery-hot blasts of delight, he sank deeply into the bed and allowed himself to relax.

When she lifted her leg and slipped his shaft free from her cunt, a small, nameless sound worked at the back of his throat. It quivered down into a sigh when the two of them curled up either side of him, tucking themselves against his body.

He'd always known that he'd be the foundation of such a relationship. Be it because he was the partner who had brought the trio together, or simply because of his age. But these two were his to love, his to protect.

He'd done a piss-poor job of it by not paying the blackmailer, even though deep down he'd never wanted to pay the ransom. As Devvy had said, that was no way to live a life. Forever waiting for the next demand.

When he had the strength to actually move, sit up and read the headlines, he knew he was ready for whatever hit him.

He had to be. It was his job to safeguard these two.

He sighed at the thought, one that filled him with pleasure rather than irritation. There was nothing else he wanted to do, nowhere else he wanted to be than here. Right at this minute.

When he considered all the euros he had in the hundreds of banks around the world, none if it held any value in comparison to this. The fruition of a long held dream, where reality was sweeter than the original aspiration.

A stubbled jaw rasped against his arm, jerking him from his thoughts. Alexei's silent nudge made him sigh. "Go on, *cher.* Hit me with it."

He grunted. "It's both worse and better than we thought."

"Straightaway, it's pretty damned shit. That means there's definitely something in the papers!" Devvy complained, although she didn't sound too perturbed. He watched her sit up, noticed the delightful sway of her tits as she moved. His mouth watered, but he pushed the spark of arousal to the sidelines. Now was not the time.

Even if his cock didn't agree.

It was probably a sign of what this woman did to him. Without even meaning to, she switched his attention from a major calamity and reverted it to herself, and the delight he found in her.

The papers rustled as she read the headlines, and with a sigh, he focused on the article. "Well, I don't understand all of it."

Alexei snorted. "I need to enroll you in a French course. Either that, or coerce you with sex to learn it."

She blew a raspberry. "Some of us can't walk on water, Saint Alexei!"

"*Enfants, enfants*!" Bastien chided.

Devvy chuckled. "I understood *that!*" She rubbed his leg. "Like I said, I don't understand the headline, but the picture says it all. Honey, you didn't have a hope in hell of stopping the blackmailer from releasing this. One of the pictures is from yesterday afternoon. It's of Alexei and me coming into the house."

At that, Bastien frowned. He shot up, relieved that the action didn't have his head pounding, and grabbed the paper.

Ménage Material read the headline. He grimaced as he sloughed through the text, reading gossip and rumor, all of it libelous.

"You'll make a pretty penny out of the libel court," Alex remarked.

"Like we need more money!" Devvy retorted, leaning over to slap her hand down on Alex's calf.

"You can give it to your favorite charity," he defended himself. "My foundation is always in need of more donations."

"One of your better ideas, Alex," he told him and turned to page three, where more pictures could be found.

There was a picture of "Madame Jacques" entering the building where "Monsieur Ivanov's" mother lived. Another picture of Sebastien and Alexei at a charity function, stood beside each other as they watched over the event. They'd never hidden their relationship from the press, nor had they made anything public. The shadowy depths of their partnership enabled the papers to form an opinion of their own and create a slant that suited the headline.

"At least they haven't come out and called you gay, Bastien," Alexei said. "I mean, that would be a lot worse for Devvy, wouldn't it?"

Devvy grimaced. "Let me see, I can be painted as the poor wife, having to endure a cheating husband's affairs. And not just with other women, but *men*! Or I can be a slatternly wife, too greedy just to have the one man in her bed. I need two!" She paused a second, obviously thinking her words through.

The minute she laughed, Bastien felt faint with relief.

She climbed onto her knees and knelt in front of them, bold, proud, and uncaring of her nudity. She clapped her hands in delight. "Oh yes, I far prefer this angle. I can't wait to hear what my mother has to say." Devvy grinned. "She can hardly accuse me of being unattractive now, can she? I've got two men in my bed!" She rubbed her hands together. "And not just any men. Sebastien Jacques *and* Alexei Ivanov!"

"I think she's far too happy about this," Alexei commented wryly.

Bastien shot him a quelling look. "Don't complain," he muttered under his breath in French.

Alex shook his head, a wide grin creasing his jaw. "I'm not," he told him. "Look at her, she's brimming with confidence."

"Stop talking in French, you two!" she complained, her head bowed over the papers. "Don't you know it's rude?"

"In fairness, *petite*, we can't always help it," Bastien told her softly, tugging the second paper from her hands to study its contents.

A La Belle sans la Bête Marriage Or Merger? read the next headline. The article following this one was far more cautious, not as libelous and damaging, even though they had mentioned the company.

The pictures were the same, although they'd dug up a few from five years ago, when Bastien and Alexei hadn't exactly separated, but had taken a time out from one another. There was nothing blatant about the image, but Bastien was surrounded by men in a nightclub filled with men and a handful of women. Where the hell they'd managed to get such a photo, he wasn't entirely sure. That was probably more damning than the other pictures put together!

Alexei, thanks to never going out, was relatively unscathed from the photographic attack. Aside from the pictures of his and Devvy's visit to his mother's apartment and their entering *Les Fenêtres*, that was it.

He grimaced at the picture of him in the gay nightclub. "The one time I even go into such a place and some fucker took a photo."

"Should I be jealous?" Alexei asked, brow cocked as he studied the photo.

"Hardly!" Bastien snapped. "That was the time I went to London, remember? For that conference. The one where, the night before, you decided you needed some space." He glared at Alex, still affronted by the memory. "Space! God, we've never even lived together and he asked me for space," he complained to Devvy, who merely patted him on the knee.

Alex grunted and reached for the two final papers. He glanced through the articles, looked at the photos, and sighed. "I think we are relatively safe. Although, it's unusual for each paper to have the same shots of yesterday, *non*? They're hardly exclusives."

"I don't know. That's the only way they can infer something's going on. They've made a big deal out of the fact my wife was visiting your mother. And that the two of you are holding hands."

Devvy snorted. "I didn't realize because I'm married, I wasn't allowed to go into other people's mother's homes! For all they know, we could be friends!"

"The images are hardly damaging, Devvy," Alex told her. "It's all fabricated anyway. The only reason it's in some of the more conservative papers and not just the gossip rags is because of Bastien's position. Plus, the fact I'm a recluse. This will all blow over, especially when Bastien sues them for damages."

"As long as my mother can't handle the shame, that's all that matters." She rubbed her hands together again, suddenly looking very bloodthirsty. "I was rather looking forward to being banished."

When he and Alex shook their heads, she just grinned. "Liberation, *mes chers*. Crossing the Atlantic didn't do it. It just took you two to corrupt me."

With that, she bounced over, presenting them both with a delicious image of her jiggling tits, pressed kisses to both their mouths, and then leapt off the bed.

Her direction, the bathroom.

Her intention, to start her day.

Her mood, jubilant.

Bastien realized no matter how long he lived, he would never understand women. More importantly, Devvy would never cease to stop surprising him.

Chapter Fifteen

"Hmm?" Devvy muttered into the phone as she looked down at her notes and highlighted a formulaic error in the recipe for her anti-acne soap.

She'd finally settled on a reason why the tea tree oil and witch-hazel combination was drying out the skin and wanted to test out the concoction with reduced levels of tea tree oil but with an added extra—salicylic acid, which would help with acne breakouts. She was also interested in a recent study that indicated thyme, the herb, could also help treat acne, and one of her new tweaked recipes included the herb oil.

With Alex working at her back, the mood in his salon was studious. Her mind was focused on her formulae, this morning's headline drama well-forgotten.

"Devvy?"

Bastien's voice had her smiling as she added another note to the margin of her recipe. "Hey, sweetie. You don't usually call so early."

"No."

The one word answer finally got her full attention. She frowned, her eyes flickering over to Alex as he worked on his huge-ass whiteboard in the lounge of his penthouse. As soon as they'd breakfasted this morning at *Les Fenêtres*, Bastien had gone out to face the world, and shoving two fingers up at society and the potential photographers following them, Devvy and Alex had returned to the penthouse. With a lot less drama than yesterday's excursion, too.

It had taken Alex only five minutes to work up the courage to cross the threshold. Twice, he'd tried to turn back, but she'd persevered and walked him to the car. Shutting him in before he could jump out and rush into the house again.

She wanted him there on a full-time basis, but not because he was stuck. She wanted him to *want* to be there.

That wasn't too much to ask, was it?

Snorting at the thought, she murmured, "Is everything okay, honey?"

For a second, Devvy thought her husband was crying. Considering she'd never seen or heard him being anything less than strident, *strong,* in control of himself and the others around him, Devvy found it hard to imagine. Not that she would have judged him for showing his emotions. Hell, she'd have inwardly celebrated, seeing it as being a step forward in their relationship.

What with the blackmail and Sebastien finally telling them the news that he was interested in pulling out of *La Belle sans la Bête*, it was safe to say he wasn't a natural *sharer*.

"What's the matter?" she asked, starting to get concerned at the prolonged silence, and the faint muffled sounds of what she thought was him crying.

Sebastien wasn't the sort to just call and then say nothing. Everything had a purpose. He was too busy to waste time on meaningless phone calls.

Alex's back was to her, his study on the whiteboard fierce as he glared at the mumble-jumbled mass of letters, words, and numbers.

She managed to stand and make it out of the room without disturbing him or attracting his attention.

The instant she made it into the kitchen, she grabbed the kettle, turned on the tap, and filled it. Using the sound of running water to cover her, she asked, "It's something to do with the blackmailer, isn't it?"

A harsh breath was her only reply and then, her earlier suspicions were confirmed as Bastien finally retorted, his words thick with tears, "Yes."

"I didn't think he'd get in touch so soon." She shook her head at her naiveté, because when else would there be a better time? With all of them having to deal with the repercussions of today's headlines, when better to remind them of what the fucker was capable of doing. "What is it? Another threat? Or a demand? What?"

More silence.

Knowing that whatever the sick fuck who was intent on playing with their lives for monetary gain wanted was bad enough to drive her stalwart husband to tears had Devvy feeling sick.

At the same time, she knew if Sebastien was weak, she had to be strong. Just like he was strong, when she was the frail one.

She couldn't afford to snap at him, demand he talk to her. She had to be patient.

This was the first time he'd come to her with a real problem. It was the first time he'd needed her. She didn't want to let him down.

"Talk to me, sweetheart," she told him, her voice low. With the kettle overflowing, she turned off the faucet and switched it on. The sounds of the machine working replaced the water.

Whatever it was, she felt sure it had to do with Alexei. For Sebastien to call her and not come to the apartment to speak with them both, the threat had to revolve around their absentminded genius. She needed Alexei's attention to remain fixed on his work, while she dealt with the repercussions of whatever Bastien had to say.

"I didn't know," he muttered eventually. "Nineteen years together, nearly twenty, and he never told me."

Rather than ask what Alexei had never shared, she murmured, "Whatever's been sent through might be lies. You can't automatically trust in the words of a blackmailer."

Bastien released a shuddering breath. "I hope to God it's not true. But they were right about Alex and me."

She scoffed, "A friend of my parents over in the US was spreading gossip about the two of you. You might have managed to keep your relationship on the down-low for a long time, but word still spread. You know what they say, there's no smoke without fire."

"Exactly. That's what frightens me the most," he rasped. "Threatening to out the pair of us…it was something I might pay blackmail money for, just so I could protect my marriage, my good name.

"This is different. This is…it has to be the truth. Asking Alexei would immediately provide me with the answer."

"Not if the blackmailer worded it in such a way as to tug at your heartstrings, make you want to protect him," she pointed out. "And what have you done? You called me, not him. If it was as easy as asking him, you'd have done it already."

"I don't dispute that, but think about what you just said. Our relationship, Alex and I, that was slander. The threat had no real base. Outside of my wanting to protect my name and my marriage.

"This is…you're right, it's worded to make me want to protect him. Why, if I weren't in a relationship with him, would I want to protect him? Why would I care enough to pay off this fucker?"

Devvy's stomach started to churn at his reasoning. "You're saying that he wasn't guessing, when he made the original threat. He *knew* you were together."

"Exactly. If he knew that, then why shouldn't this be true?"

She nibbled her lip. "Can you tell me what *this* is?"

"*Dieu,* Devvy. The threat…it says Alex was abused as a child. Raped by his mother's partner. For years," he breathed, sounding on the verge of sobbing. "Years!"

For a second, the words didn't penetrate. She stood, in Alexei's kitchen, another expanse of space filled only with the basic requirements to make the room a cooking space.

More minimalism.

As the words sank in, Devvy thought back to that first time they'd slept together. When, out of nowhere, Alex had had a panic attack. When he'd curled on the floor, as naive and as frightened as a child. The next morning, vowing to share his *secret* with her someday. She looked back to her own reaction to his mother's odd behavior…

She thought of the open, empty spaces of his penthouse. His need for freedom. Yet, his inability to leave the penthouse. His safe zone. Where no one could touch him. Where he was perpetually safe.

Devvy was no psychologist, but she was pretty damned certain child abuse could explain a lot of this away.

"Devvy?" Bastien asked, smashing through her thoughts like a hammer slammed through the icy covering of a lake in winter. "*Mignonne?*"

"What do they want?" was all she said, not sure if she could even talk about this until she'd processed what it meant.

What the ramifications were.

Alexei's obsession with finding a third, someone he considered untarnished and capable of loving Bastien the right way.

This morning wasn't the first time she'd heard mentions of Alexei breaking the two of them up in the past. Bastien had said he'd been heading out on business, when Alexei had called wanting a break…

The way he distanced himself from them. Hiding in his lab, when he ought to have been with them.

His relationship with his mother…her obsessive ways and his veiled scorn of who and what she was as a person.

A ragged sob tore through the kitchen. It was timed perfectly with the climactic whistle of the kettle. It covered the sound and enabled her to sag against the kitchen counter, before slowly sliding down to the floor.

In her gut, deep down, she knew this was true.

She prayed to God she was wrong. She'd pay off the blackmailer, pay him millions to keep something like this hidden, and wouldn't care if it was all lies. She hoped it was. But she knew it wasn't.

Alex thought the two of them were similar, because they shared similar backgrounds educationally. They'd both been raised in classes where their so-called peers were a good two, three, or four years older than they. They'd both had to survive in an adult world at too young an age. They'd both mastered their sciences, and were at the top of their game.

And while Devvy had her little quirks, like hating the mornings and never wanting to get out of bed, they were nothing in comparison to the systematic routines Alex had.

"You believe the threat, don't you?" Sebastien whispered down the line, his voice strangled.

"You do, too," she retorted, knowing Sebastien had followed the same reasoning as she herself had. Reasoning that made it very easy to believe Alexei had been sexually abused as a child.

"I do, God help me. I keep thinking, if it were true, then he'd have told me. But he wouldn't. I know him. This explains so much and leaves me with nothing but questions."

She sucked in a breath. "You never told me what the bastard wants."

"For us to stew. He or she will contact me in five days' time."

"The only thing he can do is threaten to release the news to the press. It's all well and good dealing with the aftermath of today's headlines. But I'm not having him go through it all again. He's kept it a secret for so damned long. He obviously doesn't want it to define him.

"On top of that, the invasion of privacy…we'll be lucky if we ever get him out of the penthouse again! This time, we'll pay. Whatever it takes. "

"I agree, but what if this time the blackmailer doesn't want money?"

Frowning, Devvy asked, “Why should that have changed? That’s what all blackmailers want, right? Money!”

“This is different, Devvy.”

“How can you say that?” she snapped.

“Stop thinking with your heart, dammit,” he griped. “Think logically. You’re right. Alex has kept this a secret. So secret even I don’t know about it. So, who does know? Who could know?”

“The abuser. It has to be him. Or, maybe somebody in Child Protection Services. The abuse must have been reported. I mean, surely his mother…?” Devvy hesitated. “She would have found out, right?”

A long, shuddery sigh blew down the phone. “I have a small file here. If it is someone in Child Protection Services, then they would have access to this information. But why sit on this info for so long? Alex made his money a long time ago. Why not go to the source? Why come to me?”

“I don’t know.”

“There’s too much about all of this we don’t know. According to this file, the abuser’s dead. Saves me going after him and castrating him, I suppose.” He hissed as though the idea of missing out irritated him.

For the first time, non-violent, pacifist, and peace-loving Devvy entirely agreed. She’d always known that everybody had a trigger, something that would free them from the cage society’s mores bound them in, and set them loose.

The idea of Alex, her amazing, astounding lover, being abused as a little boy…. Put a knife in her hand and she would have done some damage.

Serious damage.

And she wouldn’t have felt an iota of guilt.

This entire situation, the revelations and then the waiting…. Devvy didn’t like where her thoughts were leading her. She didn’t like what was popping into her head.

All she kept seeing was Alex’s mother yesterday. How she’d hovered and doted on her son. How she’d obsessed over the tiniest things. How each time Alex had made a veiled insult, she’d flinched as though mortally wounded.

How could a woman, so obsessed with her son, so meticulous and so aware of him, fail to spot the signs her child was being abused.

The only answer Devvy could come up with was Antoinette hadn't failed.

She prayed she was jumping to conclusions. But what part of this situation didn't make a person do that?

Devvy remembered her parents being entirely unaware that for most of fifth grade, Rosie Simmons had been her tormentor. At six to Rosie's eleven, with nearly twenty pounds of weight difference between them, Devvy's suffering had only come to an end when a teacher had discovered Rosie doing what Rosie did best during recess. Using Devvy as a human cushion.

Until the school had notified her family, her mom and dad hadn't had a clue. She was certain that was the same for a lot of kids, where bullying was concerned. Even more so for those who were being sexually abused. Parents tended to find out too late to protect their children and then were ridden with guilt at not having spotted the signs.

She tried to imagine Antoinette not spotting the signs and knew that if the woman could notice the button on Alex's cuff was loose, go so far as to offer to stitch it back on while they were having coffee, then she'd notice her child's withdrawal as he was abused by someone who should have protected him, someone his mother had brought into the household.

"What are you thinking, Devvy?"

Closing her eyes, she whispered, "Horrible things."

"This is a horrible situation to be in, *chérie*. If he'd told us, instead of keeping it a damned secret, we could have regrouped.... I don't know, be dealing with the actual threat rather than the repercussions of his secrets."

"Hey! Don't say it like that. He has every right to keep this to himself. There's nothing in the relationship handbook that says every single secret has to be out in the open."

He grunted. "Don't be ridiculous, Devvy. Things like this can't be kept hidden. They're too huge. They're bound to have an effect on the relationship as a whole, which, in this instance, it sure as hell has! Twenty years and I still haven't shared a roof with him!" he blasted.

"Did you know when I was seven, I was bullied? Or that in tenth grade, when I was twelve and my classmates were nearly sixteen, Lewis Goodman tried to grope me?" Silence whistled down the line. "No. You didn't. I didn't tell you. I'm sure there is something you haven't told us. That's your right.

"It isn't your right to start blaming Alex for protecting himself against something that should never have happened to him. So, before we confront him with this, you need to get your head in the right place. You need to cool off."

"What do you mean confront him? We can't let him know about this new threat!"

She snorted. "We have to tell him, Bastien. We can't hide this from him. He has a right to be involved, to know that his history is being used as a pawn in some fucker's sick game. I won't hide this from him," she warned.

"I can't confront him about this, Devvy. I just can't."

"You have to. You have to support him, to let him know this doesn't change things between us."

"Of course it changes things!" he snapped.

She stiffened. "You can't mean that."

Bastien groaned. "Not in the way you're thinking. I love the infuriating bastard as much as I ever do. I wish the fucker who abused him was alive so I could go and kill him. I'd spend twenty years in prison to avenge him. But I can't sit there and let him know I know about his past, when he wasn't the one to share it with me.

"You said it yourself. He's kept this from us. Not once did he ever say or do anything that might have led me to believe this happened to him. I can't watch him crumple, when he finds out I know."

"I'd share the cell with you if I could," was all she said, after taking a second to process his words.

A strained chuckle was her reward. "You're not supposed to make me laugh. This is serious," he chided with a sigh.

"Who's not being serious? I'd kill the fucker, too. And I understand. I'll tell him, but there's something I want to do first."

"What?"

"We've got five days until we hear from the blackmailer. As long as I tell him we know and what's being threatened before then, it's okay. And I want to go and visit his mother."

Sebastien blew out a breath. "You…" He paused. "You think she knew about his abuse?"

"You should have seen her yesterday, Bastien. You wouldn't have believed her. She was totally obsessed. She watched him, constantly. It was unnerving. The attention she gave him. I never realized how focused someone could be on someone else.

"I swear to God, she only looked away to blink! It's no wonder he can't stand being there. It was the creepiest thing I've ever seen. How could she not know what her son was going through, when she pays that amount of attention to him?"

"She might not have been like that when Alex was younger."

"You think that kind of behavior happens overnight?" Devvy glared down at the white tiles beneath her feet. "Bull. If this is true, if what that file says is true, then she can confirm it before I go to Alex about this."

"I hope to God she says it's all lies."

Devvy's sigh juddered out of her. "So do I, *cher.* So do I."

Disconnecting the call was tough. She wanted to remain connected to Bastien, needed his silent support and understanding. Shell-shocked, before it had become a cliché, was the only way to describe the way they were both feeling.

In the end, Sebastien's PA called him and he muttered into the phone, "I'll see you later, *mignonne.*" Before the phone cut off and before she could return the sentiment, he whispered, "*Je t'aime.*"

The phone felt like a ticking time bomb in her hand and she shoved it onto the kitchen table and backed away from it as though it could explode any minute. The phone wasn't at fault, but still, she wasn't feeling very rational at the moment.

Her hands shook as she switched on the faucet and ran the cold water over her wrists. She felt hot, nauseated and trembly, like she'd just run a marathon and was on the verge of collapse. Those emotions magnified at the prospect of actually exiting the kitchen and returning to the lounge.

The door became the next ticking time bomb, and it took her a good ten minutes to actually approach the jamb. Crossing the threshold was the hardest thing Devvy had ever had to do. She knew it would be the first of many hardest moments in the upcoming days, but this one still felt like flying to the moon in her nightgown.

She wanted to go over to him, wrap him up in her arms, and just love that little hurt boy inside him. But he wasn't a little boy anymore. He'd think she was trying to initiate sex, and that was the last thing she wanted at the moment. Especially as she couldn't actually tell him why she wanted to hug the breath out of him.

Eyes burning with tears she couldn't let fall, she returned to the lounge, and was eternally grateful that he was still stuck in his studies.

She managed to sneak back in, lounge back on the sofa, and pretend she hadn't just learned Alexei had been molested as a child.

Yeah, like that would be easy. Or even possible!

Devvy sat there and stared into space for only God knew how long. Around her, the squeak of Alexei's pen, the muttered curses he mumbled under his breath as he worked, the otherwise silent atmosphere all signified that the world hadn't come to a standstill for this momentous moment.

Her world had. And so had Bastien's.

Learning of something like this about a partner's past, yeah, it was supposed to stun. And you were supposed to feel a strange guilt, as well as empathy, sympathy, and pity. The whole gamut of emotions. That was the way it was supposed to be.

But this?

It explained so goddamn much.

Bastien had once labeled Alexei as quirky. He wasn't. He was disturbed. Repressed. Locked in tight and unable to free himself.

After all this time, decades had passed since his infancy, yet he still couldn't share it with the man he loved. Potentially, he hadn't shared it with anyone. She only hoped his psychiatrist knew. It meant that someone in his life was trying to deal with and heal that part of his past.

His inability to share his secrets was worrisome. Yes, it affected their relationship, because if he could hide this, what else could he hide? But that was a secondary issue and unimportant in the scheme of things. Both her lovers were, by nature, remote. They didn't share their emotions easily. In truth, their emotional intelligence was nil!

What concerned her was how he would ultimately react to finding out they knew about his secrets.

He'd said, the morning after their first night together, he'd tell her his secrets. Eventually. And she believed him. She believed, when the time was right and he was comfortable, he would have told her, and she knew this was the secret that had had him launching off the bed like he'd been shocked with a cattle prod and screwing himself up into a ball on the floor.

If he'd had the chance to share this with her, he'd have been in control. Alex liked to be in control.

In this instance, he wouldn't be the master of the situation. Devvy could only see things going downhill fast.

"You were gone a long time."

Alex's offhand comment jerked her from her thoughts. "Huh?" she asked, not really retaining what he was saying. Her eyes flickered from the sofa's linen covering and over to him. "What did you say?"

"You were gone a long time," he repeated patiently.

"Where?"

"The kitchen."

"Oh!" She blinked. Her gaze dropped down to her watch and she saw that at least forty minutes had passed since she'd staggered into the lounge. Trust Alex to notice but to comment after the fact. "I had something to eat," she lied, hating the untruth yet unable to share the real reason behind her long stay in the kitchen.

"I thought Bastien called."

"He did."

Alex rolled his eyes. "What did he want? Is everything okay?"

"Oh. Yeah, everything's fine." Christ, Devvy! Could she be more inane? "He said he's set the company's attorneys onto the papers."

Another lie. But founded on the truth. She knew that particular task would have been the first on his agenda today.

"My cancer foundation could do with the funds," he remarked.

"Sure. Whatever we win will go to fight the cause." Devvy's smile was strained.

"Are you all right, *chérie*?" Alex asked, taking a step away from the whiteboard and plugging the lid back on his marker pen. He strode over to the sofa, climbed over the back, and pushed himself in the small space between her and the cushions. "You look sad."

It was a relief to touch him, to have him squished so closely to her. He reached for her hand and tucked his fingers between hers. When he squeezed, it was almost as though he'd squeezed the tears out. She burst into sobs, the racking, whooping, convulsive waves of weeping just exploded out of her. She didn't wait, she jumped up, straddled his thighs and threw herself against his chest, trusting him to take her in his arms and hold her close.

He did just that, and in French, and sounding extremely confused, started to murmur soft whispers in her ear. That *he* was soothing *her* felt so unjust. She should be cradling him. She should be the one tending to him. But the tears just wouldn't stop. They left her trembling, a quivering mess on his lap, and they only ceased to fall when exhaustion hit her first.

The gasps that came in the aftermath of her sobs left her even more tired. He said nothing, asked no questions, but she sensed his perplexity and ignored it, unable to come up with an adequate lie as to why she'd gone from happy to sobbing after speaking with Sebastien. He let silence reign, only clucking his tongue or humming to soothe her. She let him rearrange her limbs, felt no surprise as he stood with her clutching limply to him and strode out of the lounge. When seconds later, he laid her down on the bed and climbed beside her, she immediately latched onto him, tucking her head underneath his chin and taking comfort from his scent.

When tiredness threatened to keel her over, to put an end to this sorry scene, she mumbled against his Adam's apple, "I love you."

As she said the words, only then did she realize how deeply she actually did love him. With all her heart and soul, and down to her bone marrow.

This was her man, and she'd protect him with her last breath.

Chapter Sixteen

Staring up at Antoinette Ivanov's apartment building, Devvy squinted as the afternoon sun reflected off the polished glass balustrades lining the balconies and the rays cascaded into her own personal lightshow. The bursts of sun were temporarily tattooed on her retinas as she finally crossed the busy road and made it onto the building's side of the street.

Either side of her, polished perfection made her feel even more uneasy. The pavement had large rectangles of lawn adorning the curb, and each expanse of grass looked as though it had been hand cut with a pair of scissors.

A few steps away, the concierge's glass walls showed her tousled and messy reflection. She'd gone to sleep in Alex's arms, woken up without disturbing him from his own rest, and come directly here.

The minute she'd awoken, she'd needed to have some answers. Waiting until tomorrow was like asking for a decade to pass. She had to know *now* if this blackmail attempt was a lie or if it was the truth. And asking Alex was totally out of the question. There was no way she could that to him, especially if the blackmailer's information was, God forbid, correct.

Devvy sucked in a breath, seeking the strength to go through with this interview. She just knew Antoinette was going to be a pain in the ass. She sensed that getting answers from her was going to be tougher than getting blood out of a stone.

She had to stay calm. She had to put the old witch at ease. Otherwise, she'd never find anything out, and Christ, she had to *know*.

Striding into the concierge, she smiled as the same woman from yesterday sat behind the desk. Smiling was the last thing she felt like doing, but Devvy had to play this role. Striding in there like Joan of Arc, demanding answers, demanding to know why Antoinette hadn't done more to protect her son wasn't the way forward.

The prospect of grabbing Alex's mother by the shoulders and shaking her, just shaking and shaking and shaking until the answers spilled from the older woman's mouth, was infinitely pleasing.

She ignored it, pushed it away, and brightened her smile as the concierge stood, neat as a pin in her uniform, and returned the smile. She made Devvy feel all the more unkempt, but by God, what the hell did appearances matter when she had important issues to deal with?

"Madame Ivanov is expecting her son. He's just parking the car," she lied.

The woman nodded, picked up her phone and dialed the connection to Antoinette's room. Devvy's French was limited, but even she could understand the woman as she told Antoinette her son and his companion were waiting to be invited up to the apartment.

The older woman's excitement literally throbbed down the line.

The concierge smiled again and nodded. "She is waiting for you. I'll send Monsieur Ivanov up, when he comes in."

"*Merci*," Devvy murmured, already on her way to the elevator.

As the doors closed behind her, she keyed in the floor number and waited to be spat out onto Antoinette's story. Seconds later, she was walking down the corridor and Antoinette was standing in the doorjamb, a huge smile creasing her jaw.

A smile that disintegrated as Devvy neared.

"Where is Alexei?" she demanded.

"He's parking the car. The concierge says she'll send him up when he comes in."

Antoinette eyed her suspiciously, and Devvy knew, if she hadn't used that excuse, there wasn't a snowball in hell's chance of being invited into the apartment. Only the threat of Alexei finding his girlfriend waiting out in the hall made his mother move away and allow Devvy to enter.

"It's busy out there. God knows where he'll have to park," Devvy stated, perpetuating the lie. "Do you have some water, please, *madame*?"

Eyes on the corridor, Antoinette ignored her. Devvy rolled her eyes at the woman's back, and took it upon herself to go into the same room as she'd been led into yesterday. She didn't bother to go out on the terrace. The instant Alex didn't stride down that corridor, Antoinette would be in here like a shot, demanding to know what the hell was going on.

She looked around the room, grimacing at the stuffy and fussy interior. The same flowery fabric, a hideous shade of ochre and fuchsia, had been used for all of the soft furnishings. On the back wall, there was a picture of Christ weeping. A crucifix sat above the modern mantelpiece, a fixture that looked out of place in the old-fashioned lounge. She had little statuettes dotted all over the room, ornaments that Devvy considered dust collectors. Pieces that held little to no value, outside of emotional.

The room suited the woman.

Uncomfortable.

Knowing it was cheeky and not caring, because Christ, she needed the boost, Devvy walked over to Antoinette's drinks tray and poured herself a small measure of whisky. She sank it back, and then poured herself another two fingers, and swallowed that as well.

The burn at her throat made her want to hop up and down to relieve the fire. Instead, her sore eyes watered all the more, and she started to cough.

By the time her coughing fit was over, Antoinette was striding into the room, glare glued in place, demanding to know, "Where is my son? It does not take this long to park, unless he has decided to drive over into the next arrondissement!"

"I lied. He isn't coming," Devvy told her easily.

Antoinette scowled. "What do you mean he isn't coming? Why on earth would you be here otherwise?"

"I wanted to ask you a question."

"Well, I'm afraid I'm short of answers."

"Tough shit," Devvy hissed, ignoring Antoinette's gasp of outrage, as well as her earlier vow to be calm and pleasant. "I have questions in need of answering, and you're the only one who can give them to me."

As Devvy took in Antoinette, she shook her head at the sour look being aimed her way. Where Alex was concerned, she was all sweetness and light.

Dressed head to toe in black again, her hair was neatly tucked in a bun. Two chopsticks kept the tight roll pinned to her head. She wore a black, calf-length skirt, and a black blouse with a pussy bow. It was way too hot to be wearing the arm-length sleeves, but Devvy supposed the air con blasting out at polar temperature was keeping Antoinette from sweating.

At around thirteen, in an effort to please her mother, Devvy had attempted to read more fictional novels. Sneaking the books her mother had read so as to have something to talk about with her parent. A fan of romantic suspense, as well as her beloved Georgette Heyer, Devvy was quite accustomed to the book's bad guy being described as having an insane glint in his eye.

Technically, Antoinette wasn't insane. She was extremely odd, incredibly peculiar, but not insane. Christ, Devvy and Alex were hardly the leaders of the board of normality! But, for the first time in her life, after having scoffed at some of her mother's favorite authors for dismissing and excusing the bad guy's behavior with wicked, crazy looks, Devvy could understand.

That sour look shot her way wasn't merely displeasure. It was…vacant. It was disturbing. She looked like she was quite capable of sitting down to tea after murdering a kitten or something.

The thought made Devvy shake her head at her own foolishness. She was freaking herself out and for no reason at all.

But still…. She'd seen it yesterday and recognized it as being *not right*. Today, it was confirmed, and all the more evident without Alex to buffer the situation.

She didn't feel in danger, just on edge. Discomforted by the weirdness the other woman seemed to radiate.

When Devvy continued to stare at Antoinette, not backing down, the other woman pursed her lips and bit out, "Well, what kind of questions?"

"Was Alex happy as a boy?"

The question disarmed her. A soft smile graced her lips, her thoughts obviously on the son with whom she was so besotted. "He was such a serious boy. So studious. As he grew older, he only got worse."

"Worse in what way?"

Antoinette frowned. "He's a genius. It wasn't unusual for him to be secretive."

"About what?" she asked, feeling like she was pulling teeth.

"Just things. He didn't like me in his bedroom, wouldn't let me touch his things. He was rude to my partner, but Pierre, well, he was no match for Alex's intelligence. Even though Alex was only a boy."

Pierre. So that was the sick fuck's name. "They didn't have a good relationship?"

Antoinette's eyes turned shrewd. "Alex did as he was told. Pierre saw to that."

Devvy could only imagine, and she didn't even want to consider how Pierre had controlled and punished Alex. She swallowed back the nausea that punched her in the gut and asked, "Did Pierre hurt Alex?"

Scowling, Antoinette slashed her hand through the air. "You have no right to say such things."

"He's my partner. I have the right to ask about things that concern his welfare."

"Partner," Antoinette scoffed. "I know who you are, even if Alex tried to hide the truth from me."

"We hid nothing from you," Devvy lied, calling the other woman's bluff.

"You think I'm a fool? I knew even before this morning's shameful headlines! You are Sebastien Jacques's wife. I can only assume you are corrupting my son."

"I think you'll find he's corrupting me," she retorted with a snap, unable to help herself.

Antoinette sucked in a sharp, outraged breath. "How dare you!" she spat.

"Easily," came the quick retort. "Alex is not perfect. Even he makes the admission. But whatever he is, you and your sick fuck of a partner created."

"I don't know what you mean." Antoinette toyed with the long loops of the bow about her neck.

"I had to come and speak to you today. I saw the way you were yesterday and I knew, the way you obsessed over him, you'd have spotted the signs as a kid.

"There's no way he could have suddenly turned and you wouldn't have noticed the difference. And even if he became less important to you when you got a partner, you'd have noticed your boyfriend's odd behavior. You're too obsessive not to!"

"You come into my house and accuse me and insult me. I would like you to leave!" Antoinette snapped snootily.

"I'm not leaving until you tell me if Alex was abused as a child. If your partner molested him."

Antoinette's cheeks turned bright pink and then, papery white. But unlike before, her gaze was cast downward. Just beneath Devvy's line of sight. Not direct and glaring at her straight in the eye.

"How dare you!"

The words didn't ring true, and there, in that moment, Devvy had her answer. Everything inside her unraveled as sheer, unadulterated horror at what Alex had had to endure as a child throttled her. "I dare, I fucking dare, you old bitch. You knew, didn't you? You *knew*, and you didn't say anything. You just let that bastard rape your son, and you let him. You actually let him." Devvy staggered backward, almost falling onto the sofa behind her.

"I won't listen to this anymore. Please leave!"

"If you think I'm going to do as you say, then you're sadly mistaken. I hope that bastard is rotting in hell, and that you do, too. You're as sick as he was. Sicker! How could you? How could you let him hurt Alex?"

"I don't know what you're talking about!" Antoinette cried out. She clapped a hand over her ears, looking more like six than sixty.

"Bull. You know exactly what I'm talking about. What happened? That first night you felt him creep out of your room but you didn't say anything. You just thought he was going to the bathroom. But he didn't come back, did he? Not straight away. I bet you knew from the very first night and you let it happen."

The more she spoke, the more Antoinette trembled, shaking her head in a furious rejection of everything Devvy was saying. But Devvy couldn't stop. The words just poured out of her. They tumbled free, vitriolic poison that couldn't be withheld.

As the words gathered on her tongue, she spat them out. Her hands shook, trembled with the need to maim, to do harm. To punish the sick bitch.

For the first time in her life, Devvy was out of control. And the woman had yet to confirm or deny anything!

But just like Devvy had known, in her gut, that Alex's childhood had been severed by being molested, she also knew this woman had hidden the truth. Had perpetuated the horrors of Alex's past.

"Admit it!" she shrieked. "Tell me the goddamn truth! You *knew*, didn't you? Didn't you?!"

"Yes!" Antoinette cried, immediately bursting into racking sobs. "Yes! Yes! Yes! I knew. God help me, I knew."

The other woman's shrieks acted like a pinprick to Devvy's fury.

She deflated. Immediately. Sinking in on herself, almost falling into the sofa.

It was one thing being dead sure, of feeling it in your gut, but having it confirmed?

It was far worse than she'd imagined, because this meant the blackmailer had something over them. They would have no choice but to dance to his tune in order to protect and shelter Alex.

She sagged against the flowery sofa, staring almost blindly into the fireplace. Antoinette's sobs echoed around the room, throbbing through her in a way that made her heart pump angrily.

How dare she cry?

What right did she have?

She was as much a monster as her partner. How dare she shed tears when she was guilty? How dare she cry when she let her baby be used in such a way?

"I just wanted his attention," the older woman whispered, almost imploringly.

Sickness flooded Devvy. "What? Your partner's?" she sneered. "You thought the way to get it was to sell your little boy out?"

Antoinette shook her head from side to side. The pace so fast, the pins supporting her bun fell out. "No. Alex's."

Devvy sighed. "What the hell are you talking about?"

"No one had to know. No one ever had to know. But he wouldn't visit. When he does, he's mean. He leaves almost immediately. I can't visit him. He won't let me.

"I'm only allowed to see him when he schedules me in. That's not right! I'm his mother," she cried. "I had to do something. I want to see my son. I have a right!"

Devvy growled. "You lost that right the day you condoned Alex's abuse. How can you even speak like that? After what you've done. Why aren't you ashamed of yourself? How the hell can you even bear to look at him, knowing what you let happen to him?"

"It wasn't my fault," Antoinette almost pleaded.

"No, it wasn't," Devvy agreed. "But the first time you knew something was wrong and you did nothing to stop it, *that* was your fault. The minute you knew and let it carry on, you took as much of the blame for all this as that perverted bastard.

"You're lucky Alex even visits you at all, never mind bitching about wanting more attention! Well, I guess yesterday's disaster was the last time you'll be seeing him." She took great relish out of laughing and seeing the other woman's suffering. "The minute I tell him you were involved, that you actually knew what he was going through, that's the last you'll see of him."

A wildness overcame Antoinette. It reminded Devvy of yesterday, when over nothing, she'd suddenly converged on her poor maid and start yelling at her in French. "You can't do that. You mustn't do that!"

"Just give me one reason why not," Devvy sneered at her, feeling her upper lip curl with repulsion at the other woman's desperation.

"I'll go to the papers. I have contacts now. I know who to send the information to."

For a second, Devvy wasn't entirely sure what she was hearing.

But the statement, "I have contacts now," suddenly started revolving around her mind.

"You're the blackmailer," Devvy said in a breath, astonishment clouding her tone. She jumped up, filled with energy again. It took every ounce of her control to not grip the woman's throat with her bare hands and squeeze the life out of her! "You fucking bitch. You would send that kind of information to the press? About your own son?"

"I can't lose him!" Antoinette yelled.

"You lost him the day you condoned him being raped!"

She flinched and drew back. "You can't tell him. If you do, I swear to God, I'll go to the press. Everyone will know. This rests in your hands."

Devvy sucked in a breath. "I'd prefer the entire world know Alex's secrets than let him come near you again. And I'm sure he'll agree.

"You sell your secrets to the press. We won't be held ransom by a sick bitch like you."

With that, she made to walk past and go on her way. She needed to get out of this room, of this apartment, of the goddamn building. Just being close to Antoinette made her feel like she was standing in toxic territory. As though she were breathing in the sickness in the other woman's soul.

As she neared her, Antoinette reached for her arm, gripped tight, and with a surprising amount of strength, pulled her to a halt. “You mustn’t tell him,” she muttered feverishly.

“I’ll do whatever I goddamn want,” Devvy spat. “If you don’t let me go, I’ll feel no remorse in slapping you. It will give me the excuse I need.”

“You mustn’t tell!” Antoinette screeched.

Out of nowhere, a long pin appeared in her hand. Devvy recognized it as one of the chopsticks used to keep her bun in place. Antoinette pointed it at her, wielding it as though she were wielding a knife.

At that moment, Devvy realized two things.

One, she could easily overcome Antoinette.

Two, she could let Antoinette hurt her and use whatever injury she incurred as a valid excuse for self-defense. The idea of doing the woman serious damage was infinitely appealing.

Then, Antoinette’s arm was crashing down and her thoughts fled. As Devvy raised an arm to shield herself from the other woman’s aim, she realized it wouldn’t be as easy to overcome her as she’d thought.

Antoinette’s strength had Devvy groaning with effort as she grabbed her shoulder and tried to push her away. When that didn’t work, she shoved with one hand and with the other, slammed it down with a knife-hand blow. When the side of her palm connected with the other woman’s head, smacking her ear with as much force as she could, the bitch staggered back, arm still raised, pin still pointed down. Looking like something out of the Hitchcock movie she’d mentioned to Sebastien that morning.

Hand ringing with pain, Devvy stared at Alex’s mother and she had to withhold the urge to laugh. The scene definitely channeled Hitchcock, with a bit Tom and Jerry thrown in.

What the hell Antoinette thought she could do with a hair chopstick was beyond Devvy. She decided not to find out.

As soon as Antoinette had backed off, Devvy reached for her cell and did the only thing she could do.

Call the police.

Chapter Seventeen

It felt pathetic calling in the *gendarmes* for what, essentially, was a bitch fight. But Devvy knew if she didn't do it, Antoinette would, and the older woman would give it a whole different slant.

She would have probably put all the blame on Devvy, making up some bullcrap about how Devvy had been the aggressor.

As it was, she knew when the police did arrive, she'd have to be cautious. Antoinette could fill them with her poison and she wouldn't be able to do a damn thing.

Shit, it really was time she learned French.

And not just pidgin French, a smattering of words that enabled her to say *urgent* and then an address. The whole nine yards. She vowed to one day talk stocks and shares with Bastien, discuss cancer research with Alex, and finally talk dirty to the pair of them.

Resolution made, she called Alex. He was the only one who could control Antoinette. After today, she made another resolution. This was the last time mother and son would see each other.

Discovering Antoinette was the one behind the blackmail attempts changed the situation. Alex needn't know Bastien and Devvy were aware of his past. She knew she'd try to protect him from that truth as much as she could, hoping that one day, he'd share it with her in his own words, and at his own pace.

Knowing that his mother had tried to hold them hostage with threats would hopefully be enough to cut the ties between Alex and Antoinette.

If not, then she'd have to think of something.

She refused to let him have any relationship with the sick bitch.

"Alex?" she snapped as soon as he answered the phone. "I need you to come to your mother's apartment."

"Devvy? My mother's flat? What the hell for?"

"She's the one blackmailing us, Alex. She just admitted it to me."

Silence pounded down the line. "You're joking."

"No. I'm not. I wish I was. She just came after me with a hair pin, for God's sake. I don't know what she was trying to do, just shut me up, I suppose. I've called the police and I need you to come here and handle her." Devvy eyed the woman who was still clutching her head and sobbing brokenly on the sofa. She refused to feel pity. Even though it was hard.

Alex cleared his throat. "Y–You mean you want me to come over there? Actually *go*."

Devvy sucked in a breath and begged for patience. "I know it's hard, Alex. But you'll have to. I need you to speak to the police for me. God only knows what she'll say. *She* came after *me*, but if she talks to them first, it will probably be the other way around, and I'll be the one being cautioned!"

More silence. This time, throbbing with Alex's panic.

She closed her eyes and whispered, "I love you, Alex. Baby, you can do this. It's just like yesterday. You did it then and you can do it now." Her eyes flickered open as the sofa fabric creaked. Antoinette was moving, away from her, thank God, and toward the drinks tray.

"Please, darling. I need you."

Devvy watched as the other woman nearly filled a glass full of brandy and began to sip it as though she were drinking water.

A quivery breath sounded in her ear. "I'm on my way."

"Thank you."

His chuckle was self-deprecatory. And to be fair, more of a groan than a laugh. "You shouldn't be thanking me. I should be there. I—I'm going to try, *chérie.* I'll do my best, and I don't want to let you down, but call Bastien. Just in case. Please."

She didn't want to call Sebastien. She wanted to rely on Alex, but knew she couldn't. Not yet. Not with his past still completely unresolved and directly affecting his day-to-day life.

There would be time in the future, time to get him the help he needed, with support from two people who couldn't love him more if they tried.

"I will. Either way, if you can manage it or not, I have faith in you, Alex."

She disconnected the call not wanting to put him under more pressure, yet hoping like hell he'd make it here. Pressing her speed dial for Bastien's office, she waited for him to pick up. As she waited, she continued to stare at Antoinette. Not trusting this sudden placidness.

Her eyes trained on the other woman's spine as she stared out of the balcony window, she murmured when Bastien answered, "Do you know where Alex's mother lives? Exactly, I mean."

"Yes. Do you need the address? I take it you're going to confront her?"

She snorted. "Consider the confrontation done. She attacked me with a hair clip! But I've called the police to stop her from telling them a whole different story. I need you to come here and translate for me." A few months ago, she wouldn't have dreamed of making such a demand. Asking Bastien to leave the office? To help her? Never!

Stunned silence was her reply and then a flurry of French. She heard *merde* repeated quite a few times and totally agreed. This was a shitty situation.

"I'll be there in fifteen minutes."

"Thank you. Stay safe. Don't break any laws to get here. It's not worth it. Alex is on the way, or at least, he's trying."

"Good. If he can make it, then all the better. If not, we can cope."

Before she put the phone down, she said, "By the way, I've discovered our blackmailer."

Another bout of French curses. She vowed, once again, to understand those goddamn swear words if it was the last thing she did!

When he eventually spoke in English, his voice was grim. "Ten minutes."

The second she tucked her phone back into her pocket, Devvy was immediately on edge. Antoinette had turned around to face her. It was strange looking at the completely ordinary woman and feeling as though the woman she was seeing didn't look right.

She should look evil. Insane. Crazy and disturbed.

It was like she was wearing a mask of normalcy, now. Devvy kept on expecting to see the Mr. Hyde side of her personality again. The nut job who wielded a hair accessory as though it were a dagger.

"You did not tell my son."

Her statement could only be about one thing. Devvy shrugged. "It's not something I feel comfortable discussing over the phone."

Antoinette shook her head, and Devvy was disturbed to see hope glinting in the woman's eyes. "You won't tell him. Not if you love him."

She sounded so sure, Devvy wanted to slap her for having read the situation so well. Although, maybe not well. After all, what woman in their right mind wanted to be the one to tell their loved one they knew they'd been abused as a child? What woman wanted to say their lover's mother had known all along?

It was hardly happy news!

And Alex was, in so many ways, so strong and stubborn. So proud.

It was how he'd dragged himself from the horrors of his past and made himself into one of the world's leading cytologists.

It took guts to do that. Pride and ego.

He had phobias and flaws, personality quirks that were head-scratching and fears so deeply entrenched they made her want to weep, but he'd risen above them.

In many ways, telling him what she knew would be all the harder for his strength.

She would be breaking the shell he'd created years ago. The thin veneer that protected him, kept his vulnerabilities caged. If she were to do anything to damage it, God only knows what his reaction would be.

She feared it would only ever be negative.

That didn't stop her from lying to the woman who had enabled her son's childhood to be destroyed. "Because I love him, I'll tell him. Just not on the phone. If you think he'll talk to you now I've told him you're the one blackmailing Bastien, you're crazy. Oh wait, you already are," she remarked with a roll of her eyes.

"I'm not crazy," Antoinette immediately denied. "I love my son."

Devvy snorted. "No mother who loved their son could let him be abused like that."

"Pierre was a good man. A good provider," Antoinette snapped. "Alex's father was no use. He left when Alex was just a boy. Divorced me, took up with another woman with children of her own, forgot about Alex. He might as well not have existed! I was alone, a child to care for. I had to pay for the roof over our heads, put food in our bellies. Pierre helped me do that."

Devvy sneered. "You think the end justifies the means? You pimped out your son to keep yourself in rent and to pay for food." She shook her head.

"How the hell can you stand there and tell me that? Almost as though that reasons it away.

"You stood by while his innocence was taken from him. While a pervert distorted your son. Look at him, Antoinette. Look at the man you helped forge.

"I love him, God help me, I do. More than I imagined possible. But he can't leave the house without having a panic attack. His penthouse is empty. It's huge! You think this place is spacious? It's nothing in comparison to Alex's place. He's surrounded by space. That's it.

"He's been in a relationship for nearly twenty years…"

Antoinette butted in, "With that pervert, Sebastien Jacques."

The disgust in her voice had Devvy shaking her head. "You call Sebastien a pervert, but your fucking child abuser of a boyfriend was a "good" man? Lady, you need to get your priorities in order."

Antoinette sniffed. "My priorities are very well organized. Don't think I didn't realize what was happening between you three the instant you started staying the night at Alex's penthouse."

Disgust crawled up Devvy's spine. She remembered Alex saying how she'd stalked him, following him about town, watching his every move from the café across the road from his penthouse. Apparently Antoinette had never stopped her surveillance even though Alex had stopped going out completely. The idea that this woman had been keeping tabs on her and her lovers' behavior made her feel queasy. "We're adults. We're consenting. We can do whatever the hell we want."

"I will not be dictated to, lectured by a woman who sleeps with two men."

Devvy couldn't help it. She smiled. "That's the nicest thing you could possibly have said to me. If you think I'm going to be judged by a woman like you, you're mistaken.

"I just wanted you to realize the way you've fucked up your son. *You* did that. Your partner helped, but you let it happen. You created a child who is so scared to live and love, he locks himself away. I just hope you're proud of yourself, of your achievement."

Antoinette's mouth pursed. Her lips flexed for a second, and Devvy could see she was contemplating how to reply. As she was waiting for the retort, Devvy heard a slight noise from the hall. The sound of steps. It was hardly noticeable, but Devvy knew what she had to do.

In a zip code like this building's, she knew the *gendarmes* would be quick to respond. And if it was a neighbor, so be it. She'd have a witness.

Devvy screamed.

She screamed like she'd never screamed before, and, calling on the years of drama class where she'd stood by embarrassed as hell, she sobbed through her screams.

Antoinette looked at her like she was the crazy person, but she didn't mind.

She had a purpose.

Over her screams, she couldn't hear any noises coming from the hall, until bangs sounded on the front door. She ran toward it, made her fingers scramble at the door as though she were panicked, and opened it to find two concerned-looking boys in blue.

She threw herself at one of them, saw his surprise, but noticed his arms opened automatically. "She just attacked me," Devvy cried. "Started hitting me."

She was telling the truth, just adding a dash of melodrama. She should have felt guilty, but how could she? Antoinette would have done exactly the same thing had she heard the police.

That sick, twisted bitch was not going to have anyone on her side.

When the police tried to calm her, one of them speaking in garbled, pidgin English, the other went to investigate. He called out, and the one embracing her coaxed her forward.

The instant she walked into the room, Devvy was glad for her melodrama.

A paper knife.

A goddamn paper knife.

Right through the shoulder.

What Antoinette hoped to achieve, Devvy didn't know. Apparently, she'd never watched CSI. Devvy had no blood on her, her fingerprints wouldn't be on the knife's hilt but the wound's location had definitely been "chosen." At first glance it looked as though Devvy could have been the one to stab her. The old woman, gushing fucking blood on the floor, looked as pitiful as could be.

Any sympathy the police had shown her disappeared with the blink of an eye. Their faces were now covered in masks of professionalism. They had a different job to do now.

All Devvy could say was if it weren't for CSI, and her minute knowledge of blood spatter patterns, she'd be peeing her pants.

And not with amusement.

Chapter Eighteen

Sirens glaring, flashing.

Horns being honked. Chaos. It was worse than usual.

The lights, the sounds, the smells…they filled him with sickness. Made the panic already winging its way around his body surge like an adrenaline rush gone wrong.

As the taxi braked to a halt, with shaking hands, Alex handed over a wad of five euro notes. Leaving the car was the hardest thing he'd ever done and the easiest. Devvy's earlier bout of weeping combined with this impromptu visit to his mother's, something that could hardly be considered a pleasure visit. Alex had questions he really needed answering. He also really needed to save his lover from his mother.

Now there was a sentence he probably wouldn't say often!

Sucking in a shaky breath, he took in the police cars nestled on the verge outside of his mother's building. An ambulance was parked askew. The sight of that ambulance chilled him to his core.

His mother wasn't *right.* She wasn't normal. He knew that, and at that moment, seeing the ambulance, Alex was sure she'd hurt Devvy.

He expected to see a body in a black bag roll out of the luxury condo and he knew, just *knew* his woman would be in there.

That belief gave him the strength to leave the taxi. He focused on his breathing. Each step seemed to take him backward, rather than forward. Being outside, the late afternoon sun gleaming overhead, burning his head and making him squint behind his glasses, cars toing and froing in front and behind him…. The panic was there. At his chest. Ready and waiting to blow. To overcome him.

He felt like a complete and utter pansy. Completely weak and useless. What kind of man could only make it out of his flat and felt sick as he did it?

Why she loved him, why Bastien did, Alex couldn't understand.

His weakness was ingrained.

Impossible to fix.

His self-hatred and the focus it took to not vomit made it so that he failed to spot Bastien. Not until he'd almost walked past him. All of a sudden, arms were there, embracing him. Thanking him. Praising him.

He felt like a fool and completely undeserving. Both of his partners had thanked him for something that should have been as easy as breathing. He'd have shrugged off the praise, but he was too focused on not vomiting.

Bastien's arms were like a beacon, though. They supported him. Helped him across the road. The words whispered into his ears made little to no sense, but Bastien kept him grounded. He was outside, but Bastien gave him the security of inside.

They crossed the street. Neared the empty ambulance. Both of them stiffened as they passed it, and entered the foyer.

The concierge spotted them, her face white with panic. She blurted out something, but Alex's ears weren't working. Bastien retorted and guided him over to the elevator. Within thirty seconds, they entered the corridor that lead to his mother's quarters.

More noise. More shouts. More chaos that was hyperlinked to his already churning stomach.

The smells, now, were worse than downstairs. There, the scents of tar and gasoline fumes and pollution had filled his nose.

Now, feet away from the door, he could smell blood.

A lot of it.

A trolley careered out of the doorway and, God strike him down for it, but when he saw his mother hooked up to a portable IV, his legs quivered with relief.

She stared at him, her eyes beseeching him as they always did. Begging him to be nice to her. To be kind. And as he always did, he felt guilty for not caring. For feeling nothing.

He was damaged. He knew that. On the brink of being broken. The only thing keeping him glued together was Bastien, and now Devvy.

Devvy.

God, he needed her.

He ignored his mother's husky pleading. The soft words that become loud cries and shrieks of fury as the trolley moved down the corridor and to the service elevator. Her yells ricocheted off the walls as she realized he wasn't going to go with her. She cursed and swore, but her words were wasted on him.

His knees knocked as they walked through the door, relief and terror coursing through him as his imagination went to work on what they'd find the deeper they went into his mother's apartment.

There'd been only one ambulance. That meant Devvy was well.

He didn't even care that she'd done something to his mother. He was just glad his mother hadn't done something to her!

Spying her looking pissed off on the sofa almost made him collapse with thanks.

As soon as she saw them, she jumped up and ran over to them. Throwing an arm over their shoulders, she buried herself in their embrace. For a second, her shaking made him see red. His mother had done this. More damage. More distress.

She pulled away, mouth a taut line and glared back at the *gendarmes*. "Your mother is a psycho," she exploded, her gaze returning to Alex. "She stabbed herself. Can you believe that?"

Alex frowned. "She stabbed herself?"

"Yeah! I went to let the police in and by the time we got back, she's on the floor. Blood everywhere, a goddamn paper knife sticking out of her chest." She tapped the soft fleshy bit that connected the arm to the shoulder and the shoulder to the chest.

Bastien spoke to the police. "You are questioning my wife?" he asked, voice stern, his arm wrapped firmly about Devvy's waist.

The cop nodded. "Just routine questions."

"How routine? I don't want you upsetting her."

The *gendarme's* partner stood overlooking the pool of his mother's blood retorted, "I don't think this could get any more distressing. She's angry, not upset. Look at her."

"What happened?"

"My English is not so good," the first cop said. "But from what I can tell, your mother attacked her, Monsieur Ivanov. Came at her with a…" he hesitated. "She said chopstick. I think this is a *baguette*. You know, the stick women put in their hair? Could you ask her to confirm?"

Alex's voice was a rasp as he did as bid. "The policeman says Mother attacked you with a chopstick. Is this right?"

Looking mutinous, she took a step away from them, folded her arms over her chest and nodded. "The frigging things you put in your hair." She harrumphed. "She must have shoved it back in her bun."

He tried to look supportive, but it mustn't have worked because she turned away from him and stepped over to the balcony door. "I need some air."

She walked out onto the terrace, leaving him to stare at her back. "She said it is a type of hair accessory," he told the officer.

"I guess that makes a weird kind of sense," the cop confirmed with a shrug. "She came at her with the chopstick, tried to attack her, but she managed to defend herself. We arrived, and your wife, sir…" He turned to Bastien, although his eyes flickered over Alex. The newspaper headlines this morning as well as Devvy's greeting had just confirmed the gossip down at these *gendarmes'* precinct. "…She was hysterical. My partner came into the lounge and found your mother on the floor." His gaze switched over to Alex, managing to look sympathetic.

"She isn't covered in blood," Alex pointed out, his voice still hoarse.

On an everyday basis, he hated his mother's apartment.

Add in a pool of blood, some police and his furious girlfriend…yeah, this wouldn't be adding to his bank of happy memories.

"No. It is our belief that your mother stabbed herself. Once we have the fingerprints analyzed, that will be confirmed."

The cop kneeling near the blood asked, "Is she capable of something like that, sir? Of stabbing herself?"

Alex huffed, relieved that the police truly didn't think Devvy had anything to do with the farce only his mother could have fabricated, and mocking the idea that his mother *couldn't* manage something like this. "Very."

The *gendarme* frowned. "She is ill?"

Alex shrugged. "She has never been diagnosed with any kind of disorder. My mother distrusts doctors, so even if something was wrong, we'd never know.

"On top of that, she is a very jealous woman. Manically so. I brought Devvy here yesterday to meet her. The *rendezvous* did not go well."

"Have you any idea why she was here?"

When Bastien stiffened against him, Alex ignored the minute gesture and shook his head. "No. No idea. This morning, she was with me. Then, this afternoon, when I woke up, she'd gone."

The look the cops shared once again told Alex they were well aware of this morning's gossip.

"This conversation, gentlemen, is in complete confidence," Bastien gritted out, obviously spotting that shared, amused glance. "If anything, *anything at all*, makes its way into the papers, I will sue your *département*. Do you understand me?"

The two stiffened, but nodded. Their faces turned to stone as the first one replied, "Of course."

"Good." Bastien moved away from Alex, making him feel like he'd been stranded in an ocean, and his lifeboat had decided to sink. "This is also completely confidential. I am being blackmailed. This morning's headlines were my punishment for failing to deal with the payoff."

"Did you report this to the police, sir?" The second officer started to look interested.

Alex just knew this would be a fascinating topic of discussion over his dinner table.

Confidential or not.

Bastien shot him an impatient glance. "No, of course not. I had my security team deal with it. I believe Devvy came here to speak with Alex's mother about the blackmail. We spoke, earlier on today. She inferred that she'd like to smooth over troubled waters with Antoinette.

"As Alex has already said, she is a very jealous woman. She didn't take to Devvy at all yesterday, and with the news this morning…well, we didn't want to upset Alex's mother any more than necessary. Apparently, it was poor timing for Devvy to visit. None of us realized just how unbalanced Antoinette Ivanov actually is."

The first officer scrubbed a hand over his jaw as he took in the scene for the last time. As he did, he shook his head and muttered, "I think we have all we need, sirs. Thank you for your honesty.

"The department will be in touch regarding the blackmail attempt. We will need you to come down and make statements."

Bastien shrugged. "Honesty causes less hassle and embarrassment in the long run. I'll have my attorneys contact the precinct. They will liaise on our behalf."

As the cops started to turn away, Alex asked, "Devvy is free to go?"

The first one huffed out a laugh. "Yes. She didn't do anything. Like I said, the prints on the knife will only confirm what the lack of blood on her clothing did.

"It is not my place, but I would recommend, sir, that you make your mother see a psychiatrist. At the moment, we're still investigating the allegations your wife has made, but if she's telling the truth, well…the medics said the level of force to make something as blunt as a paperknife slip through flesh…it took a lot of effort." He hesitated. "Your…" He settled on, "…Madame Jacques implied that your mother actually stabbed herself, while she was talking to us at the door. She did not cry out. We did not hear anything.

"Once we confirm the story, the hospital will arrange for psychiatric treatment. She's obviously a danger to herself and the public, but after that, unless she truly is ill and this wasn't just an aberration caused by difficult circumstances, it will be up to you to arrange for some kind of treatment."

"My mother is a very strange woman, capable of anything. I will see to her care," was all he said.

He stepped away from them and headed over to the balcony. He didn't stop until he stood beside Devvy and wrapped an arm about her tense shoulder.

"I didn't hurt her. I swear."

The tension in her voice and frame had him frowning. "I know you didn't. But I wouldn't have blamed you if you had."

"How do you know I didn't?" she asked, still a little frosty.

He frowned. "The evidence says so."

"So you don't believe I didn't hurt her because I said so?"

Alex sighed. "Please, Devvy, let's not get into this. It was hard enough getting here. I don't want to argue with one of the two people stopping me from throwing up."

At his candor, her lips softened out of their tight clench. “You made it, didn’t you, though?”

He grunted. “With a statement like, ‘I have faith in you,’ how could I have let you down?”

She stood on tiptoe and pressed a kiss to his cheek. “Thank you.”

“You and Bastien keep on thanking me for something so pathetic. I don’t deserve your thanks.”

“We all have our issues, Alex. No matter how small, large, petty, or serious. Overcoming them deserves a reward. Even if it’s just a kiss and a ‘thank you.’”

He sighed. “You are too good for me. Both of you.”

Tears made her eyes sparkle in the golden glow of the early evening sun. She soothed her fingers over his cheek, ran them up over his jaw, and combed at the hair curling over his ears. “I know,” she retorted, deadpan.

It took a second to absorb her meaning and he glared down at her, the tears having disappeared only to be replaced by mischief.

“Are you teasing him, *chérie*?” Bastien’s voice broke into their conversation. He crossed over the terrace and stood beside Devvy. As he passed her, he tapped her on the butt and said, “That’s naughty.”

She grinned. “I wouldn’t have, but he was getting all serious on me. We’re too good for him, apparently. Shall we dance off into the sunset together?” She spun around, grabbed Bastien’s hands, and in a totally un-Devvy-like move, began to waltz on the terrace.

Even though Bastien moved with her, he stared down at her as though an alien had just taken his wife’s place.

She finally came to a stop, when she forced Bastien’s arm up into the air, and did a little twirl. “I don’t care how inappropriate that was. I don’t care that your mother’s blood is staining the carpet. I had to do that. Twenty minutes ago, I wasn’t sure if I was going to be arrested!” She laughed, but her face held the earlier echoes of her panic. “She’s a nutcase. A total and utter psycho. And I thought my mom was bad making me take dance class.”

“It came in handy for something,” Alex remarked, brow cocked.

She moved over to him, pressed herself against his chest and whispered, “If you’re not careful, I’ll make you dance, too.”

Alex snorted. “I’ve got two left feet.”

"I'll make a dancer out of you, yet," was all she said before burrowing her arms between his and embracing him. Tightly. "I don't ever, *ever* want to hear you say that you don't deserve us. Do you understand me?"

At her fierce command, what could he do but smile at Bastien and retort, "I do."

Chapter Nineteen

As Bastien worked at his desk, Alex looked out onto the garden where Devvy stood watering her herbs. She'd been out there for the last two hours, straw hat on her head protecting her from the sun as well as shielding what he expected were tears from him and Bastien.

This morning had started off with the shittiest of bangs. A call from Devvy's mother. At five a.m.

Miranda's shrieks of outrage had burst down the line, her fury and shame at the news spreading about her daughter almost tangible as they sat there, half-dazed and sleepy.

When Devvy had just taken the abuse, motionless aside from the tears rolling down her cheeks, making no move to cut the call, in the end, Bastien had taken the phone out of Devvy's hand and disconnected the line on her behalf.

He'd held her against his chest, pressed a kiss to her temple and said, "The next time she calls, I'll handle her."

She'd refused breakfast, and he'd grabbed a coffee and a croissant, taken a seat on the sofa in Bastien's study, and had been watching over her for the last two or so hours. Her earlier bravado had disappeared in the face of her parents' vitriol, and it hurt him to see her so down.

It was a few days since his mother's attack and subsequent arrest. After they had left her apartment building, they had headed home to *Les Fenêtres,* and he'd been there ever since. He'd had no desire to return to his lab, no desire to be anywhere else but here, with the people who mattered most to him.

They had been odd these last few days. A time where they had come together, but also a time where he'd had the chance to think. Had a chance to take stock of his life and realize he had amends to make.

He'd hurt Bastien so many times over the years. Been a bastard and been totally undeserving of the stalwart love Bastien had given him.

It was time, he'd realized, to stop being selfish, to focus on Bastien. Devvy, too, but Bastien was the one who had suffered through the decades of their relationship. He could only imagine how often he'd caused him pain.

He'd come to a decision last night, when the two of them lay in bed beside him, snoring away. The silence in the room, the circle of trust he'd been in, the meaning behind being under Bastien's roof and in his bed…all of it, the security, trust and the love, had made him see it was time to cut ties with his mother. It was time to stop hedging his bets and to liberate himself from her.

He'd do what he could, when he could, to help her out of the mess she'd created when she'd decided to blackmail them. He'd been hard-pressed to believe her obsession had risen to such heights, that she'd intended to blackmail him to make him visit her more often.

When Devvy had told him that, had repeated verbatim the words his mother had screamed at her as she'd attacked, he'd known enough was enough. It had taken a few days of processing to realize what had to be done, though.

He was ready. Ready to tell the truth.

After what happened at his mother's apartment, things had changed. He'd changed. It was time to make amends.

"I'm sorry, Bastien." The minute the words popped out, he regretted them. They weren't what he'd wanted to say. He'd wanted to tell him he loved him. Instead his subconscious had made the decision for him.

He watched as his lover's head shot up. A glare aiming his way, Sebastien spat, "What for?"

There was a stillness about the other man that told him he was expecting to hear bad news. Alex supposed he deserved such a reaction. He'd hardly been as steadfast as Bastien. His anger told him he expected another rejection, only this time, Devvy was involved, hence the anger. In the past, Bastien had always closed in on himself.

The times Alex had said he needed a break, Bastien had always nodded quietly, listened to his reasoning, and then left. Not a word spoken.

For Devvy, he was attacking.

The notion pleased Alex. The three of them were really tying together. The connections knotting and taking a firm hold. A forever kind of hold.

"For having to put up with me through the years. For dealing with my selfish bullshit."

Bastien's glare lessened a little, but there was still tension in his shoulders. "I love you. You were worth it."

"*Were*?" Alex asked, a teasing smile on his lips.

"Are," he corrected. "What's wrong? You're looking at me strangely."

"I need to tell you something, something about me. I was going to tell Devvy, but I'm not ready for her to know. And this…" Alex sucked in a breath, terrified at what he was about to reveal. Horrified at what Bastien's reaction would be. "I need you to know, because I need you to understand why I've been the way I've been. All these years, you've loved me. You've supported me, and I've been a shit. I've treated you terribly, and even the fact that I love you and have loved you almost from those first months together, doesn't excuse the way I've behaved."

Bastien frowned. His chair screeched as he stood up and strode over to Alex. He knelt in front of him, reached forward and cupped Alex's trembling chin. "No tears, *mon cher*."

Alex's mouth still quivered, but he braved a smile. "Please, Bastien, don't pull away from me once I tell you this."

A strange look appeared in Bastien's eyes. Alex couldn't describe it, and it disappeared before he even had a chance to name the emotion hidden within the amber depths. "You need never fear I will stop loving you, Alex. You had me that first day and you'll have me until my last."

"You say that now, but you don't know what made me *me*, Bastien."

"I know the man sitting here today. I don't necessarily understand him, but I know, deep down, I *know*."

"I was raped. As a child." The words blurted free and Alex's eyes clenched down, blocking out Bastien's reaction. "Not a week passed where he didn't come for me. Where he didn't touch me. For years, Sebastien," he breathed out the word, his eyes fluttering open. He saw his lover's face through a blur of tears. "Years."

He gulped. "I'd just lie there. Every night. Waiting. Mother always used to leave the hallway light on. I can remember her always doing it. Even when I was really young. But the light would shine under the door, and I'd wait to see his feet making shadows on the floor. I'd wait for the little creak on the floorboard outside my bedroom.

"The door would always open without a sound. Not even a whisper. His socks would slide against the floor, then he'd be standing there. Over my bed. Every part of me would freeze, praying tonight would be different. But it never was." His voice was hoarse when he continued. "That is what turned me into the man you see before you. A man scared of his own shadow. Terrified to leave his own home, too cowardly to be with the man he loves. I don't deserve you. And I certainly don't deserve, Devvy."

His eyes closed again, but he felt the warm brush of Bastien's breath on his lips, before he was kissed. Gently.

"Are you going to move into *Les Fenêtres*, Alex?"

The question, after his confession, stunned him. He was silent, unsure of how to answer.

"Are you going to let Devvy and I love you, free you from the past?"

The soft words had a sob building in his chest. "I don't know if I'll ever be free. I can't stop thinking about it. Every day, it's with me. No amount of therapy, nothing, takes it away. I'm in a prison up here!" he yelled, banging his temple with a fist. The dull thudding ache he caused was nothing to the agony deep inside. "I'm broken, Bastien. Nothing will fix me. Nothing."

"You've shared the truth with me, Alex. That's the first step. Do you think it doesn't kill me to know that someone abused you? Do you think I'm *okay* with it?" Alex looked at the fierceness on Bastien's face and shook his head. "Do you think I don't want to kill the fucker who touched you? Avenge the little boy who would become the man I love?"

"He's dead. He died a long time ago."

Bastien sucked in a breath. "I never believed in heaven or hell, but I do now. Simply so that bastard can rot in hell." His top lip curled in a sneer. "I would kill for you, Alex. That's how much I love you.

"Bruised, battered, broken, I need you, and Devvy does, too. We can't fix the past, we can't change the present, but we can work on the future.

"Be with us, Alex. Not tomorrow, maybe not in six months' time, but get used to the idea. You can't heal, darling, until you accept what happened to you, and know that I love you more for telling me something so painful to you."

Alex swallowed. "I don't deserve you."

"You do. And you deserve Devvy."

His chin wobbled again. "Are you my reward, Bastien?"

Bastien smiled. "We're whatever you need us to be."

The word "salvation" whispered through Alex's head, but he didn't repeat it. He leaned forward and whispered, "I need you to love me. I need you both to love me."

"We do. We always will. Don't pull away from us, Alex. Don't push us away because you're frightened. When you're ready for Devvy to know, tell her. It won't change a thing, except make her understand you better."

"I—I will. I swear. I don't know when, but I will. I just needed to tell you. It was the only way, the only real way I could apologize to you. You're right. I have pulled away from you, and I've pushed. I won't do it, ever again. I swear."

Bastien's eyes grew moist with tears, and Alex realized that was one of the first times he'd ever seen him cry. Molding their mouths together, they kissed for endless, timeless moments. They sat there, awkwardly holding each other, imbuing the kiss with regrets soon to be forgiven, and the need that was always there.

When Devvy's amused voice broke them apart, their eyes were dry, but the connection still held fast. "You two starting without me?"

Alex's lips twitched into a wide, cocky grin. For the moment, he would hide behind his mask, until he was ready to share that side of himself with her. It would come, and it wouldn't take the two decades it had taken him to reveal the truth to Bastien. But not yet, not yet. He couldn't stand for the love and trust, the lust and the need he saw in her eyes, to turn to pity. Or horror.

In time, he told himself, in time. "Want in on the action?" he teased and laughed as she strode over to them both, a pout on her lips.

"Am I invited? Or a gatecrasher?"

Bastien shook his head. "What the hell is a gatecrasher?"

Devvy grinned. "Never mind. I don't care if I am one. Keep on kissing, you two."

Noticing her slight tremble, Alex cocked a brow and asked, "Getting you hot and bothered, is it?"

"Always, babe. Always." She sat beside him on the sofa, knelt on the cushions and watched the two of them expectantly.

Bastien laughed at her. "Do you expect us to kiss to order, *chérie*?"

"Well," she mumbled, nose crinkling. "Not to order, exactly. But now. Yes, please."

Before Bastien could tease her anymore, Alex connected his mouth to his. With his hand, he reached for Devvy's leg and squeezed, touched when her fingers pried at his grip and made a bridge with his own. As Bastien's tongue twined with his, he felt her move closer until she was inches away, and her breath was brushing his chin.

Her lips suddenly connected with his cheek, her tongue slid down over the curve of his jaw and to his throat. His skin prickled in reaction and the tiny moan that escaped was swallowed by Bastien's kiss.

Suddenly, two sets of hands worked at his shirt, the buttons popping free of the holes as hungry hands sought to caress his chest. A hand slid down to his crotch and, while Devvy's confidence had increased, the slight hesitance told him it was her burrowing into his fly. Bastien was always sure of his each and every caress.

He pulled away to catch a breath and saw the heavy-lidded look on Bastien's face, the one that spoke of his need. He saw the lift of Devvy's chest, the quick breathing that told him of her excitement.

He reached for her, pulled her to him by clasping a hand behind her neck and tugging her forward. "I want you both. I need you both," he admitted hoarsely. "So badly, so much you'll never know."

Devvy's lips twitched. "The feeling's mutual, Alex. It might be crazy and unusual, fucked up and weird. But it's my kind of weird. It's my kind of crazy." Her gaze flickered over to Bastien and, whatever they shared with that one glance, it urged her to stand. She reached for Alex's hand and said, "Come, there are better places for what we want to do to you."

He accepted the clasp of her fingers to his, and allowed her to lead him from the room, down the hall, and toward the bedroom all three of them had been sharing the last few nights.

It might have happened in a blur. He could have passed countless members of staff. At that moment, his head was abuzz. Relief, fear, need, unease, love. They battled for supremacy. The huge hole inside him, the hole created out of the young Alex's despair was nowhere close to being filled, but having shared it with Bastien, the black hole seemed to lose its power over him. It made him feel less empty inside.

The bedroom door closed the instant Bastien crossed the threshold. Immediately, without a word being said, they methodically stripped. This wasn't frenzied need, but a clinical baring. Exposing themselves to the other. Devvy, in her T-shirt that she considered baggy and showed a delectable amount of tit, and the shorts she thought were comfortable and cupped her ass to perfection, stripped off first.

She climbed onto the bed, giving him a delicious glimpse of glistening pussy. He licked his lips, mouth salivating with the need to taste. He followed her onto the mattress as she spread her legs and began to touch herself. Her eyes were on his, no shame hidden in the depths as she strummed her clit. Cock in hand, he stroked himself in time to her movements, as he crawled over to her. Only stopping when she was between his thighs and he was looming over her.

Her mouth opened, her eyes on his cock, but he didn't want that. He wanted *her*. He needed to be inside.

His head turned to the side, wanting to make sure Bastien was behind him, and what he saw made his heart shudder in his chest. Bastien's cock was gleaming as he stroked himself, and the lube he'd poured over the shaft made a squelching sound with every touch.

Alex's ass quivered with the knowledge of what was about to happen, and his body reveled in the idea. He bent down and pressed a kiss to Devvy's mouth. His tongue speared deep and she groaned as he fucked her mouth, sliding the flexible muscle against hers, inciting and exciting her.

Her hands gripped his hips, her nails spearing into the sparse flesh there. They raked upward, making him shiver as his spine tingled at the touch. His cock bobbed with the need to be inside her, and with their mouths joined, he pushed her legs open, settled himself between them, and then grasped for his shaft and nudged it against her opening.

The sweet, hot, clean depths of her called to him and he pressed himself deep, groaning with delight as her pussy swallowed him in one go.

He thrust, slightly, getting as deep as he could go and enjoying the delicate little ripple of her inner muscles as they quivered at his intrusion. Apart from that, he didn't move. His blood was hot, boiling with the knowledge that Bastien would soon be at his back, fucking him and helping him fuck Devvy.

He wouldn't have to jerk himself off as Bastien took him. Devvy's muscles would pull and tug at him, drag him to the point of no return.

He shuddered at the thought.

With a few inches between them, he pressed one hand against her breast, cupping it and teasing the nipple, pinching it and then rubbing softly. He quivered against her, his lips pausing for a second as the bed shifted with Bastien's arrival.

Hands gripped his hips, fingers pulled his cheeks apart and probed at his ass. Wet digits touched and caressed, jerking every single nerve ending awake as he rubbed the pucker before spearing him with a finger. He cried out and into Devvy's mouth. Her chuckle was naughty and satisfied, as his hips had rolled forward in reaction to Bastien's touch and he'd thrust deep.

His eyes clenched shut, his mouth unable to focus on kissing Devvy as Bastien's fingers devastated him. He felt the little gland deep inside quiver as it was rubbed and touched, knew it wouldn't take much stimulation for him to burst inside Devvy.

The thought had him pressing his forehead against hers. He felt her breath as it landed against his lips and she whispered, "I love you, Alex. I need you, Bastien needs you. Stay with us, never leave us, never."

The words penetrated his brain, but he couldn't respond. Feeling the hard nudge of Sebastien's cock at the pucker of his ass, a keening cry escaped him as the shaft pressed deep, forging into welcoming tissues.

When the thick girth filled him to bursting, his eyes once again grew moist with tears. As Bastien began to move, overloading him with a sensation that was only trebled as the jerking thrusts pushed him in and out of Devvy's warm, welcoming pussy, Alex whispered, "Never, never, never."

Epilogue

Six months later

As Tiesto's *A Beautiful World* pumped from her stereo, Devvy's butt shook and wriggled to the beat. The beauty of soundproofing. She could have it as loud as she wanted, so loud it hurt her ears, and not feel guilty about annoying anyone else.

Not that the staff would have complained about their employer's sudden desire to play music loud enough to wake the dead. But still, she didn't have to be a total pain in the ass, just because she could.

Through the window overlooking the garden, she saw Bastien on the terrace. He had a tray of coffee at his side, as well as his briefcase and a stack of papers. Some kind of weird hybrid takeover was happening at *La Belle sans la Bête*. It meant that Bastien was still CEO of the company, but he could work from home. He could take things slower, and as a result, he was happier.

She thought he'd be bored. Staying at home, away from the office and the fast pace. Instead, he was thriving.

She hadn't realized, until he'd started going to the office only twice a week, how drawn he'd been. How taut and pale.

As she watched, he tilted his head up to the sun and absorbed the rays. She'd always loved her view from the lab, but now it was even prettier. He had this lovely tendency of working on his papers shirtless. Sometimes dressed only in a pair of boxers.

Yum.

It was a shame that would change now that fall had taken hold, but Bastien was making the most out of today's surge in temperature.

Sighing with pleasure at the glimpse of his bare chest, she strode over to the sink and just stood there for a second. Watching him work.

He seemed so much happier now. So much more at ease.

She knew that was because their relationship was now a fixed part of all their lives. He didn't have to run himself ragged between the business and his two lovers. With Alex starting to move in, and still bitching about it, they were all on the brink of being under the same roof, and Devvy knew how much that put Bastien at ease.

At heart, Bastien was a protector. An old-fashioned man who provided for his loved ones. When he couldn't protect or provide, he felt impotent. And while she knew there was still some strain, because neither of them had told Alex they knew about his past, it was different now. Almost as though the knowledge of why Alex was the way he was, what made him tick, enabled Bastien to relax.

She could understand that.

Alex wasn't an easy man, outside of the bedroom, that was. At the same time, he was loveable. Charming, amusing, honest. He could be quieter than a church mouse, and then be the noisiest when he was happy.

His quirks were a part of his nature, and she knew Bastien had always accepted them but never really understood his lover. It had hurt him that Alex always tried to put distance between them, either by asking for time-outs or by refusing to live with him. In a way, it was that that had hurt Bastien the most, she thought.

His traditional soul had quivered with the pain of not being trusted by a man so important to him, and while his love had been strong enough to push all that to the side, it hadn't been enough to soothe the ache.

Devvy could only imagine how hard it must have been for Sebastien. For twenty years, not understanding why Alex pushed him away, but enduring it because he loved him. As painful as their discovery had been, finding out why Alex was the way he was, what had happened to him to make him this way, had been illuminating.

That sounded like a positive reaction, and when dealing with the aftermath of Alex's childhood, positivity was hardly the case. However, just knowing the answers made it easier to accept the oddities in their lover. It made it easier to adapt to him, to mold themselves to protect him.

That his mother wasn't rotting away in a jail cell burned a hole in her stomach lining every time she thought about it. Bastien and she had made the decision to keep quiet about Alex's past, preferring to let him settle, to let him come to them with the truth, if he ever decided to do that, anyway. He'd spent too large a part of his life out of control. They decided to hand him the mantle of power, even if he was unaware of it.

The problem with secrecy was the fact she couldn't tell him his mother *had* known what her partner had done to him. She'd tossed and turned before making her decision to keep quiet, preferring to leave his secrets well alone. In the future, she might regret it, but as Bastien agreed with her, she felt a little more at ease.

Devvy would admit that she only felt comfortable hiding Antoinette's part in her son's abuse because of her admission she'd been the one blackmailing them. The police had found more evidence to prove this was the case in her apartment, and her role of blackmailer had ensured that Alex had cut all ties with her.

He *had* paid for her legal team, and he'd done his best to ensure she'd have the lightest sentence possible. Combined with a certificate of diminished responsibility, Antoinette was currently serving a suspended sentence while she underwent psychiatric treatment.

As horrible as it made her feel, Devvy knew and rejoiced in the fact that Antoinette's biggest punishment was not seeing Alex.

Only the fact that he was no longer in contact with his mother made her feel in any way happy with the situation. If he'd remained in touch with her, Devvy would have had to tell him of his mother's awareness of his abuse.

She couldn't have stood for him to keep on communicating with the fucked-up bitch.

As it was, she could rest easily. Knowing he was safe and away from the toxicity that was his mother.

To society, it was the woman who was the weak partner. She needed the strength of a man to give her a backbone. But in their relationship, Alex was the weakest. There was no shame in that, but it was the truth. He needed them, and he didn't exactly know why or what to do with them. They just had to be there. They had to love him, protect and care for him.

It sounded like a selfless role undertaken for a selfish man. But Alex was anything but selfish. He gave of himself without even realizing it. He boosted and lifted their lives, because he flourished in their care.

Being with these two men had made her realize how strong she was. She might still be shy, and hardly the most confident woman on the planet. She might not be the most beautiful or the sexiest. But she was needed. And she was loved. What else mattered?

Suzette was the only parent at ease with their ménage. Her mother refused to speak to her, something that was a blessing in disguise, and Devvy's father had also cast her out. Henri, Bastien's papa, was totally perplexed, but on the whole, forgiving.

In a way, they'd created an exile of their own making, and she'd never felt happier. Or freer.

A smile had her lips twitching as she watched Alex hovering at the doorway that led onto the terrace.

He hadn't moved in. Yet.

More and more of his stuff was appearing in one of the spare rooms. A room he'd demanded so he could have his own space, which had subsequently remained unused because he always slept with them.

It was still a nightmare trying to get him out of the penthouse, and he was stubbornly refusing to speak to a new psychiatrist, insisting he was happy with the one he had.

A few days ago, she'd actually jerked him off in the elevator, then told him she'd let him come in the limo waiting outside, just to get him over here.

The power throbbing through her as she'd made that statement had made her feel like electricity. He'd let her take the lead, submitting to her care. With his broken sighs in her ears as she rubbed the head of his shaft, enticing the cum out of him, only to grab his balls and gently twist, she'd manipulated him out of the elevator.

He'd been here four days now. Every step was like crossing the Brooklyn Bridge in one go, but it was worth it.

She tapped the window and watched Bastien's head jerk up. She pointed behind him, nodding her head to urge him to look behind him. Squinting at her, he turned around and, seeing Alex stood behind the French doors, jumped out of his seat.

Devvy watched the silent movie unraveling before her. The two of them were talking, normally at first. As she watched, Alex started to glare at Bastien, then shot a glare over at her. She didn't know if he could see her, but she grinned, just in case he could. His scowl deepened, so she reasoned he'd spotted her amusement and almost as though that was the trigger, he stalked outside.

For a second, he looked as though he regretted the move. Then, as the peace of the garden settled on his shoulders, as the tweeting of birds and the calmness of the serene yard overcame him, she watched as he took in a huge breath and started to relax.

She was a long way away from fucking him in her herb garden. He was far too fraught to even tease. She knew because she'd tried! His lack of a hard-on, considering he was like a jack-in-the-box for most of the time, told her of his stress even out here in the peaceful surroundings of their enclosed land.

Time would ease this particular wound. And she'd help, too.

Bastien had enabled Alex to get worse. He'd let him do what he pleased, when. It had been out of love, as well as helplessness, so she could understand why he'd acted the way he had. Not that she'd allow it to continue. Devvy was intent on dragging Alex out of his comfort zone, and, inadvertently, had found another aspect of her nature.

When Alex finally took a seat, looking like he'd sat down on a bunch of hot coals and could leap off any second, she turned around, content for the moment that he was outside with Bastien, and returned to the concoction she was brewing. Thanks to Alex, the anti-acne soap was complete and she was working on the final trial product.

One night, while Sebastien fucked her and Alex ate her pussy, alternatively licking Bastien's shaft and slurping up her juices, the answer had come to her.

The teeniest, weeniest addition of olive oil.

Okay, it was weird to come up with the solution to her dry-skin problem mid-coitus. The thought had just popped into her head, and then slowly popped out again, when Alex had sucked on her clit.

The memory made her smile, and tingle.

That was the beauty of being with two men, especially two men who weren't afraid to touch one another. Nothing was taboo. Everything was an experiment, and if it created pleasure, then it was all to the good.

Devvy had discovered a naughty streak in her nature, something that had led Alex to nickname her "Dirty Devina." The alliteration, according to him, was too delicious to ignore.

When he called her that, she just rolled her eyes at him.

But inside, she soared.

Why?

Because of these two guys, she *was* dirty. She'd been liberated from a lifetime of boredom between the sheets by meeting Alex and Bastien. She'd avoided being humped away at by a scientist as geeky as herself, lights out, curtains closed, and under the covers, all the while accepting the fact she'd never experience an orgasm because there was something wrong with her. It couldn't possibly be the guy's fault, right?

They'd saved her from that.

She'd teased Alex when she'd told him that in the photo, from the magazine interview that had started all of this, she'd been pissed off at having to change so many times for the photographer. A part of her wondered if her yearning for something more, something better than what she'd always known, had burned brightly in her eyes.

He'd interpreted it as a promise.

She thought of it as silently pleading for someone to drag her out of herself, to help her experience a life outside of the lab. To experience love and acceptance with no repercussions.

They'd done that for her.

As Tiesto's song went, "If you close your eyes, it's a beautiful world."

For Devvy, eyes open or closed, her world truly was beautiful. It wouldn't be perfect, and with Alex there would always be a few bumps in the road, but to her it was a dream come true.

Thanks to her two men, and the life they'd given her, the doors of opportunity they'd opened, and the love so deep she could drown in it and still breathe, Devvy Jacques realized she was the luckiest botanist in the whole world.

THE END

WWW.SERENAAKEROYD.COM

ABOUT THE AUTHOR

Serena Akeroyd is a romanceaholic. She won't touch a book unless she knows there's a happy ever after at the end of it. Pathetic as it may be, because of this addiction, Serena decided to craft her own tales, stories that suit her voracious need for raunchy romance. After all, a love story ain't a lurve story without a bit of raunch!

A citizen of the world, Serena is a nomad at heart, and her novels enable her to travel the globe and all behind her computer desk. Naturally, she'd prefer the option of a private jet, but still, if wishes were horses, eh?

Always feel free to connect with Serena, she'd love to chat with her readers, as well as fellow raunch addicts!

Siren Publishing, Inc.
www.SirenPublishing.com

CPSIA information can be obtained at www.ICGtesting.com
Printed in the USA
LVOW04s1546160815

450313LV00027B/1094/P

9 781632 589552